RISE OF THE MAGES

RISE
OF THE
MAGES

SCOTT DRAKEFORD

TOR

A TOM DOHERTY ASSOCIATES BOOK
NEW YORK

RISE OF THE MAGES

Copyright © 2021 by Scott Lofgren Smith

Maps by Jennifer Hanover

A Tor Book
Published by Tom Doherty Associates
120 Broadway
New York, NY 10271

www.tor-forge.com

Tor® is a registered trademark of Macmillan Publishing Group, LLC.

Library of Congress Cataloging-in-Publication Data

Names: Drakeford, Scott, author.
Title: Rise of the mages / Scott Drakeford.
Description: First edition. | New York : TOR, 2022. |
Series: The age of Ire ; 1
Identifiers: LCCN 2021035823 (print) | LCCN 2021035824 (ebook) |
ISBN 9781250820150 (hardcover) | ISBN 9781250180070 (ebook)
Subjects: LCGFT: Fantasy fiction. | Novels.
Classification: LCC PS3604.R36 R57 2022 (print) |
LCC PS3604.R36 (ebook) | DDC 813/.6—dc23
LC record available at https://lccn.loc.gov/2021035823
LC ebook record available at https://lccn.loc.gov/2021035824

ISBN 978-1-250-82015-0 (hardback)
ISBN 978-1-250-18007-0 (ebook)

Our books may be purchased in bulk for promotional, educational, or business use. Please contact your local bookseller or the Macmillan Corporate and Premium Sales Department at 1-800-221-7945, extension 5442, or by email at MacmillanSpecialMarkets@macmillan.com.

First Edition: January 2022

Printed in the United States of America

0 9 8 7 6 5 4 3 2 1

For Kailey. Always.

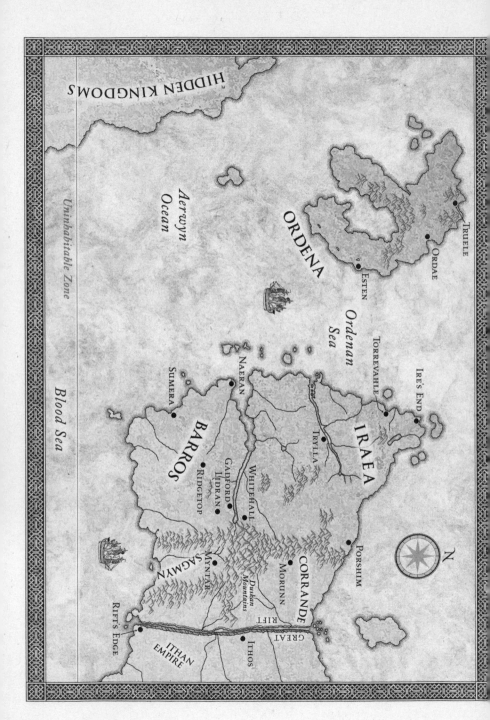

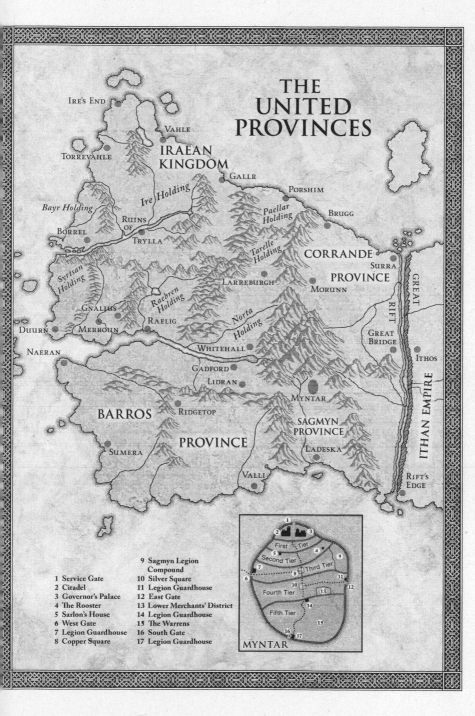

THE UNITED PROVINCES

IRE'S END

VAHLE

IRAEAN KINGDOM

TORREVAHLE

GALLR

PORSHIM

Ire Holding

Paellar Holding

BRUGG

Bayr Holding

RUINS OF

BORREL

TRYLLA

Tarelle Holding

CORRANDE

SURRA

Syrtsan Holding

LARREBURGH

PROVINCE

MORUNN

Raehren Holding

GNALIUS

RAELIG

Norta Holding

DUURN

MERROUN

GREAT BRIDGE

NAERAN

WHITEHALL

ITHOS

GADFORD

LIDRAN

MYNTAR

SAGMYN PROVINCE

BARROS

RIDGETOP

PROVINCE

LADESKA

SUMERA

VALLI

RIFT'S EDGE

GREAT RIFT

ITHAN EMPIRE

1 Service Gate
2 Citadel
3 Governor's Palace
4 The Rooster
5 Sarlon's House
6 West Gate
7 Legion Guardhouse
8 Copper Square

9 Sagmyn Legion Compound
10 Silver Square
11 Legion Guardhouse
12 East Gate
13 Lower Merchants' District
14 Legion Guardhouse
15 The Warrens
16 South Gate
17 Legion Guardhouse

First Tier
Second Tier
Third Tier
Fourth Tier
Fifth Tier

MYNTAR

RISE OF THE MAGES

Fire falls like rain
The stones return to earth
Fair Justice, Mercy wane
And each shall prove their worth
For Glory will men conspire
Be born the Age of Ire

—The Book of Ages
(Temple at Truele, Ordena)

PROLOGUE

Savian sat at his small desk, in a cramped room, inside the dilapidated stone structure that had been his home—his prison—for five long years. He stared at the night sky through his tiny, wood-framed window.

The full moon glowed with a brilliant blue light, partially illuminating the Temple grounds Savian guarded day and night. It had long been his habit to sleep by day in a windowless room in the cellar in order to spend his waking hours enveloped in the peace of the night.

He still didn't believe that there was anything in this Glory-forsaken corner of the world to guard, but he had no choice but to stay, if he wanted to keep his rank. And his life.

Keeper of the Temple of the Fallen, they had said. No higher honor! None higher, indeed. His lips twisted into a sneer. His long, powerful fingers, callused by years of Crafting wondrous devices only he could conceive, gripped an ivory pen until it cracked under the strain.

Liars. Thieves.

They had used his own ambition to exile him. It had taken him years to see it, but he had eventually realized that he would never fight the Ordenan devils, never rule the Hidden Kingdoms as one of the Seventh Circle, never ascend out of this hell-pit.

So it was that he came to be the Keeper of the Temple, an ancient holy site about as far from civilization as one could get in the Hidden Kingdoms. He was the most powerful outcast in the Malithii Priesthood. His only consolation was the fear he saw in the eyes of the few brethren who visited him.

He ran his hand through his thick black hair and contemplated his own image, reflected in the windowpane. He had been practically a child when he had arrived there, but the strong lines of his face had sharpened, his excess flesh wasted away while guarding the Temple of the Fallen.

Outside, through his reflection in the window, Savian thought he saw a faint flickering light on the side of the Temple, a huge, peaked building, square at the base and triangular on each side.

Probably just moonlight reflected by quartz in the stones, he told himself. *I'll have the slave investigate.*

"Kyrit, attend me!" Kyrit was technically his understudy, hoping to raise himself from the Third Circle under Savian's tutelage. He was Savian's Mindless now, and the Keeper had no intention of ever releasing Kyrit from the mindbinder he had designed. He felt a twinge of guilt at that but felt much better when he reminded himself that the boy was an irredeemable idiot.

If his brethren ever found out he had Bound one of their own to mindless servitude, there would be trouble. Never mind that Savian's new Crafting was likely the greatest invention in recorded history. Well enough that few of them visited the Temple, then. None of them even knew this type of binder existed, and Savian planned to keep it that way. Not that any of them would be able to replicate it anyway.

Kyrit appeared at the doorway to Savian's study, stopping before entering the room to look in hesitantly. His eyes had the cold, lifeless look of those who wore one of the new mindbinders, but with a slight, sharp gleam that implied some retained intelligence. More importantly, it wouldn't mutate his body into one of the living dead like the ancient soulbinders his brethren coveted. A bit of drool seeped from the corner of Savian's mouth to fall in his thick black beard as he grinned to himself.

He had set out to re-create the ancient soulbinders—though they had tens of thousands to spare, the secret to making them had been lost to the Priesthood for longer than anyone could remember—but was almost as excited about these that had gone wrong. He suspected that these new binders, mindbinders that sacrificed a certain amount of control for a subject that appeared autonomous, would be incredibly useful. Their like had not been seen for centuries, if they had ever been more than legend—a true work of genius. He would show the Seventh Circle yet. He would repay them their treachery. Soon he'd run the entire Malithii Priesthood—maybe the world—with his mindbinders.

"Kyrit, go take a look outside. Be sure no one has entered the grounds. No dawdling."

Kyrit ducked his head in a pathetic cringe and plodded toward the door. Savian turned back to staring out the window at the spot on the Temple where he had seen the twinkling light.

Kyrit approached the Temple without the apprehension even Savian felt near the monument to Fallen Glory. The mindbinder did not allow Kyrit to act on the fear he undoubtedly felt. Good.

As Kyrit began to inspect the outside of the building, Savian saw the flash again, stronger this time. An intense blue light outlined the heavy stone slab that had sealed the entrance to the Temple for centuries, perhaps even millennia.

Savian drew in a sharp breath and stared in shock. What could be causing the light inside the Temple? He had heard the claims that the Fallen God of Glory rested here, that the whole reason for the Malithii's existence was to prepare for his return. He had even used these tales to intimidate and coerce his brethren when convenient. But not until this moment had he truly believed it himself.

He rushed out of his room and into the courtyard that separated his building from the Temple. The pulsing light emanating from the Temple entrance grew stronger as he crossed the courtyard with sweeping strides of his long legs. He could hear a humming, feel a vibration in the ground that reverberated deep in his chest. It was almost as if the Holy Power had taken a life of its own, right there inside the Temple.

Kyrit stood just in front of the entrance to the Temple, staring at the light coming from the cracks around the large stone slab like the imbecile he was.

"Kyrit, come away from there! I'll have your skin—"

Savian's furious shout was cut off as the vibration culminated in a blinding pulse of blue light and a deafening blast that blew the stone-slab Temple door outward in a rush of flying chunks of stone.

Savian coughed as he rose unsteadily from where he had been thrown to the ground. Ears ringing, he stumbled across the courtyard toward the now-dark entrance to the Temple. Only a faint glow came from the building now, but the powerful pulsing of raw power continued.

He stepped over Kyrit's motionless body and crossed the threshold of the Temple, sparing only a brief remorseful thought for his servant as he was drawn to the source of unimaginable power.

He paused just inside the doorway, peering cautiously inside. The interior of the structure appeared to be one enormous room. Vaguely familiar symbols and script on the walls pulsed, illuminating the interior of the Temple intermittently with a deceiving, pale blue light. The air was stale, but surprisingly . . . sterile.

A huge, rectangular enclosure made of stone lay in the exact center of the structure. The stone slab that appeared to have covered it was strewn about the room in chunks of various sizes.

An oversized throne carved from translucent crystal sat at the far side of the large, open room. The throne pulsed with the same rhythmic blue light as the script on the walls, only more intensely. A huge grey stone statue of a bald but otherwise perfect specimen of a man sat on the throne. The statue had more of the same overlapping, angular script inscribed into its surface, almost like the tattoos that covered the Malithii priests. Except that these were glowing and pulsing in tandem with the crystal throne, and seemed somehow more . . . complete, making it impossible to determine a beginning or end to the script.

"So. My children attend me this time." A rushing tide of a voice swept over Savian; the vibrant power dropped him to one knee. He peered fearfully at the statue. It stared back at him with pale eyes—eyes that shone with life. How could this be? What was this sorcery? He staggered to his feet and drew holy *infusori* Power from a gold *infusori* coil in his pocket, prepared to direct it at this charade, to bring down whoever thought to fool him. He would make them pay.

The statue *moved*, pointed at him. "I prefer you on your knees, loyal one." There was a hint of amusement in the deep, powerful voice.

As it spoke, furious energy, primal *infusori* on a scale he could hardly comprehend, tore through Savian, driving him back to his knees.

A sudden realization chilled him to his core, an icicle to the heart. Could the legend be true? He wanted to scream, to run from this place and never look back, but found himself unable to move.

The Being rose from the throne and drew near with heavy steps that reverberated throughout the chamber.

"Rise, child. Tell me your name."

Savian took a shuddering breath before he rose. He could now see that what he had first thought was a statue of stone was in fact a being of living flesh, flesh an ashen grey color. The script inscribed into its skin still pulsed but changed colors and rhythm slightly as he watched. He could feel *infusori* energy emanate from the Being to pulse through him in perfect sync with the pulsing of the inscriptions in the Being's skin.

"My . . . my name is Savian," he croaked, finally daring to look up to the face of the magnificent Being that towered over him by a foot or more.

The Being regarded him with calm eyes. It reached out, fit its large grey fingers around Savian's neck, and said, "I have been called many things in this world. God of Glory. Father of All. Fallen One. You shall know me as Master."

Intense cold shot from the Fallen's touch around Savian's neck and through his body. Savian had known the touch of his own experimental binders and had thought it the height of pain and despair. This was worse than anything even his dark mind could have imagined.

As the icy pain reached his heart and brain, however, Savian found his emotions calming. The pain turned to intense pleasure. He looked up to his Master. The ice was power flowing through his veins. The power he had so craved all his life. His Master had made him whole.

Savian knelt on the gritty, dusty floor and proclaimed, "I live to serve, my God."

The Fallen God of Glory smiled, stalked back to his throne, and sat once more.

"Come, Savian. We have a great work to realize. A Son of Glory has drawn his first breath, one who will taste the white flame and prepares to seize my power as his own. My Sisters ever seek to replace me, but I will prevail as I ever have. But . . . perhaps this time will be different, my Savian. I tire of this pitiful world. We have much to prepare, only short years until our young charge is of age. We will test him, to see what he may yet become."

The Fallen God's smile became a deep, mirthless chuckle. "My Sisters will yet lament imprisoning me on this earth."

O

Emrael Ire and his father Janrael were the first to step from the barge onto Iraean soil. Janrael breathed in deeply, then spat to the side. He flexed his powerful hands as he stopped to survey their surroundings. "Every time I set foot here, I remember my fool father. Too proud to join the United Provinces, too weak to defeat them."

Emrael had often been told he didn't look much like his father. His pure white hair—the result of a training accident years ago, and the subsequent healing—was a stark contrast to his father's dark brown hair and beard. He still felt short standing next to his father, though he was only an inch or two shorter by now, and neither were all that tall. It was his father's presence that embellished his stature, an aura of command that made him seem the biggest man in the room regardless of physical size.

None would say that Janrael was a small man, however, and Emrael shared his father's build. Wide, powerful shoulders built through long hours of training with sword and shield; broad backs that had lifted many a supply crate; sturdy legs shaped by long hours of marching with the Legion. They were built to be warriors.

A thrill of excitement coursed through Emrael at finally being allowed to visit his ancestral homeland. He had just seen his twentieth summer, graduated from the Barros Junior Legion, and would be assigned a post soon if he chose to enlist in the Barros Legion right away. He couldn't contain his eagerness, despite his father's foul mood. The Iraean countryside looked much like the northern Barrosian countryside, giant pines, oaks, and maples quilted between large swaths of farmland and pasture. Still, it *felt* different to him. He stepped closer to his father so they were shoulder to shoulder. "I don't understand why you and Grandmother never returned, after the war ended."

Janrael chuckled darkly, hand now gripping the rune-carved hilt of his sword, the ancient sword of Ire kings, passed down from father to son for centuries. "We didn't have many options, son. My mother and her guard fled just before the Corrandes and the armies of the

Provinces besieged Ire's End, and Corrande would have killed our entire family. We've had to rebuild our lives from nothing."

"But you're the Commander First of the Barros Legion now. Why don't *we* go back?"

"The Iraeans that stayed in Iraea don't like us much either, Em. Many don't see us as true Iraeans, despite the blood of Mage Kings in our veins, and they're right. I was born at Ire's End but raised in Naeran, as you were. The Iraeans would likely throw us to the Watchers or kill us themselves as soon as help us take our ancestral Holding back, never mind handing us a throne. A throne that doesn't exist anymore, mind."

Before Emrael could ask more questions, Janrael clapped Emrael on the back. "Let's go help our men."

Emrael followed his father back to the barge to help the four squads of fellow Barros Legionmen unload their horses and gear for the campaign. "But you earned your Mark as a Master of War at the Citadel, you could have gone anywhere you wanted and been respected after that. Even Iraea, right? Why do we still fight for Barros?" He said that last quietly, not wanting the other men to hear.

Janrael grimaced, staring at the tattoo of the Citadel's sword and *infusori* coil crest on his forearm for a moment, then responded in a grim tone as they led horses from the deck of the ferry. "Many in the Barros Legion are Iraeans like us, who've fled the Watchers' brutality and taxes in our homeland and can't go back. I'm lucky my mother's guard joined the Barros Legion and supported us until I was old enough to go to the Citadel, then join myself. I couldn't leave them behind after what they sacrificed for us. For me. We might have starved, without them. Many did."

He grunted, facing Emrael to grip his shoulders. "We are Barrosians now, and we dance to Governor Barros's tune. Just the way it is. Right now, he wants these bandits run out of this stronghold of theirs on the Iraean side of the river. Lord Holder Syrtsan—that's your friend Halrec's bastard of an uncle—exiled his own brother to appease Corrande and Sagmyn after the war. He and the Watchers won't deal with bandits on the river like they're supposed to, so it's us."

His father spat as he hoisted a crate and turned to take it to one of the waiting wagons. "Still don't understand why he'd send me to see to it personally, though, other than to get me out of the capital so he can turn more of my subcommanders against me while I'm away. He's regretted allowing the Legion to make me Commander First from the day it happened. Can't have Corrande thinking he's giving an Iraean power to lead a rebellion," he growled with a mirthless chuckle, then spat again.

They arrived at their target after a half-day ride on a dirt road barely wide enough for the small wagons they had brought with them. The bandit stronghold turned out to be a vine-covered castle, most of which was an empty, crumbling shell. Emrael supposed that once, only a generation or so earlier, before the War of Unification, it had likely been home to some Iraean noble and scores of his retainers. Now the roof had caved in and the windows had all been broken out, leaving only the large main hall intact. A wisp of woodsmoke rising from one corner of the structure was the only sign that any living thing inhabited the place.

Janrael, Emrael, and the four squads of Legionmen that had accompanied them waited at the tree line of a ridge above the castle. Emrael's father shook his head, anguish darkening his eyes.

"These are probably remnants of the Whitehall rebellion. That Norta boy asked me to join he and the Raebren heir, you know. To 'take my crown and rightful place as a Mage King.' If not for your mother, I may have been tempted," he mused. "I may have, but I'm no more a king than I am a mage. Now I hunt them. Such a fickle world."

A scout on foot made his way through the trees, saluting when he reached them. "Commander First, Sir!"

Janrael nodded. "Captain First Loire. Report."

"The hills are clear, sir. Only this one set of recent tracks leading to the ruins and another on the other side of the castle. Judging by the traffic, there's a dozen in there. Two dozen at most."

Janrael nodded. "Thank you, Captain. Gather your scouts and hold here. Emrael, stay with them." He raised his voice so the soldiers gathered behind him could hear. "Squads one and two on me, three to the back gate, four on cover."

Emrael and the small group of scouts waited a few hundred paces away at the tree line as two squads of Legionmen moved into position in front of the main gate, which hung askew but still partially blocked the entrance. They formed up, shields overlapping and swords at the ready. Another squad trotted around the structure to block any escape from the rear service gate. The last squad, crossbows slung across their backs, crouched near a pile of pitch-filled jars and torches a few dozen paces away.

Oddly, there hadn't been so much as a warning shout as the Legionmen advanced. Emrael watched as his father approached the ruined castle, shield-less, sword still in its scabbard.

"Aho the castle!" his father shouted.

No response.

"If you're in there, surrender yourselves and you'll come to no harm."

Still nothing.

"Last chance! We'll burn you out if you do not surrender!"

The Commander First shrugged, then gestured to his men nearby.

The waiting squad of Legionmen lit jars of pitch and tossed them over the walls. Smoke soon billowed from several places within the castle, but still no motion from inside. Emrael saw his father's brow crease in puzzlement.

His father's confusion turned to shock and dismay as black crossbow quarrels soared from the tree line nearest the front gate, cutting down a large portion of the Barros Legionmen, who were facing the wrong way. A quarrel punched into Janrael's unprotected thigh. He fell to one knee.

Emrael shouted his surprise and anger, punching the first solider who tried to stop him from running to his father. A second Legionman tackled and pinned him to the ground before he could cross more than a dozen paces of the open ground. Some of the enemy crossbowmen had noticed them, and a few quarrels whistled through the air above Emrael's head. He watched helplessly as more quarrels flew, lodging in the shields of the few Legionmen who had managed to pull into a defensive circle around Janrael.

Just then, a group of mounted riders burst from behind the ruined gate of the castle. Emrael could see more formed up in the castle's courtyard behind these, at least fifty of them. They had been ready for this attack, had laid a trap for them. How?

Emrael struggled harder against the men who restrained him as the riders crashed into the Legionmen surrounding his father, hacking with swords and axes, trampling with hooves.

He threw one Legionman to the ground and tried punching the man that held his other arm, but he was grabbed by several of the squad of scouts with him and dragged to the nearby horses. They quickly tied his hands and feet and hoisted him to the back of a horse. Emrael spend the next hour bouncing along on the back of a trotting horse, still bound hand and foot. He was too proud, too shocked to resist further or call out to his fellow Legionmen.

The captain of the scouts called for a halt an hour or so later, apparently judging that they had escaped immediate danger.

Emrael, still draped across the back of a horse, stared at the pine needle–strewn dirt beneath his horse's hooves as the sound of footsteps drew near. He looked up to see Captain Voran Loire staring at him, pity in his eyes, though there was anger in the set of his jaw.

"Are you done sulking, boy?"

Emrael stared at him a moment, then lowered his head. He was embarrassed. Angry. How could they have walked into such an obvious trap? "How did you miss them, Loire?"

"I am Captain First Loire to you, boy. Have you come to your senses?"

"How did you miss them?" Emrael said, nearly shouting now, squirming against the ropes that bound him. "They were ready for us, Voran. How did you miss them? How could you turn tail and run?"

Anger flashed in Captain First Loire's face, and he stalked back out of view. "So be it. Bounce like a sack of grain all the way back to Naeran."

⚬⚬⚬

Emrael sat in the dining room of his mother's house inside the Legion compound of Naeran, the capital of Barros. It had been several weeks since they had been attacked in Iraea, and they had yet to find his father. Not even a trace of him.

He pushed away the remnants of a fine meal—beef steaks from the Tallos Holding in the south of the Barros province, cooked over an oak wood fire—and fixed his eyes on his mother, Maira, who sat at the head of the table just to his left. Nearly as tall as he and well-built for a woman, the only sign of her age was the grey beginning to streak her hair. She stared back with red-rimmed eyes.

She broke the heavy silence after a ragged sigh. "What now, my sons? Your father has been missing for weeks; it's time we thought about relocating. I fear it will not be long before we find ourselves unwelcome in the Legion compound."

Emrael's younger brother Ban sat next to him, head down, melancholy and silent. Emrael put a hand on his brother's bony shoulder and squeezed gently.

Captain First Voran Loire, the same that had brought Emrael forcibly back to the Barros Province after the attack on his father's expedition, sat at the far end of the long table, having just returned from another search expedition across the river. He spoke in a hushed, gravelly voice. "Aye, you may be right, Lady Ire. The governor has no strong love for Iraeans like us. With Commander Ire gone, you would be wise to make yourselves inconspicuous for a while."

Emrael pounded his fist on the table. "He isn't just 'gone,' Voran. Those were no ordinary bandits. You and I both know it! Bandits don't set traps for four squads of Legionmen, and they Fallen well don't win! Something else is going on, and I intend to find out what. I'll not give up on Father. His body hasn't been found; there must be a reason."

The scout stared at him hard but glanced at Maira and took a deep breath, obviously struggling to be polite. "I'm sorry, son. Your father and his soldiers were lost. We've seen none of the missing yet, and it's been weeks. Like as not, the bastards dumped his body in the river when they realized who they had killed. You've been with us on many of the rides; there is no sign of your father. Commander Second Anton is leading an entire battalion across the river as we speak to continue to search for him, but hope is dim. No one can understand why the Commander First led the expedition himself."

Emrael's mother murmured softly, "Stubborn fool."

Emrael shook his head. "He told me that the governor himself asked him to. This doesn't feel right, Mother. I'm going to help Corlas find Father."

Emrael's mother put her hand on his arm. "You may be right, Emrael. I'm afraid that your father's death may be no coincidence . . . there are many Sentinel priests and their Watcher soldiers in the city. Janrael was not the only prominent Iraean to disappear these past few weeks. This province is no longer safe for us. I have arranged for passage to Ordena and a place for us at the Ordenan ambassador's residence until the Ordenan cruiser arrives."

Voran nodded his agreement. "Lady Maira says true," he said in a gruff, quiet tone. "Many of the officers from Iraean families are already planning to return to Iraea, shame and taxes be damned."

Maira waved to the other side of the room, where bags were already packed. "I had some things gathered. It should be all we need. Take a few minutes to gather any personal items dear to you, but we leave within the hour."

Ban lifted his head and stared at Emrael expectantly, eyes red with grief. When Emrael said nothing, Ban slowly stood and walked toward the hallway to their rooms.

Emrael took a deep breath to calm himself. "No. Father could still be out there. I won't leave him behind and run to Ordena. Besides, this is my home. I can't just leave."

Ban stopped in the doorway and looked to Emrael, then to their mother.

Maira sighed. "Emrael, I love your father too, and your intentions are noble. But what can you do? If your father can be found, the men loyal to him—like Captain Loire here—will find him, and we can return straightaway. Look at it as a vacation just until your father turns up."

Emrael shook his head again, his mind made up. "No, I won't leave the Provinces while he could still be alive. If the Barros Legion isn't safe, I'll go to the Citadel and study there like Father did. They'll let me in because Father earned his Mark there; he told me so himself. I'll become the most fearsome warrior the Provinces have ever seen, and I'll find my father or exact my revenge myself."

"I'll come with you," Ban squeaked.

Emrael started, surprised. Ban usually did whatever their mother asked.

Judging by the look on their mother's face, she was equally shocked. "You *what?*" she screeched.

"I'm going with Emrael," Ban said calmly. "I'm going to study *infusori* Crafting with Elle. The governor is sending her to join her sister there next year."

Maira recovered her ability to speak, if not her temper. "That's preposterous, Banron! The Imperial Academy in Ordena can teach you everything the Citadel can and much, much more. I studied at the Academy myself and can assure you: the Imperators of the Academy far outclass those . . . *Crafters* and mercenaries at the Citadel."

Ban shook his head, calmer than anyone in the room. "I'm staying, Mother. I understand if you need to go back to Ordena, but Emrael and I will go to the Citadel. The Provinces are our home, and we can't leave while there's still a chance to find Father."

Emrael crossed the room to put his arms around his little brother, nearly moved to tears. "Thank you," he murmured to Ban. "We'll find him someday. We'll make a grand life for ourselves."

1

Three years later

Emrael sat in the main dining hall of the Citadel, absently wiggling his big toe through a hole in his worn-out right boot as he stared at his little brother, Banron.

"I still don't get it, Ban," he said.

Ban rolled his eyes from across the table and sighed. "I don't see what's so complicated. I'm calling it an Observer. The transmitter interacts with a receptor via latent *infusori* fields—" He finally noticed Emrael's intentionally bored stare. "You know what, never mind. Em, it's a device that allows one to talk to someone far away using another pair-tuned device. It uses the earth's natural *infusori* both as a power source and mode of transmission."

Emrael nodded, ignoring his brother's playfully condescending tone. "Why didn't you just say so? Glory, I don't need all of the details. Just tell me what it does. Now, how far away can these things transmit?"

"About fifty leagues, depending on the strength of the natural *infusori* fields between the devices."

"Using *infusori* fields? I didn't even know there were *infusori* fields outside of *infusori* Wells. How do you calculate their strength?"

"The fields are simply weaker at the surface of the earth than they are at subterranean loci—known commonly as Wells, obviously. There's no way to measure exactly, but the math is fairly accurate if I have readings from the areas in question."

Elle, the younger daughter of Governor Barros and Ban's friend since they had both apprenticed with Emrael and Ban's mother as children, smiled and patted Ban on the back. "I think the Observers may be the first Crafted devices to utilize latent *infusori* fields . . . ever. Even the Ordenans haven't managed anything like this—that we know of. So the calculations are still far from certain."

Emrael chuckled. "Fallen Glory and his Absent Sisters, we've only been here three years and you two are already making things the Master Crafters can't?"

"Well, yes," Ban said, blushing. "And you should try to keep up. If you put even a tenth of the effort into Crafting that you do fighting, you'd be well ahead of most of the students here. Knowledge of Crafted devices and being able to sense their use is going to set you apart when it comes time to take a commission in a Legion or a Lord Holder's guard . . . or even a mercenary company in the Ithan Empire. You'd take command within a year or two, tops."

Emrael pursed his lips. "Yeah, well. I'll start studying more with you if you'll start taking your sparring with me more seriously. I'm here for a Mark as a Master of War. I can learn Crafting from you later. And as for your Observer, we can make that into something. I'll talk to my friend in the Sagmyn Legion stationed here at the Citadel compound, see if he thinks the provisions subcommander would buy it for use on the city walls. I bet we get a lot for this one. Though we'd get more from the Watchers, since they have so many men stretched across the Provinces' eastern borders and all across Iraea."

Ban got an embarrassed look on his face. "Em . . . you can't have this one. Master Throsden knows about it. I'm to present it to him today."

Em grunted sourly. "Oh. Old bastard will steal it for sure."

Elle chimed in. "Emrael, it's really very good. I doubt half of the Masters could replicate it, let alone conceive the idea. Ban isn't just presenting it; he's testing to become a Master-in-Training."

"What!" Emrael exclaimed, leaning forward. He looked back at Ban. "When did this happen? Your tuition will be outrageous as a Master-in-Training under that man. Once I'm a Master of War, money won't be an issue, but I'm not sure I can pay for that right now. I've already taken as many shifts in the kitchens and at the *infusori* Wells as I can handle."

Elle again spoke up in Ban's stead, brushing her curly golden hair away from her face as she talked. "If Ban passes, the Citadel will manufacture and sell his device. Half of the proceeds from this project are his and will more than make up for the increase in cost." She looked pointedly at the fraying sleeve of Emrael's shirt. "Besides, if you truly need funds, I can always—"

"I'm not a beggar, and neither is my brother. We're fine. Thank you," Emrael interrupted gently, plastering a smile on his face in an attempt to cover how awkward he felt.

Elle's expression suddenly grew sour and Ban's face darkened. Emrael didn't think he had been overly rude, but was about to apologize to Elle anyway when a hand gripped his shoulder painfully from behind.

"What's this you say, Emrael? Tired of laboring at the Wells and kitchen duty already? If you need money, I'll hire you as my errand boy. I pay very well."

Emrael stood quickly and turned to face the newcomer, knocking the hand from his shoulder with a sharp slap. "Trying to play tough in front of your friends, Darmon?"

Darmon laughed and smoothed his immaculate black hair with one hand. The small group of equally well-groomed and finely dressed young men gathered behind him chuckled as well. He leaned in close but still spoke for the room to hear. "I hear your heathen friends in Iraea are calling for independence again. Didn't learn their lesson with that fool of a Lord Holder's son in Whitehall a few years back. Nor when your idiot father disappeared, it seems. Has he turned up yet?"

Emrael shook with rage as he stared the smirking Darmon in the eye but stopped himself from punching him—barely. He would risk expulsion and could lose everything he had worked so hard for these past years.

Darmon was determined to push him over the edge, as usual. His father could buy his way out of any trouble with the Masters of the Citadel, and he knew it. "What do you say, Ire? Do you have it in you to lead your people against mine, like in our grandfathers' day? I would relish the opportunity to gut you like my grandfather gutted yours. You heathen piece of shit."

Emrael smiled, but inside he was cold rage. "The Ordenans sank your idiot grandfather and his entire fleet when he attacked them— after he *murdered* my grandfather. And the Ordenans have cut your province off from sea trade for decades. I hear your father is running out of money, getting desperate. Weak." He clenched his fists and stepped closer to Darmon, aware he was severely outnumbered but not caring. "The people of Iraea have as much right to freedom as any. Those Iraean peasants you mock are each worth ten of you, and word is that they are growing mighty weary of your father's repa- ration taxes. Be careful what you wish for. But if you are so eager to fight me, Darmon, why don't you meet me at Tournament? Live blades."

A hushed chorus of whispers trickled from the students all around them, who had now turned to watch the confrontation.

Darmon looked around, face twitching. His eyes burned with cold hate as he turned back to Emrael. "Men like me have nothing to prove to vermin like you, though I'll relay the message to my father. I'm sure he'll be very interested to hear about your feelings for the

Iraeans . . . and about your brother's work here. The High Sentinel will want to take a look at the almost . . . *magical* work little Ban here is doing."

Despite himself, Emrael froze. Fear knotted his stomach. Darmon's father, Governor Corrande, had more than enough power to make someone like Emrael or Ban disappear. The High Sentinel's palace was right next to the Corrandian palace, after all, and the High Sentinel had an entire Legion's worth of soldiers at his command in the form of the Holy Provincial Legion—the Watchers. The Watchers were ostensibly a neutral force, tasked with guarding the United Provinces' borders. Everyone knew that the High Sentinel and his Watchers were Corrande's puppets, however. With two Legions at Corrande's command, the other provinces tended to go along with whatever he wanted. Worse, Corrande wouldn't be the only governor who would be more than happy to get rid of the last living Ires on charges of rebellion or heresy, fabricated or not.

Elle came to his rescue. "You wouldn't dare bring those zealous lunatics here, Darmon. The Masters of the Citadel would have your hide if they thought you caused any scrutiny of their very profitable *infusori* Crafting operations. Besides, my father and Governor Sagmyn would never allow such reckless accusations. Even you aren't above the rules."

Darmon laughed again and kept his eyes locked on Emrael's, though he spoke past him to address Elle. "Arielle," he said, addressing her by her full name, "the Masters of the Citadel have no power over people like us. The governors and the High Sentinel control the Legions and therefore make the rules. You'd do well to remember that. You can do so much better than these pitiful heathens. Worse, they're spawn of an Iraean rebel and an Ordenan bitch; I'm sure your father would not approve."

Emrael again shook with anger, but Darmon ignored him, turning to pull a girl from among his gaggle of sycophants. "Ah, well. At least I have your sister's good company."

Emrael's heart sank.

That's what this is about. Damn him. What is she doing with the likes of him?

He hadn't noticed Elle's older sister, Samille, during the confrontation. Darmon must have found out Emrael had been—and to an extent, still was—fond of her. Likely from Sami herself. Where Ban and Elle had always been inseparable friends, Sami had always been an object of distant admiration for Emrael. Which was embarrassing, because he was fairly sure she knew it. He flushed as he met her eyes briefly.

Apparently, Darmon now knew it as well and had come over just to flaunt the relationship.

"Come, Samille. We have . . . better things to do."

Darmon's lips twisted in a lecherous grin and he turned to depart without looking back.

Sami continued to look at Emrael for a moment before following Darmon, leaving Emrael trembling slightly with sullen anger.

Elle approached to lay a hand on Emrael's arm. "Don't mind him, Em. Your Iraean heritage is something to be proud of. Your grandfather was a king, for Glory's sake. And . . . I love her, but you can do better than my sister."

Emrael forced a smile and patted her hand without looking at her, too embarrassed to meet her eyes. "Thank you, Elle."

He turned to his brother and said tersely, "I'm not hungry anymore. I'll leave my food here. Eat what you want. I'm going to see what news the merchants have from Iraea, then I'll be at the weapons yard."

~~~

"Emrael!" Ban called.

Emrael glanced at his brother just long enough to see him trotting into the Citadel's combat practice courtyard. Ban hurried through the oversized wooden doors into the yard, his wavy brown hair slightly disheveled. He had an excited look on his handsome face.

Before Emrael could respond, a fist connected solidly with his left cheekbone, knocking him to the ground.

"Damn it, Ban," Emrael said after he rolled back to his feet, backing away to give his legs time to steady. He brushed dirt and sawdust out of his short white hair and spat blood as he watched his opponent, Jaina. She regularly beat the shit out of him. It was her job as his mentor and sponsor at the Citadel, and the only person who could grant him a Mark as Master of War. She allowed him to regain his wits but all too soon prowled like a wild animal preparing to kill its next meal.

Jaina's eyes gleamed dangerously as she feinted toward Emrael.

"Do not blame others for your weakness and lack of focus, Emrael Ire," Jaina said, then lunged at him.

Emrael circled quickly and barely escaped her attack. He figured her to be nearly ten years his elder, but she certainly hadn't lost any speed to age. If anything, she had gotten faster in the three years since Emrael had arrived at the Citadel and started training with her.

Without taking his eyes from Jaina, he said, "Ban, what is it? Are you trying to get me killed?"

Ban's voice was excited as he replied. "Em, I passed! Master Throsden said my Observer was more than good enough to earn my Apprentice's Mark. He said I'm to receive the Mark next week and begin work as a Master-in-Training, just like you."

"Seriously?" Emrael asked, so surprised he glanced over at Ban again. "A Master-in-Training at twenty?"

"Ask him yourself! I'm to propose—"

Emrael stopped listening to his brother and mumbled a curse under his breath as he dove away from a vicious combination of punches and kicks from Jaina. He grunted as her leather-slippered foot hit him in the ass.

"I'm to propose a project to start my training to be a Master Crafter!" Ban repeated.

Ban paused as Emrael struck futilely at Jaina, and then continued in a more solemn tone. "I want to make something to help you once you become a Master of War."

Emrael threw another tentative kick to keep Jaina at bay.

"I won't live to be a Master of War if I keep talking right now. Wait," he said between heavy breaths while pacing backwards, trying in vain to keep a safe distance between him and his attacker.

He focused, determined to end the sparring bout quickly with a win. He feinted, then followed as she circled to his left, cutting off her escape. He had her.

Without any warning, Jaina shot forward and grabbed hold of both of his legs before he could react. She twisted her body as she lifted him, slamming Emrael to the ground with a *thud*.

Emrael immediately struggled to gain the upper position, but Jaina secured his arm and sprawled across his midsection, pinning him to the ground with a painful arm hold that threatened to tear his shoulder from its socket. He tapped her shoulder with his free arm, admitting defeat.

"Shit, you're fast," Emrael said through gritted teeth, attempting to save what little pride he could as he waited for her to climb off of him.

Jaina scrunched her face in anger and rammed her forehead into Emrael's nose, causing him to squeal, then struggle out of her grasp and to his feet.

"I think you broke my nose!" Emrael exclaimed, clutching at his face. Thick red blood bubbled between his fingers.

"I did not break your nose," Jaina said, "but perhaps I should. You are good enough to best me at least three times in ten, but you are lucky to win one! You are capable of much more than this, Emrael, and I do not have time to waste. I have been too lenient."

"Does this look lenient to you?" Emrael held out his bloody hand to his brother, his eyebrows raised incredulously.

Ban simply laughed and said, "Jaina is right, Em. I would have thought you could at least win a few against Jaina—she's half your size. You fight well enough against everyone else."

Jaina pointed a threatening finger at Ban and said, "I am Mistress Jaina to you, boy. I will remind you of the respect a Master of the Citadel is due if I must. It would be a shame to scar the face of such a pretty young man."

Ban backed away quickly with his hands raised, eyes wide. "Sorry, Mistress Jaina. I meant no offense."

"And you," she said, turning back to point a finger at Emrael, "are to report to my office this evening at dusk. You are to prepare a written explanation of why you petitioned me to train you as a Master of War. I will not mentor one who refuses to use the talents given him."

Emrael locked his light grey eyes to hers of brilliant green. Her anger seemed to shine physically through her irises, brightening their color briefly. He nodded after a tense moment, not having an answer he was willing to voice. He wanted to tell her he was tired from losing sleep and working too many shifts in the kitchens and at the *infusori* Wells, that he pulled punches against her because she was half his size. She would only see those as excuses, however, and might literally kill him next time they sparred.

Jaina stalked out of the courtyard, her short, sweat-darkened hair swaying as she walked towards the Citadel's living quarters.

Ban looked at Emrael with a smirk and said, "If you tell her your real reason for wanting to be a Master of War, she will beat you bloody. Again." He looked up at the open sky visible between the walls of the courtyard with the thoughtful expression he assumed when trying to be especially clever. "You have a few hours to come up with a decent argument before your shift at the Well; I'll come with you. I'm supposed to meet Elle to write an essay on '*infusori* and its use as spiritual metabolization of energy' for Master Throsden to preface my proposal for a Master's project, but I suppose I can cancel with her to help you. I'd not want to leave you to your own devices and feel responsible for you ending up just a kitchen worker and *infusori* Well laborer for the rest of your life."

Emrael stared after Jaina for a moment, one hand gripping his short, pure white hair in frustration. Finally, he gathered his boots, tugged them on quickly, and used his shirt to wipe the blood from his face before responding to his brother's banter. "So, you were going to 'write an essay' with Elle, huh? Is that what you kids call it these days?"

He laughed when Ban blushed and stammered that Elle was just his friend, then punched his brother playfully. "And I'm the assistant to the head chef, thank you very much. You'd be the one suffering without the stipend from my shifts."

Ban's mood sobered quickly. "I know. Thank you, Em." He reached into his pocket and extended his hand. "Here, this is for you. It's one of my Observers, only it's got some additional features I've been working on. Not everything I want to add, but better than nothing. Wear it around your neck and we can talk even if we are at opposite ends of the city, maybe further. I'm going to make its twin for me while I work on my proposal."

Emrael took the pendant from Ban and studied it momentarily. Intricate twisted metal loops of swirling copper, silver, and gold formed an hourglass shape that shimmered in the afternoon sunlight. Something like this would have taken Ban hundreds of hours and was likely worth more money than he had ever held in his hands.

"Thank you, Ban," he said quietly. "It's the most beautiful thing I've ever seen. I'm proud of you, you know. I had almost a decade in the Barros Junior Legion with Father to prepare me for my training, but you are still earning your Master's Mark as quickly as I am. You might be the fastest to achieve the Crafter's Mark in the history of the Citadel. Three years is unheard-of."

Ban answered with a silent smile, eyes shining. Emrael clapped his brother on the shoulder and they headed back to their room side by side.

❦

Back in their room, Emrael sat at his small desk beside their bunk beds, counting their coin while Ban tinkered at the big wooden worktable that dominated their moderate space. His brother focused diligently on his work, pouring molten raw metals from his benchtop smelter into the forms he had created for his latest Crafting idea.

Dozens of such projects lined crude shelves they had put up in their small room.

"I might have to take up weekend shifts laboring at the *infusori* Wells, at this rate," Emrael said, separating the Provincial coin from the larger Ordenan coin that their mother sent to cover Ban's tuition—she had sent a letter nearly a year before, explaining that she thought it would be good for Emrael to earn his way through the world. That had been the last letter of hers he bothered to open. He knew his mother had money from his father's time as a Commander First of the Barros Legion if nothing else, though he admittedly knew little of her new life in her native Ordena. It was just like her to punish Emrael for not following her there, however.

He knew he should be grateful that she at least paid Ban's tuition—they would have had to leave the Citadel long since, otherwise—but couldn't help but envy the other students who lived in relative ease and luxury, their tuition and a comfortable lifestyle paid for by wealthy parents. They certainly weren't working shifts as laborers while trying to earn a Master's Mark at the same time.

Emrael's labors covered his own tuition and other necessities like food, clothing, and the many, many supplies for the work that Ban did in their room. He was proud of that especially. Ban's Craftings were nothing short of miraculous and were going to make them rich sooner or later. He didn't need his mother or anybody else to fund their dreams.

"We can always go find Mother in Ordena if we can't make it here," Ban said distractedly. The contraption he was working on sparked, then flared bright blue as *infusori* escaped with a pop and the smell of scorched metal. "Damn it all!" Ban cursed. "Should have been more careful with the receptor array . . ."

Emrael chuckled at the mishap despite the anger he felt at Ban's suggestion. "Ordena wasn't an option three years ago when we came here, and it's not an option now. Anything you Craft would belong to their government, and if I joined their Imperial Army, I'd be shipped off to fight their holy war in the dark lands across the West Sea. We'd be little better than slaves. No, thank you."

Ban shrugged, replacing a now-spent *infusori* coil connected to his apparatus with a fresh one—the last charged coil they had. The coils Ban used were very small and of poor quality, but they were all Emrael could afford, even with the discount he received for working at the Wells where spent coils were sent to be recharged. Ban never complained, but Emrael was sure that the lack of proper equipment and *infusori* to fuel his devices and the Crafting process itself were hampering his efforts at least to some degree.

Ban placed one hand on the glowing *infusori* coil as he began to tinker once more, and murmured, "Do you ever feel it, Em?"

"Feel what?" Emrael replied.

"The *infusori* . . . Sometimes, I swear I can almost feel it, feel where it should go, like I could Craft directly with *infusori* instead of using it just as a fuel for my tools."

Emrael leaned forward, speaking quietly now. "I've felt it too, though I'm not nearly the Crafter you are. But don't let anyone hear you say that, Ban. You remember what happened to that kid Jeras who claimed he had discovered the ancient magic. The Sentinels had their Watchers club and drag him off like a sack of grain, and the Masters didn't do a thing about it. He never came back, and nobody knows where he went."

"Mmm," Ban mumbled. "But I'm not setting a Master's clothes on fire, now, am I? Still not sure how he managed to do that; maybe it was magic after all. That book I'm reading, *A History of the Arcane*, briefly mentions widespread use of magic, a few centuries ago. It says mages could use *infusori* directly, without any devices at all!"

Emrael snorted. "If it was magic, he would have been wise to hide it until he could get out of the Provinces. Just keep talk like that to yourself, especially with Darmon and his gaggle of assholes around. They'd love to turn us in for using witchcraft, and Corrande would be quick to let the Sentinels and their Watchers make us disappear. But maybe once we have our Master's Marks, we can find someplace to learn this magic. We can probably earn our Marks within a year or two at this rate, then we can head for Iraea. Or maybe the Ithan Empire and whatever lies beyond that."

Ban looked up from his work, smiling. "Father used to say we were part of the Descended Lords of Iraea, the progeny of the ancient Ravan mages. That has to mean something, right? You really think we can learn?"

"I don't know, Ban, but it's worth a shot, isn't it? We can do anything we want, just as soon as we're done at this damned school."

"Let's do it, then. But first, you have to write a paper convincing Jaina to keep you as a student. Get to it."

"Just one game of Reign first?" Emrael asked, already moving to set the carved pieces on the board that never left their small side table.

Ban smiled again, his eyes lighting up. "Fine. I think I finally know how to beat you."

~~~

Emrael stopped next to the small window across the hall from Jaina's door, sweating after running up several flights of stairs to make sure he arrived on time. He leaned against the cool stone wall and took a deep breath. It had been a stressful day, and he was anxious to resolve this whole mess with Jaina. It wasn't quite sundown, however, and he didn't dare risk angering her by knocking early. After how she had reacted earlier at the sparring grounds, he wasn't about to push his luck.

Large gold *infusori* coils set in copper sconces that enhanced their glow lined the upper halls of the Citadel, casting a clean blue light into the growing dimness of the late hour. He idly tried to calculate how much the *infusori* energy contained within each coil was worth. Coils this large and pure required days of sitting deep within an *infusori* Well to charge fully—a costly endeavor, as *infusori* Wells were scarce, and even the largest Wells could only house a few thousand coils at a time.

The heavy gold coils themselves were not worth the trouble once the *infusori* trapped within had been exhausted, of course, but the amount of *infusori* energy each of these fresh high-grade fist-sized coils held could pay for several weeks' worth of fine dining and carousing at the nicer taverns and inns in the second and third tiers of the city, or even a meal at one of the exclusive restaurants in the first tier. He had heard other students speak of them often but couldn't fathom spending such vast amounts of money on one meal. Besides, the money would be better spent on some new shoes, and on Ban's supplies—the charged *infusori* coils, precious copper, silver, and other wiring for the circuitry were going to cost Emrael a fortune. The cost of *infusori* had soared in recent years with the increased popularity of Crafted devices, especially those made there at the Citadel.

He sighed. He wasn't going to stoop to stealing. Besides, he didn't really know to whom he could sell the coils without getting caught. He'd just have to keep working like a dog until either he or Ban earned their Master's Mark and could start making some real money.

Jaina's door still stood closed, and the last of the sun's rays still shone through the windows into the hallway. He turned from contemplating the lights to look out the small window next to him. The window sat propped open, and occasional gusts of wind supplied cool, sweet air that smelled of rain and the new life of spring to the stuffy hallway.

The top floor of the Citadel provided an incredible view. The Citadel was the tallest building in the highest tier of Myntar, towering over the city and the vast Sagmyn Valley below it. On clear days like today, it was easy to imagine he could see the sparkle of the sea if he peered southward hard enough. The peaks of the Duskan Mountains to the north shone pale and cool. The governor's palace, which sat on the east side of the expansive courtyard, gleamed blood-red in the dwindling spring sunlight. Laborers milled at the small service gate at the north end of the courtyard, unloading the day's shipment of glowing *infusori* coils shipped down from the Wells.

The rest of the city already lay in the shadow of the surrounding mountains. In the wealthy upper tiers, steady blue light from *infusori* coils gleamed at him through the windows of large buildings, and high-peaked slate roofs reflected the steady light of the *infusori* lamps that lined the paved avenues. That so many in the upper tiers could afford *infusori* as a light source shone as a literal beacon of Myntar's status as the trade center of the world. Wealth beyond Emrael's wildest dreams flowed through those streets, shops, and warehouses.

The windows of the more modest wood-shingled dwellings in the sprawling lower tiers glowed with the soft, pulsing orange light of candles and traditional lamps. The hard-packed dirt streets of the lowest tiers wallowed in darkness save for an occasional torch that cast a flickering pool of light. The inhabitants of the lower tiers—the laborers, the working class—could not afford *infusori* to light their homes, let alone to light their streets.

Have I really been here three years?

It was his home now. He would not give it up without a fight.

Emrael withdrew from his contemplation with a worried start as he realized that the sun had finally slipped behind the mountains. He hurried to the door and knocked, hoping Jaina would not accuse him of being late.

He heard measured footsteps and a brief pause. The door opened with a slight *click,* and Jaina appeared in the entryway.

"I was wondering how long you would stand there before knocking," she said with a wry smile. Emrael blinked in surprise, not knowing what to say.

A modest but formfitting robe draped her lithely muscular figure, and her short, shoulder-length hair formed a small tail at the nape of her neck. Her light caramel skin was flushed, and Emrael could smell bathing soaps. Her smile became warm, relaxed. It was an odd but pleasant contrast to the usually strict demeanor she maintained with Emrael during their training—and extremely confusing, given the circumstances.

"I was just waiting until dusk as you asked, Mistress Jaina," he said uncertainly.

"Well, come in. Have a seat." She gestured to the chair before her rose-carved desk. "I am looking forward to reading your argument. I trust it is not too lengthy?"

Emrael shook his head. It wasn't. He and Ban had deliberated at length about what argument Emrael should present to Jaina. They had only been able to come up with a few that had not seemed ridiculous or self-serving.

Emrael handed his written argument over and took the chair she had pointed to. She sat down in her chair behind the desk and took what seemed to be a very long time to read through the single page of paper.

Emrael became nervous. There wasn't that much material on the page to digest, and he thought it was fairly good. Ban had helped, after all.

Finally, she looked up. Her face was calm, betraying no emotion.

"This is well done. I would accept it from any other of my students."

When she failed to continue and the staring match grew awkward, Emrael said, "What do you mean? Why not from me?"

"Because I have nothing left to offer you. And I am fairly certain your brother wrote most of it."

Emrael remained silent—he could protest, tell her that Ban had only helped a bit, but it would only make him look more guilty. After an awkward moment, Jaina continued. "It says here that you want to become a Master of War, just to join a Legion as an officer?"

"That's right."

Becoming a Master of War was only a means to an end but would be incredibly valuable if his goal was to get to the top of a Provincial Legion like his father had, or if he was going to build a mercenary company of his own out in the Ithan frontier or the Free Cities near the Rift. It was best not to mention such out loud, however. People wouldn't take too kindly to the thought of an Iraean building his own army, for all that it had been nearly two generations since the War of Unification.

"But you left the Barros Legion to study here. Why return to a Legion afterward?"

He sensed her skepticism and felt he needed say something to damp her irritation. "You are one of the best instructors in the Provinces, maybe the world, Jaina. You are the youngest Master of War I've ever heard of. You have bested the Commander Second of Lord Governor Sagmyn's Legion at a Tournament, and he is the best sword in this province, maybe all the Provinces. You are the one I want to instruct me. I intend to make something of myself, leave a mark on the world. When you grant me your Mark as a Master, everyone will know I'm the best, and no doors will be closed to me."

Jaina raised one eyebrow and shrugged. "Hmm." She rapped her fingertips on her desk several times in rapid succession, staring at him thoughtfully. "I have witnessed *you* defeat the great majority of classmates you have faced, Emrael. In fact, you have never lost to other entrants, not that I recall. I even witnessed you defeat Master Graton, breaking his arm in the process. You have the potential to become what you desire, and much more. But you do not apply yourself to the other disciplines. Your knowledge of *infusori* Craft is mediocre at best, something I expect any Master I mark to take pride in. I expected much more of you, given your Iraean and Ordenan heritage."

"I'm not that bad," he protested. "I just let Ban handle most of that."

She continued without acknowledging him. "I would almost think you lazy, if I had not seen how hard you work to keep your brother in coin. I know for certain that you are not stupid. Frankly, I suspect your motivations in training to become a Master. You have potential, but as things stand, I cannot accept you back under my tutelage."

Emrael stared at her, unable to speak for several seconds. "What? Mistress Jaina, you know this means everything to me. I am likely within a year or two of earning my Master's Mark by even the highest standards . . ."

He trailed off as he realized that he was rambling. He needed to get his wits about him, or this was going to go badly.

"Do you think I care a whit about other Masters' standards?" Jaina asked with an odd look in her eye and one side of her mouth upturned. She did that when she thought something entertaining.

"Uh . . . probably not?" he said, watching her carefully. "What I mean to say is that I am capable of being everything that you require, and willing to do whatever it takes. I am performing well in Tournaments and I attend all of your lectures and lessons. I can improve my *infusori* Crafting."

"Abilities are worse than useless if the intentions are less than honorable," she declared, cutting him off. "I require a test of your dedication if I'm to share the full scope of my knowledge. I must know you are worthy, for your safety and my own."

He had a sinking, suspicious feeling forming in the pit of his stomach. She was starting to sound far too much like his mother, speaking as she was of dedication and worthiness. Ordenans were notoriously attached to their religion and its moral code, but until now, Jaina had never made it an issue. His fear turned to anger.

"What do you want me to do, swear to your Silent Gods? I don't know what else I can do to convince you, Jaina, but I'm here, and I'll do anything you ask of me." He said, gesturing to the copy of the Ordenan Book of Ages on her desk. "I'll swear on your holy book if you wish, though they are no more than fairy tales to me."

Jaina flashed an amused smile. "You might be surprised by how real many fairy tales turn out to be."

"I've seen your hidden tattoo, Jaina," he challenged further, glaring at her. "You have three interlinked circles, one solid black below two hollow. It's inked just above your hairline on the back of your neck, just like my mother's. What is this really about? Do you know her somehow? Is she finally trying to chase me out of the Citadel?"

Jaina did not respond immediately. She sat behind her desk, pursing her lips while giving Emrael a hard look. "That is simply the Mark of a full Ordenan Citizen. I know of your mother, but all Ordenans know of her."

Emrael's eyebrows lifted in surprise. "What do you mean, all Ordenans know of her? Why would they care about the wife of the dead Commander First of the Barros Legion?"

"You truly don't know?" She shook her head in exasperation. "I don't have time to correct your ignorance of our people, nor to correct your mother's mistakes. Suffice it to say that your mother is a leader of sorts in our empire."

He squinted at her skeptically. "You damn Ordenans love your secrets. My mother is a Master Healer, some sort of teacher at your Academy, nothing more."

Jaina fixed him with a glare. "Enough," she said, cutting him off with a wave of her hand. "Are you sure you wish me to be your instructor, and no other?"

"Yes," he answered with absolute certainty, despite his confusion about the rest of their conversation.

She surprised him yet again by standing abruptly. "Emrael, as you are no doubt aware, tomorrow night the Tournament of Arms will be held. You were planning to compete this month—that match will have to be cancelled. I hereby challenge you to a formal duel of arms, which will supersede your planned event. Live weapons are to be chosen at random at the commencement of the duel."

He couldn't believe what he was hearing, but she continued as if challenging him to a real armed duel—out of the blue—was the most natural thing in the world.

"The challenge will be published to every hall of the Citadel. If you defeat or so much as disarm me, I will consider you worthy of my continued mentorship, free of any tuition."

"If I defeat you, however, I will stop just short of killing you. I will beat you, break you. Then you will be stripped of all possessions, flogged, and turned out of the Citadel for as long as I remain a Master here. People will tell stories for decades about the beating I give you. And if you refuse the challenge, I will refuse you as a student and you will be forced to find another mentor. How do you respond?"

2

Emrael's mind reeled.

What in the name of the Fallen just happened?

Jaina wasn't just being unusual; she was insane. She was challenging him to a formal duel in front of the entire Citadel? Usually, these things were planned, formal occasions. There was preparation, and the duel was always fought with blunted weapons. Almost always.

He would be the talk of the school, no matter the outcome. He certainly had no desire to fight Jaina with real weapons, but being denied tutelage under Jaina was as good as being cast out. Master Graton and the other Masters of War would never accept Emrael as their student—a lowly Iraean with hardly a copper penny to his name. Not to mention the whole incident with Emrael breaking Master Graton's arm.

The Citadel was his best chance at earning real wealth. Real freedom. Maybe his only chance. Emrael had no choice.

"I guess I accept," he said after a moment, stunned. He stood.

"Good." She smiled, a concerned look in her eyes. "I am sorry it came to this. The Silent Sisters, they will watch over us. Prepare well and sleep early tonight," she said, standing.

He turned, and as he approached the door, she said, "Emrael?"

"Yes, Mistress Jaina?"

She closed the space between them to put a hand on his shoulder, face suddenly serious again. "Though I am sure this seems sudden and harsh, this is very necessary for reasons I can't yet explain. You must trust me." She gave his shoulder a strong squeeze.

Emrael could only manage a confused look, then quickly exited the room. He headed down the nearly empty halls toward his quarters, the thought of having to fight his mentor so preoccupying his mind that he didn't even see the two men lurking in a side hallway.

⌁

Jaina stared at the door after it shut behind Emrael. Silent Gods, she couldn't help but see her younger self in the boy. So ambitious, so confident—yet so far from his true potential, blind to what he could be. She had been much the same a decade before—maybe even worse. Of course, that was before graduating from the Ordenan Imperial Academy and meeting Welitan on deployment in the Dark Nations.

Twirling the ring on her heart-finger unconsciously at the memory of Welitan, she approached the door on soft feet, opening it a crack to see that Emrael had gone and the hallway was clear. She closed the door with a soft *click* and secured the lock. She was sure there were still Citadel guards—or men pretending to be Citadel guards—watching her apartments, but they stayed out of sight. They thought they knew who—what—they were watching, but they had no idea. These children at the Citadel—and the Masters who taught them—fiddled with *infusori*, never realizing the true potential of the energy that powered their devices.

Smiling to herself, she slipped back into her bedroom on silent feet, then moved her sitting chair and the carpet under it to reveal a trapdoor that appeared to be solid stone unless one knew where to find the precise spot that acted as an actuator. She sent a pulse of *infusori* energy into the stone and pulled the hatch open to reveal steep stairs that led to a series of passageways hidden in the walls and between floors. Most had forgotten the ancient Ravans had built the Citadel. The ancients had built it as a fortress with secure, often secret, passageways in and out for the mages who had lived here. Even if one did find an entrance, one needed to be able to find and open many *infusori*-actuated doors hidden in walls and dead-end rooms to reach a useful destination. She was the only true mage in the Citadel and thus the only person who ever haunted the secret passageways.

Several such hidden doors later, she arrived at a door that let out into the Citadel courtyard just behind the stables. Though most of the courtyard was bright with the glowing blue light of *infusori* coils, this particular corner of the courtyard was kept dark to allow the horses in the nearby stables to rest. Looking about to ensure nobody was near, she secured the door behind her and made her way quickly to the small gate on the far side of the stables.

A small jitter of anxiety heightened her senses as she passed through the gates with the hood of her robes up, but the Sagmyn Legion guards made no move to stop her. Once out of sight, she shed her robes and stashed them in a barrel inside an upscale apothecary shop she frequented—the shop owner had been perplexed when she asked for a key and to rent space in the back of her shop for an empty barrel, but had been happy to oblige when Jaina offered twenty copper rounds, more than even most first-tier merchants could hope to earn in a busy week. She hastily applied some heavy makeup that she kept in the barrel, let her hair loose, and secured a purse over one shoulder.

Now free of her robes, Jaina swished down the moonlit street in a loose black trouser-dress that ended in snug pant legs around her knees—stylish enough that she wouldn't be out of place at a restaurant in the first tier of the city, but functional enough to allow her to fight her way clear of a messy situation. But most importantly, between the makeup and finery fit for a young lord's daughter, nobody would mistake her for the austere Master of War who rarely, if ever, left the Citadel grounds.

She made her way through the broad streets of the first tier, down a long, wide marble staircase into the slightly dimmer second tier, and into a luxurious but outwardly unassuming restaurant called the Rooster. The dull brick exterior and small black door hid a large, richly decorated reception room that led to several private dining chambers in the back. Exotic hardwoods from the frontier reaches of the Ithan Empire covered the floors, elaborate tapestries and original paintings covered the walls, and the *infusori*-coil lighting sconces were clearly of Ordenan design, despite the Rooster's proximity to the Citadel, where such commonplace Crafted devices were easily obtained for less than half the cost of buying wares shipped all the way from Ordena.

The ostentatious nature suited the place, as it catered to wealthy first-tier patrons seeking a more private location to settle various . . . affairs away from the prying eyes of their equals.

Jaina walked in and handed a stamped copper plaque, her token of reservation, to the young male attendant dressed in silver-and-white livery. He accepted it with a shallow bow and led her to her reserved room.

Jaina took a seat before addressing the young man. "I will have the Sweet Valley red now, and you will fetch my supper in exactly one hour. I'll have the roasted piglet, sautéed vegetables, and the sweet rice pudding. You will knock before entering, and I am not to be disturbed for any other reason."

The young man, knowing his place, nodded and left with a fixed smile, closing the door behind him. Jaina crossed the room to lock the door, then went immediately to the wall her room shared with the adjoining chamber. She removed a painting of a horseman in front of some lost castle and pressed her hand to the wood beneath. The walls were of thick oak, designed to silence any sound coming from the rooms.

She reached in her bag to grasp an *infusori* coil hidden in a steel sheath and closed her eyes for a moment, palm to the wall. After a moment of focusing her *infusori* energy into the wood just so, a dull *thud* emanated from beneath her palm. She moved her hand to reveal a tiny circular hole burned clean through the wall. A faint smell of smoke permeated the air, so she pulled perfume out of her bag to dab about the room, hoping it would cover the smell enough for anyone nearby to assume that the smoke had come from the kitchens. Replacing the perfume, she extracted a collapsible metal cone that she inserted into the newly created hole.

Her informants had assured her that her quarry would be there tonight at the second hour of moonlight, and she was not disappointed. Less than ten minutes later, she heard a faint noise in the hall. She pressed her ear to her amplification cone and could clearly hear three voices.

"He'll be here in a moment, Headmistress. Please take a seat; we'll order dinner shortly," a man's deep voice said in clear Provincial common.

"Call me Dorella, please, Corlas," Headmistress Dorella said with a light laugh. "Or should I address you as 'Commander Anton'?"

Jaina rolled her eyes. Dorella continued when Corlas didn't respond immediately. "Who is this man we are meeting? I was under the impression it would just be the two of us."

"Ah, well. Dorella, you know I would love that," Corlas said smoothly. "I think you'll find my associate well worth meeting. You know that I've had some men stationed in your school the last few weeks for security purposes—the High Sentinel has grave concerns about that Ordenan woman you hired—"

"It wasn't me!" Dorella objected. "I can't possibly be held accountable for every hire. It was that fool Yerdon and his group."

"Be that as it may," Corlas continued, "my men have found reason to be concerned, very concerned."

A light knock at her door jerked Jaina away from the wall as she scrambled to hide the amplification cone and to replace the painting. She stalked to the door, ready to give her attendant a tongue-lashing. When she threw the bolt back and opened the door, however, she stepped back in surprise.

Her handler, a burly bear of a man named Sarlon, pushed her aside and stepped inside quickly.

Jaina locked the door quickly behind him. "What are you doing here?" she hissed. "You know who I'm tailing tonight!"

Sarlon placed a finger to his bearded lips and smiled. The infuriating man had the audacity to *smile*. "Dear girl, I am not here on a whim. The situation is more urgent than we thought. We need to leave, quickly. Malithii priests are here. One is coming to this meeting with Corlas and Dorella, right now."

Jaina drew a sharp breath. "The dark ones are here? I *knew* there was something odd about the ring I found on Master Loran. It must have been a new form of mindbinder. Where in the Fallen hell did they get *mentai* after all these centuries? What does it mean? And how did they come to be in the Provinces, or this continent, for that matter?"

Sarlon shook his head, dark shaggy hair swirling about. "Corrande and the High Sentinel—along with his Watchers, of course—are declaring war on Ordena and have allied with the Malithii. They likely found some previously uncharted route across the Lost Sea and into the lands beyond the Ithan Empire. I cannot believe that the Ordenan fleet let them through the Aerwyn ocean after centuries of successful blockade. Never mind all that; what we do about these mindbinders is what matters now, if they indeed have them."

Jaina spat a curse. "They have them, though likely not many. The one I found looked rudimentary, handmade. I suspect one of the Malithii bastards has discovered how to make them and kept the secret for himself. Maybe if I kill the priest here in Myntar, I'll kill the secret to making *mentai* with him."

She drew a knife as quickly as thought, already preparing herself to enter the room next door when the Malithii arrived. She could likely kill both the priest and Corlas without taking an fatal injury, if she took them by surprise.

Sarlon shook his head again. "Not one Malithii. There are at least a dozen in Myntar, and several battalions of Watchers. You must retrieve the Ire boys as quickly as possible. Tonight, as planned. We cannot risk a confrontation here tonight. We will wait until the Malithii priest meeting with Corlas and Dorella arrives, then sneak out. No fighting, Jaina. I mean it this time."

Jaina put her hands on her hips and glared at him.

Sarlon rolled his shoulders, annoyed. "Don't you glare at me. There are just too many of them to kill quietly, Jaina. Councilor

Maira will not be pleased if we let her sons be harmed." He approached her on surprisingly quiet feet and calmed his voice. "I've already sent the Order's intelligence network underground. This is no time to play games; you know how cunning the Malithii can be. Bring the boys to my house tonight if you can, tomorrow morning before the Tournament at latest, hear? I would bet my beard the Watchers will make their move tomorrow, and they want those boys."

She sheathed her knife slowly, reluctantly. "What if I can't get them out, Sarlon? If they're already here, they might already have the boys. I may have failed already."

"You must, Jaina, and it must be you. I cannot reveal myself, no matter the outcome."

Jaina threw up her hands in exasperation but nodded, then shushed Sarlon and went back to the wall. She carefully removed the painting again and put her ear to her listening piece. For a time, she heard nothing but idle chatter from Corlas and Dorella, but soon enough another voice joined them.

"Ah, this is the Headmistress, yes? I am very happy for meeting you, Lady Dorella," a voice said in a harsh but oddly musical accent. An accent she knew well from her time fighting the Malithii and their undead soulbound in the Dark Nations. A slow anger built in her, and she had to work to control it to keep from charging into the next room to murder all three of them, consequences be damned.

Sarlon must have seen something in her face, because he put a comforting hand on her shoulder. "The time for killing will come soon enough, dear Jaina. Now is the time for calculated decisions. The boys must be taken to Ordena safely, quietly."

Jaina ignored him and moved to the door. If there were multiple Malithii in the city, there would be more than this one priest there tonight. She cracked the door to peer out quickly, then stepped into the empty hallway. Sarlon followed, muttering curses in old Ordenan. He hurriedly tossed the attendant at the front desk several Provincial paper notes as Jaina strode out the door.

The faint blue light of the moon illuminated the alleyway across from the restaurant just enough for Jaina to recognize another Malithii priest, all robed in black, a weighted copper cable twisted about his waist like a belt.

Jaina controlled her breathing and walked down the street toward the alleyway, memories of her Welitan flashing through her mind. She kept her eyes downcast to avoid detection, should the pulsing emotions inside her cause her eyes to glow with uncontrolled *infusori* energy.

Just as she drew abreast of the alleyway, she lunged, securing the Malithii priest's wrist before he knew what was happening. Rather than fight physically, Jaina took advantage of the physical contact and opened her *infusori* senses to draw on the life energy of the Malithii with all her force of will. He resisted for a time—a strong one, then—but soon began to wilt as she drew the very life from him. Before Sarlon could get close enough to feel what she was doing, she drew a knife from her sleeve and sliced through the Malithii priest's neck. Blood sprayed her as the priest fell writhing and gurgling into the dark alleyway.

All of this happened in the space of a few furious breaths. A few passersby were looking their way, peering through the darkness to see what had caused the commotion. She could hear Sarlon hurrying toward them, now cursing aloud in Ordenan.

"Fallen take you, Jaina, what happened to calculated decisions?" he panted, staring at the dying Malithii. "We've got to go before anyone summons the Legion, and you can't go through the Citadel gates looking like you've just slaughtered a pig."

Jaina smiled, relieved that Sarlon hadn't felt her pulling the priest's life source *infusori*—a serious crime among Imperators of the Order. "That *was* calculated, dear Sarlon."

He shook his head and gave her a gentle push to get her moving. They made their way quickly to Sarlon's residence in the second tier of the city, where Sarlon hustled her inside. The servants of his household didn't even give her a second glance as she hurried to a washroom to clean the blood spattered across her face and clothing.

After washing up, she hurried to an *infusori*-activated door at the back of Sarlon's house that led through an ancient tunnel into the Citadel's now-unused dungeons.

Sarlon stopped her with a hand on her shoulder before she went through the doorway. "Be careful, Jaina. If you aren't out by tomorrow evening, we'll leave without you. Councilor Maira may kill me for leaving her boys, but we must get word to the Order about the Malithii and their *mentai*."

"I'll be back with them, one way or another. The Watchers will believe that Emrael and I will be at the Citadel until our match at the Tournament tomorrow; I issued a formal challenge. If I can't get them tonight, we'll try to fight our way free during the Tournament. I arranged to fight Emrael with live blades, just in case."

Sarlon chuckled. "Of course you did. Go on, then."

She crept through the dungeons and dark halls of the Citadel as quickly as she could, finally arriving in the students' quarters where Emrael and Ban shared a room.

As she drew within a few dozen paces of Emrael's door, she heard footsteps behind her. She slunk into the shadows between *infusori-coil* sconces just as a group of men entered the hallway. Several of them wore the blue uniform of the Watchers, but not all. She recognized Master Graton, another of the Citadel's Masters of War—a weathered man in his forties with a limp in one leg and a hand that didn't work quite right, though still a capable warrior for all that. A few of his best students tagged along behind him.

Jaina was trapped. The men would see her within moments if she stayed where she was, but if she ran for Emrael's room, it would almost certainly start a fight even she would not win. These men were not patrolling this hallway by chance; they had swords at their hips for a reason. There were likely several squads of Watchers standing by as well. Jaina had only a pair of small knives, and though her training as an Imperator put her at a clear advantage, she wouldn't be able to fight her way clear by herself.

She made up her mind and walked straight toward them. "Graton," she called. "What are you doing, armed in the halls? You know weapons stay in the armory and practice yards unless there is urgent need. Why are those Watchers here?"

Graton smirked and pushed his way through the group of Watchers, who had stopped several yards away from Jaina, hands on the hilts of their swords. "Mistress Jaina, I might ask the same of you—are you perhaps paying a visit to your favorite student here? How scandalous, after hours like this, and in his room. If you are looking for entertainment of the carnal sort, I can do better than that runt."

Graton reached toward her, but Jaina stepped away. She smiled as she stared him down. "I seem to remember that runt breaking your arm and making you look a fool, Graton. If you ever try to lay a hand on me again, I'll gut you like a stag."

She drew both of her knives in a flash and flourished them for dramatic effect. Graton scurried back, and the Watchers behind him crouched, swords half-drawn in the blink of an eye. Jaina slipped her knives back into their sheaths and raised her empty hands. "Easy. You can be on your way."

The Watcher in the lead clucked his tongue and shook his head.

"I don't think so, lady. The halls are to stay clear tonight, on orders of the Commander of the Watchers himself."

Jaina sneered and looked to Graton. "Since when do the Masters of the Citadel take orders from the Watchers?"

It was the Watcher who replied, his dark eyes glittering as he smiled. "Since the High Sentinel and Commander Corlas parked an entire battalion of us in the Lord Governor Sagmyn's palace, that's when. You'll let us escort you to your rooms where two men will stay with you to ensure your safety. Or I can throw you in a cell. Your choice."

Jaina spared one last glance back at Emrael's door, then nodded to the Watcher. She quickly made a mental note of his features: high cheekbones, square jaw, thick eyebrows. Handsome, in a harsh way. She would kill this one slowly if she got the chance. "Lead the way."

She realized as she walked that there was very little chance she would get the boys out before the Tournament tomorrow, and that they'd have to fight their way clear when the Watchers occupied the school. If Sarlon was correct about their plan, it might even happen during the Tournament itself. They'd be lucky to escape alive, but at least she had arranged for her and Emrael to have real weapons for their match. Tomorrow, there would be blood.

⚔

The wind blew erratically that night, rattling the windows in their casings enough to keep both Emrael and Ban awake to worry over the events of the next day as they lay in their small bunk beds.

Ban was as taken aback by Jaina's decision as Emrael. "How could she challenge you to test for your Master's Mark without warning like this? She has taken one too many blows to the head, if you ask me. We could always try turning her in to the Sentinels. They might have the Watchers arrest her, whether our allegations are true or not."

Emrael sighed and said, "We aren't rats, Ban. I'm not going to get those preachy bastards to solve my problems for me, and they'd probably arrest us with her besides."

Ban rolled onto his side to give Emrael a pointed look. "What other options do you have?"

Emrael punched his pillow in frustration. "I have no idea, Ban. In almost three years as Jaina's student—and I'm by far her best student, maybe the best in the Citadel—I've never seen her like this. It's unheard-of to fight your own Master. With edged weapons to boot! There is something else going on. I think Mother might be involved somehow. Jaina has a tattoo on her scalp just like Mother's."

"Mother wouldn't continue to pay our tuition only to have your Master try to kill you. We can ask Elle whether she's heard anything tomorrow before the Tournament. She seems to pick up on rumors better than anyone I know. She certainly understands politics better than either of us. Besides, she'll take any chance she can to talk to you, even if it is about another woman. Maybe she could tell us why Jaina would act like this."

"What do you mean, Elle will take any chance to talk to me?" Emrael replied.

Ban rolled his eyes. "Maybe you *are* as dumb as everyone thinks you are."

Emrael glared at him. "Watch it. Talking to Elle won't help now. It doesn't matter what Jaina's reason was. Either I win or my life is effectively over. I have no choice but to be on that field tomorrow, and she knows it."

"We could always go back and live with Mother in Ordena, or maybe you could join the Sagmyn or Barros Province Legion. You're good enough already to make at least Captain Second, Em."

"Thanks, Ban, but no thanks. Captain Second isn't enough, you know that. It'd take years to get to a position of any real power—if I could do it at all—and we'd be stuck selling your Craftings for pennies on the dollar if you quit before you become a Master Crafter. Becoming a Master of War means joining any Legion I want as at least a Captain First if not a Subcommander, and is the only way I— we—are going to earn the respect of the Iraeans. We belong in our ancestral home, Ban, and this is the way we return with some shred of honor. Now all I have to do is beat Jaina."

Ban guffawed. "Good luck. I'll have Elle ready to tend to your wounds."

Emrael laughed, though he didn't find it very funny. "I wouldn't be surprised if Jaina's a full-on mage, the way she fights."

Ban was silent for a time, and when he spoke, his voice was hushed. "Was our grandfather really a Mage King, Em? Could they really channel *infusori* directly, without the help of any Craftings?"

"How should I know, Ban?"

"Elle says it's true too, the king part at least. Don't know about the mage thing," Ban mused.

Emrael clicked his tongue. "The king part I know to be true. The mage business may be nothing but folktales, but I guess it's possible.

I sure wish I knew how. It was probably just another lie that the Corrandes made up to justify creating the Watchers and invading Iraea, though."

"Do you ever think about what life would be like if our Grandfather and the Iraeans hadn't lost the war?"

Emrael growled. "It's not worth thinking that way, Ban. Our lot in life is what it is. Whining about the past won't help us climb any faster. Doesn't help that Mother ran back to Ordena as soon as Father died."

"She didn't abandon us, Em. You were there; the Sentinels threatened her and the Ordenans sent a ship to take her home. And she still stayed to see us safely to the Citadel. In the three years since Father died, she's sent you at least a dozen letters. How many have you answered?"

Emrael took a deep breath. "Fine. If I live through tomorrow, I'll write to her."

They settled into silence for the rest of the night. Emrael could hear Ban in the top bunk above him, tossing in his sleep throughout the night. Perhaps Elle and her sister could take care of Ban if Emrael was expelled or killed tomorrow. If nothing else, Emrael could join the Sagmyn Governor's Legion there in Myntar and stay relatively close to Ban. If he lived. But his dreams of wealth and status would be dead.

Emrael finally drifted off to sleep and dreamed of the first time he was picked on for being an Ire as a boy. Such a silly dream to still trouble him so often all those years later, but trouble him it did.

◦━━◦

Emrael kicked at a stone as he walked the cobbled path that passed through the Barros Palace grounds' well-manicured stands of trees, groups of hedges, and flower gardens before reaching a large gate that let out into the Legion's compound. The day's lesson about the history of the Barros Province had just about put him to sleep, and he was not looking forward to the math and letters work he was supposed to finish by tomorrow. He'd much rather be playing at swords with Halrec—one of the other boys born to a father who had fled Iraea and ended up in the Barros Legion—or escape the compound to roam the city streets for a few hours.

As he was walking and daydreaming, a group of older boys jumped out from behind the hedges. It was likely part of some game they were playing, but he was surprised that these older boys would choose to include him. The other students who took lessons in the palace typically ignored him.

He shrugged off his initial surprise and started walking again. As he passed, one of the boys grabbed him around the neck from behind, securing him while another of their group hit him first in the face, then the gut, before shoving him to the ground.

Emrael struggled to his knees, gasping for air. His mind reeled, trying to make sense of what had just happened.

One of the boys in the group—he couldn't see who, as he was very busy inspecting the grass that grew next to the garden path—spat at him and said, "Serves him right, the filthy Iraean. He has no right taking lessons with us. You hear that, Ire? Commoners are not welcome here. Stay in the barracks where you belong."

Emrael shook off his shock enough to stumble to his feet, blood dripping from his nose.

Only then did Emrael notice that one of the boys held Ban, who had been walking with his friend Elle some distance behind Emrael. She was the governor's daughter and naturally lived in the palace, but often walked Ban and Emrael to the gate that led to the Legion compound. Elle was nowhere to be seen now, however.

Two of the boys moved toward Emrael again, but Emrael darted away from them to tackle the boy who held Ban.

"Run to the gate, Ban! Run!"

Thankfully, Ban didn't hesitate. He dashed down the path toward the gate, his long limbs carrying him faster than the group of older bullies could match.

Things got even worse for Emrael. He wrestled with the boy he had tackled, punching wildly and doing well for himself until something smashed into the side of his head.

He rolled away groggily from whatever had hit him. A spiteful, thin-faced boy raised his booted foot for another kick at Emrael. Emrael felt fear, but for the first time, he also felt something else boiling inside him, drowning out the pain and fear: white-hot rage.

He scrambled to his feet and dove at the new assailant, flailing his fists, intensely focused on causing him as much harm as possible.

Emrael got in a few good shots before the rest of the group jumped in again. By the time Ban led a group of Legion guards back to the scene, Emrael was in pretty bad shape.

The boys who had ambushed Emrael scattered when they saw the guards, who helped Emrael to his feet. Ban pressed a rag to a particularly bad cut above Emrael's eye as they headed toward their house, Emrael stumbling along with the help of a guard.

"Does it hurt bad?" Ban asked, touching Emrael's head with a gentle hand.

Emrael couldn't answer for fear of crying.

When they arrived at the Ire home inside the Legion compound, the guards escorting them home timidly asked his mother to speak with Emrael and Ban's father, Janrael—Commander First Ire, to them.

Emrael's father arrived at the door with a grim face. He looked at his sons, his face calm as he took in the blood all over Emrael's face. "Get inside. Your mother will take care of you."

Janrael ushered them inside and closed the door behind them, already asking the two guards about what had happened.

Emrael limped in the door, and to his relief, his mother helped him to a chair and began tenderly cleaning his cuts without a lecture. He had worried she would blame Emrael for the encounter, maybe even punish him further. Ban assisted her with a determined look on his face and sympathy in his eyes.

His father entered the room a short time later and walked over to where Emrael was being tended.

He went to one knee in front of Emrael and put a hand on his shoulder. "I'm proud of you, boy. Thank you for protecting your brother. No matter what else you do, always fight for your family."

His father smiled, a smile sweeter for appearing on his normally severe face. "My men told me that more than one of the little bastards ended up bloodied as well. That's my boy."

He stood and rubbed the rune-etched hilt of his sword like he often did when thinking. "I think it's time that you begin military training. From now on, you—and Ban, for that matter—will report to the junior officers' training sessions in the sparring yard at midafternoon, right after your lessons at the palace."

His mother opened her mouth, but his father spoke over her. "No, I know you don't like it, Maira, but I'll be damned if I allow an Ire—my boys!—to be unable to defend themselves!"

Emrael spoke up, though it hurt his swollen jaw to do so. "Father? Why did they do this?"

"Well, son, sometimes boys are that way. We'll show them that Ires can hold their own. That's the way of things. You will be fine, and stronger for it. And I'll make sure you have guards to escort you until you feel you can handle yourselves."

Emrael looked down at the floor. "I mean, why do they hate the Iraeans? They said that we don't belong in those lessons, that commoners aren't welcome. Are we commoners?"

His father's face froze momentarily before twisting into a mirthless smile. "Is that what those low-bloods think, then? Hmm. We may not have a title or even an acre of land to our name these days, but you have the blood of lords, the blood of kings, Emrael." His smile turned to a sneer. "I ought to gut those damn kids and their bastard parents. I ought to take the men loyal to me and raze this whole pathetic city."

"Janrael . . ." Emrael's mother, Maira, began in a pleading tone. She never pleaded for anything.

Janrael looked at Maira with a shining anger in his eyes that Emrael had never seen before. His eyes almost seemed to glow. She grew quiet, very unlike her.

Emrael's father's voice hardened. "I will not stand for it, Maira. Their grandfathers were kings, and I still carry the sword and blood of my Iraean fathers. I can't go a single year without receiving a letter from some Iraean lord or another, asking me to raise the banner of the Mage Kings again. The war between Iraea and the combined provinces was a close thing, and I am not the only one it still rankles. And now my sons are ridiculed, beaten by cowardly low-blood Barros nobles? For the sake of peace, and for you, I have tried to forget my home, my blood. But it has not forgotten me—nor my sons, it seems."

"Janrael!" Maira barked, forcefully this time.

"Damn it, Maira, they're almost grown. They'll find out soon anyway. You can't keep them sheltered here forever."

Now his mother's eyes seemed to glow with anger. "I could shelter them forever in Ordena, like I have suggested for years. Or have you forgotten who I am? What I am?"

Emrael must have hurt his head worse than he thought if he was seeing people's eyes glow.

Janrael stared angrily at Maira for a tense, awkward moment, then turned then to fix his intense gaze on Emrael. "I've changed my mind. You are done with the palace lessons, Emrael. From now on, you train with me full-time. Your mother can give you lessons in the evenings to teach you everything you need to know about the world outside of the Legion."

He placed a large hand gently on Ban's head. "Ban, you will continue lessons at the palace but will be escorted by my men. And you will still join in afternoon training with Emrael and the other junior Legionmen."

Their father kissed them both on the head and marched out of the room, punching the wall next to the doorframe as he went. His fist left a noticeable dent in the wooden paneling.

Emrael woke with a start, breathing hard. A single hot tear rolled down his cheek at the memory of his father.

I'll show them.

After a long day of healing supplicants from the city with her mentor, Master Healer Yerdon, Elle entered her suite of rooms she shared with her sister. The sleeves of her fine linen shirt were specked with blood, and she had her shirt halfway unbuttoned as she crossed the foyer to the hallway that led to her and Samille's dressing chamber and separate bedrooms.

"Sami?" Elle called.

She heard her sister giggle behind the large, dark wood of her bedroom door just before it opened. Darmon Corrande and Sami exited the bedroom hand in hand, Sami blushing, Darmon smirking. Darmon's smooth chest showed through undone shirt laces, and Sami's hair had been thoroughly tousled. Elle stared at them, eyebrow raised in disgust.

"What, Elle?" Sami protested. "Get over yourself. You'd do well to have some fun yourself, you know."

Elle snorted, holding her unbuttoned shirt closed with one hand. "This is fun, is it?"

"You wouldn't understand, healing peasants and running about with those vile Ire boys all day," her sister retorted.

Darmon laughed as he settled in on one of the fine leather sofas in the spacious dressing room. "Honestly, Arielle. You do your family—and yourself—a great disservice hanging about with those outcasts. Trust me when I say that you would be far better off distancing yourself from them immediately."

Elle glared at him. "I don't choose my friends based on their political station, Darmon. They are good, talented people." She raised her eyebrows and glanced at Sami. "Besides, their family is just as noble as either of ours."

Darmon stared at her, eyes flicking to her open shirt and back to her eyes. "Not since the War of Unification, Elle, and you'd be wise to remember that. This is more than a game. Being seen with them could get you hurt."

"Is that a threat, Darmon? Perhaps I'll let my *vile friends* know you are threatening me, and we'll see what Emrael has to say about it."

Darmon lay back, closing his eyes and flicking his hand in dismissal. "He has other things to worry about right now, I think.

Though I almost wish he would try something. We should just make an empire out of these silly provinces already and take possession of the Iraean lands in truth, do away with their kind for good."

"With your father as emperor, no doubt?" Elle retorted.

Darmon's eyes opened in a flash. "I didn't say that." He glared, obviously bothered. "You know what, Arielle, maybe you *should* go find your Ire friends. Stay nice and close to them tomorrow, see how that works out for you."

She exchanged a confused glance with Sami. "What's that supposed to mean? What's happening tomorrow?"

Darmon's lips squirmed into a small smile as he leaned back into the sofa and plumped a down pillow to put behind his head. "Nothing. Forget I mentioned it."

3

E mrael Ire," Emrael called after knocking at the door to the students' equipment chamber, which adjoined the Citadel's large formal combat yard. He eyed the two Sagmyn Legionmen standing fully armed on either side of the door. There had been two at his and Ban's room as well. They'd never been stationed in the Citadel proper before that he could remember. It made little sense, as none of the students were allowed to carry weapons in the school, but he was too preoccupied with his own problems to give it much thought.

Master Graton answered the door a moment later, an expression on his grey-stubble-covered face somewhere between a grimace and a smirk. He flexed his arm and said in a gruff voice, "Surprised you showed up. The drums will let you know when it's your turn. Take these leathers if you want them. Not going to help much."

The old weapons master handed a pair of worn combat leathers to Emrael and returned to doling out the necessary gear and instructions to the various groups of combatants. The participants were segregated by round; several matches would occur simultaneously in each round, and there would be ten rounds of contests. Or would if it were a typical Tournament. Today, there was an eleventh round—his and Jaina's duel.

People died in tests for their Master's Mark with some regularity, at least in the stories Emrael had heard about the ones that took place with live blades. He was going to take any advantage he could to make sure he wasn't one of them. He didn't like being sliced open. He removed everything but his smallclothes and the pendant Ban had given him, then set to putting on the smooth leathers that smelled of oil and old sweat.

Emrael took a stool in a vacant corner of the equipment chambers, trying to lace up his unfamiliar dueling vest with shaking hands. The gear was made from thick, supple leather. It fit but was a little small at the chest. It and the accompanying bracers were designed to keep edged weapons from penetrating without restricting the fighter's movement. They weren't necessary with the blunt-edged weapons typically used at Tournaments.

Trumpets blared, sounding the beginning of the Tournament and sending alternating jolts of panic and determination through Emrael.

Some of the other students preparing themselves for their contests peered over at him with wide eyes but soon went back to their raucous conversations and boasting of who would beat whom. He was friendly with some of them, but they could see he was in no mood for talking. Besides, none of them wanted to be seen with the man Jaina intended to beat bloody. Or kill.

Emrael had always hesitated to harm Jaina in training, but now that his life was on the line, he would give Jaina everything he had. Even at his best, however, he had a very slim chance of defeating her. He was proud to have earned a place as Master-in-Training, but Jaina wasn't just any Master. Her combat skill rivaled or exceeded that of any living warrior, as far as Emrael knew.

Emrael squatted to do up his bootlaces and leg guards. He trembled so hard that it took three tries before he could get his bootlaces done up.

Emrael went back to his stool and sat down. He closed his eyes, breathing deep to calm himself. The air smelled of dust from the combat yard, the musty sweat of combatants returning from the Tournament, and the oiled leather he had donned. The noise from the crowd outside surged intermittently as rounds of contests came and went, classmates cheering on their friends as they won or lost in various competitions occurring simultaneously in multiple sparring areas in the combat yard.

After some time, the crowd outside grew quiet. Deep drums began to pound an ominous song.

Emrael rose, tucked Ban's pendant under his leathers, and walked toward the wooden doors that almost certainly led to his demise. Sunlight blinded him briefly as he pressed the latch and swung one of the double doors open to the combat yard.

Hundreds of students watched as he stepped through the doorway onto the dirt field. A low murmur started. The anticipatory energy of the silent crowd hung in the air, almost palpable.

Emrael strode towards the sparring court at the center of the yard, catching bits and pieces of conversations among the spectators. Most students attended, of course, and wealthy citizens from the city paid to watch each Tournament—the stands were full today. He was sure that word of his duel with Jaina had spread like wildfire.

"An actual duel . . ."

". . . ought to be good."

". . . white-haired Iraean prick . . ."

Emrael kept his face still and tried to focus on the combat field ahead of him, the center square reserved for this event.

His confidence built as he moved across the large yard. The weakness drained out of his legs. His hands steadied. He held his head high and met the eyes of the spectators. If this was his last day at the Citadel, maybe his last day alive, he refused to live it as a coward.

Emrael arrived at the center sparring square and stopped at the chalked edge. The dirt had been freshly raked and smoothed. A pleasant aroma emanated from the pine shavings that had been spread on the ground to soak up any blood spilled.

He lifted his eyes to the platform where several dozen Masters of the Citadel sat. Each of them were expert Crafters of devices that utilized *infusori*, or healers that used such devices to heal people who would have otherwise been untreatable. A few, like Jaina and Graton, were also Masters of War, the last vestige of a legacy of war in a world turning its eyes to industry and peace—or so the Provinces claimed.

Emrael noticed kindly Headmaster Yerdon arguing with the pinch-faced Headmistress Dorella. Headmaster Yerdon gestured toward Emrael with a flailing arm, and Headmistress Dorella pointed angrily at Yerdon. She said something, and Emrael could see spittle fly from her mouth from where he stood over a hundred paces away.

Yerdon stood abruptly and stormed down the steps to one side of the platform and out of the combat yard, forcing two of the Citadel's private Peacekeepers at the main doors to move quickly out of his way.

I wonder what that was about, Emrael thought.

He found Ban's familiar face in the front row of the bleachers, as close to the center of the field as he could be. Elle was with him. She appeared to have been crying recently. Odd; she wasn't the one about to be mauled by a Master of War. Ban gave him a thumbs-up and an encouraging smile.

The drums stopped momentarily when Emrael reached the field, but they resumed their deep rhythm only moments later. Emrael looked toward the doors that opened to admit Jaina from the dressing rooms reserved for Masters of the Citadel.

She stepped onto the field, dressed in leathers much better made than the ones Emrael wore. The deep-crimson, almost-black leathers fit her well. Emrael wondered if Jaina dyed the leather in the blood of unsuspecting students she had killed in Challenges. In hindsight, he should have suspected that an Ordenan might hold to odd—and dangerous—traditions like actual duels with their students.

Stern and alert, Jaina crossed the distance to the center field. Her head moved from side to side as she scanned the windows and roof overlooking the courtyard. She searched the crowd with her eyes, stopped for a moment when she saw Ban nearby, then settled her gaze on the Masters' platform. She no doubt carefully noted the location of each person in attendance and any possible threats—as usual. Emrael had never met anyone more paranoid.

Emrael watched as his mentor reached the opposite side of the field and focused on him. He inclined his head, and Jaina winked back at him. How could she take this so lightly? There was a very good chance she was about to ruin—or end—his life.

Up on the platform, Headmistress Dorella prepared to address the assembled students and onlookers. Her rather overweight man-servant handed her a speaking cone, an *infusori*-Crafted device designed to amplify her voice. She placed her finger on the actuator, and the attached *infusori* coil began to emit a low blue light as it powered the speaking cone. There would be copper, gold, and silver wiring inside, twisted into myriad components that amplified the speaker's voice with the *infusori* energy pulled from the attached coil.

Dorella lifted the cone to her mouth and said, "Assembled Masters and students! Today, we have a very special event! It has been some time since the Citadel has seen a formal duel at arms. The old laws still apply. The Weapons Master for this Tournament will draw colored disks to determine the weapon given to each contestant. All three traditional dueling weapons—sword, staff, and spear—are valid. Weapons Master, please proceed."

Master Graton came forward with two assistants in tow, each with a set of the three named weapons in hand. Graton approached Jaina first and extended a hat toward her.

"Mistress Jaina, please pick your weapon."

Jaina drew a blue disk carved with the image of a sword.

"Sword!" Graton declared, replacing the disk and pushing the hat at Emrael.

"Son of a bitch," Emrael spat. The sword was Jaina's strongest weapon. He quickly reached in and withdrew a yellow disk carved with a straight line.

"Staff!" Exclaimed Graton. "Combatants, take your places!"

He could have drawn worse. His Father had forced him to practice the staff frequently in the Junior Legion, and the reach compared to Jaina's sword might give him a slight advantage.

Emrael and Jaina accepted their weapons and took their places in opposite corners of the court. Emrael pulsed with nervous energy.

"Commence!" Graton commanded.

He and Jaina stepped forward and began to circle each other inside the chalked lines of the combat field. They feinted and weaved as they tested each other.

Energy surged through Emrael's body. He controlled it, focused it all on the mentor who had become his adversary.

Emrael tried his luck with a quick combination of strikes with his staff. Jaina was too fast, parrying easily and launching an attack of her own. He narrowly missed being skewered by turning his body and stepping into Jaina. That earned him a slice across the front of his leather vest and an elbow to the face. Jaina kicked him away to create space.

Emrael threw a few more fast thrusts and sweeping strikes to keep her at bay. She appeared content to keep her distance for now. Oddly, she still cast quick glances at the crowd.

Jaina never *breaks focus,* he thought.

The spectators screamed with excitement.

Emrael decided to take what advantage he could, striking as Jaina once again snuck a glance at her surroundings. She seemed particularly concerned with the Masters' platform.

Emrael swung hard at Jaina's knee, aiming to sweep her from her feet. Jaina managed to bring her sword down to parry the blow just in time, but the blow knocked her off balance.

The crowd was chaos.

Emrael followed up with a jab to Jaina's midsection, landing a solid blow that made her grunt and hunch over. Emrael continued his attack, his staff a blur as he fought for his life. Instead of parrying as Emrael expected, however, Jaina thrust toward his leading shoulder just as he struck for her head.

Just as the staff connected, Emrael felt the point of her sword lodge itself in his leather vest. He tried to twist away, but it was too late. The momentum from his aggressive attack carried him forward, and the sword passed through his vest and bit into his shoulder. He stumbled, rolled, and hit the ground with a cry.

He looked up and found Jaina hunched over, shaking her head as if to clear her vision. Blood trickled from a lump above her left eye where his staff had connected. Her sword lay on the ground.

Emrael lay on his side and quickly inspected the wound in his left shoulder as he kept an eye on Jaina. Jaina had not followed through with the thrust, and the sword didn't seem to have penetrated deeply. His shoulder ached and felt strangely numb, but he could move his arm.

As Jaina straightened, Emrael rolled to one knee. "Ha! I disarmed you. I win!"

Something flew in front of Emrael's face, causing him to flinch. He followed the path of the object and saw a thick black quarrel stuck in the dirt in front of him. That had come right near his face! If he had continued to his feet, it would likely have taken him full in the chest.

He looked about and finally took in the pandemonium occurring in the courtyard. There were people running everywhere. The Masters scrambled from their platform. Several figures wearing Citadel Peacekeeper uniforms lay in pools of blood near the doors to the combat yard, quarrels protruding from their bodies at odd angles.

Students poured from the bleachers into the yard, attempting to exit through the large double doors on either side. They must have been locked from the outside, as a mass of people were pounding at them to no avail.

The screams from the spectators that he had taken for excitement had in fact been screams of terror.

Emrael quickly found the source of their panic. There were figures on the roof of the Citadel, ringing the open courtyard. They wore the blue military uniforms of the Holy Provincial Legion, commonly called the Border Watchers or just Watchers—the military arm of the Church of the Holy Departed.

Emrael cursed as he recognized the *infusori*-Crafted crossbows they carried, the kind only the Provincial Legions or public Peacekeepers were allowed to possess in the Provinces. Those would be hard to avoid.

Emrael's mind raced. *What in Salvation are the Watchers doing here? They should be off guarding the borders with the frontier cities and the Ithan Empire. Could their Sentinel priest overlords really be so bold as to attack the Citadel itself? They aren't supposed to raise a hand to any citizen of the Provinces. Where are the Sagmyn Legionmen?*

His thoughts turned immediately to his brother. He would die before leaving without Ban.

"Emrael! Quickly, bring your weapon!" Jaina's shout brought his attention back to his mentor.

Jaina already ran towards the Masters' equipment room door, sword in hand. Emrael grabbed his staff and followed slowly while searching the crowd where Ban had been.

He couldn't find his brother but spotted Elle racing toward him. "Emrael! Master Throsden took Ban!"

She pointed to the Master's platform, where Throsden and his assistant each had Ban by an arm. Elle's older sister Samille was next to them, held by Darmon Corrande, who appeared to secure a bracelet around her wrist as Emrael watched. Ban struggled, but Sami appeared dazed, her head drooping slightly.

Emrael had almost reached where Jaina had stopped next to the closed door to the dressing room, but pushed Elle toward Jaina and turned back toward the Masters' platform to get his brother.

Several of the Watchers on the roof shot at him as he sprinted to the wooden steps of the Masters' platform, one quarrel grazing his leg as he ran. The cut burned but wasn't serious. He knew from experience that it was very difficult to hit a moving target from any distance, so he kept moving and dodged from side to side to throw off their aim.

More Watchers on the roof noticed him running and raised their weapons. There were now dozens of Watchers coming through the main doors right next to the platform as well. Emrael realized that he was never going to make it to Ban alive.

Forgive me, Ban.

He dove to the ground and rolled over his staff, hoping to throw the shooters off aim. Sure enough, at least one quarrel whistled overhead as he dove.

He rolled to a crouch, already pushing off the ground and sprinting back to Jaina and Elle, who stood outside the equipment-room door that had just opened to admit a half dozen more Watchers. These wore light armor over their blue uniforms and had swords in hand as they poured into the courtyard. They immediately focused on Emrael, thus neglecting to see Jaina behind the now open door, also with a sword at the ready.

Jaina thrust her sword expertly through a Watcher's back just as Emrael was forced to engage the first two Watchers, keenly aware of the crossbowmen likely still aiming at his back. He had to hope they wouldn't shoot while he was so near their comrades.

The first Watcher was a large man with a very crooked nose, the

other a lanky man who moved like he knew what to do with the
sword in his hands. Emrael parried the first blows from the large
man, then dipped his staff under the man's sword and swept his
legs at the knees with a powerful stroke. As he followed through,
he knelt and spun just in time to knock away a whiplike swing from
the second Watcher.

Emrael feinted, then took a step back and quickly finished
crooked-nose by clubbing him in the temple hard enough to crack
his skull.

The skinny Watcher was now alone, as thankfully none of his
companions had attacked Emrael. The Watcher feinted aggressively,
struck, and changed the direction of his attacks so fast that Emrael
suffered two cuts on the arm before finally knocking the sword out
of the Watcher's hand with a hard blow to the wrist. Emrael followed with a hard jab to the belly and finished with a swing to the
back of the Watcher's head that connected with a satisfying *thud*.

He took an instant to survey the remaining attackers, trying
to ignore the burning ache from his wounds. The encounter had
taken a very short time, but Jaina had already finished off her third
Watcher, and the final assailant had turned his full attention to her,
having rightly decided she was the greater threat. Emrael darted
forward and hit the man behind the ear with his staff.

The Watcher stiffened and lurched to the ground. Emrael had
most likely saved his life. Several of his fellow Watchers lay motionless, bleeding out onto the dirt from various wounds carved by
Jaina's sword. That could have been him just moments before on the
combat field. He still kept a wary distance from Jaina as he surveyed
the courtyard.

More Watchers poured into the courtyard through the doors near
the Masters' platform and began rounding everyone up, putting
those odd bracelets on all but a few. The students and faculty who
remained free seemed to be helping the Watchers—Headmistress
Dorella and Darmon Corrande among them.

Several Watchers were already running toward Emrael, Jaina,
and Elle. Emrael paused as he recognized one of the Watchers, this
one striding calmly toward him instead of jogging with weapons
drawn like the others.

It was his father's old friend, Corlas. Emrael knew that Corlas
had joined the Watchers after Emrael's father had been killed. He
had been his father's Commander Second and had not been named

the replacement Commander First as everyone had expected. He had left the province to join the Watchers shortly thereafter. Emrael had not seen him since. Why was he there with these men, attacking his school?

Emrael had little time to wonder. More quarrels would soon start flying from the men on the roof, and Emrael had no choice but to flee after Jaina and Elle as they darted through the door into the Masters' equipment chamber. Emrael slammed the door shut behind him, sliding the lock into place and throwing a bench behind the door for good measure.

Emrael turned around to find that Jaina and Elle had already left the main equipment chamber. Emrael had never set foot in the room and became disoriented in his panic. He could see three doors. One of them stood slightly ajar, so he took a guess and ran for it just as the Watchers began beating against the stout door behind him.

He ran through the open door and pulled up short as he almost ran into Elle. He put one hand on her back and stepped around her to find Jaina wiping her sword on Master Graton's motionless body—now detached from his head, which lay a few feet away. An awful lot of blood pumped from Graton's severed neck to pool on the floor.

Emrael had never seen that much human blood. It fascinated him, in a sick way. He had to pry his eyes from the gruesome scene to focus on Jaina.

"You stabbed me!" Emrael growled at Jaina when he had recovered his voice. "You. Stabbed. Me."

"You rolled into my parry, you fool. And hit me in the head. Couldn't you tell I was just stalling? If I wanted to stab you, you'd be dead," Jaina replied.

Elle made a high, strangled noise from behind Emrael. He looked back to see her ashen-faced and wide-eyed, still staring at the now-headless Graton, tears welling in her big blue eyes.

"Everything will be okay, Elle, I promise. I'll make sure you're safe," Emrael said, taking her cold, clammy hand in his.

He turned back to Jaina, still irate. "What do you mean, *stalling*? You challenged me to that insane duel! You threatened me—a lot."

Jaina shrugged. "I needed the Watchers to think we'd be here at the Tournament. I tried to get you and your brother out last night, but the Watchers were one step ahead of me. I had only a day's warning that the Watchers were going to attack the school, but not when, and if it happened to be during the Tournament, I needed someone I could trust with a real weapon. Just follow me. We have little time."

Jaina strode to the door, clearly planning to leave without answering him further.

Emrael was still confused but followed her cautiously. "What do we do now? They must be guarding the entrances to the Citadel. Those guys pounding on the door behind us are going to break in any minute. We need to get to the governor's palace, let the Legion know we've been attacked."

Jaina turned, handed him a sword—presumably Master Graton's—and replied, "The Lord Governor and his Legion will not help us. This was done on higher orders than his. Come quickly."

Higher orders than those of a Lord Governor? Emrael thought as he dropped his staff and accepted the sword. Every ten years, a governor from one of the provinces took a turn as the Chancellor of the United Provinces, acting as the final authority on any business involving multiple provinces. That mantle had just passed from Governor Barros to Governor Corrande last year. But the High Sentinel of the Church of the Holy Departed commanded the Watchers. Had Corrande struck a deal with the High Sentinel? That thought sent a queasy feeling roiling through his gut.

"What! How could—"

Jaina ignored him, stepped to the door, and jerked it open to check the hallway outside before slipping out, sword at the ready.

Emrael growled his frustration but limped after her, pulling Elle along by the hand. They padded away from the courtyard and into a stairwell leading down into the Citadel's cellars. He was glad to lean on the wall momentarily while he urged Elle down the stairs ahead of him.

"Stop!" a voice called as Emrael started down the stairs. "What is going on? Why are you going down there?"

Emrael peeked back around the corner. A grey-haired figure was striding down the hall toward him. It was Headmaster Yerdon.

"You there," Yerdon commanded, "with the white hair. I can see you there with Arielle. Stop and tell me what is going on. Why aren't you at the Tournament, and why are you three skulking about? You were supposed to be fighting a duel with Mistress Jaina, as I recall. I expected to be treating one or both of you before long. Where are you going with my student?"

Jaina hurried back up the few stairs, grabbed Master Yerdon's elbow, and hustled him forcibly down the stairs. "We must leave. I'm sure you also have word of Bortisse Corrande's seizure of the Watchers. They obey him completely now—with the blessing of the High Sentinel—not the Council of Governors. *Infusori* Crafters are being rounded up and fitted with binders all across the Provinces. The Watchers have the school."

Master Yerdon exclaimed, *"Binders?* Where in Salvation did they get those? Binders haven't been seen on this continent for centuries! Millennia! Most scholars don't think they even existed outside of children's fables and religious texts! Are you sure?"

"Feel free to go back and look for yourself," Jaina replied over her shoulder as she continued down the stairs.

Master Yerdon grumbled but followed Jaina just as quickly as the others. Emrael headed down the stairs last. He had just reached the bottom when he heard several quick footsteps behind him. Before he could turn around, something hit him hard from behind, throwing him to the floor. He screamed as blinding pain shot from his wounded shoulder and radiated through his upper body. His sword flew from his hand to skitter across the floor, well out of reach.

Emrael twisted under the weight that pinned him to the floor and found himself staring into the dark eyes of Darmon Corrande.

4

"Hello again, Ire," Darmon said with a vicious smile. He put his knee into Emrael's stomach and slipped a knife from his belt.

"I want you to know that I plan to work your brother's life away like the slave he is. Fitting, considering our families' past. I almost wish I could keep you alive so you could see—"

He cut off as a low, warm female voice spoke from the corner. Emrael could have sworn it was Samille Barros. "Darmon, come here."

Darmon glanced over his shoulder, obviously surprised and confused. "What are you doing down—"

Emrael struck Darmon in the jaw with a closed fist. The blow rocked Darmon backward, giving Emrael the space he needed to flip Darmon off of him. He rolled, pinned Darmon's arm that held the knife, then struck him in the temple as hard as he could with a knee. Darmon's head slumped to one side, his body slack, his breath coming in ugly snorts and rasps.

Emrael heaved a sigh of relief and slumped onto his hands and knees, resting his head on the cold stone floor. Everything hurt, and he was so tired. He began to shake as the rush of battle rage trickled from his body.

Gentle hands touched the back of his neck. He looked up to see Elle kneeling beside him, her lightly curled hair falling around her concerned face.

"Emrael! Em, are you okay? Say something!" Her voice had returned to its normal pitch, higher and sweeter than her older sister's.

Emrael lifted his head to look her in the eye. "I'll live. That was very good thinking. Thank you, Elle."

She smiled in relief. "Maybe you should work on your fighting. I thought you were supposed to be good. You won't always have me around to save you." Her smile broadened to a mischievous grin as she helped Emrael climb to his feet.

Emrael stood to find Jaina and Yerdon coming back toward the stairs from where they had continued on through the cellars.

Anger and impatience were plain on their faces until they noticed Darmon lying on the floor, blood slowly oozing from his nose and one ear.

"Dead?" Jaina asked.

"No. He'll have a terrible headache, though," Emrael responded.

"Pity. You should finish him off. You will be doing the world a kindness."

"I don't have the same comfort level with killing that you seem to," Emrael said, peering somewhat regretfully down at the person he hated most in all the world. He probably should finish him off but couldn't bring himself to kill in cold blood.

Jaina guffawed. "He just tried to kill you. He helped Bind your brother and the others as slaves. Are you really going to let him live?" She stared at Emrael for a moment. "Either way, we need to move quickly."

Shouts sounded in the hall at the top of the stairs, and Jaina turned, cocking her head to listen. She put her finger to her pursed lips to motion for silence and started down the hall at a quiet run.

They left Darmon behind and made their way swiftly through the cellars, passing old holding cells from the days when the lower levels were used as a dungeon. Rusted bars enclosed small stone rooms that smelled of dank abandonment. Emrael could see black, slimy growth in the back corners by the light of the small *infusori* lighting coils that Yerdon had produced from his pouch.

To Emrael's surprise, Jaina turned suddenly into one of the old cells. There was nothing distinctive about this cell that Emrael could tell. It was just one in a long row of old cells in this distant part of the dungeon and seemed to him like a not very good place to hide.

Jaina opened the door—the hinges must have been well oiled, as it opened without a sound—and ushered them into the cell, closing the door behind them. She put her hand to the back wall, and Emrael could feel her doing . . . something. Emrael closed his eyes and tried to understand what he was feeling. He and Ban had sometimes been able to sense *infusori* in a way nobody else seemed to but had never dared tell anyone for fear of ridicule.

But this was something very different, something he'd never felt before. Jaina seemed to be using *infusori* directly, not as a fuel source for some Crafted device. She was a mage! She had to be. The idea frightened and excited him all at once.

Abruptly, the wall shifted and slowly ground its way backward.

It stopped after sinking back only about a pace. He looked to Jaina, confused. She rolled her eyes and ducked through the narrow opening exposed in the side of the recess, which had been invisible from where he stood.

Master Yerdon and Elle followed, and Emrael groaned as he limped after them down a narrow tunnel. As they started down the tunnel, Emrael could hear shouting echoing through the dungeons behind them. The wall slid shut with an audible *clunk* of stone a moment later, cutting off the sound of their pursuers.

The passageway continued for what seemed like leagues. Emrael's battered body protested each step. His left arm hung limp at his side, blood dripping slowly from his fingers. Elle held his other hand and guided him down the tunnel gently. He could barely see by the light of the *infusori* coils held in Master Yerdon and Jaina's hands and was glad for Elle's hand in the darkness.

This tunnel seemed old, but the floors were smooth, and it seemed to be perfectly straight, with no twists, turns, or elevation changes. Even still, Emrael occasionally stumbled and relied on Elle to steady him. He thought that they might be heading south toward the city. Where had this tunnel come from? Jaina had obviously known where to find it. So many unanswered questions, but the only one that truly mattered was how he was going to rescue Ban.

Eventually, Jaina called for a halt when they reached a solid wall of stone at the end of the tunnel. Emrael closed his eyes and leaned against the cold, damp tunnel wall as Jaina put her hand to what was presumably another hidden door.

Emrael could once again feel Jaina drawing *infusori* from the gold coil she held and somehow pushing it through the wall. He sidled closer to her, every whit of his attention on the magic he could feel happening right in front of him.

He had heard stories of students who had developed small magic tricks during their work with *infusori*-Crafted devices, but Jaina was doing much more than that. This must be true magic, the stuff from the histories. Where was she getting so much power from, and how? All of that power could not be coming from those small coils, could it? He had never felt anything like it.

Tired to the point of being delirious, Emrael reached out with his uninjured hand and grabbed the coil in Jaina's hand, drawing on the remaining *infusori* like he had felt her do.

Jaina grunted with surprise and displeasure, but it barely regis-

tered in his mind. He shook with the power of it. This was the power
of gods. He was invincible.

He put the other hand to the wall and could feel something . . .
a spot inside the wall that seemed more receptive to the *infusori*
energy. He gathered the *infusori* swirling within him and *pushed*
the energy to that spot. It flowed from him in an avalanche, fire
and ice passing through his flesh, his soul, to soak into the stone in
front of him.

He heard the stone door crash open with a violent *crunch*, and all
went black.

⟶

Darmon Corrande sat at the foot of the large rectangular table in
the Masters' Hall of the Citadel, a damp rag tied around his throbbing head. That damn Ire rat and the little Barros wench would pay
for this. He was going to see to it.

His father, Bortisse Corrande, sat at the head of the table. Three
men occupied the chairs to his father's right: High Sentinel Burlahn of the Church of the Holy Departed; Corlas Anton, the Commander of the Holy Provincial Legion—the Watchers, the military
arm of the Church; and one of his father's new foreign allies, a priest
in a dark hooded robe. To his left sat another three: Governor Sagmyn, a Barros Legion Subcommander representing Governor Barros, and some lord or other likely representing the Iraean province,
as if their opinion mattered.

"Gentlemen," his father said, placing his large hands on the table
in front of him. "Thank you for traveling all this way for a formal
vote. The Ordenan threat has become so severe, to my own province
and each of yours, that we can wait no longer. I've called you here for
a vote on a formal declaration of war. We must break the stranglehold they have on the United Provinces. Trade has all but stopped
through Corrandian ports, and I know your people suffer as well.
The devils will not negotiate; they will not compromise. We need to
take action, and we need to join together as never before."

The Barros Subcommander and Governor Sagmyn shifted uncomfortably but said nothing. The Ordenans allowed trade to flow
through their ports, and if they joined his father in a declaration of
war, that would cease.

Bortisse continued. "As you have no doubt noticed, with Governor
Sagmyn's blessing, Commander Corlas and I have taken possession

of the Citadel. The Masters and students here will be offered prestigious work in support of the war effort. We need their technology if we are to stand a chance against the Ordenan devils and their navy. Any questions before we move to the vote?"

"Who the Fallen is he?" the Barros Legion Subcommander asked flatly, pointing at the man in the robe.

Darmon's father's hard face cracked into a slight smile. "This is our greatest ally, my Barrosian friend. He is an emissary from the lands across the Aerwyn Ocean, a land also plagued by the Ordenan devils. They have been at war with the Ordenans for centuries in their homeland and can help combat the devils' use of arcane magic. He insists we address him as simply 'Priest'."

Priest lowered the hood of his robe, revealing a man with dark hair and a pale white face framed by angular tattoos that climbed his neck to cover his face. "We will get to know each other very well, I'm sure, my friend," he said, addressing the Barros Subcommander in a nasal, accented voice. "We Malithii welcome brotherhood with all who oppose the Ordenan plague."

The Subcommander gave a slight nod after a moment. "Very well."

Bortisse smiled again. "Good. Now. All in favor of a formal declaration of war, granting me, Bortisse Corrande, command of the combined Provincial Legions as the current Provincial Steward?"

Corlas, the Commander of the Watchers, pounded his fist on the table excitedly. "You shall have the full might of the Holy Provincial Legion behind you, Lord Corrande."

The Barros Subcommander didn't look happy about it, but he pulled a sealed letter from the inside of his jacket. "You have my governor's pledge," he said, tossing the letter on the table.

"Aye," Governor Sagmyn proffered, a bit too eagerly. "I'll gladly lend my support, Lord Corrande."

The Iraean lord sat quiet. Bortisse glared at him. "Haven't the Iraeans learned to cooperate yet, Lord Syrtsan?"

The Iraean pursed his lips, never looking away from Bortisse's stare. "We'll offer no dissent, Lord Corrande, but we have no Legion to offer. Do as you wish."

Bortisse stared a moment longer, then turned to address the room. "Good. Let's get to work, gentlemen. I'll have orders for each of you to take to your Legion Commanders by this evening. You are excused."

The Iraean lord and the Barros Subcommander stood and exited, but Governor Sagmyn lingered awkwardly.

Bortisse sighed. "Yes, Governor?"

"Oh. Ah. Nothing really, I just wondered . . . will you be staying long, Lord Corrande?"

"As long as it takes, Governor. You know as well as I that the Crafters of the Citadel need careful oversight. I'll be here with the Malithii priests to oversee the research efforts."

Governor Sagmyn bobbed his head, seeming to shrink in on himself as he backed toward the door. "Oh, yes. Very well. You are most welcome, Lord Corrande. Please allow me to assist you in any way I can. My Legion is at your command."

He slipped from the room quickly, leaving Darmon, the Malithii priest, and Corlas with Bortisse. Darmon's father turned to consider him with pursed lips and serious eyes. "Come here, boy."

Darmon approached his father with slow, wary steps. "Yes, Father?"

His father put a hand to the side of his head. Darmon was forced to crane his neck to meet his father's eyes as he loomed over him. "You let Ire escape?"

"I was ambushed! Corlas and his Watchers were the ones that couldn't handle Emrael and that Ordenan bitch in the combat yard," Darmon spat. "Besides, we got his brother, Banron. He's the valuable Crafter. Emrael is nothing."

His father's grip on his head tightened. "Emrael Ire is a loose end. I do not like loose ends, especially not loose ends with claims to an Iraean throne, however tenuous. We can't afford any disturbances from those barbarians if we are to solidify Barros's acceptance of my command of this war. You saw how insolent Lord Syrtsan remains even after all these years. You will not fail me again."

"Yes, Father."

Bortisse pursed his lips again, his expression hard as he stared Darmon in the eyes. He nodded and pushed Darmon away gently, turning to loom over the hooded Malithii priest. "Priest, I am not pleased with your abuse of our arrangement. My men assigned to accompany you disappeared without a trace, you've brought those . . . *monsters* into my Provinces without my permission, and now you've let one of my most dangerous rivals escape your grasp. I struck our bargain to rid the world of the Ordenan devils that killed my father and put a stranglehold on my province, not to spread your abominations to my empire. You are dangerously close to exhausting my benevolence."

The Malithii cocked his head. "I'm sure your men will turn up eventually, Your Excellency. I already have men tracking the young Iraean. He will be found."

Bortisse stared at Priest for a long moment. "See that he is. Accompany my son to the stables. The two of you will be leading a squad of Watchers in pursuit of the boy. Now you'll excuse me; I must speak with High Sentinel Burlahn and Commander First Corlas about our next steps."

The Malithii bowed, face still. "As you wish, Excellency."

Darmon followed Priest through the door into the hallway and flinched violently when the dark-robed man turned quickly to grab him by the shoulders. "It is obvious that I can sit in the shadows no longer," he hissed in Darmon's ear. "My brethren and I will be taking a more . . . direct approach."

His breath smelled strongly of lavender. Odd that such an unpleasant man should maintain such a pleasant aroma.

Priest's eyes glowed briefly as his hand shot out to grasp Darmon by the neck. Darmon tried to slap the hand away, appalled at the foreigner's insolence, but found himself frozen, unable to move. He had never felt so helpless, so instantly terrified. His already-aching head now felt like it was about to split in two.

The dark priest leaned very close. "You answer to me now, boy. Do we understand each other?"

Darmon's headache began to fade as Priest removed his hand, and he found himself nodding in fear.

"I thought we might. Now come. Our quarry is fleeing as we speak."

———

Emrael opened his eyes groggily. He was being carried somewhere, and not gently. Jaina had hoisted him on her shoulders and was lugging him through a finely furnished house. He could smell her floral perfume. The wooden floors were burnished and gleaming, and there seemed to be many fine copper pieces in the place. Each must have been worth a fortune.

Damn, Jaina is strong, he thought. She seemed to be having no trouble with his weight.

She turned into a room and put Emrael on a bed. Without hesitation, she set about stripping him of his clothing. Elle followed Jaina into the room and helped her undress him with a worried look in her eyes.

"What are you doing?" Emrael protested feebly. He tried to fend them off but had little strength in his arms. He couldn't remember ever having been this tired.

The women ignored him, undressing him like they would a child. Dried and congealed blood from his wounds covered his chest and shoulders. His leg still bled from the gash caused by the Watcher's arrow, smearing crimson all over the sheets.

Elle picked up a bowl of steaming water and a cloth from a side table. She began cleaning Emrael while Jaina exited, calling for Yerdon.

Elle murmured as she wiped the blood from Emrael gently, cleaning the cloth in the hot water every so often. "Jaina wasn't too pleased with whatever happened with that wall slamming open. I wouldn't have known you had anything to do with it except that your hand went cold as ice, then she looked at you like you had slapped her in the face. I don't know what that was about, but I'll keep you safe." She said that last with a small laugh.

Jaina reentered the room and thanked Elle. Master Yerdon appeared at the bedside shortly after. He brought a tray of surgical instruments, including a wooden case full of intensely bright gold *infusori* coils.

These were high-grade *infusori* coils, the blue glow emanating from them stronger than from any coil Emrael had ever seen, even stronger than those he'd seen his mother use for healing at the Barros Palace when he was younger. Each was set in a copper casing that covered the bottom half of the coil. Thin, short needles that would penetrate his skin protruded from the bottom of each copper casing. He hated needles, but these allowed for better transfer of the *infusori* from the coils into the body. The *infusori* contained in the coils was akin to energy the body used to heal itself, and the body would slowly accept the *infusori* to replenish any it had lost due to sickness or injury.

Emrael had needed healing with *infusori* coils like these once before as a young man, back home in the Barros Province. He and his best friend from the Barros Junior Legion, Halrec, had been practicing dueling with real swords sneaked from the armory after hours. Emrael's arm had been sliced open to the bone. He had lost a great deal of blood, and Emrael's mother had produced coils and healing apparatus similar to these.

The coils that Yerdon had on his tray would have cost a fortune. Coils had to be of a very high quality to hold enough *infusori* to heal effectively, and that made them—more specifically, the amounts of *infusori* they held—expensive.

Yerdon proceeded to clean and sew shut the larger wounds on Emrael's shoulder, chest, and leg while Elle mixed something in a cup and forced it down Emrael's throat. Emrael soon grew too tired to keep his eyes open, despite the nearly overwhelming pain. As he closed them, he felt the prick of the healing apparatus's needles being inserted into his body.

Jaina spoke quietly as he drifted off to sleep. "He will need to be guided by someone with the proper abilities. We cannot let him loose now that he's shown ability with the Art."

A deep voice that Emrael did not recognize answered. "You are the best qualified, at least here in the Provinces. I trained you; I know how good you are. Besides, you have worked with the boy. He will listen to you. He *must* listen to you."

There was silence for a short time. Finally, Jaina sighed. "I suppose you are right. He's occasionally insufferable, but we all make sacrifices for the sacred Order." There was more than a little bitterness in her voice.

Emrael had all sorts of misgivings about their conversation but could fight off sleep no more.

⌇⌇⌇

Emrael woke to see Jaina and Elle speaking softly on a sofa next to his bed. The healing-grade coils Yerdon had used on him lay on a bedside table, completely devoid of their blue light.

Before his foolish accident several years earlier, his hair had been a dark brown like his father's. His hair had turned stark white after his mother had exhausted similar coils to heal him. He wondered whether it had gone back to brown this time.

He swung his legs out of bed and sat up. He blushed and pulled the sheet over himself as he discovered that he was still completely naked. He rolled his shoulder to feel the effect of his injuries. He was still sore and could feel the stitches tugging at his sutured lacerations, but he felt almost whole, as if he had healed for weeks.

"How long was I out?"

"Since yesterday afternoon. It is now almost midmorning," Jaina said, handing him his pendant. Emrael thanked her and slipped it over his head. Had they really needed to strip him completely, even his underpants and pendant?

He looked from Jaina to Elle, rubbing his hand absently through his hair. Elle smiled at him. "Your hair is still white, same as before. The *infusori*-assisted healing didn't change anything this time."

He stopped feeling at his hair, embarrassed she had guessed his thoughts—Glory, he was surprised she remembered at all. He gave her a bashful smile, then squinted at her in confusion. "I felt like I was dying last night, but now I could run a lap around the city. I wasn't that gravely injured; why did I pass out?"

Elle looked to Jaina, who raised one eyebrow as she surveyed the two of them before answering. "You are a mage, Emrael. You can manipulate *infusori* directly, and you tried to use too much last night. It happens sometimes the first time a mage uses their abilities, though most aren't quite as . . . dramatic about it." She arched an eyebrow at him and pursed her lips in a wry smile.

"Wait wait wait," Emrael interrupted, leaning forward as panic froze his heart in his chest. "I'm a *what*? I can do *what*?"

Jaina nodded calmly. "You can manipulate *infusori* without the aid of a Crafted device," she confirmed. "You may even know or have heard of students at the Citadel who learned to control *infusori* in some small fashion, after extended study of *infusori* Crafting. I'm positive you have heard stories of mages of old—including your own Iraean and Ordenan ancestors. This is the same thing."

Emrael closed his eyes and rubbed his face with one hand. This was the stuff of fairy tales—or nightmares.

Elle shifted on the sofa and asked calmly, "How did he do that, Mistress Jaina? He used more energy than your coil contained. Or so I would think. It was nearly drained already."

Jaina smiled and stood to address them both. "Excellent question, Elle."

She pointed her finger at Emrael and stared at him for a long moment, head cocked. "He accessed another energy source besides the *infusori* he rudely stole from my coils—he drew on his own life source, the *infusori* energy that all living beings possess."

"Okay . . ." Emrael said slowly. "Mages can use their own life source as energy? That seems dangerous."

She nodded, pacing back and forth as she had when lecturing at the Citadel. "Indeed. Mages must be touching a source of *infusori* to pull it into themselves and in turn use it to manipulate an external object. Once you exhausted the *infusori* in the coils, your first instinct was to access the energy with the least resistance." She leaned toward Emrael to poke his chest with one finger. "You used your own life source to power the actuator in that door until your body could no longer sustain itself. It nearly killed you, in fact. Pulling large amounts of *infusori* from yourself can be traumatic, and you used a large amount indeed. That door weighs at least a thousand pounds."

Emrael snorted, still trying to make sense of what Jaina was telling him. "Does that mean I'm an Imperator, like in the stories?"

"An Imperator?" Jaina guffawed. "Hardly. Forget everything you think you know about Imperators, boy. The title of Imperator is an honor given only to those who earn it in the service of the Ordenan Imperial Order. We alone have preserved the glory of the Ravan Imperators of old. But a mage, you most certainly are."

"I can't be," he muttered, shaking his head. It made no sense. He had always liked to believe he could feel *infusori* but had never been nearly as good as Ban at *infusori* Crafting or anything like it. Glory, he could name dozens of students who were better Crafters. Could he really have some special ability even beyond Crafting?

"Shit," he groaned, louder this time as he recalled leaning against the cold wall, reaching toward the energy that seemed so warm and inviting, the wall slamming open as the lights in Master Yerdon's hand extinguished.

"I see you remember now," Jaina said, a smirk on her face. "You gave me quite a surprise, you know. My only consolation is that Sarlon nearly shit himself when his door crashed open like that."

The smile slipped from her face as she locked her gaze to his. "Next time may not be so harmless. You can deplete someone's energy to a dangerously low point, like you did to yourself yesterday. You could even kill them, if you deplete their *infusori* completely. It happens now and then with poorly trained mages. You will kill yourself—and others—if you aren't careful."

Emrael felt sick to his stomach. His mind reeled. "Justice, Mercy, and Fallen Glory. You are telling me that magic is real, mages and Imperators are real, and we are as dangerous as the Sentinels preach?"

Elle stared at him with pity in her eyes, but Jaina's eyes were stone, her gaze unwavering. "We are very real, Emrael. Your own Iraean ancestors practiced 'magic' not two generations ago. You are a liability, and I'm tasked with making sure you do not hurt yourself or others until I can turn you over to your mother and the rest of the Council of Imperators."

"My mother is one of you?" Emrael asked in a squeaky voice.

Elle followed quickly with a query of her own. "She's part of your governing Councils?"

Jaina quirked a small smile at them both and nodded. "Maira's secrets are her own to share, but she is our best chance of securing help to rescue Ban, which is why you will both accompany me back to Ordena immediately. Sarlon has an Ordenan *infusori*-powered vessel in the harbor at Ladeska waiting for us. We can be in Ordena within weeks, and back with a few dozen of my Imperators to rescue your brother and the others before the month turns."

"But I can't go," Emrael replied incredulously, wrapping the bedsheet around his waist and standing to confront Jaina. Anger surged through him, pushing rational thought to a distant corner of his mind. "I can't leave my brother to the Watchers! A month is far too long—who knows what they'll do to him, where they'll take him. They just killed people at the Citadel! I've got to do something now. I don't care if all the Provinces and the Watchers together try to stop me."

Jaina gripped her hair in her fists as she shook her head in frustration, then she laughed softly. "What exactly would you do to rescue him from thousands of well-armed Watchers, Emrael? They will be crawling all over the dungeons now that they know we escaped them. Corrande has declared war on Ordena and seized control of the Provinces with the help of the High Sentinel and his Watchers. There is no one else in the Provinces who will oppose him. Worse still, they have help from evil mage-priests called Malithii, the ancient enemy of the Ordenans against whom we fight a centuries-old war in the Dark Nations across the Ordenan Sea. I can do nothing without reinforcements. Which means that *you* can certainly do nothing to help your brother right now."

Emrael sat back down on the narrow bed, put his head in his hands. "I don't know, Jaina. I just know I can't leave him, *especially* if what you say is true. I heard you tell Yerdon that the Watchers and these Malithii are using binders on their prisoners. The stories Sentinel priests tell say that binders did horrible things to people."

He looked up, staring desperately at Elle. "Elle, help me here?"

Elle shifted again on the sofa, looked at Jaina, then back at Emrael before speaking. "I don't understand what's going on at all, Emrael. I think we need to listen to Mistress Jaina, at least until we have a better idea of how to help Ban, Sami, and the others."

Jaina let out a long breath. "Exactly. Unless I am terribly wrong about what is occurring, it is well beyond your ability—or mine, for that matter—to change what is happening. We need trained mages—Imperators—and an army, and that means gathering help in Ordena. Your brother should be safe enough in the meantime. The binders they are using are not the ones from your stories. Believe me, I know something of losing loved ones to soulbinders. The one

I found on Master Loran was removed easily enough and caused no lasting harm. Your brother is not in immediate danger; I am almost sure of it."

Emrael could feel his anger building, hot tears of indignation welling in his eyes. "I won't go, Jaina. My place is here. I will die here before I abandon my brother."

Jaina's expression didn't change as she said, "I cannot allow it, and my Order will not allow it even if I tried. I *will* stop you, and you *will* accompany me to Ordena if I have to beat you and stuff you in a barrel to get you there."

She paused to let the threat sink in. "Since you seem to be back in good health, we are having a meal with our hosts in half an hour. We will also be discussing travel arrangements. You may want to wear pants."

Jaina stalked from the room without a backward glance. Emrael stared after her in consternation, tears finally wetting his cheeks.

Elle rustled on the sofa. Emrael ducked his head quickly, wiping his tears roughly with one hand. He had forgotten she was still in the room.

"I can't leave him, Elle. I just can't."

He looked out the window at the street below and realized that they were in the second tier of the city, very near a little café where he and Ban liked to spend off-days when they had spare money for coffee and pastries. He could be back to the Citadel within minutes. He turned to look Elle in the eyes. "Do you think you could find me some clothes and cover for me while I slip out?"

Elle rose from the sofa and settled next to him on the bed, voice soft but firm. "Emrael, what would you do? I want Sami and Ban back just as badly as you, but what can we do?"

"Do you really think that Jaina cares about rescuing Ban and Sami, Elle? If she will leave them to their fate now, what will stop her from doing so in the future? All they are likely to care about is continuing their war with these foreign priests and their binders. I don't even trust my mother to come back for Ban. She left us here alone, after all. I don't know what I can do, but I have to try."

"But if we run, we'll have Jaina *and* the Watchers after us," Elle mused.

Emrael shook his head in exasperation. "Why do they care so much about keeping me close? It's not like I'm the only *infusori* Crafter to ever manifest a magic trick or two."

"I think it's more than that," Elle whispered, glancing at the open door. "You heard Jaina. Your mother is one of them, and I think she's in a position of power. They won't let go of you easily."

"Fallen take the lot of them, I'm not leaving Ban. We'll go down to eat, but when we get a chance, we run. Maybe we can get word to your father and ask for his help. Jaina may have been wrong about his allegiance, especially if Corrande and the Watchers took Sami too."

Elle hesitated. "Em, I've heard things . . . My father may not be very happy to see you or any Iraean at the moment."

Emrael scowled and picked at the blanket. "You mean what Darmon said the other day in the dining hall? He was just saying that to make me angry. The Iraeans aren't a credible threat to mount a serious rebellion, and I'm certainly not involved even if they are. I'm nothing to them."

Elle pursed her lips, clearly not convinced. "Perhaps."

Emrael ignored her skepticism. "I'll escape tonight. You're welcome to come if you'd like. I think I might be able to get through one of the Citadel's service gates if I can find the right crew coming back from the *infusori* Wells. I can get inside and find Ban."

Elle raised her eyebrow. "You're going to sneak around, evade hundreds of Watchers, and rescue your brother—someone they know to be a skilled Crafter and are sure to be guarding—by yourself?"

"It's worth a shot, Elle. I'm not helpless, you know. They'll probably be holding him either in the Crafting laboratories or the cells in the basement."

Elle drew a deep breath. "I really don't think you are thinking this through, Em. You'll need a better plan than that." Her eyes glazed as her mind went elsewhere, chewing on her lip as she pondered.

Worried she'd only reach the safe, *smart* conclusion that they should listen to Jaina, he broke the silence. "Elle . . . could you help me find some clothes? And perhaps stand outside for a moment while I dress?"

Elle's attention snapped back to the present, and she let out a little giggle. "I already saw . . . what there is to see."

"Elle!" Emrael yelped, mortified and blushing as she handed him some nondescript clothing that had been laid in the corner of the room.

She giggled again. "Oh, please. Get over yourself. I've seen plenty of men as an attending healer."

She waited outside the room while he dressed, then they headed down the hall and a short flight of stairs together. Heavenly smells wafted from the kitchen, reminding Emrael and his empty stomach that he had gone almost a full day without food.

They followed the sound of dishes clattering and people talking to a room with a large wooden table beneath an inverted copper dome. The burnished copper reflected and magnified the light from *infusori* coils set into the fixture, filling the entire room with a steady light blue glow.

Four people sat at the table talking quietly, serious expressions on their faces. Jaina sat next to a large man with a full dark beard and the caramel skin of an Ordenan. Across from them sat fatherly Master Yerdon and a beautiful middle-aged woman with the olive skin and dark yellow eyes common in the southern Ithan Empire. He'd have to ask her about the Ithan frontier—he'd heard that the mercenary companies that forayed into the Ithan Wilds paid very well for someone with Citadel military training, and even better for someone with knowledge of *infusori* Crafting.

All fell silent as Emrael and Elle paused in the doorway.

After a moment, the large Ordenan with the beard grunted and said with a noticeable Ordenan accent, "Welcome, welcome, both of you." He paused and stared at Emrael for a moment. "White hair on a man barely able to grow a beard. Things you see these days."

He was the owner of the deep voice that Emrael had heard speaking with Jaina while Master Yerdon had operated on him. He must be part of Jaina's Order, judging by the way he had talked to her. He wondered what business the Ordenans had owning a house with a tunnel leading to the Citadel.

The eastern woman gave a throaty chuckle and fixed her calculating yellow gaze on Emrael like a fox eying its prey. "Oh, I think he is cute, Sarlon. Nice strong jaw, broad shoulders. I like the hair, the honey-colored skin, the whole thing. Though I liked him better without all of those clothes."

Emrael tried not to blush but rolled his shoulders uncomfortably and cleared his throat. Had everyone come up for a peek at him? Elle giggled again, elbowing him playfully.

Jaina spoke as they stared into the room without moving toward the table. "This sack of hair next to me is our host, Master Merchant Sarlon. The fine, ever-so-tactful Ithan is Yamara, his wife. They try very hard to seem crass and uncouth, but they have some redeeming qualities. At times."

Sarlon and Yamara smiled. Jaina rolled her eyes but continued.

"They are two of the most respected Imperators operating in the Provinces. They are going to help us get to Ordena. Sarlon has already arranged safe passage out of the city tonight with an Ordenan fleet ship. Enjoy this moment of respite; we leave immediately after dinner."

Sarlon cleared his throat and slapped the table gently. "Come, please, young friends. Share my table; we can discuss the details as we eat."

Emrael and Elle took seats across from each other at the table, Emrael next to Sarlon and Elle next to Yamara. Sarlon rang a small bell mounted to the wall behind him, and liveried servants with the tan skin and dark features common to Ordena brought dishes of wilted greens, roasted meat, and large dumplings in a brown sauce. They carried in a cask of amber-colored ale next, and each of them soon had a full mug set in front of them—all except for Jaina, who received a glass of dark red wine.

She flashed a quick smile at Sarlon as she swirled the wine gently in her glass. "You remembered. Thank you, Sarlon."

Sarlon winked in return, then turned to Emrael as he took his first bite. "This is a new recipe I used on the rib roast. What do you think?"

Emrael looked at his plate as he swallowed a mouthful of food, then back to Sarlon. "I like the mint leaf and peppers. What is the sweetness I taste? Dates?"

Sarlon's lips curled upward slowly into a large, toothy grin partially hidden behind coarse black hair. "You know food! Maybe you aren't so bad after all. I included some powdered molasses in the rub for the beef. Do you like it?"

"I do. I bet it would be even better on pork."

"Perhaps we can try that," Sarlon said, nodding approvingly. "Where did you learn to cook?"

"I have been a chef in the Citadel kitchens for a few years," Emrael replied. "Once I have my brother back, I'll stop by and show you how it's done."

"You have a deal!" Sarlon proclaimed with a deep belly laugh. "Though you'll have to come to Ordena. My lovely wife and I are moving back to my homeland. I've already purchased an inn. I'll be working the kitchens while my lovely wife runs the establishment."

Emrael bit into a dumpling and smiled. "I'll visit, if the Ordenans will let me in. Sometime after all this."

He turned back to his plate and ate in silence for a while, in large part to process his situation. It was hard for him to believe that this man sitting next to him was an Imperator, a real practitioner of magic. His wife Yamara, and Jaina as well. The Sentinel priests and their military arm—the Watchers—would hunt and kill them like animals if they knew the truth of what they were, what they could do with *infusori*. Come to think of it, Emrael himself was likely now as much a target as the others. Even if he rescued Ban and escaped the Corrandes, he could never go back to anything like his old life.

Emrael had been half-listening to a conversation between Elle and Yamara while lost in his thoughts.

". . . I saw the way you looked at me when I was admiring him. I'm not trying to steal your man, just gauging him. And you," Yamara was saying.

Emrael glanced over discreetly and saw that Elle's fair complexion had turned a dark shade of red. A kind, motherly smile graced Yamara's face, quite different from the predatory one she had directed at Emrael earlier.

Emrael felt his own face heating and feigned ignorance, but when he turned back, Sarlon winked at him. Emrael quirked an uncomfortable smile, then stared at his plate in embarrassment.

Truth was, he was caught by surprise. He had always thought of Elle as almost family due to her close friendship with Ban, and he'd never taken any of his brother's hints as more than jest. He looked at Elle in a new light, like sunlight at dawn revealing an unnoticed flower. He couldn't deny that Elle was a beautiful young woman. She was very intelligent, her work with healing and *infusori* Crafting brilliant, according to Ban.

He set his jaw and shook his head. What was he thinking? Elle was a Lord Governor's daughter. Her father probably had some powerful noble or rich merchant's son lined up for her. Besides, Emrael found it hard to get too excited by the prospect of a new romance right then. The weight of leaving Ban to the mercy of the Corrandes and the Watchers left him sick to his stomach, threatened to crush his soul.

"Jaina," Emrael said in a strong, serious voice, lifting his head to meet his mentor's eyes.

The table quieted, everyone turning to look at him.

"I am grateful for this meal, for the gracious company, and especially for the healing. But I must disappoint you. I am not going to Ordena."

Jaina shook her head, flicking a glance at Sarlon. "We discussed this, Emrael. It is our only option, *your* only option. Only the Order can help now that the Malithii priests and their new binders are involved. We leave for Ordena tonight. Please do not force me to resort to less-than-civil means. I'll have Sarlon pack you in a crate for the voyage if I must."

Emrael glanced at Sarlon, who shrugged as if to say, "*I've done it before.*"

Emrael chortled mirthlessly. "I hardly think you need Sarlon's help to subdue me, Jaina."

Master Yerdon shifted in his seat, clearly uncomfortable with the tension in the room. "I'm afraid I don't understand any of this, Mistress Jaina. Why would Corrande and the Watchers allow these vile things into our Provinces? And what do these Malithii fellows want?"

"The High Sentinel and the Malithii want the same thing Corrande does—the eradication of the Ordenans," Jaina replied. "Bortisse Corrande is desperate to break the Ordenan blockade but likely does not know what he has done by involving the Malithii. It will not end well."

Yerdon grimaced and shook his head. "Why would the Watchers attack the Citadel, though? Why move on it first? Why take students prisoner?"

Jaina pursed her lips and stared him in the eye. "Corrande wants the students and staff for their abilities with *infusori* Crafting. He's going to arm his soldiers with weapons the likes of which haven't been seen on this continent in centuries, millennia. For this reason, I believe Banron and the other Crafters are relatively safe—"

She cut off as glass shattered in the front room of the house. They turned as servants began shouting about fire. A heavy *thud* announced someone throwing a shoulder against the front door.

Sarlon stood quickly and snatched a staff made entirely of copper from where it rested in the corner just behind him. Jaina and Yamara followed him out of the room, drawing weapons of their own as they dashed toward the front of the house.

Emrael was left standing at the table with Elle and Master Yerdon, perplexed. The others had disappointingly low levels of panic on their faces. Yerdon looked nervous but in control of himself, and even Elle looked calm. He felt as though his stomach were trying to leap out of his throat, but he moved to position himself between the front of the house and the two healers anyway.

"Run if you can!" Sarlon bellowed back into the house as they heard the door burst open with a cascading *crack* of splintering wood. Metal rang on metal and boots stamped loudly on the floor. Cursing, screams of pain, and grunts of effort filled the air.

Emrael dashed to the hallway to see the commotion for himself. More than a dozen Watchers were pushing their way into the house, swords bared. More waited behind them in the street.

In the entry room of the house, Sarlon swung his copper rod expertly, sending a weapon flying or body reeling wherever he landed a strike. Jaina, sword in hand, had several Watchers pinned at the door. Two lay bleeding on the ground, motionless. Meanwhile, Yamara sent projectiles into the Watchers who tried to climb through the broken windows with what looked to be a small version of an *infusori*-Crafted crossbow—but curiously, it had no staves to propel the quarrels and apparently didn't need to be reloaded between shots. The Crafting technology in Ordena must have been centuries ahead of what they were making in the Provinces.

The house smelled of smoke due to the burning torches that had been thrown through the broken windows. Sarlon's servants were nowhere to be seen. The Ordenans seemed to be holding their own, despite the odds, but couldn't hold for long.

Emrael turned to gather Elle and Yerdon. "To the back of the house, quickly."

Emrael ran ahead of them into what must have been Sarlon and Yamara's personal quarters and flung open the ground-floor window to peer down the alleyway outside.

The late-afternoon light revealed a pair of Watchers standing guard at the end of the alley beside the house. They shouted as Emrael drew his head back into the room.

Emrael spoke quickly, going to the fireplace to arm himself with the fire-poker. "The alleyway runs behind the house next door. Go quickly, while I hold off the Watchers outside."

Emrael was already climbing out the window as he finished speaking. The two Watchers were running one behind the other down the narrow alley and had almost reached them.

"Run!" Emrael cried as he threw himself at the Watchers.

He managed to knock away the first Watcher's sword and plant a hard kick in his chest, sending him tumbling back into his companion. Emrael took the chance to sneak a glance behind him. Elle and Yerdon were nearly to the alleyway behind the building next door.

Elle stopped and called to Emrael. "Come on!"

"I'll meet you tomorrow, one hour before sundown at the spot where we ate lunch with Ban last weekend. Go!" Emrael called over his shoulder.

There was no way for him to disengage long enough to get away from his assailants. They would stab him in the back if he turned to run. He had no choice but to defeat these two before making his own escape.

As Emrael swung a great overhand sweep with his poker, another figure entered the alleyway and walked calmly toward the fight. This man had greying hair and an authoritative bearing. Emrael recognized him as he strode closer. It was his father's old friend, Corlas.

"Emrael! Em, is that you? For Mercy's sake, lad, put your weapon down. Men, put up your weapons! The boy and I are friends," Corlas called, sheathing his own sword.

Emrael kept his poker trained on the men in front of him, who lowered their weapons with a confused look on their faces. They moved aside to let Corlas pass between them.

"Friends knock before they throw lit torches through the window, Corlas. What in Glory's name is wrong with you? You took Ban! I saw you kill Citadel guards. Those were good people who posed no threat!"

"Lad, you have it wrong, I assure you. I'm not here to hurt you! Your brother and the others are being treated well. Please, put down your weapon and I'll take you to him. We were only here for those Ordenan devils. Our war is with them, not you."

Corlas extended his hand and inched toward Emrael.

Emrael hesitated. "What are you doing with Ban? Why are the Border Watchers attacking a school?"

"Look, Emrael. *Infusori* Crafters are being recruited for the war with Ordena. The Ordenans are preparing to invade us, and the only chance we have of defending ourselves is as a united empire, a true unification of the Provinces. Crafters give us a fighting chance against the devils. We need advanced weapons that can offset their advantage of numbers and their filthy, unnatural magic. The Ordenans have been abducting *infusori* Crafters faster than we can round them up to protect them, and we had to act quickly."

"You could have just arrested the Ordenans, Corlas. You took it too far."

Corlas hung his head, contrition on his face. "Yes, the casualties at the Citadel were unfortunate. My men who were responsible are being disciplined. Your brother and the others are being held at the

Citadel for their own safety and will be well compensated for their contributions. I need you, too, Emrael. You can join my personal command staff. Please, Em. Let me show you to your brother."

Emrael slowly lowered his poker. This man had been like an uncle to him, once, his father's closest friend and a frequent visitor in their home. While it had been years since he'd seen Corlas, he trusted him a hell of a lot more than he trusted Jaina and the others right now.

"You will take me to Ban? He is still in the city?"

"Yes, I'll take you to your brother. Right now, in fact. Those cursed Ordenans escaped, and I can't do much about them today." He slammed a fist into the open palm of his other hand. "I was so close!"

"Okay, Corlas, let's—"

Emrael cut off with a shout as Corlas lunged and secured Emrael's arms in a two-armed bear hug. After a brief struggle, the two Watchers grabbed Emrael's arms, took the poker, and shoved him to his knees.

Corlas's face turned cold once more. "Put him in the wagon with the others. Put one of the foreigner's contraptions on him, but don't injure him. We have more work to do, more heathen-magic Crafters to convert to the cause of the Holy Departed. Find the others that were with him. They will be trying to leave the city."

Corlas did not look back as Emrael tried to jerk out of the Watchers' grasp.

"Corlas! You son of the Fallen! I trusted you!" he screamed as the Watchers dragged him toward an enclosed wagon parked in the street. He managed to ram his head into the face of one of the Watchers, but the man recovered quickly and painfully twisted Emrael's arm behind his back while his companion held the other arm. Emrael struggled but could not wrench free.

Something cold touched his wrist, and he heard a *click*. Instantly, his vision went white with pain.

Emrael screamed in agony. He would have dropped to his knees if not for the two Watchers supporting his weight. His head was splitting open, and Ban's amulet seemed to be burning a hole through his chest.

"What's wrong with this one? The others didn't whine at all," one of his guards said as they hoisted him into the wagon. "Bastard's heavier than he looks, ain't he?"

They set Emrael down on a rough wooden bench in the enclosed wagon next to several other people, presumably other fugitive Citadel students like him. Or perhaps they had just crossed the Watchers in some way. The guards closed the doors at the back of the wagon and paid him no more attention.

His head cleared and the pain receded to a dull ache over the next few minutes, though the pendant hanging against his chest still burned with the same fire it had since the Watchers placed the bracelet on his wrist. The bracelet must have been one of the mind-binders Jaina had talked about. It was still cold as ice.

He looked around and found that his fellow prisoners all stared blankly, occasionally blinking but otherwise motionless. He thought he recognized a few of them from the Citadel, but checked each of them and was disappointed—but not surprised—to see that none of them were his brother. He quietly tried to talk to them, to ask where they were being taken, but got no reply. They just continued to stare aimlessly, even when he prodded them in the face.

What in the Fallen hell is going on here?

He looked through the cracks in the back doors of the enclosed wagon and could only spot one Watcher riding his horse just be-hind the wagon. The rest must have stayed behind to chase Jaina and the others. They didn't seem to be worried about their prisoners escaping. No wonder, with his fellow detainees rendered comatose by their binders. Why hadn't his done the same?

Emrael tugged at the binder on his arm and found that it dis-engaged easily. His pendant stopped burning the instant he took the binder off. They must have interfered with each other somehow, protecting Emrael from the effects of the binder. Could his brother have guessed he would need protection from an *infusori* Crafting like this binder, or was it just a fortunate side effect?

He tried pulling at the other prisoners' binders, but they wouldn't budge. After a few minutes of futile attempts to free the others, he gave up and tried the doors at the back. The catch was unlocked.

Anxiety bubbled in his stomach as he wondered where they were taking him and how he could escape without a Watcher stabbing or shooting him immediately. He briefly considered waiting until they arrived wherever they were going and trying to sneak in to find Ban, but immediately dismissed it as a terrible idea. Without the element of surprise, he would be cut down in a matter of seconds.

He tugged frantically at another prisoner's binder one more time, trying to find whatever secret had allowed him to remove his own, but it wouldn't come off no matter what he tried. He even touched his pendant to the other young man as he tugged on the binder. Nothing.

Finally, he gave up and went to the back of the wagon, dragging a fellow prisoner with him by the wrist, a young man Emrael recognized from the Citadel as one of Darmon's lackeys. One he had faced—and beaten—at Tournament.

He looked through the cracks in the back door once more, trying to judge the best time to jump. The Watcher would be able to draw his crossbow in seconds, so Emrael would have very little time to close the distance and attack.

He waited until the wagon turned a corner, holding the latch in one hand, his fellow prisoner's arm in the other. As soon as the Watcher was out of sight, Emrael threw the door open and tossed his unwitting accomplice off the back of the wagon.

Sorry, kid.

As the senseless young man rolled limply along the cobblestone lane, Emrael jumped down and sprinted toward the Watcher on horseback, who was looking in shock at the prisoner who had just tumbled from the wagon.

The Watcher tried to pull his crossbow from where it hung across his back as he realized that Emrael was alert and charging at him.

"Hey! St-stop!" he stammered.

Emrael reached him just as he swung the crossbow around. Emrael jammed the crossbow upward and leapt, using the Watcher's arm to pull himself up onto the horse. He struck the man hard in the throat with a closed fist.

As the Watcher gurgled, Emrael grabbed him by the collar and pulled him from the horse violently, jumping backward as the Watcher slammed into the ground face first.

For the first time in his life, Emrael hoped that he had killed his opponent. He had no time to continue the fight, however, as the two Watchers driving the wagon had noticed the commotion and had just started shouting. They paused briefly to consider the prisoner that Emrael had thrown to the ground, but soon stalked his way with swords drawn. Emrael wanted nothing more than to fight these two, slaughter them for taking his brother. He wanted to hunt Corlas down like a hound tracking a fox.

But if Emrael was to have any chance of escaping to meet up with Elle and then to rescue his brother, he could not stick around and allow any more Watchers to catch up. Besides, facing two Watchers on his own was a big risk, though he hated to admit it.

Emrael hurriedly gathered the crossbow from the motionless Watcher and jumped onto his horse, keeping the crossbow trained on the two Watchers until he was far enough away to kick his horse to a gallop. He left the two Watchers behind quickly, racing through the crowded streets of Myntar with only one thing in mind: how to get out of the city so he could regroup with Elle and save Ban. He would stop at nothing to get his brother back.

5

When Emrael felt he was a safe distance from the Watchers, he slowed his horse to a walk. He passed through a raucous market that smelled strongly of fish and rotten fruit. A street crier shouted from behind a table stacked with bound leaflets that contained the news of the day. "War with Ordenan devils! A new empire is forming! Read it all here!"

Emrael shook his head in wonder as he passed. The world had turned on its head overnight.

He needed to get to the spot he had arranged with Elle, an oak tree just off of the road to the West Pass where they had eaten lunch with Ban the week before. The Watchers were undoubtedly aware of his escape by now, however, and Corlas would expect him to make a dash for the west gate and straight into the Barros Province where he had grown up. He'd have to find another way out of the city, even if it meant riding all the way around the outside of the walls. That also meant he'd need supplies.

A few streets later, he came to a stop in front of a two-story inn. He dismounted and rifled through the Watcher's saddlebags, finding nothing of use but a belt knife, a few rations, and a plain oiled canvas jacket. He wrapped the rations and the crossbow he had taken from the Watcher in the jacket, tucked it under his arm, and entered the inn.

As he stepped inside, he assumed a stern, commanding posture that he associated with people of authority like his father, Jaina, and Corlas. He approached the bar and rapped on the wood top with his knuckles. The husky man turned from loading a cask behind the bar and hurried over to greet Emrael with a practiced smile.

"Can I help you, young sir?"

Emrael set his things on the bar, staring the innkeeper in the eyes. "Yes, you can. I require a room for the night and some travel rations, enough for a few days. I seem to have lost my coin pouch, but I have no need for my horse now that I have arrived in the city. You see the handsome brown out front? He's yours in exchange for the supplies and a Provincial copper round in return."

The innkeeper narrowed his eyes at the offer. He looked outside to the horse, biting his lip.

"I can do a room, the rations and eight silvers," he offered. "And I'll need to check him over, of course."

"You have a deal at ten silvers, but I want a good room with a window," Emrael said after a pained pause. The horse was worth twice what he had just bargained for—at least a full copper round, the equivalent of twenty silver pennies—but he needed to offer a price good enough that the innkeeper would hand the money over before inspecting the horse. There was a chance he would recognize the tack as Watcher issue and call the Sagmyn Legion patrols.

The innkeeper, eager to close such a profitable transaction despite any misgivings, counted out the silvers—some Provincial, some the smaller coins from the Ithan Nations, but none of the larger Ordenan coins—and shouted to the back for one of his servers to wrap some bread, cheese, and salted meat.

Before long, Emrael was following the innkeeper up the narrow stairs, coins in his pocket, his jacket and rations under one arm.

As soon as he had shut and locked the door to his room and ensured that the innkeeper had left, Emrael went to the bed and threw back the cover. He drew the belt knife and cut a large square and several strips from the linen sheet, bundled his belongings in the large linen square, and slung it over his shoulder. He stepped to the window, opened it with only a little difficulty, and propped it open with a piece of wood that lay on the windowsill for that purpose.

He watched the yard below until the innkeeper had finished inspecting his new horse. Apparently satisfied with his purchase, he called to his stable man and pointed toward the stable. The stable hand, a thin older man, obediently led the brown horse into the stable to be unsaddled.

Emrael waited until the innkeeper had returned to the inn, then leaned out the window to gauge the height. The drop looked to be less than ten paces to the ground but still higher than he would have liked. He dropped his things out the window and grabbed the windowsill, exiting backward.

Sweat rolled down his forehead as he hung from the side of the inn for several moments. He looked over his shoulder at the ground, momentarily regretting the decisions that had led him to be hanging from a second-story window. He hated heights. The half-healed wound in his shoulder began to ache and burn, the stitches threatening to tear free.

He drew a deep breath and let go of the windowsill, dropping to the bare ground and trying to roll as he hit the ground. It didn't work quite as well as he had hoped. Instead of rolling like he had been taught in training, his weary legs collapsed as he landed. He tumbled backward and managed to land hard on his ass.

He limped slightly as he scrambled to his feet, suddenly very aware of the many partially healed wounds he had earned the day before. A small amount of blood seeped through his shirt at the shoulder where stitches must have torn, but his arm worked fine despite some pain, thanks to Yerdon's *infusori*-assisted healing. Grumbling to himself, he gathered his bundle and hurried into the stable.

Emrael paused briefly just inside the doorway to allow his eyes to adjust to the dimness of the stable, where the stable hand was just tying the brown horse to a post to begin taking the saddle off.

Emrael drew his knife and tiptoed swiftly towards the man, keeping the horse between them. He rounded the horse and approached the man from behind. One hand went over the man's mouth as the other held the knife to his throat.

Emrael growled in his ear, "Please don't make me hurt you. I am going to take this horse, one way or the other. I'm going tie you up and you stay quiet, or I slit your throat."

Emrael slowly released him, lowered the knife, and moved so he could keep his eyes on the man's thin, wrinkled face. The elderly man watched with dark, concerned eyes beneath thick grey eyebrows as Emrael pulled the strips of cloth he had cut from the bed out of his bundle.

The old man met Emrael's eyes and nodded slowly, kneeling and putting his hands behind his back for Emrael to secure with the cloth. Emrael tied the man's hands, then his ankles, and a strip connecting them so that the man could not stand. Finally, Emrael wadded a cloth, stuffed it in the man's mouth, and tied it in place gently.

Emrael rolled the man over and said, "Thank you for being reasonable. Wait a few minutes before calling for help. It could save my life and yours. I'm going to slip some coins in your pocket for your trouble. I'm truly sorry for all this."

Emrael stuck two of his precious silvers in the man's pocket and hoped that the stable hand would not be punished too severely for letting Emrael steal the horse.

He hurried over to the still-saddled horse and secured his belongings behind the saddle. He snagged the reins and walked out of the stable next to the horse, using it to shield him from view should the innkeeper happen to look out one of the rear windows.

"Taran! Damn you stupid, worthless old coot!" the innkeeper shouted from the back door. "I told you to get that horse ready to sell to Darik! I've sent a messenger; he'll be comin' before sundown. Get that horse back to the stable! I'll throw you there myself if I have to!"

Emrael angled toward the voice of the innkeeper, keeping his head down and face hidden. He could hear the innkeeper stomping toward him, clearly in a rage.

The innkeeper came into view, and his eyes widened in surprise and outrage. "You! Sneaking little thief! I knew there was some demon about you! I—"

He cut off with a *hmmph* as Emrael swung a fist into his gut.

Emrael quickly wrapped an arm around the large man's neck while using his other arm as leverage to choke the man and cut off the blood flow to his brain.

When the man had stopped jerking and struggling, Emrael grabbed one of his ankles, not sparing a moment to check for a pulse. The innkeeper groaned feebly as Emrael dragged him into the stable and dumped him next to the stable hand. It seemed the innkeeper was still alive, for which Emrael was thankful. He had no desire to kill the man, disagreeable though he might be.

"Hello again," Emrael grunted cordially, nodding to the tied-up stable man as he similarly trussed the innkeeper. He got an unsure nod of the head in return from the old horse handler. "Tell the innkeeper when he comes to his senses that I'm sorry, and that I'll be back someday to settle up with him."

He hurried to the horse once more, stepped into the saddle, and exited the inn's yard at a calm walk.

Emrael stopped a few hundred paces from the east gate just before sundown that evening. Grateful that the rain gave him the excuse to keep his hood up, he dismounted and walked his horse slowly toward the gate. At least a half-dozen Watchers mingled with the Sagmyn Legionmen that normally guarded the large wood-and-steel gates, and he'd draw attention riding through on his own. Best to wait for other travelers to provide him with some cover.

Emrael could now feel as well as see the glow of *infusori* emanating from the huge coils mounted in the wall next to the mechanism that moved the enormous gates. He wondered how much the governor spent on the *infusori* to power just this one gate. Likely more coin in a week than he'd ever seen in his life. If only he could harness that power at will like Jaina could. She could probably use it to break out of the city no matter how many soldiers were guarding the gate. He was tempted to try but didn't know where to start. When he had used the *infusori* to open Sarlon's tunnel door, he had just . . . *done* it.

He noticed a merchant's wagon train in the distance, trundling down the wide cobblestoned street toward the gate, and he lounged against a shoulder-high wall lining the street while he waited for it catch up to him.

Too late, he realized that the wall belonged a Provincial Church of the Holy Departed—the church of the Sentinels. Two-headed torches sputtered and spat in the rain, their light illuminating two figures of indeterminate gender with long hair, blank faces, and elaborate crowns carved into two marble pillars framing the entrance to their church. They were the Gods of Mercy and Justice, called the Holy Departed by the Provincial priests known as Sentinels. The Ordenans called them the Silent Sisters, and claimed to know their true identities. They were simply the Absent Gods to those like Emrael that didn't give a shit one way or another.

Emrael strained to inspect the church from the corner of his eye, searching for any Watchers that might be accompanying their Sentinel counterparts. He nearly shat himself when a Sentinel priest called out to him. "Come inside, young brother, and be saved from the hell of this world. The Holy Departed will soon reveal themselves, and Mercy's arms are open to all believers."

"I'm sure Mercy would love to save me, for a price," Emrael said sarcastically, though under his breath so as not to draw attention. Damn Sentinels and their threats in the name of Mercy. These bastards would likely hang him—or have the Watchers do it for them—if they knew he was a mage. Or whatever he was.

Emrael took one last look back at the Citadel, contemplating its dominant presence over the city. He stared so long, replaying memories in his head and imagining Ban locked up in the Citadel dungeons, that he nearly missed his opportunity to follow closely behind the merchant's wagon train exiting the east gate. He tugged the hood of his jacket up further to hide his white hair as he fell in line behind them.

So many things had gone wrong in the last day that he was almost surprised when he made it through the gate unnoticed by the Watchers and Sagmyn Legionmen standing guard.

6

Emrael rode his horse off the highway and into the foothills to the north of the city as the sun sank behind the mountains. The rain continued to fall steadily, soaking every inch of him that wasn't covered by the oiled canvas jacket he'd stolen from the Watcher.

He was surprised to see dozens—maybe hundreds—of campfires burning in the clear space just outside the north wall of the city, near the Citadel's service gate. Corrande and the Watchers must have brought a significant force with them. Jaina had been right; he wouldn't stand a chance trying to get in to rescue Ban on his own. He felt a pang of guilt as he wondered what had become of Jaina and her Ordenan friends, but his thoughts soon turned back to Elle and his brother. How was he going to get Elle to safety, and how was he to rescue his brother from such a large army intent on keeping him prisoner? Elle should be safe if he could get her to the Barros border and hand her over to Barros Legionmen, but if the Provinces had joined Corrande in attacking the Citadel, they'd be of little help in rescuing Ban.

He turned west once he reached the forest that stretched into the mountains above the city, several leagues outside the city walls—hopefully far enough to avoid any Sagmyn Legion or Watcher patrols.

He rode through the night, stopping only for a few hours of soggy rest once he judged he was near the Toryn River, where he'd need to turn south. The rain continued until just before sunrise, making sleep a difficult proposition, even with the waterproof jacket. Eyes grainy from lack of sleep, he continued west at first light, and near midmorning he heard the rushing headwater of the largest river in the Sagmyn Valley, the Toryn River. He dismounted and tied his horse to a small tree in a stand of pines.

Stiff muscles and chafed legs protested as he crept toward the sound of water. It had been far too long since he had last ridden a horse for any distance. He emerged from the trees and found himself on a small bluff overlooking the Toryn. The sound of rushing water and the invigorating smell of water vapor filled his nostrils, helping chase the fog of weariness from his mind.

He would follow the course of the crystal-clear water down to where it intersected the Barros road less than a league from where he was to meet Elle at the large oak.

He began to unlace his pants to take a piss, then froze when he heard a faint noise from a different direction than where he had left his horse. He went to one knee without a sound, lacing his pants quickly as he peered intensely at surrounding forest, hoping to catch a glimpse of what had made the noise. It had sounded like a footfall on hard ground, probably rock. Had the Watchers followed him all this way?

After several minutes of no movement or further sound, he crept silently at an angle and uphill from where he had last heard a noise, hunting his pursuer like he would wild game.

There was another faint noise off to his left. He held perfectly still until he was certain that there was only one person following him. Whoever it was, they were close and coming almost directly toward him. He took cover behind a large partially fallen pine and waited tensely. He was tired of being chased, being hunted.

He saw the tip of a booted foot as his would-be pursuer rounded the fallen tree. Emrael lunged forward, grasped the person following him, and drove toward the ground. As he pushed, he wrapped his leg around his prey, taking them both to the ground, Emrael atop his target. His despair, his fear fueled his primal rage as he brought the fore of his elbow down on the attacker's head.

Just as his strike landed, his mind registered the dark, shoulder-length hair and delicate features of the person he was fighting. Jaina.

She managed to block his arm but not the full weight of the blow. He watched as her expression turned from startled to terrified.

She let out a short, high-pitched cry and recoiled as if injured deeply. She lay dazed, limp beneath him, her eyes still open but unfocused.

Emrael froze for a moment, confused and stunned. His blow had been hard, but she had partially blocked it even as he pulled the strike. Very little of the force had hit her head. But he had felt something else, something very similar to what he had felt when he had thrown open the stone door in the tunnel that opened to Sarlon's home. It was as if *infusori* had been generated from his extreme emotions, then physically flowed from him and into Jaina.

What is happening to me?

He leaned down and pressed two fingers to her neck, feeling for a pulse, then put his face in front of her mouth to feel for breath. Thankfully, she was breathing fine and her heart was beating normally, if fast.

"Jaina? What in Glory's name are you doing? Why would you sneak up on me like that? Jaina?"

He gently cradled her head in his hand, afraid he had done something awful.

"Jaina, please say something. What did I do? How do I fix it?"

He sighed with relief when she blinked and groaned softly, then moved her head slightly to look at him. He expected to see anger, or even hatred in her eyes, but was surprised to see a very different emotion—respect.

She lay still, staring at him for a time, saying nothing. He began to feel awkward holding her sweaty head in his hands, so he rolled off of her gently and rested her head on the dark soil but stayed kneeling by her side.

"What are you doing out here?" he asked again. "Absent Gods, Jaina, what did you think would happen, sneaking up on me? I'm just glad I didn't kill you! I thought you were a Watcher or something." He scrubbed his hand through his short white hair as he shook his head.

"I underestimated you," Jaina croaked finally. "I should have been more careful. I did not know who else might be tracking you, so thought it best to follow behind you. Now fetch me some water. I have some in my pack over behind that large flowering bush."

He left Jaina lying on the ground and went to fetch her pack, grumbling to himself about tracking and people lacking common sense. What if he'd stabbed her instead of tackling her? And he was almost sure he had used *infusori* somehow when he'd attacked her—that could have ended as badly or worse than a stabbing.

He made his way back to where Jaina lay. She had her eyes closed again but opened them as he neared. Her eyes tracked him as he knelt next to her and opened the cap of her waterskin.

"Are you able to sit up and drink?" he asked.

"Why don't you help me up?"

Emrael put his hand under her neck and helped her sit up to sip the water. After a few swallows, she pulled away from him and sat up enough to rest her head on her knees. She looked up after a deep breath and stuck her hand out, silently asking him to help her to her feet. He obliged but had to steady her when she stood.

He picked a few twigs and leaves out of her hair with his right hand as she held tightly to his left. She stamped her feet in an attempt to steady her legs.

"Jaina . . . how did you escape? Are Sarlon and Yamara okay?"

A mischievous look shone in Jaina's deep green eyes. "It would take more than a few Watchers to put us down. They are fine. I sent them after Elle and Yerdon."

Emrael smiled, relieved. "Good. Hopefully, we'll find them at the spot I asked Elle to meet me. But now I want to know why you look as if a horse kicked you senseless. I know I did something with *infusori*, and I want to know what. I felt . . . I felt so angry. My emotions seemed to *surge* toward you, and . . . What happened? I've never felt anything like that."

Jaina sighed and looked him in the eyes. "*Infusori* is closely tied to your emotions, Emrael. Now that you've used it, you'll continue to do so reflexively. You need training, and you need it soon. I suppose I have no choice but to train you myself, the Order's rules be damned."

He nodded slowly. "Great. Show me."

She laughed, low and guttural, then closed her eyes and tipped her face up to the sky. "Imperators study at the Imperial Academy for years—decades, even—to learn *A Me'trae*—'the Art,' in Old Ordenan. One of the first skills an Imperator initiate learns is to use *infusori* to boost their own strength and endurance briefly to give an edge during a fight."

"You can do that?" Emrael blurted. "No wonder you are so damn strong when we spar. How do I learn that? What else can you do?"

Jaina tried—poorly—to hide a wry smile at his excitement. "In time, Emrael. I will coach you through it when we have time—and when I think I can trust you with such knowledge."

Emrael thought back to a conversation with his mother years before, when she had tried to convince him to attend this Academy instead of the Citadel. Maybe he and Ban should have gone with her after all, if they taught all this. He probably owed his mother an apology.

He took a deep breath, thinking through the ramifications. "Do your Imperators make *infusori* Craftings as well, then? Are they as good as what we make at the Citadel?"

"Better. Much better. *A Si'trae*—the Craft—is central to an Imperator's training. Ordenans rule the seas for a reason. We possess

Craftings the likes of which you could not dream. Our Mage-Healers can cure diseases and treat wounds that would be fatal anywhere else, including here at the Citadel."

He nodded, thinking of the famed Ordenan naval forces. Nobody in the Provinces knew much about the Ordenans, though, besides their naval supremacy and religious fanaticism. Ordenans were a secretive people. Though his mother was an Ordenan, he had never thought her any different from other Citadel-trained healers in the Provinces, and she had been less than forthcoming about her upbringing and training. "Do your Mage-Healers—or Imperator Healers, whatever—use better Craftings to heal?"

Jaina hesitated. "I am not skilled in the art of Mage-Healing, but anything that can be done with a Crafted device can be done with direct manipulation of *infusori*, usually much more effectively. If we had a true Imperator Mage-Healer with us, they could have Healed you within minutes instead of days, and would have used no Crafted devices at all. Did you never see your mother Heal so? She is a renowned Mage-Healer."

Emrael shook his head, but then thought back to when his mother had healed his arm when he was a boy. Not only had he woken up with stark white hair, he had woken up completely healed. His parents had made him wear a bandage for weeks, but there had been no need—it hadn't pained him at all, and there was barely even a scar. He had thought she had used an apparatus similar to the one Yerdon had used, but now that he thought back, he couldn't remember the needled *infusori* Crafting having been left in him like Yerdon's had been.

"I mean, I guess she could have, now that I think about it. Can you really not Heal at all?"

"I'll show you. Give me your hand."

He placed his hand in hers, and before he could react, she gripped tight, drew her belt knife, and scored a clean slice across the back of his forearm.

"What the hell!" he yelped, pulling his arm away from her, his anger rising. "Have you lost your mind?"

She just chuckled darkly as she put her knife away. "This way, you won't forget. My first teacher gave me the same lesson. Give me your arm."

He took a step away from her, incredulous. "Uh. No thanks," he said sarcastically.

"Don't be a child, Emrael. I won't hurt you this time. Give me your arm."

He pursed his lips, then took a slow step back to her, allowing her to take his arm again. Her eyebrows drew down in concentration, then crinkled in puzzlement. "Relax, Emrael. You are making an already difficult task nearly impossible. I cannot Heal an unwilling patient."

"But I am relaxed . . . Ah," he said sheepishly, tugging the pendant from around his neck. "Ban made this for me. It's a sort of communication Crafting, but I think it interfered with the binders the Watchers were using. It might be interfering with this, too."

Jaina studied it for a moment, nodded thoughtfully, then handed it back. "It is not impossible but would be extraordinary. I haven't heard of an *infusori* shield like this being created outside of Ordena for millennia, even by accident. And to interfere with a binder? Many Imperator Crafters would consider it the pinnacle of their career to build one of these, even by accident. Leave it off for now, and we'll try again."

Infusori gathered in Jaina as she gripped his arm in both hands, then a cold, prickling sensation as she pushed the *infusori* into him. His wound throbbed with pain, then it was done.

He looked at his arm as she released him. A red scar covered the spot where the long, shallow cut had been, but it was still painful to the touch. "You barely Healed it."

"That's your lesson, Emrael. Not every mage, even an Imperator, is capable of all forms of the Art. Healing in particular is complex, nuanced. Though some can work miracles, Healing a minor scrape pushes the boundaries of my abilities. But most Mage-Healers cannot use the Art in battle like I can, for example."

Disappointment made his chest tight, his gut heavy. If Jaina barely knew something as useful as Healing after years and years of training as an Imperator, how long would it take him to become proficient at even simple skills?

She sat abruptly, holding out her hands expectantly. "Now, one more lesson before we continue. This will only take a moment and may prove to save your life. Or mine."

He sat down opposite her and took her hands in his. She continued to look him in the eye, her new expression of grudging respect still odd to him. He wondered if it was because he had managed to surprise her as she tracked him or because of his newfound ability as a mage.

She squeezed his hands. "Close your eyes. You have *infusori* within you; all living creatures do, even the earth herself. Feel your own *infusori*, your life essence. Feel mine. I'm going to draw a small amount of your *infusori*, then pass it back to you. It may not come easily, so be prepared and do not act rashly. Control your emotions and relax. You need only feel what I'm doing and follow suit. Are you ready?"

Emrael nodded and closed his eyes to concentrate, excited about what he was feeling. He could feel his life energy like it was a new-found body part, and hers as an extension of his awareness of her. The *infusori* that comprised the life source of a living being felt different from the *infusori* that was pulled from the earth via *infusori* Wells and stored in gold coils, but similar at the same time. This new sense felt like nothing he could have imagined—familiar, natural, yet fantastic. It dissolved the borders of his previous reality, like sprouting a third eye.

She squeezed his hands to give him a gentle warning, and he immediately felt a pull of *infusori*, a tug at his life essence, his soul. It was hard not to react defensively as it left him. He felt sick to his stomach.

"Now draw it back, gently."

He obeyed, reaching toward her *infusori*, though he did not know how he reached. He tugged gently, trying only to replace the *infusori* that Jaina had drawn from him, then released his hold on her life essence.

"Good. That was *very* good. We may be able to teach you to control yourself after all."

She narrowed her eyes slightly as she chewed on one cheek. "I want to try one last thing."

Emrael interrupted before she could continue. "Can I use that trick to give someone energy if they are hurt, or sick? It should work just like the healing Craftings, right?"

Jaina's lips twitched upward in a smile. "Yes. The *infusori* from a living being can replace the life essence from another living being, provided the Mage-Healer can replicate the patient's life source *exactly*. This is the most elemental aspect of an Imperator Mage-Healer's art, and the secret to how they Heal so effectively, even compared to a Crafting made for healing. The best ones are also able to accelerate the body's own healing mechanisms."

"That doesn't seem so complicated," Emrael said carefully, rubbing the raw scar on the back of his hand. "Why can't you Heal?"

Jaina rolled her eyes and muttered something about smartass children. "I can transfer *infusori* better than most, but I cannot *feel* the other person enough to be in tune with their own life essence. It's not a skill easily learned without endangering the very person you aim to save. Most Mage-Healers are born with a knack for feeling minute differences in *infusori*. In the days when your provinces were still kingdoms, backwater mages killed or crippled their patients as often as they Healed them, and that is a large part of why the Sentinels and other religious folk are so strongly prejudiced against mages of any sort."

Emrael nodded thoughtfully. He had heard plenty of Sentinel sermons about the evils of magecraft, and could see how their hatred might have developed over centuries of uneducated mages inflicting their ignorance on those who didn't possess such powers.

Jaina gripped his hands tighter. "Now, no more interruptions. I want to do one more exercise. This is one of the tests that the Ordenan Council of Imperators administers before granting entrance to the Imperial Academy. I'm going to try to draw *infusori* from you, and you are going to resist. Then you will try to draw from me as I resist. Ready?"

Emrael nodded and closed his eyes. He did not know what to expect, but he tried to imagine his life energy as being solid, stable, and untouchable. He realized he was flexing his physical muscles as well. Embarrassed, he relaxed his body but tried to stay concentrated on detecting Jaina's unseen attempt to draw his *infusori*.

Emrael grunted as Jaina struck. He thought for a moment that he would withstand the onslaught, as they held at a stalemate. Sweat dripped down his face. Slowly but surely, Jaina's probe worked its way through his resistance. His defense broke before her attack in a rush, like a faulty dam bursting under the huge weight of a reservoir. It hit him hard, and he thought he might empty his stomach.

He opened his eyes and found Jaina sweating heavily as well, though she smiled with the same predatory look she wore during weapons training. That look lit a spark of anger inside Emrael, prodding his pride and competitive nature.

"Now try to do the same to me; break through my shield," Jaina said.

He gathered his emotions, his irritation and anger, and launched his *infusori* sense at her as hard as he could. He felt resistance as she tried to keep him away from her life essence but punched through much quicker than he had anticipated.

Once through her shield, he froze. His senses were enveloped by Jaina's life essence, her *infusori*. He felt her emotions, her fears, her hopes, everything that made her *her*, just like he felt his own emotions. She was surprisingly soft, warm, and lovely—below a hard, scar-like shell of emotional numbness.

He heard her gasp as he floundered, lost in the connection that had formed between them. His eyes opened, and he saw Jaina pulling out of his grasp, saw her trembling, but could not sever the connection.

Jaina reached a hand toward his face. "Release it, Emrael! Release it, you blundering oaf!"

Emrael frantically tried to relax his *infusori* sense. He imagined opening a closed fist, and suddenly the connection between him and Jaina was gone. He felt dizzy momentarily and had to fight to stay sitting up, but his strength returned quickly.

Jaina, who had already been weakened by their earlier encounter, did not fare so well. She swayed where she sat on the ground, though her gaze was as piercing as ever as she squinted at him.

"I am a fool," Jaina whispered.

7

Emrael pulled on the reins, stopping his horse next to the clearing with the giant oak where he hoped they would find Elle and the others waiting.

Jaina still hadn't recovered fully from the episode in the woods and had spent the last several hours clinging to his back as they found and traveled the road to the West Pass.

She released her grip on him as they stopped. "You are positive she will know this tree from all the others we've passed?"

"I'm sure," he replied. "Ban, Elle, and I met in this very clearing just last week. She'll remember. Stay here while I look around."

When he looked back to Jaina, he found her regarding him with a raised eyebrow and what he could only call a smirk.

"What?" Emrael demanded.

Jaina laughed. "You think you are in charge now, do you?"

Despite his plentiful insecurities, her attitude goaded him into false audacity. "Last I checked, you followed me through the woods. You can go your own way, but I'm going to find Elle, then I'm going to get my brother out of the Citadel."

The sarcasm was heavy in Jaina's voice as she replied, "So, where is your girl? We are here, but Elle is nowhere in sight. And how exactly are you going to get Ban out of the Citadel without any help? And how do you know he's even still at the Citadel? Have you given that any thought, *Commander Emrael*?"

"I've given it *plenty* of thought. If the Watchers are using the students for *infusori* Crafting, the only place in the entire province they can access the right equipment and close *infusori* stores is at the Citadel. And if I send Elle to Governor Barros, she may be able to enlist his help in case I don't succeed in getting Ban out myself. She might be able to convince him to negotiate my brother's release. He is her best friend, after all. There's no way Governor Barros leaves Samille with Corrande. With any luck, I'll be able to extract Ban well before Governor Barros gets involved. If I fail and Barros won't help, maybe my mother will send someone after all."

"You know as well as I do that Governor Barros will do nothing.

He is a coward. He wouldn't dare move against Corrande and the Watchers even if Corrande won't release his heir—which I'm positive he will, if he wants Barros to fall in line with his plan of creating his new nation. So, that leaves you to rescue Ban yourself. And when you find a full battalion of Watchers inside the Citadel? And what if you encounter experienced Malithii mages? What will you do then? How will your death help your brother?"

"I'll figure something out. It's better than sitting here doing nothing, or going to Ordena, thousands of leagues away, while my brother is in the hands of those bastards. I'll never forgive myself if I don't do anything to help him, and that's worse than dying. Besides, we don't know that Corlas has any Malithii mages with him, do we? And if he does, I guess it's a good thing I've got you, isn't it?"

Jaina paused, then flashed a surprisingly warm smile. "While I appreciate your vote of confidence, I can only do so much. I know there is at least one Malithii mage here in the province, and Sarlon said there were more. What we truly need is a contingent of Imperators. I cannot counter Malithii in significant numbers by myself, and I'll not die for your fool plan. We should follow the original plan. Sail to Ordena, return with help."

He felt Jaina shift her weight behind him, and she dismounted with a noise somewhere between a grunt and a sigh. Perhaps he wasn't the only one unused to hard riding. He had set a hard pace, trying to get to the meeting place as quickly as possible.

Jaina stamped her feet and bent at the waist to stretch. "I sent Sarlon and Yamara after Elle and Master Yerdon. If she's not here—and it looks like she is not—I have faith they will have found her. We should take a look around."

Emrael could see his mentor's legs wobble slightly. "You can stay here and rest, Jaina. I'll take a look around for tracks."

She nodded gratefully and leaned against a nearby tree. She must have been truly exhausted.

The soil beneath the grass in the clearing was soggy with spring thaw. Muck squished beneath his boots as he dismounted and walked over to the oak.

"Elle? Master Yerdon? Sarlon?" He called. He looked around briefly, but the clearing was indeed empty, as were the woods surrounding the small clearing. Fear and anxiety roiled in his stomach as he was forced to choose between continuing to look for Elle and going back to rescue Ban. He couldn't leave Elle, but with every moment, the chances he could recover Ban dwindled.

Checking the ground near the oak, he noticed boot prints in the soft loam, both large and small. They were recent and led to a small boulder near the base of the tree. He crouched down, careful not to get his knees wet—he had just gotten dry, and nothing was worse than wet, itchy clothing—and found a white strip of cloth wadded up underneath an overhang of the boulder. It had a series of knots tied into it, some larger than others and of varying complexity and shape. He had no idea what it meant, if anything, but it didn't seem accidental.

He turned to walk back to Jaina, studying the handkerchief as he walked.

"Jaina, does this look familiar to you? I have no idea what it is, but there were recent tracks leading to the stone where it was left."

Jaina smiled again as she took the handkerchief from him and fingered each knot.

"I told you Sarlon would find them. For whatever reason, he must have thought it better to leave the valley and wait for us on the other side of the pass. It looks like we are on our own until we get to the other side. I'm sure he will leave us some sort of clue."

"How do you know that? That handkerchief said all that?"

"Well, he couldn't leave us a letter or painted sign, now, could he? These knots tell me that they were here, they went west, and to expect further communication. It's not so complicated."

"That will leave Ban at the Citadel for days before we can get back to save him," Emrael protested.

"Emrael, you will die if you go back to the Citadel alone. You can go if you wish, but I'm following Sarlon and Yamara."

Emrael grunted his defeat. "Fine, let's go find them. Maybe you can teach me about these knots?"

"Depends. What do I get from you in return?" Jaina lifted her eyebrow.

"I suppose I could continue to pay you for instruction . . . although I did disarm you in the duel, and you promised to continue my instruction free of charge if I won."

Jaina laughed softly and said, "So I did. Very well, I'll continue instructing you when we have time. But the knots will have to wait. We'd better hurry if we are going to get to the pass before they close the gates at sundown. Come here; let's do something with that hair so you don't stand out quite so much."

She reached down into her pack and pulled out a wax-paper packet of a black powder.

Emrael regarded the packet skeptically. "What's that? Don't we have a cloth I can tie around my head or something?"

"They will likely be watching for a young man with white hair, Emrael. A hat or cloth intentionally covering your hair would bring attention. If we can make your hair a different color, they won't think twice when we go through. Now get your hair wet."

He wet his hair from his waterskin and allowed her to massage the powder into it. She finished by wiping any extra from his hair and face with a piece of cloth and stepped back to look at him, one corner of her mouth upturned as she squinted at him.

"Are you laughing at me? Really?"

"I am not laughing."

"You do that half-smile thing when you think something is funny. Does it really look that bad?" Emrael felt at his hair until Jaina swatted his hand away.

"Stop that. You'll rub it off. Just let me do all of the talking. Maybe in the fading light, they won't notice you."

With that, she turned and mounted the horse, leaving him to scramble up behind her.

As they reentered the roadway, she looked back at him as he was trying to keep himself steady. "Emrael, I'm not going to bite. You can hold on to me." Embarrassed, he carefully wrapped an arm around her firm midsection.

The farms they passed turned into larger and larger villages, with only farmers, merchants, and odd travelers sharing the road—no sign of any Watchers or Legionmen, which surprised Emrael. They finally reached the section of road that inclined steeply upward and curved slightly to the north before reaching the West Pass, just out of sight. The ancient, weather-worn twin statues of the God of Mercy and the God of Justice were just visible, reminders of the distant past when the ancient Ravan Empire had hewn the West Pass from the stone of the mountain by some unfathomable method. The statues' facial features—and most everything else—were indistinguishable due to centuries of erosion. They were the inspiration for the Sentinel's faceless statues of the Holy Departed that adorned every Church of the Holy Departed throughout the Provinces.

The road turned from hard-packed dirt to well-fitted paving stones as they climbed out of the small but extraordinarily fertile Sagmyn Valley to the pass that led west to the much-larger Barros Province. The horse's shod hooves rang on the hard surface in rhythm with the fluttering of the butterflies in his stomach.

"Remember, Emrael, just keep calm and let me do the talking. All will be well."

Easy for her to say. She wasn't the one trying to hide in plain sight by putting dye in her hair.

He should be grateful that she was helping him. She was putting herself in harm's way just to help him find Elle. She had no reason to be here instead of sailing away from this whole mess without him.

"Jaina, thank you."

"For what?" she asked without turning around.

"For finding me, for helping me find Elle. You could have just left all of this—and us—behind, especially after our argument at Sarlon's house. So . . . thank you."

Jaina grunted softly and said, "The Order—your mother especially—wouldn't be pleased with me leaving you here. With the Watchers all over the Sagmyn Province, getting a ship from another port might be my best option to travel to Ordena, anyway. For *us* to travel to Ordena."

"Maybe," he replied noncommittally. Truth was, he couldn't see how to rescue Ban without outside help either. If his mother could provide that help . . . he didn't like it, but Ordena might be their best option after all.

The sun perched on the tips of the snow-capped mountains when they reached the Sagmyn Legion guard post that stood watch over their side of the pass. The outpost building sat on the right side of an enormous forged-steel gate, supported by hinges secured to the rock face on either side of the hewn canyon so that the gate opened in the middle. Even with its robust *infusori*-driven mechanism, the large gate would not shut quickly.

Sagmyn Legionmen in dark red uniforms manned the nearest guard post and the checkpoint at the gate. The Barros Legion, dressed in river-stone grey uniforms, had a post of their own with a similar checkpoint on their side of the gate. Both Legions inspected those entering and leaving their provinces, evidently not trusting the Legionmen of the other province to weed out smugglers and other law breakers. They were certainly not going to miss out on collecting the tariffs for goods entering their provinces.

There were no Watchers present. Emrael couldn't believe it. Could they really have left the West Pass unwatched? Why go through the trouble of tracking down escapees in the city only to neglect major routes out of the province?

A small group of people waited to pass through to the Barros

Province while a clerk inspected a wagon full of fresh beets at the head of the line. Other travelers waited impatiently in a line behind the wagon, likely hoping to get to the safety of a walled town or at least a decent campsite before dark.

Emrael grew more nervous by the minute. He thought he might vomit. He was worried that being last in line would bring too much attention to them, that the Legionmen attending the clerks would recognize him for sure, that they wouldn't make it through before the Legionmen closed the gates for the night. He tried to slouch so that his off-color hair wouldn't be overly obvious. It didn't appear to be doing much good, however. One of the Sagmyn clerks was looking at him with an intense expression on his face.

Emrael leaned forward and murmured, "Jaina, I think that clerk over there by the guard house is on to us. He's staring right at me."

"Relax, Emrael. Stop squeezing me so tightly. I can barely breathe. I see him."

He tried to relax but still watched the clerk out of the corner of his eye.

Emrael's stomach dropped as he lost sight of the man. Great. Where had he gone?

Jaina kicked the horse forward without warning just as the clerk reappeared, clutching at their horse's bridle.

Time seemed to freeze, each moment turning into hours.

Now that they were close, Emrael could see that the man had a paler complexion than was typical in the Provinces and had dark, mesmerizing tattoos under his robe—overlapping sharp angles covered his hands and peeked out from under the collar of his shirt.

The robed clerk stopped trying to grab at the bridle when it became obvious that he could not control the horse. The clerk—who was clearly no ordinary clerk—reached into his robe and snatched out a copper dagger.

Infusori built in the clerk as he slashed at Emrael with the odd dagger.

In a panic, Emrael tried to gather *infusori* of his own, trying to respond to the dual threat of the dagger and the *infusori* that he felt building in the tattooed man. Any ability he possessed escaped him in the moment of terror and he kicked desperately at the man as they galloped past instead, hoping to keep the copper dagger from his flesh.

The tattooed man tried to twist away from Emrael's kick but snarled in anger as Emrael's foot took him in the shoulder. The dagger had been darting toward Emrael's chest but only grazed the back of his hand as the man's aim was thrown off by the kick.

The instant the copper blade bit into his flesh, however, Emrael felt *infusori* surge from the tattooed man, through the copper blade, and into him. He clenched his will, resisting the attack for a moment, but was quickly overcome even with the aid of Ban's pendant. He began to tremble uncontrollably as the mage's *infusori* coursed through him.

His vision dimmed as the attack threatened to consume him. He lost track of time as he struggled to hold on to Jaina with one numb hand while fighting to retain consciousness.

Then, as quickly as it began, the knife broke contact with his skin and the pain and tremors were gone. His head still buzzed with the aftereffects of the attack, his body trembled, but he seemed otherwise unharmed.

Jaina twisted in the saddle to throw a knife with a flick of her hand. Emrael watched over his shoulder as it sailed true and struck the robed man square in the neck. He crumpled and fell as Jaina urged their horse onward.

Time continued to lurch as they left their attacker behind, rushing past stunned Sagmyn guards and other travelers at the checkpoint.

"Hey! Get back here!"

The guards shouted behind them; one even threw his spear, though it fell well short of their now galloping horse.

However, the Barros guardhouse sat at a second gate at the far side of the pass, leaving a sizable distance of paved road—enclosed by the sheer rock walls of the Pass—between them and the entrance into the Barros Province.

The Barros Legionmen there saw and heard the commotion, and had plenty of time to draw up into a line in front of their gate, shields interlocked and spears leveled at Emrael and Jaina as they charged forward.

"Halt!" one of them called.

Jaina reined in sharply and turned the horse to the side when the soldiers didn't budge. They came to a prancing stop no more than five paces from the nearest spear tip.

"You want to be the hero. Go talk to them, Emrael," Jaina said as they came to a halt.

"What!" he protested, pitched so the Legionmen wouldn't hear.

She responded with a flick of her hand and a nod toward the men holding spears as if his course of action should be obvious.

He shook his head in disbelief but dismounted and shuffled toward the Barros guards with his hands raised over his head. He was still shaking from the *infusori* attack at the Sagmyn gate. He took a deep breath to calm himself and shouted toward the guardhouse as loudly as he could.

"Post Captain! My friend and I mean no harm! I am a citizen of the Barros Province seeking aid. My name is Emrael Ire, son of late Commander Janrael Ire."

While Emrael shouted, a tall man in Barros Legion leather and steel plate armor with two steel straps riveted on the left shoulder exited the guard post. The two riveted straps identified the officer as a Captain Second. Emrael could not make out the man's face in the dim light of the deep canyon, but his bearing seemed familiar. There was a slim chance that one of the officers he had trained with while studying under his father was going to be somewhere in this detail, but most officers would at least recognize his name. And if he was really lucky, it would count in his favor, not against him.

He continued walking slowly, very conscious of the Barros Legion guards who still aimed bows and crossbows at him. Regular crossbows, not the *infusori*-Crafted type—Lord Governor Barros didn't like spending more than necessary on his Legion. There hadn't been a war in more than two generations, after all.

He kept walking forward, empty hands raised. "We mean no harm. I swear it. Please, we need your help. The Citadel has been attacked."

He stopped as he came close enough to see the captain's face, stunned by who it was. He recognized this officer, sure enough. He was a hand taller than Emrael and had a slightly slimmer build. His stark but handsome face matched his short, dark hair, which was cut precisely to Legion standards.

"Halrec?" Emrael exclaimed.

The officer responded with a scowl and moved forward threateningly as he spoke. "Did I hear this scoundrel claim to be Emrael Ire? Everyone knows that lout has white hair and is ugly enough to turn your hair white, too. All I see is a short, dirty scholar."

Emrael froze, not knowing quite how to react to his long-time friend's cold manner.

Halrec laughed suddenly, a toothy smile splitting his face as he caught Emrael in a rough embrace.

He released Emrael to hold him by the shoulders at arm's length.

"Em, what did you do to your hair? I almost didn't recognize you. The Legion just stationed me here. I was going to send a messenger and arrange a meeting."

Emrael let out a relieved laugh and gripped Halrec's arms. "I'm compact, not short, you lanky bastard. I see you've gotten even taller—and uglier—since I left the Junior Legion."

Halrec chuckled but raised his eyebrows and gestured to his Legionmen, still standing at the ready. "What have you done now, Emrael? Why are you trying to charge through a border post?"

"Halrec, please, have your men put their bows down. The Watchers have attacked the Citadel, and one of those Sagmyn clerks just tried to kill me as we waited in line to cross the pass. We need help, Hal. We are looking for Arielle Barros and some others that fled with her. Have you seen them?"

Halrec shook his head in confusion, and Emrael's hopes sank. "Oh, Gods, Hal, they have Ban. They have them all."

Halrec furrowed his brow, pursed his lips, and let his hands fall as he listened to Emrael. "Why would Watchers attack the Citadel, and why do they have Ban? A clerk tried to kill you? Are you sure? You always were a bit dramatic."

Emrael stared hard at his friend.

Halrec threw up his hands defensively. "Fine, fine. We did have some Watchers through here recently, but nothing terribly odd about that. Bring your mount and your friend to the guardhouse and you can tell me about it there."

Halrec shouted an order for his spearmen to stand down and called one of them over. "Sergeant Abath. Take first squad up to the midway gate for night duty. On second thought, take fifth squad as well. See that no one passes through that looks like military without calling for me, not even Watchers. And make sure the boys stay good and awake tonight. Understand?"

"Yes sir, Captain Syrtsan."

Emrael waved Jaina over from where she was still sitting on their horse. They converged on the guardhouse, where Jaina dismounted and tied their mount to a hitching post. They entered the stone block building to find Halrec waiting for them in the doorway to a small office.

"Come on in; we'll get this all sorted out. Just my luck. Raised to Captain Second only to be sent to a post that even Captain Thirds try to avoid, and now this." He sighed.

The three of them entered the room, Halrec sitting in a large chair behind a sturdy desk, Jaina and Emrael in the two smaller wooden chairs on the other side of the desk.

Emrael waited for Jaina to sit, then took the remaining chair gratefully. It had been a very long day, and the fatigue and half-healed wounds in his shoulder and leg were catching up to him. "First, since you so politely inquired outside," he said sarcastically, "this is Jaina, Master of War at the Citadel and Ordenan Imperator. She helped Elle and me escape from the Citadel when the Watchers attacked."

Halrec's eyes widened, and he bowed deeply. "It's a pleasure to make your acquaintance, Mistress Jaina. I apologize for not introducing myself sooner." His eyes flitted between Emrael and Jaina, and his expression hardened. "You should keep her nationality to yourself from now on, though, Emrael. There's been a proclamation of war with Ordena. I don't think most would react well to meeting an Ordenan right now."

Jaina's face grew grim. "And how will you react, Captain?"

Halrec glanced at the closed door to his office before raising his hands in mock surrender. "Your secret is safe with me. I have no orders regarding the proclamation, and I'll do whatever I can to help Emrael. And you."

Halrec stared at Jaina for an uncomfortable moment, in what could only be described as wonder. It wasn't every day you were introduced to an Ordenan Imperator, a figure only heard about in stories for most in the Provinces.

Emrael smiled at his friend. "Jaina, Halrec is my best friend from before I came to the Citadel. We grew up and trained in the Junior Legion together. His family came from Iraea at the same time mine did. I trust him with my life."

Halrec grunted, trying not to show his embarrassment.

Jaina cleared her throat. "We must be quick, Captain. We escaped the attack on the Citadel but lost Arielle getting out of the city. She is likely with some friends but potentially in grave danger. Last we knew, they were headed this way."

Halrec just stared at them for a moment, eyes squinted in confusion. "Why did the Watchers attack the Citadel? It doesn't make sense, capturing so many sons and daughters of powerful nobles and merchants."

Jaina responded again. "Governor Corrande is using the Watchers to make himself the leader over all the Provinces. He took the

Citadel and Bound the students to make *infusori*-Crafted devices to fuel his new war with Ordena—and any here in the Provinces who oppose him."

Halrec put a hand to his head and leaned back into his chair. "Gods. It's going to get bad if that's true. We have no business fighting Corrande's war for him."

Emrael leaned forward. "I know it sounds crazy, Hal, but it's the truth. Corlas is the Commander of the Watchers now and he's helping Corrande. He tried to imprison me himself."

Emrael proceeded to tell his friend about the attack at the Citadel and the subsequent attack at Sarlon's house. He told him about his escape, carefully leaving out anything about his newfound ability with *infusori*—he wasn't ready to tell a member of a Provincial Legion that he was one of the dreaded wielders of *infusori* that they were supposed to abhor, friend or no. He finished by telling him about the man dressed as a Sagmyn clerk that tried to attack him.

Jaina spoke as Emrael finished. "The man dressed as a clerk was a mage-priest from the Dark Lands across the Ordenan Sea. They call themselves Malithii, or 'Hands of Glory' in their language. He must have been prepared specifically for this type of assignment, or his tattoos would have extended to his hands, face, and scalp. We would have noticed immediately."

Emrael nodded slowly, remembering the tattoos that had peeked out from underneath the collar and sleeves of the man's clothing. "*That's* a Malithii priest? How many of them are here in the Provinces?"

She shook her head. "I do not know. We only found out days ago that they were here at all. I do not believe they have been on this continent since before the collapse of the Ravan Empire, and I do not know how they've finally arrived here. My people fight to keep their evil contained in the West Lands, but we have failed. Silent Sisters help us all."

Emrael closed his eyes, trying to gather his thoughts. "We'll figure out what all that means later. For now, we need to make sure Elle and Ban are safe. Hal, we think that Elle came this way, probably with another woman and two men. We need to find them before the people who attacked us catch up, especially if these Malithii are after them."

Halrec pursed his lips in thought. "Hmmm. My men likely wouldn't recognize her, and I've been inside doing paperwork all day. But I have a log here of all the people who passed through. Let me see . . ." He trailed off, mumbling to himself as he fumbled through sheaves of papers that had been in a pile on his desk, "Would have used fake names . . . two men, two women, two of them foreign . . . Ha! This could be them. The log says they are headed for Lidran just like everybody else, and it might even be true. Can't think where else they might go around here, that late. They passed through just over an hour ago, just before a contingent of Watchers."

Halrec looked up at Emrael. "So, what do we do? I should probably tell Lord Governor Barros about his daughter being abducted. About the Watchers and Ban too, all of it, right?"

"Yes. Once we find Elle, you should see to it that she makes it to Naeran to talk to her father. Barros might even be playing along, but I doubt he knows his own daughter has been abducted."

Halrec nodded slowly.

Emrael turned to Jaina. "How will we find Sarlon and the others?"

"Sarlon will leave me a sign. If there are more Malithii about, we need to find them quickly," Jaina said.

Emrael looked back to Halrec. "Hal, can you spare an extra horse? I don't have the coin to pay you, but I'm sure the Legion will understand if you tell your superior officer that it's for a messenger to the Lord Governor. I'll return it just as soon as I can make sure Elle is safe and get back here to rescue my brother."

Halrec pursed his lips and said, "I don't know, Em. They will question me giving a Legion mount to a civilian, even with your history. But if the Lord Governor's daughter is in danger . . . Those Watchers are after you, and probably her too, right? Not to mention Sami and Ban, who you say are still being held captive. Are you sure, Em?"

He hesitated, waiting for Emrael's affirming nod, then nodded to himself as if he had reached a decision. "I can't send any of my men, but I can requisition horses if I come with you. My hundred Legionmen can hold here even if the Watchers try something, and I'll send a messenger to ask the Captain First stationed at Lidran to send reinforcements. It doesn't feel right that the Sagmyn guards are acting as if nothing is wrong, though. If Sagmyn is in league with Corrande, and this really is an attempt to take over the Provinces, they will likely attack here or through the Whitehall Pass up on the Iraean side of the river before long. Unless Barros is in on this too . . ." He trailed off, mumbling to himself.

"You could be stripped of your station or even executed for desertion. I can't let you do that, Hal. We don't know enough. Just give me a horse."

Halrec shook his head, jaw set stubbornly. "You will need another sword, and I can get us through Legion checkpoints if necessary. The Legion and the Lord Governor will understand, especially if we save Elle and bring him word that might help Samille. If Barros is in league with them . . . well, it's a risk I'll gladly take in any case, Em. I didn't get to Captain Second this fast by being afraid of taking risks, you know."

"How did you make it to Captain Second, anyway? I always thought you were destined to be an eternal Captain Third. What with your inferior swordsmanship and all," Emrael responded with a perfectly straight face.

"Inferior swordsmanship? I suppose that's how you got your pretty white hair, then, eh?"

Jaina interrupted Emrael and Halrec's playful banter by clearing her throat. "We will be glad to have your help, Captain Halrec, but we really must go. You two can catch up on the road."

Halrec nodded, flushing. "Of course, Mistress Jaina."

Emrael stood and stepped around the desk to embrace Halrec briefly. "Absent Gods, Hal, I can't tell you how much this means to me. I need to get Ban and Elle back, but I have no idea what to do against an entire army holed up in a fortress."

Halrec smiled. "We'll just have to find an army of our own, then, won't we?"

"Heh," Emrael gave a false chuckle. "I'll get right on that."

Halrec waved them out of the room. "I'm sure you two are starving after the day you've had. Why don't you go over to the mess hall and grab a quick meal and some travel rations while I arrange things with Sergeant Abath. We'll leave in ten minutes."

⁓

Emrael looked back at the pass as the three of them descended the foothills in the grey false light just after sunset. His brother was still on the other side of those jagged peaks of stone, a prisoner in Myntar. He felt sick leaving him to Glory only knew what fate. He would be back soon to save Ban. He would.

He wondered if the Barros Legionmen standing guard at the gate could stop another Malithii mage-priest like the one that had attacked him at the Sagmyn checkpoint. Their torches and *infusori* coils lit the pass well and Halrec had doubled the guard, but he could not even guess what mages were capable of. If the stories people told about the ancient Ravan Imperator mages—and the modern-day Ordenan Imperators, for that matter—applied even in part to what the Malithii were capable of, he certainly wouldn't want to be the one blocking their way. Hopefully, the double guard would be enough.

They descended the steep canyon road as quickly as their horses could trot in the soft blue light of the waxing moon, and within hours they were beneath the oaks, maples, and evergreens of the Stemwood Forest. The sun had set, turning the forest into a dark sea of rustling leaves, but he could smell the fresh spring growth on the branches and the rich, dark soil as they traveled the Kingroad. Though the familiar sight of the forest was partially hidden from him by the darkness of the tree-shrouded night, Emrael felt at home. The clean, earthy aroma brought him memories of navigating the woods to the east of Naeran with his father.

The memories in turn reminded him of Ban. The image of the captives in the Watcher wagon flashed continually through his head. His heart ached, imagining his little brother abandoned to the same fate.

"Stop," Jaina commanded, her voice cutting through his brooding like a knife through soft flesh. She dismounted to peer at the ground.

Emrael berated himself for not paying better attention as he clambered down from his horse to stand beside Jaina. She took a knee to get a better look at some tracks that had dug deep into the hard-packed dirt road, then followed them off the side of the road and into the thick trees.

"What do you see, Jaina?" Emrael whispered. He exchanged glances with Halrec, who remained mounted but had drawn his sword.

Jaina continued her quick pace until she snatched something from a low branch with a satisfied grunt. Emrael hurried to her. She was holding another small handkerchief, though this one did not have knots tied in it like the last one.

"What does it mean?" he whispered again.

"Get on your horse. Many riders were here, recently. Something is wrong," Jaina replied. She followed her own advice and ran to her own mount, trotting into the woods before she had settled in the saddle. Halrec followed as Emrael went for his own horse and was left to bring up the rear. He had no idea what to expect but readied the *infusori*-Crafted crossbow he had stolen from the Watcher in Myntar as he mounted.

They followed a small path into the forest, more a game trail than a real path. Jaina set a quick pace through the trees, quick enough that Emrael worried about his horse's footing in the darkness. He spent as much time trying to dodge low-hanging tree branches as he did looking for whatever Jaina was chasing.

Jaina pulled to a halt once more, this time silent as she pointed deeper into the forest. Emrael peered into the trees for a moment before seeing a faint gleam, as if from a campfire. He watched for another moment and saw another point of orange light, then another. They were moving. Torches, then. He doubted Sarlon and Elle would be traipsing through the deep woods with torches.

Dread weighed heavy on his limbs, but he forced himself to climb down from his horse and quietly loop the reins over a branch of a nearby tree. He gripped the crossbow tightly in one hand and crept to where Halrec and Jaina already waited for him.

"What now?" Emrael whispered.

Jaina glanced at him and the crossbow in his hand. "Halrec will come with me to the left. We will get as close as possible. The ground rises to the right. You go that way, find a clear shot at whoever is down there. You will decide how to handle the situation. Your shot will be our signal to attack."

Halrec nodded and Emrael added his own quiet consent before creeping away, angling to the right of where he had seen the light shining through the trees. He carried the Watcher-issue crossbow with him but left the sword that he had borrowed from Halrec with his horse so he could move quickly and quietly.

As he drew nearer, someone with a deep voice spoke in what looked to be a small clearing, but Emrael could not make out what was being said. He kept low, angling toward the voice until he reached a large, moss-covered boulder that looked down on the clearing.

He trained his weapon on the group gathered in the clearing as he took in the torch-lit scene below him. There were at least half a dozen blue-clad bodies lying motionless, blood staining the ground around them. Elle was on the ground, kneeling beside Master Yerdon and Sarlon. They had their hands tied behind their backs and looked haggard, terrified. Three Watchers stood behind his friends with weapons drawn. Perhaps half a dozen more Watchers stood in a ring around the clearing.

Sarlon alone did not look scared. He was bleeding profusely from somewhere on the top of his head, but his face was a crimson mask of fury. He was yelling angrily at a familiar figure in Watcher blue who held his wife, Yamara.

It was Corlas.

Corlas held Yamara on her feet with one arm around her neck, pressed close to him, hands tied tightly in front of her. Her head drooped forward onto her chest, bobbing up and down as she drifted in and out of consciousness. She and Sarlon had obviously been hurt in whatever fighting had occurred before Emrael arrived.

Corlas drew a large, heavy knife and pressed it to her throat. Darmon Corrande stood next to him, wide-eyed but sneering in triumph at the enraged Sarlon.

"You Provincial filth! Unhand her, or I'll see you and everyone you love in a shallow grave!" Sarlon roared.

Corlas showed almost no emotion as he spoke. "Tell me where Emrael is, or I'll slaughter you one by one, starting with this lovely woman. I'll count to five. One."

"I don't know! I haven't seen him since you burned down my house in Myntar. I swear it."

"Two." The knife pressed against Yamara's skin.

"By Salvation and the holy Silent Sisters, I do not know! Let her go! Take me!"

"Three. If you value your woman's life, find some answers." The knife pressed harder, and Yamara let out a quiet moan. Emrael slowly moved his crossbow to aim at Corlas.

"Please! I do not know where the boy is. Likely on a ship to Ordena by now!" Sarlon pleaded. "Please!"

"Four." The knife pressed hard enough to pucker the skin just above Yamara's collarbone. Blood ran in a small rivulet down her chest and under her arm. Emrael put his finger on the trigger, then hesitated, unsure of his aim. Only Corlas's head and shoulders were visible above Yamara's. Emrael would have to make a nearly perfect shot to hit him without killing her in the process.

"Please! You must believe me! I do not know!" Sarlon screamed. He tried to surge to his feet, but the Watcher behind him kicked him hard in the back, sprawling him onto the dirt.

"Five," Corlas said calmly over Sarlon's screams. He grimaced again, and Emrael watched, stunned, as Corlas's hand jerked suddenly, slicing the knife across Yamara's neck.

Yamara cried out weakly, jerked, and fell to the earth with a dull *thud*.

Panic surged through Emrael, overcoming his shock and hesitation. He fought the urge to vomit as he jerked the trigger.

The Crafted crossbow sent the quarrel speeding toward Corlas with a flash of *infusori*.

Blood spurted as the quarrel hit the Watcher Commander in the right shoulder, knocking him away from where Yamara lay in a spreading pool of blood. He clutched his shoulder and staggered into Darmon.

The Watchers began shouting and milling about, frantically peering out of their circle of torchlight for the hidden shooter.

From the other side of the clearing, Halrec and Jaina burst from the dark forest to cut down the Watchers guarding Elle, Yerdon, and Sarlon from behind.

Emrael reloaded the crossbow with shaking hands and put a quarrel in the back of a Watcher that was bearing down on Halrec as Jaina cut Elle, Yerdon, and Sarlon free of their bonds. The hit Watcher staggered to his knees, then fell backward in an awkward sprawl and lay squirming on the ground.

Sarlon rushed to his wife as soon as he was cut free, felling a nearby Watcher with a brutal strike of his fist as he ran. "Yerdon!" he bellowed, summoning the healer. Yerdon hurried over and began tending to Yamara, who lay clutching her throat in a slowly growing pool of dark crimson that darkly reflected the dancing light of the torches.

The remaining Watchers had retreated to form up in front of their horses, their torches planted in the dirt around them. Five had swords drawn and stood their ground while Darmon helped the injured Corlas onto a mount. Two final Watchers who stood back a few paces had retrieved *infusori*-Crafted crossbows of their own and were readying them to shoot at Jaina, Halrec, and Sarlon, who charged them rather than fall prey to the crossbows.

Emrael would not be able to reload and shoot both crossbowmen before one of them put a quarrel in one of his friends. Despite having left his sword with his horse, he leapt from the boulder he had used for cover and sprinted toward the bowmen.

The Watchers' attention was drawn to the immediate threat, and they didn't notice Emrael as he rushed toward them from the opposite direction. He reached the first crossbow-bearing Watcher and tackled him into the second crossbowman before they could loose.

All three of them went down in a heap, Emrael on top of the two squirming soldiers.

He pushed himself up enough to gain leverage, then drove his knee hard into the throat of the man on the bottom of the pile. The snap of a crushed windpipe reverberated against his knee. He immediately turned his attention to the second man, tripping him again to then rain elbows and clenched fists on his face and neck until he stopped struggling.

His panic now fully transformed to rage, Emrael's face twisted in a snarl as he drew his belt knife with a shaking hand and plunged it into the hollow of each Watcher's throat. Blood sprayed his hands as the men's dying breaths whistled through their ruined windpipes.

There was a loud *clang* of metal on metal just to the side of his head, and he threw himself to the side and forward, rolling to a crouch. He whipped his head around to find Halrec battling a Watcher who had turned from the main fight to come after Emrael. Emrael had never seen him coming, busy as he had been with the two men he'd been fighting. Halrec had just saved him from being run through from behind.

Before he could help his friend, he heard the sound of horses moving behind him. He whipped around to find that Corlas and Darmon were fleeing the clearing. Darmon rode ahead, torch and Corlas's reins in hand, while Corlas slumped in the saddle of the rear mount.

Emrael snatched a sword from one of the dead watchers and wasted no time leaping into the saddle of the nearest horse. Without looking, he shouted back at Halrec, "Follow me!"

He didn't know how the rest of the fight had gone, and didn't know whether Halrec could follow him, but he couldn't let Darmon and Corlas escape. If he captured them alive, he might even be able to exchange them for Ban, besides using them for information. Without them, he had nothing. No plan, no real hope of rescuing his brother. Corlas was already gravely injured; only Darmon stood between him and a chance to get Ban back.

He urged the horse through the trees at a reckless run, following the light of Darmon's torch. Battle rage coursed through his veins, his new lifeblood.

I'll kill him. I'll kill them both.

8

Tree limbs beat at Emrael's face and body. They threatened to tear him from the saddle and reminded him sharply of the half-healed wounds he still bore in his shoulder and calf. The short, broad, Watcher-issued sword in his hand grew heavy. His shoulder throbbed as if pounded by a hammer.

He didn't care. His brother's captors were within his reach. He pushed himself and his horse harder, and the light of Darmon's torch grew closer with every stride. The battle joy sang in his heart, pushing thought and pain aside.

Just as he came within view of his quarry, Darmon and Corlas burst from the trees and onto the main road. They veered left and started toward Lidran at a fast trot, likely all that the injured Corlas could sustain. Emrael did not slow as he exited the trees, racing forward with his sword raised.

Darmon looked over his shoulder in surprise when he realized someone was behind him. Emrael could see the fear in his face as he weighed his options, then threw the reins of Corlas's horse aside and took off at a gallop.

Emrael followed, swinging at Corlas's head with the flat of his blade as he passed the injured man, whose horse continued at a slow trot. He connected, sending Corlas tumbling from his horse, senseless.

Emrael leaned forward into his horse's neck, kicking it in an effort to catch Darmon, who now raced away from Emrael at a dead run.

He could likely get all the answers he needed from Corlas, but there was no way to know how long Corlas would stay alive after taking a crossbow quarrel to the shoulder. Besides, Darmon would be a much more valuable bargaining chip. He needed Darmon as well.

Emrael gained ground, and Darmon soon seemed to realize that he was not going to escape by outrunning him. He reined his horse in sharply and turned to face Emrael.

Emrael slowed to approach at a walk. The churned dust burned his throat as he breathed deep and hard. The urgent, anticipatory beat of his heart spurred him toward the battle. Time slowed to show his eyes every detail of the impending fight.

Contempt wrestled with fear in Darmon's eyes and in his sneer. "So. We finally meet, peasant," he spat. "You'll have your chance at me after all."

Darmon dismounted and planted the torch he had been carrying in the ground with a sharp thrust. He drew his sword with a flourish and shouted, "Come on, then, Ire!"

Emrael dismounted as well, careful to keep his own sword up and at the ready as he did. Darmon might be an arrogant, pampered fool, but he had also been one of the best combatants at the Citadel. Some said he was as good as Emrael, maybe better. And Emrael would not put it past Darmon to attack him while dismounting.

"I'll put my sword in your heart, Darmon. But before I kill you, I will peel back your skin and cut every malformed limb from your body. You'll pay for taking Ban," Emrael said, voice shaking with emotion as he approached.

Darmon laughed. "We will see, Ire." Before he finished speaking, he lunged with a lightning-quick thrust at Emrael's midsection.

Emrael deflected the thrust and stepped to the side smoothly. He shouted with effort as he whipped his own series of quick slashes and thrusts. Darmon pulled back from the attack but did not anticipate Emrael's last, lunging strike.

He felt his blade bite deep into flesh as he hit Darmon's sword arm near the elbow. Darmon drew back, clutching his wounded arm with his free hand and hissing in pain. Emrael thought he had all but won the battle and swung overhand at Darmon's sword arm again, all his rage, pain, and desperation fueling the strike.

To his surprise, Darmon anticipated the attack and danced away expertly rather than trying to meet it.

Emrael was thrown off balance. Darmon flicked his sword up impossibly quickly as he withdrew, scoring a deep cut along Emrael's left arm.

Emrael growled in frustration as he was struck, then pulled back to circle his opponent in the ruddy light of the torch. The injury was not on his sword arm but was more serious than Darmon's wound, bad enough that blood loss would slow and doom him eventually.

He angrily launched attack after attack at Darmon, feinting and bobbing in between strikes, not letting him recover.

Darmon was better than Emrael had expected. A thread of doubt wove its way through Emrael's rage-fueled confidence.

Being a skilled duelist was well and good, but it wasn't everything. Darmon had likely never been in a real fight in his life, a fight without rules and honor. Emrael would have to bet his life on it.

He feinted and struck again, but instead of pushing off after locking swords, he kneed Darmon in the groin. Darmon gasped and instinctively doubled over in pain.

Emrael pressed his advantage. He secured Darmon's sword arm with his free hand, sidestepped, and slammed his blade down, cutting through Darmon's arm at the wrist in one fluid motion.

Blood spurted as Darmon's scream pierced the night air. His severed hand fell to the dirt road, still clutching his ornate sword.

Emrael dropped Darmon to one knee with a hard kick behind the knees.

"That's more like it, Corrande," Emrael crowed triumphantly, standing over his bleeding foe. He rested the point of his blade next to Darmon's neck. "Now. Tell me where my brother is, or I'll let you bleed out right here."

Darmon, still clutching his ruined arm, looked up to meet Emrael's eyes. A vicious smile crept onto his lips, and his pain-crazed eyes grew hard. "He is supporting the war effort and is far beyond your reach, peasant," he said, panting in pain. He lifted his bleeding stump of an arm, which he clutched with his remaining hand to slow the bleeding. "I will kill you for this. I will kill you, but first I will enslave everyone you love and make you watch them suffer, cursing your name. Just wait until my father and his priests come. You'll be sorry."

Emrael snorted. "Your father isn't here to save you."

Caught in the battle rage as he was, he was tempted to kill Darmon then and there. The asshole represented his best shot at getting Ban back safe, however, so he clubbed Darmon unconscious with the hilt of his sword instead, then tore a piece of Darmon's fine shirt into a strip that he used as a tourniquet on his enemy's bleeding arm. It wouldn't do to let Darmon die before he could be ransomed for Ban. It was tempting, though.

He tore more strips of cloth from Darmon's shirt and used one to hogtie his captive, much as he had done to the stable hand in Myntar the day before. He wadded another strip of cloth and tied it around his own wounded arm to slow the bleeding as much as he could.

When he was reasonably sure he wouldn't bleed to death, he grabbed the torch and walked the few hundred paces back to Corlas's horse, but the Watcher Commander was nowhere to be seen.

Worried that Corlas may have miraculously recovered and was waiting for him, Emrael readied his sword and kept a sharp eye on the trees next to the road as he approached the horse. He frantically searched the ground for more clues as to where he could have gone. Emrael needed Corlas. Darmon might be the more valuable captive, but Corlas almost certainly knew where Ban was being held.

Emrael retraced the horse's steps a little way and found the spot where Corlas had fallen from his horse. There was a patch of blood on the ground, presumably from the wound that he had given Corlas with the crossbow, but no sign of Corlas.

He knelt to inspect the ground and found that a large swath of the dirt road had been disturbed, as if something had been dragged away. He followed the tracks to the edge of the road, where he saw at least two sets of footprints leading back into the woods to the north.

Emrael raced back to Corlas's horse, fear gripping him. Someone had been waiting to sneak Corlas away. If they took Darmon as well, he would have no chance of finding where Ban was being taken, no chance at exchanging him for Ban. He snatched up the torch before he jumped onto the horse and urged the animal to a full gallop.

He saw motion up ahead where he had left Darmon. Two dark figures. One was carrying Darmon's unconscious body on its shoulders. The mysterious figures shouted and shuffled quickly toward the woods when they heard Emrael bearing down on them.

Emrael overtook them just before they left the road. He ran his horse directly at the two shadowy figures, forcing them to jump back from the roadway, dropping Darmon in the road as they scrambled out of his path.

As the two men scrambled, Emrael leapt from his horse, already swinging his sword at the first man as he landed. The swing missed by inches as the person dodged with incredible athleticism.

I might be in for more than I can handle—again, Emrael thought, looking at the two mysterious men he faced. He couldn't see well enough to ascertain anything other than that they wore dark robes. He was exhausted and injured, and his friends had not appeared yet. He was all alone, with no choice but to face these two.

For a moment, the night was silent save for the sputtering of the torch and quiet footfalls as Emrael circled his enemies.

He charged, hoping to take one of the men down quickly, but they separated, not allowing Emrael to engage both of them at once. They were obviously no strangers to fighting.

Emrael stopped his advance, instead edging backward and to one side, hoping to lure one of them into attacking. He noticed that these men appeared dark of complexion, but only because most of their skin was covered in tattoos. Their skin was paler than he had seen on any folk here in the Provinces. He couldn't see well in the darkness, but he would bet the tattoos were similar to those of the Malithii priest who had attacked him at the West Pass. Two of them, when one had almost been enough to kill him back at the Sagmyn checkpoint.

The tattooed men uncoiled something from their belts and began to whirl them in tight arcs at their sides as they stalked Emrael. The weapons looked like thick rope with small weights at one end. What an odd weapon.

Emrael didn't know what the rope weapons were used for, but he didn't want to find out. He remembered his helplessness during the *infusori* attack in the Pass all too well. He sprinted toward the nearest man without warning, his sword already moving to strike. The tattooed man bared his white teeth in a smile and whipped his weighted rope at Emrael, not even bothering to dodge away from the attack. The heavy rope hit Emrael in the midsection, coiling around him almost magically. A painful surge of *infusori* ripped through him as before, but not painful enough to prevent him from slamming his sword down between the man's neck and shoulder. The tattooed man's eyes widened in shock as the sword bit deeply into his torso, exposing gory viscera and white bone. The smell of death filled the air, and the *infusori* wracking Emrael's body ceased. The dying priest slid easily off of Emrael's blade to land on the ground with a squelch.

Emrael already had his eyes trained on the second priest, who had thrown his hood back. The man's pale head was shaved bare, and Emrael could now see that even his scalp was covered in tattoos. Definitely one of Jaina's Malithii.

This Malithii was much more cautious now that his friend had been gutted. He discarded his weighted-rope weapon and circled his fallen companion to pick up Darmon's sword, which he handled comfortably. The man stole a few glances toward where Darmon had been dumped, then his attention snapped to the forest behind Emrael as someone shouted in the distance. Without warning, the priest threw his sword at Emrael as if it had been a throwing knife and sprinted into the forest in the opposite direction.

Surprised, Emrael batted the thrown sword from the air with his own just in time, though the hilt clipped his head as it tumbled past. Absent Gods, that could have been the blade that hit him. He'd have been brained like a cow in a slaughter yard.

Emrael knew he was lucky to be alive, but desperately wanted to follow the Malithii to find where they had taken Corlas. He chuckled ruefully to himself. He was so exhausted that he was not sure he would last more than a few hundred paces, let alone through another fight with a warrior mage-priest. He listened gratefully to the sound of the man retreating deeper into the forest.

Emrael sank to his knees, lungs burning as he breathed heavily. He had lost his makeshift bandage and blood now trickled freely down his arm. His head swam and his stomach threatened to empty itself. He wanted to lie down right there on the dirt road and sleep until the pain went away but knew that to be a nap from which he might not wake. Instead, he drove his sword into the ground and rested his head against the hilt in a dazed, trance-like state. He hoped that the shouts in the forest had come from his friends—it had sounded like Halrec—but either way, he wasn't going anywhere.

Before long, he heard horses crashing through the forest, and he started out of his trance in a panic. Fear heightened his senses once more, spurring him to one last fight. The Malithii could have come back with reinforcements, or the Watchers in the clearing might have bested his friends. He wouldn't win, but he'd spill as much of his enemies' blood as he could before he died.

"Em?" Halrec called.

Relief flooded him when he heard Halrec's familiar voice.

"Over here!" Emrael shouted weakly, voice full of emotion. He pushed himself to his feet, but exhausted and wounded as he was, he decided to let his friends make their way over to him.

They carried the torches that had been in the Watchers' possession and had horses for everyone plus a few extra, but no prisoners. Halrec led the way, torch held high. Jaina rode behind him with an *infusori*-Crafted crossbow ready to shoot. Next rode Elle, then Yerdon, who led two horses with a litter tied between them for Yamara. Sarlon rode behind the litter, watching it like a hawk.

Mercy, please let Yamara be alive. I should have taken the shot sooner.

Emrael stood, supporting himself with his sword until the light from the torches reached him. He heard Elle gasp, and Halrec said, "By the Holy Departed, what happened, Em? How much of the blood is yours?"

"My arm is bad, but I'll live if one of you can stop the bleeding for me. Oh, and Darmon is tied up over there somewhere." He waved toward the side of the road. "There were more of those Malithii priests. I killed one of them, but I think others took Corlas." Emrael half-sat, half-fell to the ground.

Elle rushed over to him while Jaina and Halrec walked over to investigate the body of the Malithii and the now semi-conscious, moaning Darmon. Emrael was relieved to see Yerdon and Sarlon stay with the litter, worried expressions on their faces as they tended to Yamara. That meant she must be alive.

Elle looked back and forth between him and the bloody scene with a horrified expression.

"Elle?" Emrael questioned tiredly.

She shook her head slightly and turned back to him, her expression now sympathetic.

"Em, you are positively covered in blood. Is it just your arm that's injured?" Elle traced her finger lightly over his face and neck, as if to make sure that the blood was not his. Now that she was closer, he could see that her eyes were red and puffy from crying.

"Yeah. Apparently, there's a lot of blood involved in killing people." He looked up at her and said in a tired, distant tone, "I've never killed anyone before."

Elle wiped the blood from his face with a rag then hugged his head to her chest gently. Her voice firmed as she said quietly, "I know. I saw you, with those men back in the woods."

She released him after a pleasantly long moment and began tending to his arm. She pulled out a belt knife and cut open the left side of his shirt, exposing the wound he had taken while fighting Darmon.

"It's deep, Em. When are you going to learn to fight without getting cut open?"

Emrael chuckled despite his pain and fatigue. "Darmon is very good with a blade. Or he was before I cut his hand off."

She widened her eyes in mild shock and pulled a canteen of water from her bag to wash his arm thoroughly. That hurt, but she soon produced a smaller vial of something that smelled like liquid fire and proceeded to pour it on the wound.

"Mercy, that burns!" Emrael roared in pain. "Are you sure you don't want to just take the arm off instead?"

Elle glared at him, this time coupled with a raised eyebrow. "I could, you know."

Halrec stomped over from where Jaina was still inspecting the dead Malithii. "I got Darmon loaded up on one of the spare mounts. Yerdon is making sure he won't bleed to death. His arm looks almost as bad as yours."

"Everybody's a comedian today," Emrael said, gritting his teeth while Elle stitched his arm shut.

Halrec smiled, then grew serious and pursed his lips. "Yes, well. It might be best to kill Darmon, you know. If we let him go now, who knows what he'll do to your brother in retaliation?"

Emrael shook his head. "We can ransom him. Besides, if we kill him, Governor Corrande might kill Ban. Gods, I hope he doesn't anyway."

Elle didn't look up from working on Emrael's wound. "Think about it. Corrande took over the Citadel as his first move because he needs the technology to compete with Ordena. Your brother and the rest are precious commodities to him. He is too smart to waste resources for revenge, especially if he doesn't know we killed his son. Halrec is right; Darmon may not exercise such restraint if he has a chance to hurt Ban. We should kill him if we can't trade him for our friends' freedom quickly."

Emrael raised his eyebrows, surprised at Elle's ruthless logic. Halrec had a similar frown of surprised contemplation on his face as he regarded Elle.

She just continued stitching.

Emrael's attention was brought back to his wound as Elle pulled the thread tight, tying off the stitching in his arm. She fingered his tattered shirt and said, "I would normally try to clean you up more, but what you really need is a bath. And new clothes."

Jaina appeared at Elle's shoulder. "I suspect that Halrec can arrange for us to stay a short time at the Legion compound in Lidran. It's a risk, but their healers are Yamara's only real chance of survival. Yerdon cannot do much without the proper coils and equipment. We can get cleaned up there."

She punched her open palm. "I would kill a god for a true Imperator Mage-Healer. A mage like your mother would have Yamara up and skipping in under an hour."

Halrec looked at her in confusion. "Em's mother used coils and Crafted devices, and hers didn't seem to work any faster than most other healers. Most of the time."

Jaina snorted. "Boy, Imperator Mage-Healers don't rely on machines. A Mage-Healer from the Order of Imperators can do work in minutes that would take Yerdon and his Craftings days. They work directly with the *infusori* to Heal. His mother would have taken precautions not to be seen Healing too well, for fear of being revealed."

For some reason, Elle had an oddly suspicious look on her face. Emrael was too tired to care.

Jaina poked a finger at Emrael. "Now. You killed that Malithii, and there were more?" She waited for his nod before pursing her lips and waggling her head back and forth. "You are good, Emrael, but not that good. Malithii priests are very highly trained mages. I've never seen one with that many tattoos before, and I spent two years fighting them in the Dark Nations."

Emrael met her gaze. "I have no reason to lie, and you see the dead priest," he said in a flat tone, waving a tired hand at the Malithii corpse nearby. "They tried to whip me with those rope things. I'm guessing they are some type of Crafting? The interference from Ban's amulet obviously surprised them."

"You were lucky in any case." Jaina held up one of the ropes with weighted ends, and Emrael saw in the flickering light of the torches that they were metal cables with copper weights on the end, not ropes as he had supposed. "Even without these, those men are extremely dangerous. Wait for help next time."

"I didn't have much choice, Jaina. Besides, we now have a captive, which is more than you managed." He met her frosty stare until she shook her head and rolled her eyes in exasperation.

"Emrael, I do not say this to undervalue your courage or skill, but you must understand what you face. If not for that pendant of yours and very fortunate timing, you would have died. That man with the dagger would have killed you back at the pass if not for me and your pendant. You are a good fighter but not practiced enough with *infusori* to withstand someone of their skill. Please be careful, for your own sake. I'm only trying to help you."

Emrael took a deep breath to calm himself before nodding silently. He knew he was being obstinate. Jaina nodded in return before walking toward where they had gathered the horses.

Elle and Halrec helped him to his feet, and Elle supported his less-injured right arm as he walked slowly to his horse. Sarlon was practically bouncing in his saddle, anxious to get his injured wife to Lidran.

"What happened to the rest of the Watchers?" Emrael murmured to Elle.

"Sarlon. He killed them before they even knew to surrender.

He was yelling so loud and hit them with his metal staff and they just . . . crumpled. I think even Jaina and Halrec were shocked. It was terrifying."

"They nearly killed his wife, Elle. Is she going to be okay?"

"I don't know. Her injury is beyond anything I dare treat, but Master Yerdon says that if we can get her to Lidran quickly enough, he might be able to help her. I don't know, though. I think at least one of her primary arteries is severed. Even *infusori*-assisted healing can only do so much—but we have to keep her alive long enough to try."

They reached his horse and he thanked Elle for helping him to his mount. As he settled himself into the saddle, Halrec drew his horse next to his and held out a sheathed sword, hilt first.

"What's this?" he asked his friend, even as he took in the fine inlay on the hilt and crosspiece of the sword.

"It was Darmon's sword. You defeated him in single combat, Em. It's yours."

Emrael hesitated only a moment before he grabbed the hilt and turned it back toward Halrec. "I don't want his sword. Let it be my payment for the horse and all of the help you have given me. Besides, you saved my life back in that clearing. It's yours."

Halrec accepted the sword after a slight pause. "Thank you, Em. I won't forget it." He slid the broad-bladed sword from its scabbard and swung it about with a flourish before replacing the blade and tying it to the front of his saddle. The sword was similar in size to a Legion-issue sword but had a slightly curved profile and was very well crafted. "Light. Well balanced. A sword fit for a lord." He smiled a large, toothy smile and winked at Emrael, who smiled and winked back.

❧

The sun had nearly risen by the time their horses' hooves clattered across a stone bridge that spanned a small river just outside the large clearing that surrounded Lidran. The city's high stone walls loomed in the early morning darkness, casting long shadows in the pale blue light of the moon. Emrael studied the city with heavy eyes. While too small to be considered a great city like Naeran, Myntar, or Whitehall, trade with the Sagmyn Province—and with the kingdoms of Sagmyn and Iraea before the War of Unification—had treated Lidran very well. The walls had been built over time to an impressive stature. It could hold off an invading army for months, and had several times throughout history.

They rode as quickly as they dared with Yamara suspended in the litter. Yerdon had an intense, worried look on his face as he hovered over her, and alternated between quietly urging the group to move faster and calling for them to slow down so as not to jostle his patient. Jaina, who rode at the front of the group, took the healer's inconsistent admonitions without complaint.

Elle rode up beside Emrael once they were clear of the trees, and leaned over in the saddle to put a hand to his face. "You are too warm. We need to get you cleaned up and in a bed."

He smiled at her gratefully and patted her hand before returning to watching his surroundings for Malithii. He knew they were out there somewhere, and if he were in their position, he'd attack them now while they were at their weakest.

As they approached the closed gate that led into Lidran, Jaina addressed the group. "Keep to yourselves. Elle, no one finds out who you are, understand? If the Watchers wanted your sister, they will want you as well. We don't know to what degree your father's Legion is cooperating with the Watchers. Same goes for Darmon. He speaks, club him."

She turned to Halrec and said, "I think it best if you lead us into the city and do the talking. Remember, we are just here for medical help after being attacked by brigands."

"Can't I even tell my superior that I'm helping escort Elle to the capital?" Halrec asked, clearly surprised. "I could be in serious trouble for leaving my post without a solid reason."

Jaina shook her head. "I'm sorry, Halrec, but you could be putting Elle in extreme danger by doing so. Please trust me."

Halrec pursed his lips but hurried to the small door set into the main gate. There were large torches set in sconces on either side of the gate and smaller ones on either side of the guard door that cast an uneven light on Halrec as he knocked. His pounding on the wooden door reverberated loudly in the still of the night.

There was a rustle behind the door, and after a moment a small opening set into the guard door opened. A bleary-eyed Legionman peered out. Halrec spoke immediately.

"Soldier! Were you asleep on your watch?" he barked. "I am Captain Second Halrec Syrtsan from the Sagmyn Pass post. I will speak with your Captain First."

The soldier's eyes widened slightly. His apologetic smile revealed a mouth missing several teeth. "Ah . . . Captain, we've orders to keep the gates closed 'til sunrise, sir. And we didn't never get no word of your coming, sir. I'm awful sorry, Captain, but I can't let ya in," he finished quietly. Resignation was clear in his voice as he refused entry to an officer well above his station.

Halrec regarded the man briefly before responding gently. "I didn't ask to be let in, soldier, but I have wounded that can't wait out here all night. Go wake Captain Gerlan."

The Legionman's face drooped in resignation at having to wake his commanding officer, but disappeared from view as he shouted for the Captain First to be advised of a Captain Second Syrtsan waiting for him at the east gate. His eyes reappeared at the gate. "He'll be coming shortly, I'm sure, sir."

"Thank you, Legionman."

"Sergeant Toerly, sir."

"Thank you, Sergeant. While we wait for the Captain First, would you please send word to your healers? We will be proceeding straight to the healers' hall once the Captain grants us entry."

"Ah, yes sir. I'll go tell her myself. Shift's changin' right now and I'm off duty. The head healer lives in the compound, near the Captain and the other officers. I'll make sure she's awake and ready for you."

"You have my thanks, Sergeant."

The sergeant ducked his head and was replaced shortly at the door by a man who studied them silently.

Emrael rested his head in his hands while they waited. Sooner than he expected, there was a commotion at the door as it opened for a half a dozen Legionmen to file out with weapons drawn. He sat up, suddenly alert despite his exhaustion, and moved his hand to his sword.

A tall man with hair as much grey as it was black stepped through the doorway as the Legionmen surrounded them. He had a large, round face that showed surprisingly little sign of his having been rousted from bed in the middle of the night. Three metal straps riveted on each shoulder of his Barros Legion officer's leather-and-steel armor displayed his rank, Captain First. This must be Captain Gerlan—likely a younger son or nephew of the Lord Holder Gerlan that owned a large swathe of this portion of the province.

Gerlan scanned the group quickly before turning his attention to Halrec, who had dismounted and was now standing at attention.

The Captain First addressed him formally. "Captain Second Syrtsan, I presume?"

"Yes, sir," Halrec responded.

"I'm Captain First Gerlan. I've heard good things about you, but I can't say I appreciate your visit in the middle of the night. Particularly when you are supposed to be at your post in the Pass. Tell me what you need."

"Captain, sir, I have wounded civilians who need immediate attention," he said, gesturing to the litter, where Sarlon was guarding his wife closely. "I also have urgent news that is best suited to a private setting. I ask your leave to enter your compound and treat my wounded before reporting, sir."

"Granted. No use letting the injured suffer. I can tell you have had some sort of trouble. The Iraean brigands have been bold as bears of late." He looked appraisingly at Emrael, who was still covered in a great deal of blood, and his gaze paused when he noticed Darmon tied up and draped across a horse. "You did well, calling for me right away. My men would not have let you pass with anything less than my word."

"I assumed as much, sir," Halrec responded. "Thank you, sir."

"Escort them to the compound!" Captain Gerlan shouted to his men.

One side of the heavy iron gates opened inward to admit them. Halrec followed immediately behind Captain Gerlan, the reins of the lead litter horse in hand. Sarlon and Yerdon were close behind, hovering on either side of the litter.

Emrael felt another pang of guilt as they passed through the gate. He should have taken the shot sooner. He could have saved Yamara.

"Come on, Em," Elle said. She and Jaina had stopped their horses at the gate to wait for him, nearly identical looks of concern on their faces. He nudged his horse through the gate. Tension drained from his muscles as he fled the night and the Malithii it hid.

He looked to the side as his horse stepped onto the main avenue of Lidran, absentmindedly studying the *infusori*-driven gears and pulleys that secured this gate and allowed it to be much larger and heavier than a manual gate. The considerable investment in such a gate said much of Lidran's importance as a trade center. It also spoke to Lord Governor Barros's—or perhaps Captain Gerlan's—acknowledgement of Lidran as an important military installation. The Treaty of the Provinces was new enough, tenuous enough that they seemed to have prepared for any eventuality. Just as well that he had. War with Corrande and the Watchers—or with the Ordenans, should Barros side with Corrande—could easily arrive at these gates within the month.

Lidran's military value notwithstanding, its current status as a trade hub between Barros and Sagmyn Province filled the city with food, goods, and people from all over the known world. As they neared the Legion compound, the buildings and their wares grew more and more opulent. *Infusori* dealers' steel-barred windows shone in the darkness, and *infusori* coils in copper sconces lit the establishments of fine tailors, bootmakers, bookstores, and restaurants. There were even a few *infusori* Craft dealers catering to the wealthiest citizens, whose palaces occupied the surrounding blocks. Even near to passing out due to blood loss, he couldn't help but inspect the finery. He would have given almost anything for a pair of boots from the window of one of those cobblers.

Jaina spat as they passed a Church of the Holy Departed, drawing his attention. The Sentinel's two-headed torches burned at all hours of the day, making sure the populace was properly intimidated by their blank-faced Gods carved into stone pillars at the entrance to their large, imposing building.

He would not mind living in a city like this, despite the Sentinel presence. They were everywhere anyhow. Perhaps once he rescued Ban, they could seek their fortunes there. A lot of money traded hands in this city, and there would be less competition than in one of the major trade capitals. The richest merchants that owned these shops and palaces would pay a small fortune for a Master of War from the Citadel to run their guard, and Ban would make them rich sooner rather than later with his Craftings.

He sat up a little straighter as they approached the Legion compound on the eastern side of the city. He was looking forward to having a talk with Darmon about where they were holding Ban.

More Barrosian Legionmen were ready for them as they arrived at the heavy timber gate of the Legion compound. They saluted Captain Gerlan and ran to swing the gate open.

Inside the thick white granite wall that surrounded the compound, several buildings lined a central square. Torches lit the courtyard, and more were being placed around the square due to their arrival. A large building at the head of the square that could only be the command post shone with the blue light of *infusori* coils—likely Gerlan wouldn't settle for his personal quarters and offices being lit by ordinary fire, like a common peasant.

Captain Gerlan stopped in the middle of the square as a middle-aged woman in white healer's robes strode from another *infusori*-lit building that dominated the right side of the square. Several young people in white robes followed closely, likely her assistants. Healers always seemed to have several assistants. Emrael could remember when Elle had served in the same capacity for his mother.

The Legion healer nodded to Captain Gerlan, then headed straight for the litter. She conversed with Master Yerdon briefly before nodding her head and turning to her students. "Unhitch the litter—carefully, mind!—and *gently* set her in the first room," she said in a high, clear voice. Her attendants leaped to obey.

Sarlon followed the litter closely, watching the healer's assistants with a sharp eye as they unloaded his wife and carried her inside the sprawling one-story infirmary. Jaina followed without so much as a glance backward.

Emrael watched gravely as Yamara was taken to the infirmary, wishing there was something he could do. Guilt weighed like a stone in his stomach once again. He could have saved her, and they could have been on their way back to rescue Ban already. Some Master of War he was.

Once Yamara had been carried inside the building, he climbed down from his horse carefully, using his right arm to lever himself to the ground. He could feel blood from the stitched wound trickling down his left arm. He probably couldn't have lifted that arm if he had wanted to.

He walked slowly to the horse that Darmon had been tied to and drew his belt knife. Darmon, now awake, had stopped struggling but growled weakly when Emrael drew near. "Ire, I'm going to—"

Emrael cut the rope that was holding Darmon to the horse without saying a word, and Darmon crashed to the ground in a moaning, sobbing heap, his arms and legs still bound. The arm that no longer ended in a hand still bled despite the tourniquet and had soaked through the bandage Yerdon had hastily wrapped around his stump. He probably needed attention from a healer soon if Emrael was going to keep him alive to barter with Lord Corrande.

Emrael bent, grabbed the ropes at Darmon's ankles, and unceremoniously dragged him across the stone-paved courtyard toward the infirmary. His shoulder ached fiercely, and he felt like he was going to collapse with every step, but the groans from Darmon as his head connected with the uneven stones made the effort worth the pain.

Captain Gerlan watched Emrael curiously from atop his horse and announced, "I think it's time to start telling me what's going on. Who is your prisoner, and who are you? You look like you need the infirmary yourself, man."

Emrael stopped and looked up to meet the Captain's eyes. "I'm a student at the Citadel in Myntar, training to be a Master of War. This here is one of the men who tried to rob us on the highway. Do you have the resources to treat his injuries? His friends made off with some of our things."

Captain Gerlan's expression grew skeptical, and he directed a questioning look at Halrec, who nodded. Gerlan responded to Emrael after a brief pause. "Take him on in. I'll see to it that a guard is posted on his room as well as on the entire infirmary; they shall watch him closely. Captain Second Syrtsan, a word in my office."

Captain Gerlan hoisted himself out of the saddle and directed Halrec toward the large command building at the head of the square. Several Legionmen followed.

Emrael continued pulling Darmon toward the infirmary. By the time he reached the front of the low building, Elle had hurried over to help Emrael, and a young male healer's assistant had appeared from the infirmary to pick the now-unconscious Darmon up by the shoulders. They shuffled inside and down a wide hallway lit by *infusori* coils. After passing several doors, the healer's assistant said timidly, "This room here on the left should do."

They entered a room with two small but clean beds, each with an accompanying worktable stocked with medical supplies like bathing pans, cloth, needles, thread, and bandages. There were several *infusori* coils set on the walls, casting a steady pale blue light on the room. Smoking torches wouldn't do in a place of healing, his mother had always said. Apparently, the head healer there agreed.

They placed Darmon on one of the beds. Emrael untied Darmon's arms and used the rope to secure his limbs to the bed, then gagged him for good measure.

Emrael sat on the spare bed and looked at the healer's assistant. "Please see to his arm. I need him in good enough shape to get answers from him as soon as possible, so don't go giving him anything to numb the pain too much. And for Glory's sake, don't undo his ropes or his gag. I'm not in any mood to chase him down or hear more of his lies."

The young man nodded and said, "Yes, sir. Of course, sir. The healer will be in soon to see to him. I'll relay your requests."

Emrael nodded his thanks, then leaned back against the wall and closed his eyes. He needed to stay awake, but his weariness and the pain of his injuries were dragging him down toward much-needed sleep.

Suddenly, he jerked awake, looking around in a daze. Everyone was as he remembered, Darmon on the bed with the healer's assistant preparing his wounds for the healer, Elle at the foot of the bed. He must have just drifted off. Elle was smiling at him.

"Come on; we need to get you cleaned up," Elle said, grabbing his hand. "Then you need rest. We both do. I'm sure we can find somewhere close by to sleep. Captain Gerlan's healer and guards will look after the prisoner until tomorrow."

She addressed the healer's assistant. "Are there baths near?"

The young man looked over his shoulder from where he was working on Darmon's bandages and said, "Yes, ma'am. Take the first hallway to the left, all the way to the end."

"Come with me." Emrael let her pull him up by the hand and lead him to the bath chambers.

They found a bleary-eyed serving woman in the bath chambers tending an enormous kettle over a fire. There were several such fire pits with kettles suspended over them on one side of the chamber, cold but ready to be lit. Two open doors led to separate walled areas occupied by tubs of various sizes, each in their own wooden-walled stall for privacy.

The woman warming water in the kettle looked up as they entered the room. She noted the blood covering Emrael and said, "Oh, goodness, you are a sight. It will just be a few moments, dears. I fired up the kettle as soon as I heard we had new arrivals. Healer Nora will be wanting some of this water for the patients in rooms one and three, but I'll have plenty for you both as well. You may choose whichever bath you'd like. Both the gentlemen's and the ladies' rooms are empty, what with it being the middle of the night. I'll bring you buckets of water as soon as it's good and hot."

She smiled and waved them toward the bathing rooms but gave them a surprised and disapproving look when they started toward a bath chamber together instead of splitting into the separate bathing areas designated for men and women.

"He is my patient. I'm going to help him clean his wounds," Elle explained with a straight face, though her blush betrayed her. Emrael would have thought he was too tired to blush, but he was wrong.

Elle led Emrael into a bathing stall near the end of the men's row and stood him next to the large porcelain tub. She considered him with a squint, then retrieved a stool from beside the wall and put it next to him.

"Sit," she commanded.

He sat, legs nearly collapsing as he lowered himself to the seat. She gathered small cloths and towels from a table set against the wall and set them over the lip of the tub next to him. She then began pulling gently on Emrael's shirt, careful to avoid his wounds as she tugged it slowly over his head. Dried blood flaked from his chest and face, making him itch.

Elle did not slow down, attacking his boots and socks next. When she had those removed, she said, "Stand up."

He gave her a confused look but stood. She reached for his belt, trying to be matter-of-fact about readying her patient for a bath, but he turned away from her with a strangled yelp.

"Stars and stones, Elle, I can do the rest myself! I'm not a child. Why don't you go take a bath as well? It's likely the last opportunity for days. Just have the good woman bring in some water and soap, and I'll wash myself. I'll be fine."

Elle had bright spots of color on her cheeks but did not retreat.

"Oh, really? You will wash yourself, will you? Touch the top of your head."

He raised his good hand to the top of his head and stuck his tongue out at her.

A thin smile sprouted on her lips despite her glare.

"Okay, now touch your toes."

He obeyed but almost collapsed as the mostly healed wound on his calf protested and his weariness made his head swim. Nevertheless, he stubbornly struggled to stay upright until he could touch his toes, and returned to a standing position. He flourished his good hand and bowed mockingly, which earned a laugh from her.

"Fine. But if you drown, I will not be held accountable," she said, lifting her chin haughtily. "Call me in if you need. I'll be just next door. Have fun in here. All by yourself."

Could she have really wanted to . . . No, I must be imagining things. I need some sleep, he thought as he watched her glide away and turn into the next stall.

"You aren't going to the women's bathing chambers?" Emrael asked carefully. The sounds of her taking off her clothing just on the other side of the thin wall were very distracting.

Elle laughed. "Why? The bathing chambers are empty, and nobody else will be arriving at this hour. Does it make you uncomfortable? You haven't given me more than a glance all these years. Surely, you don't mind now." She laughed again, louder this time.

Emrael sat on the stool and tried to jerk his thoughts away from Elle. She was right; he hadn't thought of her as anything but a friend, Ban's friend at that. But now he found it hard not to think about her—when he wasn't busy trying not to be killed, or trying to plan his brother's rescue.

The thought of Ban sobered his mood. Gods, how was he going to tell their mother? She would be furious with Emrael.

The serving woman finally entered with a knock to fill his bath with buckets of steaming hot water while Emrael stood to the side, trying to cover himself with a towel. She brought in a large bucket of cold water, a chunk of soap, a razor, and small mirror, setting them on the stool he had vacated without a word. He thanked her as she smiled and pulled the curtain to his stall closed behind her.

He used the cold water to bring the bath to a bearable temperature and climbed in gratefully, though with considerable pain as his wounds touched the hot water. He sighed, closed his eyes, and let the steam roll over his face for a long while. He could hear similar sounds of relaxed pleasure from Elle in the next stall. The buckets were not nearly as convenient as the piped-water system he had become accustomed to at the Citadel, but he was not about to complain.

He let himself sink underwater and held his breath there in a trancelike state for as long as his lungs would allow. He emerged from the water with a large, exhaled breath, then snatched the soap from the stool next to him.

"Are you sure you don't need help?" Elle called lazily. "If those wounds are still dirty after the bath, I won't be kind about cleaning them."

"Ah," he stammered. "I'm fine, Elle, thanks," he replied finally with a small chuckle. When had Elle become so bold? Tempted as he was, he was in no shape to share a bath after the fight they'd just been through, physically or mentally.

After scrubbing the black dye from his hair, he lathered one of the small cloths that Elle had set over the side of his bathing tub and scrubbed away the blood and dirt that had caked itself to him. He was especially careful with the fresh gash in his arm, but even so, it began to bleed steadily, staining his bathwater pink. Elle would not be happy with him. Shaving was not easy, as he had to use his injured arm to hold up the mirror, but it was worth the effort. He felt more and more human with every swipe of white-grey stubble.

When he stepped out of the bath, he left the worst of his fears and anxiety behind with the blood and the dirt. He felt more relaxed than he had since before Jaina had challenged him to a duel. He just needed a few hours of sleep, then he could get on with finding a way to free his brother—starting with interrogating Darmon.

He looked down at his ragged, filthy clothing that lay on the ground. He still had some coin left but definitely not enough to pay for new clothing. He would need a new shirt, at the very least.

I'll bet Darmon has plenty of coin on him. I should search his purse.

Emrael tied a towel around his waist and gathered his belongings beneath his uninjured right arm before walking out of the bath chamber. He approached the curtain of Elle's bathing stall hesitantly, but it opened just as he was about to knock.

Elle was wrapped in a towel as well. Her dampened hair curled around her shoulders and delicate collarbones. She started slightly at seeing Emrael outside her bath stall but recovered quickly. She made an irritated noise when she saw his shoulder bleeding and intently checked his stitches.

The door to the bathing chamber opened behind him, and the serving woman stood in the doorway, her arms full of Elle's discarded clothing.

"Hand your clothes over to me, young sir. I'll see that they are cleaned and mended and returned to your room before you wake. Do you two need help finding rooms?"

Elle stepped forward. "Yes, please. We'll need just one room but with two beds, and I'll need supplies to clean and bandage his wounds. And . . . do you by chance have healing-grade *infusori* coils?"

The woman smiled in a motherly way, in response to Elle's innocent tone. "Oh, dear, I can see your man is hurt, but healing coils are reserved for the officers and those that can pay for them. Sometimes for the gravely injured if Healer Nora says so. I'm afraid that won't be possible," she finished with a titter.

Elles eyes flashed and she drew herself up, every bit the Lord Governor's daughter, wrapped in a towel or not. "I'll have you know that I—"

Emrael laid a hand on her bare shoulder, and she cut off abruptly. She looked over her shoulder at him in irritation. Her mouth opened angrily, so he hurriedly said, "It's okay, Elle. She's right. We *simple* folk can't afford them, and my wound will heal. Let's get to a room. My arm hurts and I want to get some rest before we leave tomorrow."

He nodded to the serving woman. "Thank you very much for your help with the baths and our clothing. May we be shown to a room, please?"

The woman gave them one more disapproving look at mention of sharing a room but quickly reassumed her smile. "Certainly, young man. This way."

She led them back down the hallway, to a room in a different hallway than the room Darmon occupied, though the contents and layout were the same. The serving woman left after telling them that their clothes would be returned to them by morning, and that she'd return shortly with robes to sleep in.

As soon as she was gone, Elle went to one of the beds and sat, patting the bed beside her. "Sit. I need to see to your arm."

He sat next to her on the bed so she could tend to his left arm, where the stitched wound still seeped blood. He was very aware of the fact that both of them were dressed in nothing but towels. Excitement warred with embarrassment, pain, and exhaustion as she prodded his arm. He couldn't help but glance at the soft curves visible above her towel. She was seemingly unaware of anything but his wound, which was probably a good thing.

She treated the cut with a potent-smelling liquid from a jar on the table next to the bed and was just wrapping his arm in a fresh bandage when the serving woman returned with robes.

"Just set them over there, please," Elle said without looking up from her task, her blue eyes and lightly freckled nose scrunched in concentration.

Once the serving woman had left, Emrael placed his hand on Elle's bare knee. She finished the final knot of his bandage and looked up at him with big eyes.

"Thank you," he said, holding her gaze with his.

"It's no problem. I like treating wounds; it's the one thing I'm good at. I just wish I had healing-grade coils," she said, pursing her lips in thought, eyes growing distant.

Emrael leaned closer to her, and she continued to meet his eyes with an inquisitive look. They looked at each other for a moment before Emrael grew anxious and stood. He wanted to kiss her but couldn't work up the courage. It wasn't like he'd never kissed a girl, so what was his problem?

"I'll stand out in the hall and let you change into your robes. I'd like to get into mine and get to sleep as soon as I can. I'm about to drop," he said, trying to hide his embarrassment.

He left the room without waiting for a reply, feeling like a complete idiot. He closed the door behind him and waited in the hall for a few minutes while she changed. She opened the door dressed in a heavy robe, towel in hand.

"Your turn. I'll be back in a moment. Go ahead and lie down," she said, already starting off down the hall.

He shrugged to himself and entered their room, too tired to argue. He climbed into his warm, soft robe, then onto the stiff bed.

He lay on his back and was just drifting off to sleep when Elle reentered the room. She had her towel in a bundle over her shoulder, full of something that clinked softly when she moved. She set the towel on the bed between his feet and let it fall open. A steady blue glow shone from a large pile of *infusori* coils. They had been pilfered from wall sconces in the building, from the looks of it. He chuckled tiredly, closing his eyes again.

Elle snorted her irritation. "What?" she demanded.

"You don't give up, do you?"

"Never." She smiled fiercely.

"Are those even going to work? I thought healing coils had to be fairly high quality to be effective, and these are medium-grade at best. And how are you going to even use them without the healing apparatus?"

"Why don't you just leave the healing to me? I want to try something. You can thank me later."

He didn't argue further as she placed the *infusori* coils inside his robe and around his neck and head. When she had placed the last coil, she slipped her cold hand under his robe and placed it on the middle of his chest.

"Uh . . . what are you doing?" He asked.

"Just shush. And don't tell anyone about this. The Watchers would kill me if they knew I could do this, and my father might let them. I'm not very good at it, but I think I can do something about your wounds. They aren't too bad, for all your whining."

He smiled and slipped the pendant from his neck and placed it around hers.

"Whatever you are doing won't work right while I wear that, I think. Keep it safe for me, please."

She didn't say anything, but he thought her eyes shone with unexpressed emotion. She likely knew what it was, what it meant to him. He lay back, closed his eyes, and concentrated on the *infusori* within the coils, trying to feel what she was doing. He felt the power flow from the coils into Elle, who still had her hand on his chest. Was everyone around him a mage? Mercy, what else didn't he know about his closest friends?

He began to feel an odd warmth in his chest. It was very unlike anything he had felt in his exercise with Jaina, or even when he'd been healed with *infusori* coils and Craftings before.

Pain flared suddenly in his arm and older injuries, and his fatigue suddenly became overwhelming. He was pushed down into a deep sleep, a sleep filled with sickening images of dying men, blood spurting from horrible wounds. Men he had killed.

9

When Emrael woke, light streamed steadily in through the small window. He stared at the ceiling, trying to forget the nightmares. Blood pouring from Yamara's wound. Blood gushing from the necks of a pair of Watchers. Blood spurting from Darmon's severed hand. Blood and gore running down his sword as he pulled it free of the eviscerated Malithii.

Finally, he sat up. Gold coils fell from his robes and rolled to *clink* on the floor. They were dull, the *infusori* drained from them completely.

He paused on the edge of the bed to look at Elle. Her chest still rose and fell slowly with the measured breathing of slumber. Golden brown hair curled around her head like a halo. He felt warmth in his heart where there had only been despair over the past few days.

He smiled and pushed himself out of bed, then paused. He didn't hurt. At all. Whatever Elle had done had completely Healed him overnight. Not even Yerdon's healing had been so effective. The only time he'd even heard of anything similar was when his mother had Healed the wound that had given him his white hair. He hadn't thought much of it until now.

"Don't tell anyone about this." Elle's words from last night echoed in his mind. Everyone had their secrets, even innocent Elle.

His clothes, including a new shirt to replace the one that had been torn to shreds, had been cleaned and placed on the stool next to the table by his bed. He didn't know who had paid for the shirt, but he was grateful for it. It had likely been Elle. It felt good to be in clean clothes, plain and patched though they were. He left with one last fond look at Elle.

He needed to make sure no one had gone through his things and found the *infusori*-Crafted crossbow he had hidden in his packs. Some of the spare mounts had been loaded with other weapons gathered from the Watchers as well. They would invite questions that would not be easy to answer, though Halrec had likely explained everything he could to Captain Gerlan.

First, however, Emrael needed to have a chat with his prisoner.

Two guards had been posted on Darmon's room. They didn't move to stop him, so Emrael did his best to ignore them in turn, entering the room and closing the door softly behind him. There were no locks on the doors in this building, so he would have to keep things quiet. He didn't know how the guards outside would react to what he was about to do.

He crossed the few steps to the bed and stood assessing his enemy for a moment. Someone had untied him, removed the gag, and wrapped his stump of an arm in fresh bandages. Emrael hoped Darmon hadn't been able to speak to anyone—things could go south quickly if Gerlan found out that the heir to the Corrande Governorship lay wounded in his infirmary.

Asleep as he was, Darmon looked normal, peaceful. Almost human. The burning, desperate rage within Emrael calmed slightly.

Darmon's eyes opened suddenly. He struggled to push himself into a sitting position with his uninjured arm. He stared at Emrael with a calm face, held up his stump of an arm and said, "I'm going to pay you back tenfold for this, peasant. You will scream for weeks before I let you die. Mark my words."

Emrael stepped closer, looming over Darmon. "You should have left my brother out of whatever scheme you are playing at, Corrande."

Darmon started to scoff but stopped as Emrael reached toward him. He shrank against the wall, clutching his ruined arm to his chest. "Don't touch me! We are in a Legion compound; the Treaty of the Provinces holds here. I'll tell the commander of this post. I've already told them who I am." There was panic in his voice now. Fear gleamed in his eyes.

Emrael clenched his jaw in anger. "I don't care about your treaties, or the Provinces, or commanders. In here, right now, it's just you and me, and you are going to tell me where my brother is."

Emrael lunged as Darmon gathered breath to shout. His hand shot out and clasped Darmon's neck tightly, forcing his mouth shut with a *click* and reducing the shout to a gurgle. Darmon swung and kicked at Emrael, but Emrael had his weight on top of him and was more heavily built by a good margin. Not to mention he had two hands to Darmon's one.

"Are you ready to tell me where my brother is, or will I have to do some convincing?" Emrael asked through gritted teeth.

Darmon's eyes scrunched in anger, and he began resisting once more, this time clawing at Emrael's face.

"So be it," Emrael spat. He pressed harder on Darmon's throat and drove a knee into his ribs, causing the other man to crumple and rasp in pain. Emrael jumped on top of his captive and eased the pressure on his throat just enough for Darmon to draw in a ragged breath.

"Tell me where my brother is and how to get him back."

Darmon sneered as he answered in a hoarse rasp. "Your precious brother is either still at the Citadel or being taken north to my province, likely through Whitehall. There is no way to get him back, you pathetic wretch. He belongs to us, Ire. So do you—you just don't know it yet."

"You had better hope I can get him back, because trading you for him is the only scenario in which I let you live, Darmon."

Darmon's sneer turned into a wheezing cackle. "My father would likely just as soon I die as return to him now that I've been captured, especially after losing a hand to a peasant like you. You'll never see your brother again." Darmon held up his stump and spat in Emrael's face.

Emrael's rage overtook him.

He gripped Darmon's throat tightly once more. Instinctively, he used his newfound mage senses to feel the other man's life source, the *infusori* that was the source of his being. He felt his humiliation, his fear, his ambition, his loneliness, his greed.

He took hold of Darmon's life source and began to draw it into himself. He could see the light draining out of his enemy's eyes, could feel the *infusori* seeping out of Corrande and into him.

He took control of himself just before drawing the last of the *infusori* out of Darmon and snuffing his life like a candle. Emrael pushed himself off of Darmon roughly and stood up. He needed him alive if he was to ransom him for Ban.

Darmon looked at him with terror in his half-lidded eyes, his breath coming in strained gasps. His face was white, and he trembled uncontrollably.

Emrael leaned over Darmon and said softly, "Care to tell me how to get to my brother now? I *will* finish you if I must."

Darmon shook his head violently, his eyes widening. His lips began moving, but Emrael had to lean down to hear him.

"I don't know, I swear. I swear, I swear. Don't do that again, please. Please please please. They are either at Whitehall or the Citadel, that's all I know, I swear. He's safe. I swear. I swear."

A knock from outside the room made Emrael start. He jumped

back from Darmon just before one of the guards poked his head in. "Everything all right?" he asked suspiciously.

Emrael stared the guard in the eyes and drew closer. The Legionman took a hesitant step backward before finding his nerve.

"Everything's just fine," Emrael said, brushing past the guard before he could call to his companion. He exited the room and strode quickly down the hallway, shaking with the power of the *infusori* he had just leached from Darmon, feeling unstoppable but somehow uncomfortable, unclean. Darmon deserved it and more. The cretin was lucky Emrael had left him alive. So, why did Emrael feel guilty?

He stopped again as he came abreast of the door to Yamara's room. The door was ajar, and he could see Yamara in a large bed, a bandage around her neck.

A spot of blood stained the bandage where it had seeped through. Healing coils, each attached to a Crafted healing apparatus, glowed on her shoulders, chest, and other spots under the blanket that covered her to the shoulders. These coils looked to be legitimate healing-grade coils.

Sarlon sat next to the bed on a cushioned chair, his head in one hand. His other hand was underneath the blanket, undoubtedly clutching his wife's hand.

Yerdon tended to Yamara from the other side of the bed, still working to keep her alive long enough for the *infusori* from the healing apparatus to bring her back from the brink of death. His face showed grave concern. That wasn't a good sign. Emrael felt a sharp pang of guilt lance through him yet again. He longed to go in and tell Sarlon that he was sorry, that it was all his fault. However, he was also more than a little afraid of what the big man's reaction might be if he found out that Emrael could have stopped Corlas if he had taken the shot sooner. He would have to settle for finding Jaina to ask her about Yamara's recovery after he saw to his horse.

He exited the infirmary into the full midday sun, passing more Legionmen who had been posted at the door since their arrival. The square was much busier than when they had arrived in the quiet of the night. Several regiments of Legionmen trained in a yard behind the barracks. The clatter of wooden practice swords filled the compound like the sound of torrential rain on glass. The poor bastards conducted combat drills in full leather-and-steel Legion armor. He didn't miss that aspect of life in the Legion. Even in the mild spring weather, full armor became uncomfortably warm very quickly.

Emrael headed toward the command building, as he figured that Halrec would probably know where their horses and belongings had been taken, and as a Captain Second he would likely have been given quarters near those of the Captain First.

The clerk at the front desk of the command building glanced at him only briefly before turning back to the stacks of papers covering his long desk without saying a word. Emrael rapped on the golden wood of the desk with his knuckle.

"Yes?" the clerk asked without looking up.

Emrael shook his head in frustration. He was still angry from the encounter with Darmon and had no patience for pompous clerks.

"I'm looking for Captain Second Syrtsan. Can you direct me to him?" The clerk pursed his lips, then turned on his heel and strode into the recesses of the building without saying a word.

"Prick," Emrael murmured loudly enough to be heard as he stared at the retreating clerk's back, then looked around for something to occupy a few idle moments.

Just as he was settling into the clerk's chair after strategically rearranging several of his stacks of paper, he heard a squawk behind him.

"Hey! Get out of my chair, you lout! You can't be behind the desk! This area is for Legion officers only."

Emrael turned the chair with a satisfied smirk on his face—until he saw Captain First Gerlan standing behind the pompous clerk. Gerlan did not appear amused.

Emrael jerked to his feet. "Captain First Gerlan, sir. I would like to speak with Captain Second Syrtsan. Is he available?"

Gerlan considered him with a slightly annoyed expression. "Come with me," he said, turning to walk calmly down the hall, his well-shined military-issue leather boots clicking on the wood floors. Emrael clipped the smug clerk with his shoulder as he hurried to catch up to the Captain First.

He walked just behind and to the right of Gerlan, as if he were an officer just slightly junior. He was close to earning his mark as a Master of War, after all. Though not a title the Legions recognized officially, it ought to count for something.

Gerlan did not comment. He held the door for Emrael when they reached his office, which occupied an entire corner of the command building. The well-appointed office likely intimidated most who were invited there, but Emrael's father had been Commander First of the Legion since before he could remember, and his quarters and offices in Naeran had been far more impressive than these.

Emrael entered the room and stood next to one of the two cushioned chairs on the visitor's side of the large Captain First's desk while Gerlan closed the door and strolled around to the ornate chair on his side of the desk. Halrec was nowhere in sight.

"Take a seat," Gerlan said, already lowering himself into his own chair.

Emrael sat slowly, wondering why the post commander had led him to his office when Halrec obviously wasn't there.

Gerlan reached below his desk, grabbing something wrapped in a piece of canvas cloth. He set it on the desk with a *clunk* and looked directly at Emrael. Not good.

"I find your visit most intriguing. I once knew of a boy with hair like yours. The son of a good commander, a man I admired—a man who led this Legion with honor and discipline, despite his unfortunate heritage. A boy whose family was close with the Syrtsan family, another of the Iraean runaways to establish themselves in our Legion."

He waited, and when Emrael said nothing, he continued.

"Now, Captain Second Syrtsan made no mention of you or any of your companions, other than reporting that you assisted him in a confrontation with some brigands on the road from the Sagmyn Pass to Lidran. He says that's how your friend got her throat slit, and how you came to capture that prisoner of yours. Very odd."

Gerlan leaned forward, resting his hands on the desk.

"This officer of mine also claims that Governor Corrande has taken Samille Barros captive at the Citadel. The Lord Governor's daughter! Now, why would Corrande do that when Governor Barros is his ally in the newly declared war with Ordena? And why would I just be hearing of it now, in such an odd manner? Foolishness. I don't appreciate being fooled with, and your friend figures to pay for it."

Anger blazed through Emrael. Halrec had told Gerlan more than he should have, though thankfully it appeared he had kept their identities hidden. Emrael had a bad feeling that this encounter was about to go very poorly.

Gerlan held up his hand, counting off each statement by raising a finger. "You just happen to have shared a room with a striking young lass who I am almost positive is the younger daughter of Governor Barros, though why she would be with you and not identify herself is beyond me. And your prisoner—this *highway brigand*—is no common ruffian, not with those clothes. Your other friends all have the look of Ordenans, and not commoners, either. They could be mages for all I know, mixed up in their blasphemous devilry."

Emrael sat motionless. Gerlan was surprisingly astute, which made him very dangerous.

The Captain First reached over to the canvas cloth and twitched it aside, revealing a Watcher-issue *infusori*-Crafted crossbow. "And *you* show up at my gate, covered in blood, with this in your possession. Very curious, and very illegal." He looked hard at Emrael with clear blue eyes beneath his greying eyebrows. "I want to know the whole story, boy. Talk, or I'll be forced to withdraw the aid of my healers and detain the lot of you."

Emrael met his hard stare without blinking. For a moment, he considered his options, but he didn't seem to have many. Gerlan seemed to be an honest man; perhaps he could even be of help.

"Sir . . . no offense was intended," he began slowly, looking away from the Captain's gaze. "It's just that we haven't had a lot of cause to trust anyone the past few days."

He took a deep breath, and as he exhaled the words poured out of him. "My name is Emrael Ire, and the blond girl is indeed Arielle Barros. The Ordenan woman is my instructor at the Citadel, a Master of War. Her name is Jaina, and she can show you her Mark to prove her station, if you wish. The other two are her associates. They are traders, nothing more."

Gerlan's eyebrows lifted at hearing that Jaina was a Master of War. "Hmm. A Master of the Citadel, eh? No matter. I received orders not an hour ago that were very clear. All Ordenans must be apprehended and sent to the capital."

Emrael sat forward in his chair, putting his hands on the desk. "The Citadel was attacked by Watchers, sir. I was there. They captured Samille Barros and my brother, Banron. They captured all of the other *infusori* Crafters, too." He paused. "We were only here to seek medical aid, but I think you might be able to help them. This has to be a misunderstanding, one that you could pressure Lord Governor Corrande to correct. Samille, my brother, and the others at the Citadel need your help. I'm sure the governor will agree. Arielle will speak with him. We could be there with a battalion in just a few days."

Emrael tapped his fingers nervously on the desk as he looked up at the Captain First, waiting for him to respond. Gerlan sat quietly for a time, then laughed suddenly. "You're serious? You want me to attack another province without direct orders? Are you mad? How did you mix Captain Second Syrtsan up in all of this? He told me more or less the same story. He may be executed for deserting his post, you know. I am extremely disappointed, after all he did to be promoted. He had real promise."

Emrael leaned forward. "We were friends in the Junior Legion, sir. When I came through the pass, I explained the situation and Hal . . . ah, Captain Second Syrtsan, that is, figured the Lord Governor would appreciate it if he helped protect Elle and bring word of Sami's capture. I'm not suggesting this lightly—I was there. The Watchers attacked the Citadel and kidnapped Governor Barros's daughter. Halrec is a hero, doing his duty to the province, and to the governor's family."

"I see," Gerlan said flatly. "Enough of this nonsense. I don't know what to think, but Governor Barros's daughter running away from the Citadel, mixed up with riffraff like you, coming here with multiple injured, including an injured boy that claims to be Darmon Corrande?"

Emrael's pulse raced. This was bad. His hand drifted to one of the knives he kept strapped to his thigh.

Gerlan sat pensively for a moment, then his eyes lit up.

"Here's what I'm going to do," he continued, leaning forward and clasping his hands together on his desk. "You and your party will surrender your weapons, and in return I'll send you all to the capital safely—under guard, of course—instead of conducting a trial here. They'll be better equipped to sort the truth from your lies. Syrtsan is lucky he received a promotion to Captain Second, as he now merits a trial from the Legion Commanders. You'll all likely face execution for abducting the Barros girl, though. And if that young man missing a hand truly is Darmon Corrande . . . I'll pity you then, son. No matter the circumstance, you will pay dearly for that. I'll be keeping him here until I learn the truth, to be sure. I'm also holding your injured friend and her husband here as collateral until I hear that you are safely arraigned in Naeran. Do you understand, boy?"

Emrael immediately regretted telling Gerlan anything and wondered whether he should have killed Darmon after all. He stood and said stiffly, "What I understand is that we are to be carted to the capital as prisoners. I'm not lying about what happened at the Citadel and since. I just want to get my brother and Sami back. You could be a hero, Gerlan. I don't have time to travel to Naeran, and I'm sure as hell not going anywhere as your prisoner."

Gerlan smiled and shook his head. "You commoners have lost all respect for your betters, an officer in the Legion, no less. I have treated you gently for Arielle's sake, but that will change if you cause any trouble. You are surrounded by thousands of soldiers, boy. Be wise."

Gerlan stood and clapped twice, loudly. Two hulking Legionmen with the sky-blue armbands of Justicers entered the room immediately and stood at attention while staring at Emrael, obviously waiting for the command to seize him.

Emrael stalked from the room without another word, anger and desperate frustration threatening to overcome him once again. The Justicers stood aside, and Gerlan stayed silent as he exited the room and retraced his steps to the foyer of the large command building, though the Justicers followed as Emrael swept into the foyer. Likely, Gerlan wasn't very concerned about them escaping now that they were in the Legion compound, and he was treating them well just in case Emrael was right and Arielle used her influence to make sure Gerlan was punished.

The clerk hurried to intercept Emrael, a smirk on his face. He was a young man, about Emrael's age, but had the soft look of one who had accepted a position as clerk to avoid the more arduous aspects of life in the Legion.

"See what happens when you meddle in Legion business, boy? Be ready to board the wagon in one hour, or I'll send Justicers to discipline you and your little friends."

Emrael stopped abruptly and turned to the clerk, who had followed him to the middle of the foyer. He knew it was idiotic, borderline suicidal to confront this clerk with the Justicers behind him, but he couldn't seem to rein in his anger. He stepped close, inches from the clerk's face.

"You don't know me yet, but you will. If you ever threaten me or those I care about again, I'll cut out your tongue."

Outrage and a glimmer of fear shone in the clerk's eyes.

One of the Justicers shoved Emrael in the back with an order to keep moving, and Emrael turned to leave. Before he could, however, the clerk pulled on his arm and blurted, "You can't threaten me like that!"

Emrael snapped. He spun, secured the clerk's wrist in his left hand, and caught him around the neck with his right, driving him to the floor with a loud *thud*. The clerk's breath left in an audible rush.

Emrael leaned down into the coughing clerk's face. "Don't touch me. Ever."

Emrael addressed the Justicers on the other side of the room, who looked almost as stunned as the clerk, who now moaned on the floor. "My apologies."

He darted out the door before they could react and hurried across the square to the infirmary, where he found Elle just emerging from the room they had shared. Her hair was tied back and a slight puffiness around her eyes told him she had only recently woken. She greeted him with a smile that faded when he said, "The Captain is shipping us out to Naeran in one hour, under guard as prisoners— except for you, probably. There are Justicers waiting at every door. And I have no idea where Halrec is, but it sounds like he's in a lot of trouble for helping us."

"But why? Gerlan has no reason to do that. I'll go speak with him."

"It won't do any good, Elle. I told him what happened, he knows who you are, it did no good. The Provinces are apprehending Ordenans due to the new war proclamation, and Gerlan won't listen to anything outside his direct orders. He is more concerned about his reputation than helping us. Either we go along, or we fight and run. Where is Jaina?"

Elle's lips twisted into a brief grimace at Jaina's name, but she quickly covered it with a small smile. "I don't know where she is, but we can't fight our way out of a Legion compound. Even if we could, Yamara will die if she doesn't receive the proper care. The Captain will listen to me once I identify myself properly. Let's go check Yamara's room before I talk to him."

When they reached Yamara's room, Emrael noticed that several more guards had taken up positions just outside the main door to the building.

So much for running, he thought. He caught Elle's eye and nodded to both sets of guards. She just nodded calmly.

They entered the room and found Sarlon alone with his wife, who already looked better than she had. Her skin had regained its healthy glow, and she was breathing steadily without any sickly rasping. Sarlon looked up when they stepped into the room.

"May we come in, Sarlon?" Emrael asked in a hushed voice.

Sarlon nodded silently and waved them in with one large hand. He rested his head on the bed again as they approached.

"How is she?" Elle asked quietly.

Sarlon raised his head, a tired smile on his round, darkly bearded face. "Yerdon says she will live. I think it is I who needs a healer now." He chuckled softly. "I haven't been able to sleep while she might have died, but Yerdon told me not ten minutes ago that the worst of the danger has passed, that she just needs another day or two for the coils to help knit her wounds before she can heal on her own."

Sarlon looked to Emrael. "Lad, I know that you are in a hurry to rescue your brother, but I cannot leave her. You will have to go on without me. We will catch up as soon as we can."

Emrael took a deep breath. "We don't have a choice. Captain Gerlan means to take us into custody and ship us to Naeran as prisoners. You and Yamara will stay here as his hostages. He doesn't believe us about what happened at the Citadel, or at least not all of it. I think he is afraid of mistreating Elle, however, and is covering his ass by letting the Lord Governor deal with us."

"He doesn't know the daughter of his own Lord Governor?" Sarlon said, waving a hand toward Elle.

"He knows who she is, all right. He thinks we have her hostage or brainwashed or something. He has every reason to send us to the capital under guard, and no incentive to help us on our word."

"Nobles. Career soldiers. Bastards," the bearded man spat. "He'll have a fight on his hands if he thinks to hold my wife and me here after she recovers."

Emrael shook his head. "They may. Corrande has ordered the apprehension of all Ordenans in the Provinces. I don't know what to do at this point. Where is Jaina? I haven't seen her since last night. Has she left without us?"

A low feminine voice spoke from behind him. "Has who left?"

Emrael turned to find Jaina standing just inside the doorway, looking freshly bathed. She had acquired new clothing that was much finer than what he had last seen her in. They looked like clothes that rich folk and nobles wore, a billowy blouse and tight, dark pants. Her dark hair was pulled up in a tight braid that fell down her neck, just short of her shoulders.

"You, Jaina. Where have you been? I haven't seen you since last night."

She responded with a pursed smile and raised brows. "I visited a friend here in Lidran. Not that my whereabouts are any of your business."

"Well, we have a problem. Captain Gerlan is sending us to Naeran under guard and holding Sarlon and Yamara hostage," Emrael said darkly.

"That might not be such a bad thing, Emrael," Jaina responded slowly. "Do you think those Malithii have just gone home, given up because you killed one of them? Or the Watchers? We could do worse than having Legion guards to accompany us and discourage them from attacking. Assuming Elle can convince her father to let us all go free, we can take a ship from Naeran to enlist the aid of my fellow Imperators, maybe even the Ordenan Imperial Army, with your mother's help."

He shook his head angrily. "That will take too long! I don't have time to be carted to Naeran in a wagon while my brother and the others are enduring who knows what. Darmon told me that the students are either going to be at the Citadel or Whitehall, where Corrande is holding Crafters before taking them north to Corrande Province. Jaina, I won't leave my brother that long."

She looked at him with a serious but sympathetic expression. "I know, Emrael. But Corrande will treat his captives from the Citadel well. You are doing all you can, and we will find a way to get them back. It may mean recruiting more help, however. Do you really think our small group can defeat the Watchers alone?"

"I'm sure my father will help as well, Em," Elle offered with a smile. "How could he not? He wouldn't leave his own daughter a captive. She always was his favorite." She said that last matter-of-factly, but Emrael could see that the statement bothered her.

Still at the side of the bed, Sarlon raised his eyebrows and looked over at Jaina, who returned his skeptical look.

"What?" Emrael asked.

Jaina looked to Sarlon again and back to Emrael. "Barros may not be able to do anything. The Barros Legion is large and well trained, but Corrande has at least as many men at his disposal. And when the Watchers are added to his forces, he commands more men than the other two provinces together. And his men are armed with *infusori*-Crafted weapons. Or will be soon. Sagmyn has already shown his willingness to cooperate with Corrande, and the Iraean Province is already under Corrande's control—mostly. Military action could be suicide, and Barros may not have much leverage. We must gather support in Ordena to have any chance at stopping Corrande."

Emrael inhaled deeply, trying to control the desperate anger building within him. "I can't take that chance, and I can't leave Ban with them that long. I will be escaping the first chance I get and will find Ban, even if I have to do it by myself. You all can go on to recruit help without me."

He had to try.

10

A rap on the door announced a middle-aged officer with two riveted straps on his shoulder plates that identified him as a Captain Second, equal to Halrec's rank. He politely but firmly informed them that their belongings had been loaded and that they were to accompany him to the courtyard.

Sarlon opened his mouth resolutely, but before he could speak, the officer held out his hand to forestall the big man. "Captain Gerlan has made arrangements for you and your wife to remain his guests. You will not leave this room and will have armed guards with you at all times, but your wife will be treated as long as you cooperate."

Sarlon nodded gratefully. "I'd like to keep my healer here with her as well, if I may.'

Yerdon spoke immediately, shaking his head and glancing at Emrael. "No no no, I've spoken with your healers, and they will do just fine. I must continue on to Naeran with Emrael and the others. My family, you understand."

The officer shrugged, his face remaining passive. "Very well. Follow me." The officer exited the room. A full squad of soldiers lined the hallway to make sure they left.

Emrael hurried to Sarlon's side before leaving. "Watch Darmon. Gerlan knows who he is, and you could be in deep shit if any Corrande soldiers or Watchers show up here."

The big man nodded. "Aye. I'll take care of him as soon as Yamara is well enough for us to escape. I'll be at their mercy no longer than I have to be."

Emrael nodded and clapped him on the shoulder before joining the rest of his friends in walking to the courtyard under the watchful eye of the Barros Legionmen.

In short order, they were all loaded into a large, high-sided wagon hitched to a team of four large horses. Emrael noticed Halrec's new sword tied to the saddle of a riderless horse next to the wagon, but his friend was nowhere to be seen. Where in the world was he? Gerlan had said that Halrec would be shipped to Naeran with them.

Just then, Captain First Gerlan led a small group of officers and two very large guards toward the wagon. The hulking guards wore sky-blue Justicer armbands that sharply contrasted the steel-grey Barros Legion uniforms. The Justicers were the group responsible for policing the Legion and anyone who fell under the Legion's jurisdiction, which was pretty much everyone but old nobility and the Watchers. So, in this city, Gerlan was military Captain, police chief, and noble. Titles weren't supposed to carry the weight they had in the old kingdoms, but they often did. Maybe Lidran wouldn't be such a good place to settle down after all.

The group surrounded someone walking with head bowed, hands tied behind his back. Emrael peered to get a look at the prisoner, who was apparently being sent with them to the capital as well. He wondered what the poor sap had done. Judging by his Legion-issue clothing, he was someone from one of the units stationed there that must have fallen afoul of the Legion rules.

The group of Legion officers reached the wagon and parted. One of the Justicers shoved the detainee forward, causing him to stumble to his knees. Emrael edged past Jaina to the near side of the wagon to get a better look.

The prisoner raised his head slowly, as if groggy. It was Halrec. Half-dried blood streaked over one eye and down his nose. He looked as if he had been beaten half to death.

Seeing his friend in such a state sparked the anger, rage, and frustration that had been growing inside of him since his altercation with Darmon. It turned into a blaze deep in Emrael's chest, a burning that spread like wildfire and eliminated all thought, leaving only a primal, bestial need to protect his friend.

Emrael leapt out of the wagon, landing on the ground in a crouch. The *infusori* he had sapped from Darmon pulsed within him like a second heartbeat, causing his limbs to tingle and vibrate with power he didn't know how to use.

One of the enormous strongarms escorting Halrec stepped forward purposefully, one huge hand grasping for Emrael. He grabbed Emrael by the shirt, an unconcerned smile on his pock-marked face.

Emrael struck the inside of the man's elbow, stepped inside his reach, and delivered a kick to the inside of the larger man's knee, causing the leg to buckle awkwardly. The Justicer dropped heavily to one knee with a surprised grunt.

The man was not smart enough to let go of Emrael's shirt even at this point, so Emrael spun around his arm, delivering a powerful downward stroke to the outside of the Justicer's arm. It snapped at the elbow with a sound not unlike that of a breaking tree branch.

The Justicer screamed. The other giant stood stunned for a moment before anger finally registered on his face, then he rushed Emrael.

Emrael stood his ground until the last moment. He darted forward and to the side even as he threw a hooking punch at the man's face. Emrael's fist connected with his opponent's temple with a solid *thud,* like a club hitting a ripe melon. The large man immediately dropped to the ground, unconscious.

The blows delivered to the two enormous Justicers had a more devastating effect than even Emrael's hard-earned skill and strength should have accounted for. In the midst of the struggle with the two men, Emrael had felt surges of *infusori* bolster each blow, though through no conscious doing of his own. He felt like a god.

A small, rational part of him—buried deep in the recesses of his rage-drunk mind—worried that he had killed the man. If the man died, it would likely warrant immediate execution.

The officers recovered from their initial shock of the violent exchange, several of them drawing their swords, filling the stunned silence with the malevolent whisper of steel on leather scabbards. Emrael's sword had been confiscated along with his horse and crossbow, so he calmly crouched and drew a sword from the belt of each of the downed Justicers. He straightened, a sword in each hand, humming with terrible power. He began a slow advance on the three officers, who spread out and stepped warily as Emrael stalked them. Fear was plain in their eyes.

"ENOUGH!" Gerlan roared. He alone had not drawn his sword, though he had retreated several paces from the fight. "Legionmen, up swords! Ire, put down your weapons or I'll have you shot." He gestured to the side, where the officer that had led Emrael and his friends from the infirmary aimed a crossbow straight at Emrael's chest. From this distance, the shot would be a sure thing.

Damn.

Breathing heavily, Emrael waited for the officers to sheathe their weapons. When they did, he turned his own swords sideways, holding them out and away from himself as he bent to set them on the ground in front of him, though still within easy reach.

He addressed Gerlan as he rose. "What have you done to Halrec? I thought this was to be a civilized affair, Captain," Emrael said with a calm he did not feel. "This man, this officer, came to the aid of the daughter of the Lord Governor, and this is the thanks he receives at your hand?"

Captain Gerlan's eye's flashed with anger, his fleshy face turning red. "Do not presume to instruct me as to the punishment fitting an officer who leaves his post, boy. You are nothing but an insolent commoner, and you are lucky I haven't had you cut down already!" Gerlan stopped, wiped the spittle from his lips, and gestured to Halrec. "This deserter is to be tried before the Commanders' Council. They will sort truth from fiction."

Emrael shook his head in disdain, never breaking eye contact with the Captain First. "Always the easy way out for you, eh, Gerlan? The Fallen take you, you stoneless worm."

Gerlan's jaw thrust forward angrily, and he began to raise his hand to signal the officer with the bow to shoot. Emrael tensed, poised to dive to the ground and come up with the swords he had just set down. He knew he wasn't thinking clearly, but his pride and the power pulsing through him would not let him back down now.

"Both of you stop this instant!" Elle's voice rang like a bell through the courtyard. Emrael paid her no mind.

Pain flared in the back of his head before he could move for the weapons, and his vision went white.

Next he knew, he was lying facedown on the cobbled ground of the courtyard, ears ringing. Someone held him down, binding his arms with a cord. He struggled to rip free and turn over, but whoever had his arm twisted it to the point of coming free of the socket.

"Don't move," Jaina hissed. "I just saved your life, you fool. Now get up and climb into the wagon, or I'll plant a knife in you before these buffoons can even think to."

She pulled him up by his tied arms, which hurt quite a bit, and shoved him toward the wagon. The two brawny Justicers who had attacked him were being helped to their feet by a few of the soldiers that had been standing nearby. The officers that had accompanied Gerlan were standing with swords drawn and ready but made no move toward Emrael. Gerlan still looked ready to order his soldiers to shoot Emrael, but after a moment—and a grudging look at Elle—he motioned tersely toward the wagon, giving his own grudging command to get in.

Emrael looked up and saw Elle staring at him with an unreadable expression. He glared at no one in particular and squirmed his way up and into the wagon as best he could with his hands tied, not meeting anyone's eyes. He knew he had been foolish, but what was he supposed to do? He hated feeling so damn helpless.

"Load him up." The command came from Captain Gerlan just as Emrael managed to work his way to a seated position near the middle of the wagon. There was a rustle just outside the wagon, a grunt of effort, and Emrael just had time to turn his head before the full weight of Halrec landed atop him.

"Mercy, you are heavy, Hal." Emrael pushed Halrec off of him with a twist of his shoulders but immediately regretted it when his friend groaned in pain. "Hal? Halrec, are you okay?"

Halrec chuckled darkly. "Just fine, Em. Looks worse than it is. Just a cut on the head. You are really good at getting me into trouble, you know that?"

Emrael couldn't stop himself from cracking a smile. "I was just thinking the same thing about you. Your friends don't know how to host very well, do they?"

"This wasn't so bad. I've been to officers' dinner parties that were far less fun than that."

They both chuckled but soon fell silent as a Legionman attached manacles to their ankles. They were content to stay quiet for a time, lying shoulder-to-shoulder on the wagon floor. Halrec nursed his wounds and Emrael nursed his wounded pride—and the aching lump on the back of his head. The hand he had used to strike the Justicer also hurt like hell.

Why had he felt so angry? He had always had a temper, but he had never done anything quite as stupid as trying to fight an entire Legion compound full of soldiers.

He felt a bone-deep weariness and could no longer feel the buzz of the *infusori* that he had leached from Darmon. He stewed in a tangle of emotions—guilt, pain, anger, and underneath it all, a deep and desperate helplessness—and tried to figure out where he had gone wrong.

I just want my brother back.

❦

"Have a nice nap, then?"

Emrael started awake and looked up blearily. Elle stood near him, staring at him with the same accusatory expression she had given him earlier. "You'll face serious charges for that idiotic display back there, you know."

"Mmm," Emrael responded. He must have drifted off as he lay brooding on the floor of the wagon. He was tired from the Healing and the short night, but it wasn't like him to sleep under such hostile and uncomfortable conditions.

He struggled to his knees until he could just see over the side of the open wagon, difficult because his hands were still tied behind his back. Enormous, grizzled pines and various hardwood trees passed slowly with the constant rhythmic squeak of the wagon wheels as the party rolled down the hard-packed dirt highway.

A lone Legionman sat on the bench seat at the front of their wagon, guiding the team of horses lazily. Two squads of Legionmen rode in a large rectangular formation enclosing a coach that appeared to be empty, a large supply wagon, and of course the open wagon in which Emrael and his friends were riding.

"How long have we been on the road?" he asked of no one in particular. Jaina and Master Yerdon barely glanced at him from where they sat on the opposite side of the wagon on a wooden bench. Elle had taken a seat on one of the wagon benches as well, now completely ignoring him.

"A few hours," Halrec said from beside him. He had cleaned the blood from his face and was already looking much better. The swelling around his eye had gone down and he had regained his ever-ready smile. "I don't know how you could just lie down and take a nap after what happened at the compound. I thought Captain Gerlan was going to jump in the wagon to beat you himself, but you were already passed out cold."

He lowered his voice and his face grew more serious. "Thank you for that, by the way. It was probably the stupidest thing I've ever seen anyone do, but I appreciate it all the same."

Emrael gave him a sardonic smile and shook his head. "*Stupid* is right. I don't know what I was thinking."

Elle took one quick step and slapped Emrael. Hard. "You *weren't* thinking. That's the problem. I don't keep patching you up just so you can go and take every opportunity that presents itself to get stabbed, or beaten, or shot! You wise up, and quickly, or I'll . . ."

She stopped abruptly, growled, and stormed over to the farthest corner of the wagon where someone had placed a fancy padded bench that looked terribly out of place in the beat-up old supply wagon. She sat and glared at him.

Emrael was taken aback by the sudden outburst and had no good response, so he settled for glaring back.

Just as he was about to try to explain himself, a smiling—and handsome—young Legion officer pulled his horse up next to the wagon. "Is everything all right, my Lady Arielle? Your coach is still available. I'd be happy to escort you back; there's no need to stay in the wagon with these . . . friends of yours."

Elle looked to the officer—a Captain Third, judging by the single metal strap on the shoulders of his leather and steel-plate armor. She bit the inside of her cheek as she pondered. She glared at Emrael once more before turning back to the Captain Third.

"That would be lovely, thank you, Captain . . ."

"Prilan, m'Lady."

"Thank you, Captain Prilan." She laid her hand on his outstretched arm and swung easily to sit astride his horse, just behind his saddle. He called loudly for a halt and carried her the few paces over to the carriage that had apparently been provided just for her.

Emrael looked at Halrec, and they rolled their eyes at each other. The young officer was tall and had lean features that women likely found attractive but had none of the build or bearing that came from hard training. He was probably yet another lesser noble's younger son, given an officer's commission to pacify a moderately power-ful father, or perhaps following a considerable lightening of a rich merchant father's purse. He wouldn't last a minute against any of the seasoned warriors he ordered about on a daily basis, much less against Emrael or Halrec.

Just then, Emrael noticed that Halrec's arms were free. He turned slightly and wiggled his fingers at Halrec from behind his back. "Hey! Why didn't you cut me loose, too?"

Halrec chuckled. "Elle and Jaina wouldn't let me. Threatened me physically, even. I saw how well Jaina fights back there in those woods, and I'm sorry, but you aren't worth that. They said it served you right if you woke up with aching shoulders."

"See if I beat people senseless for *you* again," Emrael grumbled under his breath.

He looked at Jaina, who returned a blank look and raised her eyebrow, daring him to complain. Halrec had a point. She was quite scary. He settled for glaring at Captain Prilan instead. The pretty boy was riding next to the coach, doing his best to carry a conversa-tion with Elle, who sat at the window in the side door. She laughed loudly now and then, but Emrael noticed that she cast frequent glances his way.

He shook his head in exasperation and checked the ropes around his wrists. Between his bound wrists and manacled ankles, he was extremely uncomfortable and nearly immobile. The tight cord held his arms at an awkward angle, making it a struggle to draw his belt knife, but he soon managed to cut himself free.

Emrael watched as Prilan's eyes followed Elle's gaze back to where he stood in the wagon, stretching his arms over his head. The Captain Third's face turned a deep shade of red as he guided his horse over to the wagon, spluttering.

"You can't do that! I have authorization to execute you, you know! Justicers!" he screamed to two tough-looking Legionmen, who came to attention and trotted their horses forward from where they had been riding several paces behind the wagon. "Justicers, secure that man! He is not to be—"

"Captain," Elle called. "Captain, don't bother with him. He is more trouble than he is worth, but he *is* a friend and I'd be somewhat put out if anything were to happen to him. He will behave, and he's still chained to the wagon. Come continue our lovely conversation." She stuck her tongue out at Emrael discreetly but reassumed her smile quickly when Prilan finally broke off the glare he was directing at Emrael and turned his horse to resume riding next to the coach. He looked rather smug but still turned red in the cheeks whenever he glared at Emrael.

The Justicers were still looking at Emrael with hard, impassive eyes. These two were hardened warriors, not oversized Legion thugs like the two he had fought at the Legion compound. He shrugged at them with a calm he did not feel, and they slowly dropped back to their position at the rear of the party where they could watch the wagon.

Emrael took a deep breath and sat down next to Halrec. Jaina pinned him with a hard stare, but there was something very like pity in Yerdon's eyes. Emrael looked down, embarrassed.

"How do you always find the spirited ones?" Halrec asked from beside him. "I can't decide whether Elle or Jaina is going to kill you first. You always did have a knack for finding the most . . . interesting acquaintances. Remember that serving girl from the palace that you tried to . . ."

Halrec continued to recount several unfortunate incidents from their youth involving acquaintances of Emrael's, usually embarrassing attempts at romantic endeavors. Emrael protested at several embellished parts of Hal's stories and blushed until he thought his white hair might turn red. Jaina laughed uproariously more than once, and even stately Master Healer Yerdon chuckled a time or two.

Emrael glared at his friend. "I suppose I'm the one always singing to girls I'm hoping to bed, then, am I?"

Halrec flashed an appropriately sheepish smile and finally let it lie.

That night, the Legion squads set up camp next to a small creek that crossed the Kingroad highway. Their tents were erected quickly in the Legion's standard formation, a hollow ring with the wagons and coach pulled into a circle outside the tents. Every fifth tent had a small fire lit near it before long, and a large cookfire roared in the middle of the ring of tents. Salted hams and several sacks of potatoes, beans, and carrots were fetched from the supply wagon. Soon, the smoky aroma of Legion camp stew cooked over an open fire filled the air.

Emrael and Halrec were released from their manacles and allowed to make their beds beneath the wagon, at Elle's request. Sleeping under a wagon wasn't Emrael's idea of a good time, but it was a hell of a lot better than sleeping in the bed of the wagon, exposed to the elements. Emrael itched to wander close to the cookfire to make sure that their supper would at least be edible, but he figured he had caused enough trouble for today. Maybe tomorrow.

Halrec caught his eye and mimicked swinging a sword. Emrael smiled and nodded, and they approached the two Legionmen tasked to keep an eye on them. "Gentlemen. My friend and I would like to get some sword practice in. Care to join us?"

Their guards—Legion lifers, by the disdainful, carefree look of them—exchanged bored glances. "Captain said you two stay put. What's in it for us?"

"Well, you might learn a thing or two, for starters. And . . . you can bring some crossbows and shoot us if we try to run."

Their faces lit up a bit at that last part. To them, Halrec was a deserter, and Emrael had embarrassed their fellow Legionmen back at the Lidran compound. Every Legionman would jump at the chance to shoot either of them.

The one with a round face licked his teeth and said to his partner, "Sorli, go round up a few of the boys. Tell them to bring their weapons. Crossbows too, in case these idiots try to run."

⌐━━⌐

Within minutes, Emrael and Halrec had at least a dozen Legionmen escorting them to the edge of the camp, where they found straight, slender sticks to serve as practice swords. They took a moment to carve smooth handles and whittle away any irregularities in the practice blades with their belt knives. The Legionmen formed in a ring around them, crossbows and swords at the ready.

They found a clear space in the trees, drew up several paces across from each other, and shrugged out of their shirts, throwing them to the side. They raised their stick swords sharply in formal salute and, despite the ring of Legionmen around them, mouthed, "We the Descended" to each other, like they always had when they were kids pretending to be their noble Iraean ancestors. Emrael couldn't help but smile—a smile that Halrec returned with interest.

More of the Legionmen in the camp found their way over and looked on condescendingly, laughing as if at two children playing at soldiering, but did nothing to stop them. Emrael and Halrec paid them no mind. They had grown up practicing sword work with this game, which had evolved over time as their skill grew. They played at it the way other youths had played at hop-the-stones and field races, and it had been a large factor in their becoming two of the best swordsmen in the Barros Junior Legion. In the course of his training at the Citadel, Emrael had improved his sword work considerably in the time since he and Halrec had last played; it was time to see whether Halrec had done the same in his time in the Barros Legion.

From the salute, they stalked each other in perfect unison until they were within striking distance. They began to move in fluid, measured motions. Each strike and parry was delivered in precise unison, perfectly timed. Their wooden swords whistled and clacked with a hypnotic rhythm. They circled each other gracefully, their weapons moving ever faster.

The game continued for ten minutes, then twenty, their wooden blades clacking with incredible speed and precision. More Legionmen gathered as the game drew on. The expressions on their faces were no longer mocking.

Emrael and Halrec separated suddenly, stepping back at exactly the same time. They brought their swords up in salute once more. The smile on Halrec's face made Emrael feel as though the two of them had never parted ways.

The Legionmen drifted off quietly as soon as the two men finished—other than the two guards, who watched them like hawks watch field mice now that they understood Emrael and Halrec's ability with a sword.

Emrael looked around and was surprised to find that Elle had joined the crowd watching them. She watched with a thoughtful expression as Emrael walked over to her.

"What did you think?" He smiled broadly, hoping that he had impressed her. He was breathing heavily and sweat dripped from his brow and down his bare chest. He hadn't had this much fun in a long while.

Elle's brow furrowed and her lips pursed. She was clearly not impressed, or more likely, still upset with him. "Wouldn't it be more realistic to train with real swords?"

He shrugged and swept a hand pointedly through his hair, flexing his arm as he did. "That's how I earned this white hair when we were kids. We don't use real swords against each other anymore."

"So, you are afraid to face Halrec with a real sword?" she asked.

He gave an unabashed shrug. "Yeah, I am. I don't want to get hurt again, and I don't want to hurt him, either. Besides, the point of this drill isn't to hit one another; it is to move through the motions in perfect unison, with perfect execution. We challenge each other by moving faster, daring the other to keep up, not by injuring him. It is just for exercise and to practice form and timing, not dueling."

She nodded, a sly look now on her face as she looked from Emrael to Halrec. "So . . . who's the better fighter?"

Halrec chuckled. "I am, of course."

Emrael punched him in the arm. "You beat up on a few Legion recruits and all of a sudden you're a hardass, huh?"

Halrec glared at him, holding his clenched fist up to show the outline of a wolf's head tattooed on the first knuckle.

Emrael raised his eyebrows and chuckled. "Fine, fine. We might be equal. Maybe. We'll have to duel to find out."

"Deal," Halrec grunted, punching Emrael in return. Emrael rolled his shoulder. The lanky son of a bitch hit hard.

Elle fell in with Emrael as he and Halrec gathered their shirts and returned to their wagon, the Legionmen that had been set to guard them following a few paces behind.

"What is that mark on your hand, Halrec?" she asked.

Halrec flexed his hand but was slow to respond. Emrael could tell his friend was embarrassed, and so answered for him. "It means he beat one of the Legion's top swordsmen in a duel—blunted weapons, of course. There are likely only a hundred men living in all the Provinces who have earned the wolf's head. It's almost as rare an achievement as becoming a Master of War at the Citadel."

"Seventy-three of us, actually," Halrec said quietly.

Elle continued to her tent after a curt goodbye at the wagon where Emrael and Halrec were to stay the night, under guard. They ate and settled in under their wagon as the night grew darker, reminiscing about their childhood. As all of the Legionmen retired to their tents and their two guards grew more and more relaxed, Emrael noticed that Elle was still awake, her fire still burning on the opposite side of the camp. He needed to talk to her.

He tapped Halrec on the shoulder and whispered, "I'm going to talk to Elle for a minute. Cover for me while I crawl out."

Harlec sighed but coughed loudly to cover the noise as Emrael crept from beneath the wagon and into the woods. He stalked past the sentries and around the outside of the camp with sure, confident steps that carried him quietly to Elle's campfire.

She sat on an upturned log, whittling intently at something with a small belt knife. He stepped around her tent, clearing his throat to make his presence known. Elle looked up at him in slight surprise, but her eyes quickly narrowed into a glare. She said nothing as he slowly lowered himself to the ground next to her. As he did, he saw what she had been carving—it was a miniature bear, so detailed and lifelike it made his skin tingle to look at it.

"Absent Gods, Elle, that's really good. I didn't know you were an artist."

Her expression remained harsh, but she glanced at him. "You like it?" she asked, tone still clearly angry.

"I do." He meant it. It seemed he learned something new about Elle every day, and each time he was more impressed. She wasn't just the pampered governor's daughter he had always thought her to be.

"Here. I was about to throw it away anyhow."

He accepted it and stayed quiet for a time, content to stare into the small campfire while he ran his fingers over the precise ridges of her carving. After a tense few minutes, Elle spoke. "What do you want, Em?"

"To talk."

"So talk."

Emrael took a deep breath, still staring with unfocused eyes into the dancing flames. The sweet smell of woodsmoke and the popping of the burning wood was soothing, hypnotic.

"Elle, I've been an asshole. I'm sorry."

Elle chortled a short, mirthless laugh. "You aren't sorry, Em. You don't even fully understand what you did." She reached down to grip his hair and turn his head toward her with one hand. He had to crane his neck a bit to look up at her. "Has it ever occurred to you that your actions might affect other people, that this whole thing is about more than just you, more than just about Ban, even? That if you act like a belligerent fool, it might put all of us in harm's way? Glory, Em, I admire your dedication to Ban and your loyalty to your friends, but what's happening right now is so much larger than that. Your recklessness could get thousands of people killed. We have to do this the right way."

"You think I don't know that, Elle? I don't want that, but I didn't start this, remember? Maybe I'm desperate, maybe I'm irrational, but I can't just sit and do nothing."

"But they were going to shoot you, and you didn't even seem to care! What do you think happens to us, to Ban, if you die? If you are truly so stupid that you can't think beyond a single moment, you are going to get us all killed or worse."

He pulled his head away from her grip and hung his head, staring at the ground. "Elle, look, I wasn't thinking clearly back at the compound. I had just argued with Darmon, and I kind of . . . stole some of his life source, I think, and that had me on edge. Then they brought Hal out all bloody and beaten like that, and . . . I don't know, Elle. I just snapped. I'm tired of the people I love being hurt. I'm doing the best I can, but I just feel helpless, you know?"

"Ha! *You* feel helpless?" She laughed. "*I'm* the one that can't do anything. Everyone either ignores me or thinks that I'm some prize to be won. Even you—a week ago, you barely noticed me, and now I think you only see a pretty face just like everybody else. Maybe I *am* just a pretty face. My whole world is falling apart, and I can't do anything about it."

Emrael smiled and looked up at her again. "Hey, I don't think you're just a pretty face. You have saved my life at least once—"

"Twice," she interrupted, an accusatory gleam in her eye.

Emrael gave a quiet but genuine laugh. "Fair enough; twice. And you healed me last night. So, three times." He lifted and rolled his right arm in demonstration. "You help people. I just make bad situations worse, no matter how hard I try."

She snagged his hair roughly once more, pulling him to look her in the eye. "I like you, Em. Probably more than I should. But you need to understand that I'm more than just your healer, more than just a pretty face. I'm as invested in saving Ban and Sami as you are, but I'm not your sidekick, and I won't help you forever if you don't remove your head from your ass."

Emrael smiled, knowing he was putting his safety in jeopardy in doing so. "Pretty face or no, I won't underestimate you again."

"We might just get along, then," she said with a smile as she slid her hand to the base of his neck. Slowly, he leaned his head against her knee.

"I suppose we might at that."

They sat that way for a long, quiet moment. Elle's hand felt good against his neck, her radiant warmth more needed than that coming from the fire.

All too soon, Elle broke the stillness. "Do you think they're okay? Ban, Sami, the others?"

"I know they are," he said with a confidence that he did not feel. "I'll get away from these goons and be off to find Ban and Sami soon enough. And you will be in Naeran within a week or two to tell your father the truth about what happened."

"I don't doubt he will jump to save Samille." There was a hard note of bitterness in her voice that took him by surprise. "I only hope he'll save Ban and the others, too."

"Don't you want him to save your sister?" he asked carefully, turning to look at her.

Elle blushed and cast her eyes down abashedly. "Of course I do. But if she were gone for a while, maybe for once he would see me as more than an asset to marry off to some rich twit to strengthen a political alliance."

Her eyes widened in horror as she realized what she had said. "Oh, you must think I'm horrible. I do want Sami and Ban back, more than anything." She leaned forward, obviously anxious for him to say something.

He looked at her for a moment with eyebrows raised, then barked a quiet laugh. "Believe me, I know how you feel. Not the part about abandoning my sibling to the wolves, of course—that was a little weird—but I do know a thing or two about being an outcast, a nobody."

She pulled her hand from his neck and punched his arm, rolling her eyes in exaggerated disbelief. There was more than a little sarcasm in her voice. "Right. Emrael Ire, who had half of the female students at the Citadel melting at the mere mention of his name, who struck fear in the hearts of all of his opponents at Tournament. You are *so* neglected, *so* overlooked. Please."

"Wait, what? I could hardly get a girl to look at me twice except out in the lower tiers of the city, and sharing a room with Ban wasn't exactly ideal for . . ." He cut off as he noticed a dangerous gleam in her eye. "Ah . . . what I mean to say is, none of the girls at the Citadel paid much attention to me. If anyone knew my name, it was to snicker at me for having to work in the kitchens to pay for tuition. It's been like that my whole life. The Ire name isn't exactly a popular one these days."

Elle had a thoughtful look on her face. "I guess I never thought of it like that."

"That's because you are a noble. Not just a noble, a Lord Governor's daughter. I'm a nobody."

"But what does that matter? Besides, your family's blood is as noble as mine. Your grandfather was a king, for Glory's sake, same as mine."

"Heh. Fallen lot of good that does me. My grandfather lost the War of Unification, remember? We aren't even welcome in Iraea anymore. We are commoners now, maybe worse, even after my father worked his way to the top of your father's Legion. By Iraean law, I have no claim to any titles since my grandmother and father fled the war, no matter who my grandfather was. I'm sure you have seen that the treatment I get for being an Ire is not exactly preferential."

She paused before saying softly, "Yes, I suppose you are right." Her voice picked up a little more volume. "But you have found a way around that, become more than just your name, whatever it may be. I was trying to do the same thing. I worked so hard, and now all I have to fall back on is the life I wanted to escape. Father will have me married off within the year. I don't want to marry just to marry. It should be my choice."

As she finished her last sentence, something in her voice made him look up, and he found her staring at him. The fire's reflection danced in her eyes as their gazes met and lingered. Not knowing what else to do, he reached out and squeezed her hand, holding it for a time.

Elle looked away after a while, and Emrael stood awkwardly. "I'd better get back. Hal will be getting jealous."

Elle laughed a beautiful, tinkling laugh. Her golden ringlets swayed as she stood and tossed her head back in amusement. "We wouldn't want him getting too lonely over there under the wagon." Her eyes twinkled.

They were standing very close to one another, gazes still locked.

Emrael put one hand gently on her hip. She laid her hand on his upper arm. His heart was pounding, and anxiety made his hand tremble. What was wrong with him?

She turned her face up toward him slightly, and his mental functions stopped completely.

Haltingly, he leaned down. She didn't move toward him, however, so he placed a gentle kiss high on her prominent cheekbone instead of her lips. He felt like an idiot but was relieved to feel her smile as he rested his lips on her cheek. She stepped into him, wrapping him in a tight hug.

"Thank you for coming to see me tonight, Em." She flashed him a smile as she pushed away from him.

Before he could turn to leave, she reached around her neck and drew his pendant out. "You forgot this after I Healed you." She went up on her toes to secure it around his neck, then disappeared into her tent with a smile.

As her tent flap shut behind her, he started and looked around, suddenly worried that one of the Legionmen might catch him up and about alone. Thankfully, the camp was still quiet. They likely weren't used to having civilians in camp, or none of them wanted to poke their nose in the governor's daughter's business. He didn't blame them.

He trekked quietly around the outside of the camp, attempting to get back to the wagon without alerting the soldiers on watch. Just as he came within sight of the wagons, a shadow stepped out from behind a cluster of thick brush.

11

His heart leapt into his throat before he realized that the shadow was Jaina. The lack of moonlight under the canopy of leaves concealed her features, but he recognized her slender stature and familiar floral perfume almost immediately.

"Absent Gods, Jaina! Don't do that," he growled.

"Follow me," she said, grabbing his arm to lead him away from the camp. They passed one of the sentries, who watched them go silently.

"Why aren't they stopping us?" Emrael pitched his whisper to carry just to Jaina, who was only a few steps ahead of him.

"I don't think they mind if we disappear into the forest. They are nervous about you after what you did to those Justicers in Lidran."

"Oh." He didn't know whether to be proud or ashamed.

She stopped abruptly and turned to look at him, still clutching his arm.

The moon peeked through the clouds in the night sky briefly, giving her delicate features a specter-like appearance.

"Let me see your arm," she commanded, pointing at where Darmon had given him a rather serious wound just a day earlier.

He complied, pulling the neck of his shirt down so she could see the nearly-healed wound.

"Elle did this?" She asked quietly.

"Yes. I think so."

Though he couldn't see well, he knew that she was biting her lip and glaring at him, as she did when pondering. "Hmm," she said finally. "I'll speak with her about this. But more important is what *you* have done."

She fixed him with her piercing gaze once more, eyes shrouded in darkness but still somehow visible, as if they produced their own slight light. "I overheard your conversation with the girl. You drew *infusori* from Darmon?"

"You listened in on our conversation just now? How?"

"That is a secret you will have to earn, Emrael." Her expression darkened. "It is time for you to provide answers. I could feel a large amount of *infusori* in you in the courtyard earlier today and assumed it was an anomaly caused by your heightened emotional state. Tell me what happened at the infirmary with Darmon."

"I just did what you showed me. I was asking him where my brother was, we argued, then fought, and I just sort of took some of his *infusori*." He lost himself briefly in the memory of that moment, totally in control of Darmon's life essence. Knowing he could consume his very life source. It had been intoxicating.

Jaina drew in a sharp breath with a hiss and jerked her hand away from his arm, then jabbed a finger into his chest. "You must *never* do this thing, Emrael! It is an enormous risk to take *infusori* from the unwilling. It is of the Fallen God and can severely harm one such as you, who does not understand what he does."

She pushed him again but grabbed his shirt as she did, jostling him roughly. "*Infusori* taken this way clouds the mind and changes your emotions. It can change your very being, if you are not careful. The misuse of *infusori* in this way has caused mages to be persecuted and murdered for centuries, and often for good reason. Even today, mages must hide their gifts in these Provinces because of this evil!"

A slight Ordenan accent crept into Jaina's speech as she grew angrier, her lips curled in a snarl. She paused, obviously trying to control her anger. "Never mention this to anyone. If you do this thing and others of my Order learn of it, *I* may be forced to kill you. It is forbidden."

Emrael was taken aback by the ferocity in her voice and the dire simplicity of her statement. Her eyes were practically smoldering with fierce but quiet anger, gleaming even in the darkness of the night-shrouded forest.

"Glory, Jaina, I didn't mean to. It just happened."

"It must not happen again. No wonder you went mad. You take on the attributes of any *infusori* you absorb, Emrael. With coils charged in *infusori* Wells, the energy is pure, sterile, the life essence of the earth itself. Life essence given by a living being willingly can be received without harm, though it is still dangerous. But *infusori* stolen from another, taken by force? This is an evil thing, Emrael Ire. It will destroy you as surely as the one from whom you have stolen *infusori*. It will turn you to evil paths."

She poked him again in the chest, hard. "*This* is why I cannot allow you to go off crusading on your own. If the Order learns that I let a rogue mage loose in the Provinces and he is draining people of their life source, it will not go well for me. Or for you."

"So come with me," he offered. "Teach me."

She stalked away, growling something about "babysitting" and "fools."

~

The next day, he and his friends sat in the wagon in various states of discomfort. Emrael sat atop a pile of blankets, shackled to the wagon once more. Halrec, also shackled, seemed asleep on his own blankets but rolled about every few minutes. Jaina sat on her padded bench, nonchalant as always. Master Yerdon had large bags under his eyes and he nodded off every few minutes, even sitting upright as he was. He evidently wasn't accustomed to sleeping outdoors.

Elle still rode in her carriage. While he was disappointed, Emrael could not blame her. The carriage was undoubtedly more comfortable than the crowded, rickety old wagon.

Halrec woke up and rolled onto his shoulder to flash an excited smile at Emrael. "How did last night go? Still can't believe you abandoned me." He shook his head mournfully.

Emrael chuckled. "When you're older, I'll explain the benefits of association with the fairer gender."

Halrec grunted but smiled still. Out of the corner of his eye, Emrael noticed that Jaina had an amused expression on her face. Yerdon just looked tired.

Emrael could sympathize. He had hardly slept the night before for fear of attack during the night. At least one Malithii was still out there, and he didn't trust these Legionmen to stop even just one.

Despite the sleep deprivation, his anxiety kept him wide awake. He kept seeing phantom movements in the forest as they trundled on, movements that his mind's eye turned into dark-robed men covered in tattoos.

A flicker of movement on the southern side of the road caught his eye. The terrain sloped upward slightly, making it difficult to see through the dense tree cover, but he was sure he had actually seen something. Emrael stretched his chains taut to reach the rear of the wagon, peering into the trees, ignoring Halrec's complaints about being stepped on.

Jaina joined him quickly at the side of the wagon. "What is it?" she murmured.

"Movement in the trees. My eyes have been playing tricks on me all day, but I'm sure I saw something this time."

He thought Jaina would snort and dismiss him as paranoid, but she just nodded and scanned the trees with him.

The sounds of a trotting horse announced the arrival of one of the Legionmen alongside the wagon. Emrael barely spared him a glance, expecting to see Prilan coming over to glare at them again. To his surprise, the visitor was one of the Justicers who had been tasked with watching them.

"Trouble?" he asked.

Emrael searched the man's face briefly, but he didn't appear to be mocking them.

"Something in the woods. Big enough to be a man. There might be someone following us."

The Justicer nodded calmly. "We been seeing more and more bandits on the roads. Damned Iraeans raiding from across the river, usually. Been attacking wagon trains, especially those from the Lord Governor."

Emrael fought to keep a smirk from his face and mostly succeeded. "That's too bad."

The Justicer shrugged. "I'll pass the word around to keep an eye out. We might collect a few bounties today." He nodded discreetly toward Prilan, who was now near the front of the group. "Just stay in the wagon for now. Not likely anybody will attack two squads of Legionmen."

"If we *are* attacked, you would do well to see us freed and given weapons. Some of the best swordsmen in the Provinces are right here in this wagon. And swordswoman," he amended after a poke in the ribs from Jaina.

The man's eyes hardened even as he barked a laugh. "Orders are orders, son. You stay in the wagon. We can handle it."

Emrael held his palms to the sky and shrugged to pacify the Justicer.

Over the next several minutes, word traveled quietly among the men. Prilan made a great show of turning to watch the forest.

Leagues passed, and nothing happened. They encountered a few riders, wagons, and one merchant train, normal traffic for this highway. None of them had seen anything out of the ordinary.

Emrael grew more and more embarrassed by the league, though the greater part of him felt relieved. They were nearly two days out from Lidran and at least a day from the next town large enough to merit the presence of a Legion force. If the Malithii attacked them here, they would be too far for any hope of help.

Near midafternoon they came to a large bridge that spanned one of the many rivers that were born in the upper reaches of the Stemwood Valley. This was by far the widest they had encountered, though Emrael didn't know its name.

A large, fully enclosed wagon sat immobile on the heavy timber bridge near the far side. It was the sort of wagon that traveling shopkeepers or tinsmiths could live out of, peddling their wares and services. One huge back wheel lay broken in splintered pieces, causing the wagon to lean ponderously. The bridge was wide enough for three wagons abreast, however, leaving plenty of room for their party to pass by.

It didn't feel right.

Emrael stood again to get a better look. Where was the peddler?

To his credit, Prilan was quick to trot his horse forward. "Hello, the wagon!"

When there was no answer and no sign of people near the wagon, he signaled two of his men forward. They approached the wagon carefully, calling out as they neared. "Hullo? Hullo! Anybody around?"

They drew their swords after dismounting and cautiously inspected the wagon. One of them disappeared briefly as he flipped aside the curtain that covered the back of the wagon and climbed in for a better look. He climbed back out and shook his head, and the two men began walking back to the squad, leading their horses.

While there was nothing odd about a wagon breaking down on the road, it was odd for such a wagon to be abandoned, especially on a bridge in the middle of a forest like the Stemwood. Prilan didn't seem concerned, however, and ordered a squad forward to clear the wagon from the bridge.

Emrael exchanged glances with Jaina and Halrec, then caught Elle's eye from where she was sitting in her coach. He motioned anxiously, asking her to join them in the wagon. She had found new clothes somewhere and had to climb carefully out of the coach to maintain propriety with her knee-length skirt, but she walked quickly to the wagon and climbed aboard, her eyebrows drawn down in confusion.

He placed a hand on her arm. "Stay down behind the wagon walls. They are good and sturdy, thick enough to stop most arrows." He patted the wooden wall and nodded reassuringly. "I don't know why the wagon is empty, but it feels like an ambush."

He and the others in the wagon squatted low on their heels, just peeking over the high sidewalls. A sudden clatter at the back of the

wagon startled them, and they turned to find the two Justicers tossing a canvas bundle containing three swords into the wagon. One of
them tossed a key to Elle.

"Thought you could use these. Healer and the lady don't look like
they'll be much use in a fight, but the three of you might be. Stay
with the wagon unless this goes to shit." The Justicer—the same that
had spoken with Emrael earlier in the day—was outwardly calm,
but tension around his eyes betrayed his worry. He knew something
was off as well.

Elle was less than pleased by being dismissed as a bystander. Her
eyes narrowed, mouth turned down in a petulant frown. "You'd think
I was just baggage for carrying with you people . . ." she grumbled quietly, then sat with her back against the wagon wall with crossed arms.

Emrael turned to her. "Would you like my sword, then?"

Elle glared at him, trying to put on a brave face despite her ner-
vousness. He gave her a smile and put a hand on her knee. "We'll be
fine, Elle. It's probably nothing, but I'm far better at being stabbed
than you are."

She softened her glare and returned an amused smile.

Jaina unwrapped the swords, inspecting them quickly before
laying them on the wagon bed. They were ugly, battered things—
obviously spare weapons—but Emrael was glad for them.

Jaina considered the blades for a moment, then handed him a
heavy double-edged weapon. Halrec received a long, slender blade,
and Jaina kept a slightly smaller, one-edged blade for herself.

Prilan called for the march to resume and the squad started across
the bridge, though they fanned out in a defensive formation as a precaution. The supply wagon, Elle's coach, and the prisoners' wagon
lurched forward, the Justicers behind them. The planks of the bridge
thrummed hollowly with the passing of the heavy wheels.

The Legion teamster driving the wagon they rode in seemed content to allow the others to cross first, leaving them to cross last.

Jaina and the others still crouched in the wagon, but if an ambush
had been prepared, it would have happened by now. Emrael stood
up enough to see the coach pull abreast of the broken-down wagon
at the far end of the bridge.

As Emrael started to stand fully, believing the danger to be past,
a blinding flash of blue light and a terrible rumble erupted from the
broken-down wagon.

12

The force of the explosion knocked Emrael on his ass. His ears rang badly, but he could hear tinny echoes of screams and shouting from up ahead.

Emrael sat up groggily and looked around, trying to shake his head clear. His friends stared back at him with shocked expressions—all but Jaina, who was already moving, sword in hand, to get a look at what had caused the powerful blast. Emrael regained his feet quickly but surveyed the wreckage before him with more caution.

The explosion had reduced the broken-down peddler's wagon to a blazing heap of wood and metal, and the coach that had drawn abreast of it hadn't fared much better. An entire side of the coach was gone, now just a hole that ended in jagged, torn wood and twisted iron. The poor man that had been driving the coach lay not far away, little more than a smoldering pile of torn, bloody meat and rags. The horses, still in their harnesses, lay still and lifeless, mutilated.

The supply wagon, which had been between the prisoners' wagon and the coach, was peppered with holes and splinters of wood that had stuck in the sides. The driver and horses of that wagon were dying slowly, moaning and screaming. If not for them, Emrael would be similarly riddled with holes.

Their own wagon jerked back and forth as the team of four horses hitched to it tried to find a safe direction in which to run. The Legion teamster looked over his shoulder as if looking for the same escape but visibly steeled himself before hurrying forward to help the wounded drivers of the supply wagon.

Jaina swore and jumped quickly to the driver's bench to secure the horses with a firm hand on the reins.

"Justice and Mercy above!" Halrec cursed from beside Emrael. "What could *do* that?"

The soldiers on the far side of the wagon had fallen into disarray, largely due to their horses trying to run from the explosion. A few clutched wounds caused by flying debris.

Shocked, Emrael also wondered what had created such a powerful explosion. He was sure that the blue flash had something to do with *infusori*. But was that even possible? He'd never heard of anything exploding like that . . . on purpose.

Damn it, Ban would know.

Emrael turned his attention from the smoldering wreck when he heard a chorus of low grunting accompanied by a deep rumble that sounded like distant thunder. Several Legionmen on the far side of the bridge began shouting in alarm.

Grey shadows crashed downhill through the trees on the far side of the bridge with the force of charging bulls, snapping stray branches and underbrush without flinching. From the sound of breaking branches and wild stomping, Emrael expected the creatures causing the noise to be huge. But the shadows that exited the woods a short distance from the road quickly became ordinary-sized men.

At least, they looked like men at first glance. Upon closer inspection, they had grey skin and an unnatural gait. Most of them had no hair on their dull grey scalps, though a few had long, wispy clumps clinging here and there. No man had ever run with such a shambling, unnatural gait.

"What the hell are those things?" he mumbled to himself.

The shambling figures were oddly imposing in their ragged clothing, each one armed with poorly maintained weapons of every shape and size. They poured from the forest in a small wave of grey bodies.

Emrael's gut twisted and he heard a gasp from Elle as the nightmarish figures ran headlong into the Legionmen without slowing.

Blood sprayed and shouts echoed as clustered Legionmen met the charge of the fearless grey men with a loud crash of weapons and armor. Some Legionmen stood behind their horses and shot crossbows, but the grey monsters simply cut their way through the poor screaming animals to engage the soldiers without remorse or hesitation.

Battle joy warred with disgust and dread within Emrael at the sight of the sudden, senseless carnage.

He felt profound relief when one of the Legionmen managed to recover and put a sword through the midsection of one of the grey monsters. It screamed in pain but otherwise didn't react, didn't stop hacking at whatever it could reach. The monster's all-too-human scream cut off suddenly as another Legionman reached over to slash his sword through the beast's throat.

The grey man-thing collapsed to its knees, still mindlessly swinging while blood spewed from its ruined neck. The creature managed to sink its blade into the leg of a nearby Legionman before it bled out and collapsed.

That the blood pouring from the odd grey man-thing was the ordinary deep red of human blood gave Emrael an odd sense of comfort. They bled. They could be killed.

Emrael shook himself out of his fascinated horror to bark at Elle. "Elle, get the locks."

He turned to find that she had already freed Halrec and was almost to Emrael. She struggled to release his chains with trembling hands, but finally she managed. He grabbed his sword and jumped from the wagon, ready to join the battle. The Legionmen now held their own on the far side of the bridge, but more grey men flowed down from the tree line. There must have been close to fifty of the creatures. The soldiers would be overwhelmed in minutes. They needed to fall back to the bridge where they could fight fewer at a time.

He started toward the battle but stopped and looked back as Yerdon grasped his shoulder. The healer's dark eyes were sad beneath his unruly iron-grey eyebrows.

"Lad, we've got trouble of our own," he said, motioning behind them.

He was right. Grey shadows emerged from the pines behind them, though far fewer than had attacked the Legionmen on the far side of the bridge. Only three that he could see, though the trees were too thick to see whether there were more behind.

"Justice give us strength. What are these things?" Emrael muttered again.

"*Alai'ahn,*" Jaina spat. When Emrael stared at her, confused by the Ordenan word, she clarified in Provincial Common. "Soulbound. Take their heads."

She hefted her blade, jumped from the wagon, and walked to the near end of the bridge as if taking a stroll in the park.

Soulbound? Now that he thought about it, these creatures did match the legends of half-dead men enslaved by ancient, evil soulbinders. It was one thing to be told these monsters existed, and another entirely to see them with his own eyes.

He hurried past Yerdon and Elle on his way to join the Justicers, Jaina, and Halrec, who had already gathered at the foot of this side of the bridge to meet the soulbound trotting their way.

Just before he reached them, he noticed Prilan standing behind his horse a few paces away. He stood motionless, staring wide-eyed at the monsters striding toward them.

"Prilan!" Emrael shouted. The Captain Third didn't seem to hear him, so he ran over to scream in his face. "Prilan!"

Prilan blinked and looked over at him with wide, terrified eyes.

Emrael grabbed his armored shoulders and shook him violently. "Prilan, you need to pull your men back to the bridge. To the bridge, you hear? Go!"

Prilan nodded and turned toward the other end of the bridge, where fewer of his men remained to stand up to the massive attack than had been there moments before. He began walking, still nodding to himself. Emrael growled angrily and planted a kick squarely on his backside.

"Go! Run, man!"

Prilan ran.

Emrael had no choice but to hope that the inexperienced officer would be able to pull himself together enough to get his men back to the bridge, where they would stand a chance at holding.

He put that out of his mind and sprinted to help his friends on his own side of the bridge.

Three soulbound reached his friends before he could. The grey men hardly slowed as they swung their pitted, rusty blades. The creatures seemed to have no fear, and that would make them very dangerous.

To Emrael's great relief, instead of trying to meet the soulbound's charge head-on, Jaina and Halrec had each baited one of the creatures into swinging wildly, then ducked back out of harm's way at the last moment, jabbing and slicing as their opponents stumbled past.

The Justicers had not been so wise but had met the remaining soulbound together. While they were not having an easy time of it, they had stopped the thing's charge by brute force.

Though the soulbound didn't have the momentum of their shambling charge, they swung with reckless force, apparently without tiring.

Emrael moved to help Jaina before he saw that she easily eluded the grey man's powerful but clumsy swings. He would just be in the way. Instead, he stepped up shoulder-to-shoulder with Halrec, who eluded his own opponent's second wild attack, but only by a small margin. Sword skill was only so helpful when facing an opponent who apparently didn't feel pain or fear.

They fought the soulbound together, separating as much as possible in the space remaining on the bridge, forcing the grotesque thing to divide its attention.

The soulbound swung heavily in a wide arc, trying to catch them both, but they danced out of range. The thing's eyes widened in frustration, and the unmistakable intelligence in the wild eyes of the beast horrified Emrael. This thing was still human, on some level.

The soulbound continued pushing forward, desperately straining to catch Halrec or Emrael with its huge weapon. Each time one of them was attacked, the other would dart in to strike. It wore no armor, and their blades struck deep, tearing great rents in its flesh. Rivulets of blood soon marred the soulbound's wrinkled, dark grey skin and tattered clothing. Anger—or perhaps fear—twisted the grey man's sagging face.

They stabbed the creature a dozen times in as many seconds, and soon loss of blood slowed it. Its attacks grew sluggish. Emrael saw an opening and lunged in for a finishing strike. He plunged his blade deep into the beast's rib cage and then heaved as hard as he could, cleaving through several of its ribs and pushing it backward.

It went down more easily than he expected, and he fell on top of it as it toppled backward. Emrael found himself pressed up against the beast's stiff skin. This close, he could smell its stink, like a man unwashed for a very, very long time. Or was it more like rotting meat? The heat of its touch felt warmer than that of an ordinary person. He had expected it to feel cold.

Emrael tried to jump up and scramble away from the soulbound he had stabbed in the heart, but the mortally wounded soulbound caught him by the shoulder in a crushing grip as it surged to its knees. He squirmed helplessly as the soulbound that should be dead raised its sword. Frantic, he punched the creature over and over with his free arm, to no avail. The soulbound clung to him with impossible strength, impervious to pain, Emrael's sword stuck in its side. Emrael had no way to defend himself.

Just as he felt the deadening realization of mortal defeat, Halrec leapt forward with a guttural shout. His blade whistled in a wide arc above his head and slammed into the creature's forearm, severing the bone but leaving the hand that had been holding a rusty sword dangling from a bloody stump.

The grey man bellowed, releasing Emrael and clutching for its sword with its good arm. Halrec stepped forward again and lodged his blade in the monster's throat with a swift thrust, sweeping through windpipe and arteries as he drew it out in a spray of hot blood. The soulbound fell to the bridge with a *thud*, a stunned expression on its grotesquely human-like face.

Emrael's relief was short-lived, as two more soulbound shuffled out of the woods on their side of the bridge. Jaina still fought her first, though its slow, labored movements made it clear how that fight would end. The two Justicers had already dispatched their soulbound and engaged the first to reach the bridge. The second headed straight at Halrec and Emrael.

Halrec waved Emrael back and set his feet. "Go on! Catch your breath. I can hold this one for now."

His face grim and streaked with soulbound blood, Halrec stepped forward to meet the last soulbound on this side of the bridge.

Emrael pulled his sword free from the dead soulbound's side and took a few steps back to survey the battle. He risked a glance behind him to look to the far side of the bridge. Many Legionmen lay on the ground, but a group of almost a dozen survivors had managed to retreat to the bridge, and their wall of shields seemed to be holding against a seething cluster of grey soulbound.

He felt a stab of worry and frustration as he saw Yerdon and Elle hovering about the rear of the group where several wounded soldiers lay on the planks of the bridge. They grabbed one of the soldiers by the arms and began dragging him back out of harm's way. Elle was too brave for her own good.

A scream behind him made him whip around, a fresh rush of fear heightening his senses. One of the Justicers was on the ground, his entrails a sickening mess on the deck of the bridge.

Emrael's stomach wanted to empty itself, but he ignored it and rushed to join the remaining Justicer, who was hard pressed now that his comrade had fallen. He screamed as he engaged the soulbound, distracting the beast so that the surviving Justicer could retreat and recover. The soldier shouted his thanks as he shuffled out of the fray.

Emrael swung his sword hard, instinctively trying to push his enemy back. The grey man met his attack with a swing of its rusty, blood-streaked blade. The impact of sword on sword rang with an ugly screech, jarring Emrael's hands and arms to the point of being numb.

He ducked back out of the soulbound's reach quickly, barely hanging on to his weapon. He waved his sword in small circles to regain feeling and dexterity in his hands, preparing his next attack. Before he could launch another attack, however, the soulbound surged forward smoothly, catching him off guard once more. Up until now, all of the soulbound had fought in powerful but jerky, poorly coordinated movements.

Emrael stepped back in a panic as the soulbound pressed forward, its eyes now intensely focused on Emrael, where before they had been wild, crazed.

Emrael stumbled slightly as his boot caught on something, forcing him to throw himself backward and roll over his shoulder and to his feet. The grey man followed as he rolled and swung its blade immediately. Emrael scrambled back again, barely escaping the tip of the soulbound's blade.

Emrael's back hit something solid. The wagon.

Panic coursed up his spine. He threw himself to the side just before the soulbound hit the wagon with an overhand blow. The age-hardened wood of the tailgate exploded in a spray of chunks and splinters. The creature's sword stopped only when it cut through the wood of the wagon bed and hit the iron axle. The other soulbound had been strong, but this one was as strong as a bear!

Emrael rolled and scrambled to his feet, feeling momentary relief when he saw that the Justicer had rushed over to help. The soldier thrust his sword into the soulbound's back, but it simply glanced over its shoulder and swung a fist, sending the Justicer sprawling. He landed several paces away and didn't move.

To Emrael's great dismay, the creature continued forward as lithely as before, entirely ignoring the Justicer's sword still sticking from its back at an odd angle. Loss of blood had slowed the other creatures but didn't seem to affect this one. He felt a shiver of fear when he saw the soulbound's eyes. They had gone dark. Not just the irises: the entirety of its eyes had turned a deep coal black.

It continued forward, baring its yellow, broken teeth in a smile. Emrael didn't know what was happening, but he knew he was in trouble.

He set his feet despite his fear and cleared his mind of all thought except for his enemy. He held his sword at the ready and turned the grey man's attacks stroke by stroke when it reached him, turning its own strength against it. He had to scurry away from the soulbound's powerful attacks several times, but managed to put several large holes in its dull grey body in the process. Blood flowed in a steady trickle from the wounds, but still it continued forward without slowing, ever smiling.

Suddenly, Jaina and Halrec appeared, stabbing at the thing's back as it advanced on Emrael. It took distracted swings in their direction, but its attention remained on him.

Short of breath, Emrael shouted, "Go for the joints! Cripple it! This one doesn't slow down like the others!"

They heeded his advice and began focusing on the joints and vulnerable points. Soon, the soulbound was brought to one knee, then dropped to all fours, all of its limbs crippled. Its head drooped forward and to one side due to a deep gash in its neck that had severed some tendons. If Emrael hadn't been so terrified, he might have pitied the immobile beast. It had once been human, after all. Chest heaving with the effort of the fight, he stepped forward to end it cleanly, but Jaina stopped him with a barked command.

"Wait!"

He paused with his sword raised to strike and looked at his mentor in confusion. Her dark hair was in disarray and her olive-colored cheeks were flushed. Her skin shone with a layer of sweat.

"I need this one alive," she said, stooping to sever the creature's left arm at the wrist and pulling a bracelet from its bleeding stump with a casual, practiced motion. "Go help the girl."

She pointed to the other side of the bridge. Elle and Yerdon ran toward them, but the Legionmen had stayed behind. The monsters had pushed the line of soldiers back several paces. As Emrael watched, one of the soulbound cleaved a man almost in half from top to bottom. The grey man broke through the line and cut down another Legionman from the side. The rest of the Legionmen realized their fight was lost and began running, but too late.

Several creatures that had broken through the line of Legionmen turned and cut the men down before they had gone a few steps. Rather than face the soulbound alone, a few of the Legionmen threw themselves from the bridge and into the deepest part of the swift, churning river. He didn't see any surface.

The group of soulbound took a moment to peer off the edge of the bridge and to kill the injured Legionmen that Elle and Yerdon had been forced to abandon. Soon, however, the monsters realized that some of their quarry remained alive at the far end of the bridge and began eating the distance between them with quick, shuffling strides. Their low grunts accentuated the pounding reverberations of the bridge underneath their heavy feet.

As Elle and Yerdon drew near, Emrael brought his attention back to the sagging soulbound on the ground in front of him and threw Jaina a questioning glance. They needed to run, right now.

She shook her head violently and motioned back the way they had come. "Get everyone off the bridge, quickly!"

Perhaps it was her tone, or maybe he was overly accustomed to obeying her commands, but whatever the reason, he turned and ran toward the near bank of the river. He slowed only to snag as many packs and bags of supplies from the wagons as he could reasonably carry, and to make sure Halrec, Elle, and Yerdon followed him. A few steps later, he almost jumped over the still form of the second Justicer but noticed the man's eyes were open and moving.

Emrael hurried to the end of the bridge, threw the packs to the dirt, and sprinted back to the Justicer. He dropped to one knee and picked the man up clumsily, shifting his sword to his left hand. He hoisted the injured man onto his right shoulder, glad that this Justicer was much smaller than the two he had fought back in Lidran. His friends slowed as if to help him, but he urged them on with a shout.

When they reached the dirt road, he set the Justicer down and turned back to the bridge, readying his weapon wearily for the battle to come. He did not know what Jaina had planned, but at least a few would surely break through. At least a dozen or so of the grey-skinned soulbound shuffled toward them, muscles rippling oddly beneath their loose skin, like giant maggots just beneath the skin of a corpse.

They were getting very close to Jaina, but she stood unperturbed. She went to one knee and stabbed a short copper blade into the crippled soulbound's back, simply staring at the oncoming tide of murderous creatures.

Emrael sprinted forward, and he felt as much as saw Halrec join him. He had no hope of surviving, but perhaps he, Jaina, and Halrec could slow the soulbound long enough for Elle and Yerdon to escape.

"Elle, run!" he screamed over his shoulder.

He was a dozen paces away from Jaina when a flash of blue light erupted ahead, near where she still knelt next to the downed soulbound. He flinched and shut his eyes against the sudden brightness.

Thankfully, he had closed his eyes just in time, and the resulting blind spot subsided quickly. With a sense of relief, he saw Jaina still kneeling. The bridge, however, hadn't fared as well. Flames enveloped the entire width of the bridge just in front of Jaina and extended most of the way to the far bank. Smoke billowed into the sky, a black column twisting this way and that in the gentle breeze as it reached the tops of the trees. There was no sign of the soulbound that had been just steps away from her—where the inferno now raged hottest. Whatever magic Jaina had summoned had obliterated every remaining soulbound.

Emrael ran to Jaina's side. She remained kneeling, gripping the copper dagger that she had stabbed through the crippled soulbound's back. She swayed tiredly, teetering perilously close to the fire.

The heat from the fire burned Emrael's skin. He could smell hair burning, but that could have been the soulbound that had just been incinerated on the bridge.

He looked closer and realized that the bridge wasn't just on fire; it had burned all the way through. He could see the rushing water of the river below through the haze of fire and smoke. As he watched, a large section of charred wood collapsed into the swiftly moving water below. The portion of the bridge on which they stood began to sway on its support columns.

Suddenly worried that the bridge might not hold for much longer, he stooped to gather Jaina's slender form, but Halrec's sudden appearance made him pause. He watched, bemused but grateful, as Halrec lifted her gently from the planks.

Halrec cradled Jaina in his arms with a worried look on his still-battered face. Her head lolled limply, coming to a rest on his shoulder as he hurried to safety. Emrael followed with his sword still at the ready, his eyes alert. Soulbound had been on this side of the river, too, after all.

What remained of their party waited for them at the foot of the bridge. Yerdon tended to the senseless Justicer, and Elle stood nearby, a worried look on her face as she watched Emrael and Halrec approach.

Halrec set Jaina carefully at Elle's feet. Exhaustion made his long, handsome face sag, but he did not leave Jaina's side. Elle raised her eyebrows as she looked at Halrec, then caught Emrael's eye. When Emrael shrugged back, she smiled before turning back to her patient. She started giving orders as she knelt to take Jaina's pulse and look her over.

"Halrec, I need fresh water. Fill a skin in the river and bring it to me quickly. Em, go check on Master Yerdon and see if he needs anything."

Emrael smiled, appreciating her ability to take command of the situation as he turned to obey. How had he never noticed how strong-willed she was when they had been at the Citadel?

Not far away, Yerdon tended to the Justicer that Emrael had carried off the bridge. The older soldier seemed to have recovered some of his wits and as Emrael approached, he said in a strained voice, "You gave that thing quite a fight, lad. Thank you."

Emrael planted his sword in the ground, trying not to show the pride he felt at the compliment. "Anytime. My name's Emrael."

"Good to know you, Emrael. Name's Joral."

Emrael nodded to the soldier before turning to Yerdon. "Yerdon, is there anything you need? We need to move, and quickly. How soon can you have Joral ready to go?"

Yerdon gave him a pointed look. "I am still a Master Healer, you know, and accustomed to being addressed as such by students. But I suppose that doesn't mean much out in these Mercy-forsaken woods." He gestured dismissively at the trees around them and sighed. "Still, I suppose you are correct. I should not like to wait around for more of those . . . *things* to show up. He should be ready for a light walk within a few hours."

"With respect, Yerdon, there isn't a school at the Citadel anymore, so forgive me for skipping the honorifics. We don't have hours. Get him ready to walk in ten minutes or we'll have to carry him."

A shout came from where Halrec had climbed down the grassy bank to fill a waterskin in the river. Remembering the soulbound that had been on the bridge, Emrael pulled his sword from the ground in a flash and sprinted down the gentle slope to the water's edge. He drew within sight of Halrec ready for a fight, only to find his friend hauling a man in Legion armor from the water.

Halrec looked up at the sound of Emrael's arrival and guffawed. "Looks like we have a swimmer!"

He clapped the half-drowned Legionman on the back hard, which sent the poor kneeling soldier into a fit of coughing.

"Halrec! Be kind. They held their side of the bridge well."

Halrec just raised his eyebrows incredulously. The Legionman raised his head. It was none other than his favorite Captain Third, Prilan.

Emrael cursed. "Son of a bitch. Of all the men that could have made it . . ." he grumbled. Then louder, he said, "Can we throw him back?"

Halrec laughed a deep, genuine laugh, and motioned for Emrael to help him. "Come on. Let's get out of here."

13

A commotion outside his door jerked Darmon from a fitful sleep. He'd only just begun to feel like himself again after that bastard Ire had used that foul magic on him several days before.

"Where *are* they, Healer?" someone shouted.

"I . . . I don't know, sir; they were just here. We have been tending the man's wife. She is still very weak; they can't be far . . . I'll ask the Captain to search the compound." The voice sounded like that of the healer who had treated Darmon. Had someone come looking for that ape of an Ordenan and his wife?

Darmon's belly filled with fear as he heard heavy footsteps and the jingle of armor approach his room. Had Ire come back for him?

He almost sobbed with relief when a man in Watcher blue appeared in the doorway of his cramped, squalid little infirmary room. He'd only been there a few days, but he'd had nothing to do but despair over his horrid, useless stump of an arm.

"I've got orders from the Lord Governor himself, signed by your Captain," the man in blue retorted gruffly as one of the Barros Legionmen challenged him.

The Watcher, a Captain First, judging by his shoulder rivets, swept into the room and stared at Darmon for a moment. "Well? Did you lose a foot as well as a hand? I've come to fetch you, but I'm sure as hell not going to carry you."

Darmon scrambled to his feet, awkwardly pulled his boots on with his one hand, and followed the Watcher officer out of the infirmary, then out of the compound. The Watcher didn't speak, didn't even turn to see whether Darmon was following as they wound through the teeming streets of Lidran. Though he was equal parts relieved and confused at first, his indignant anger quickly grew.

"Hey!" he shouted at the man's back. "Who are you and where are we going? Do you know who I am, you lout?"

The Watcher glanced back at him. "Yes," he answered simply, then continued walking.

Darmon just shook his head. The man must be a simpleton.

Several winding streets later, they arrived at a manse in one of the wealthier districts of the city. It didn't compare to the Citadel or his father's palace back home, but it was a welcome sight after the tiny room he had been kept in at the Barros Legion compound.

The entry to the manse led into one large, open gathering hall. The Watchers and dark-robed men scattered about the room seemed out of place among the abundant marble and copper, but for Darmon, it was as close to home as he'd felt in quite some time.

Darmon's escort strode straight to a small cluster of black-robed men and stood at attention. "I have him." He gestured toward Darmon.

One of the dark-robed men turned, smiling. Tattoos covered a large portion of his pale skin, including the entirety of his hands. Darmon almost mistook him for his father's advisor that had arrived by ship from the east last year, known to them only as Priest. But Priest had tattoos covering his entire face, and this man's face was bare.

"Ah, good," the priest said warmly in a lilting but only faint accent, then pointed at one of his robed companions, who occupied a chair in the middle of the group. "Just in time. We are working on something special here for a moment, but soon we will be Healing your friend. I'm afraid your conventional methods of healing have not been kind to him."

The priest moved back to the huddle of robed men, motioning Darmon closer. Darmon stepped forward carefully but stopped with a sharp intake of breath when he saw that the seated man's eyes were completely black. The man sat rigidly, not moving a single muscle but almost seeming to thrum with tension. The rest of the robed men watched intently. Why were there so many of them there, in a midsized city in the Barros Province of all places?

Without warning, the priest with the tattooed hands jerked a dagger from his robes and whipped it straight through the seated man's neck. The man jerked, his head flopping backward on his partially severed neck. Lifeblood spurted and flowed from the spasming man, soaking his robes, pooling on the floor.

Darmon thought he might be sick, but he could only stare into the dying man's eyes, still the color of starless midnight.

The priest who had just slit his companion's throat grabbed Darmon by the scruff of his neck and led him firmly toward the back of the building. "I'm sorry you had to see that, my boy, but such is oft the price of failure. Had I not killed him, the Ordenan witch on the other end of that link may have killed us all."

They entered a dimly lit room just off of the main hall. Another pale, tattooed man in dark robes—a healer of some sort—tended the occupant of a cot in one corner of the room. "Speaking of failure, I believe you know the Commander First?"

Darmon walked closer, and his breath caught. Corlas lay on the cot, stripped to the waist. A blood-soaked bandage adorned his right shoulder, where he had been hit with the crossbow quarrel. His neck shone with the blue light of a glowing collar.

"What did you do to him?" he asked quietly.

The priest smiled sadly. "Unfortunately, gentler methods of healing are not working for your friend. He is too close to death, so we must resort to more extreme measures." He gestured sharply to the healer, who quickly removed the collar from Corlas.

Corlas jerked awake immediately, groaning and clutching his shoulder. His eyes bulged with pain. "Help me, boy," he rasped at Darmon. "Don't let them put that thing back on me—"

The priest pushed the healer out of his way as he grasped Corlas by either side of the head, a snarl on his face.

Corlas screamed. He screamed so loud, it seemed as though his vocal cords would burst. Just when Darmon thought it would never end, the priest tore the bloody bandage from Corlas's shoulder and stepped back. The screaming ceased.

Corlas was left panting raggedly, visibly weakened. He moved his shoulder well enough, though. All signs of his wound were gone. "What . . . have you done to me? Who are you? Where am I?"

The priest moved forward smoothly. "Not to worry, my friend. Here, let me feel your pulse." The priest snatched Corlas's arm, and all in one motion snapped a thin mindbinder on his wrist. Corlas jerked, then was still, face blank.

Darmon clutched the pendant of the Holy Departed he wore around his neck, feeling sick. "Why . . . why have you Bound him? I thought we were only doing that to the *infusori* Crafters at the Citadel as a temporary precaution."

The priest shook his head and smiled sadly once again. "You both have failed us, young prince. I can no longer trust him to do as I say without this additional measure of assurance. You will accompany our friend back to the Citadel. Free . . . for now."

The priest clapped his hands, and immediately, several dark-robed men and one woman entered the room to stand at attention.

"Yes, Master?" one of them intoned.

"See to it that these two are given horses and escorted back to the Citadel." The priest turned to the others, flexing his hands. "Take the rest of the Servants after the Ordenan witch. Take a few of your brethren with you; I want you there in person. Kill all but the white-haired boy and the golden-haired girl. Bring them to me alive."

14

Emrael and Halrec half-carried Prilan back to where the others waited in the trees near the foot of the bridge.

"We need to get out of here now," Emrael told the group. "Someone knew exactly where we'd be. We need to get off the road." He looked at each of them. "Darmon told me back at the compound that they are holding Ban and the others either at the Citadel or at Whitehall in Iraea. If I'm not mistaken, Whitehall is close to due north from here, just across the river. Seems to make sense to hit there first, then make plans for the Citadel if Ban and Sami aren't at Whitehall. We should be able to catch a ship from Whitehall if we need to get to Ordena to gather allies, Jaina."

He looked to Jaina, expecting an argument, but apparently she was too tired after her impressive feat of magic. When nobody objected, he continued. "How do we get to the Low Road? Even a game trail will do. We can't blaze a trail and move quickly, especially with Jaina and Joral wounded."

"Who the hell is Joral?" Halrec interrupted.

"That'd be me," Joral chimed in.

"Ah. Carry on."

Emrael rolled his eyes at his friend's ever-present jibes. "Once we hit the Low Road, it should be easier, but these Malithii bastards are obviously following us and trying to make sure we end up facedown in a ditch. This attack didn't happen by chance. They knew where we would be, somehow. They'll probably be watching major roads and highways. We need to travel by backroads until we find a ferry to get us across, preferably in a small crossing town where the Malithii won't expect us. We don't have horses, so we may as well cut through the forest."

Elle grimaced. "I just *had* to put on a skirt today."

Emrael shrugged. "Scratched legs are a small price to pay if it means staying alive."

He was about to ask when Jaina and Joral would be ready to leave when he saw motion across the river. He squatted down and froze, squinting to focus his eyes. His breath caught as he saw movement again and recognized the outline of a person in a hooded robe standing among the trees on the far bank, near the road and the now-burning bridge. He blinked, and the figure was gone.

"We leave now!" Everyone turned to look at him, surprised at his sudden shout. "Up! I mean it. Let's go! I will carry her if I have to," he yelled, pointing to Jaina. "But we leave now!"

Everyone lurched into confused motion, looking at him as if he had gone mad. He growled in frustration. "I just saw a Malithii priest over on the other side of the river. They know we survived. We are only safe until they figure out a good way to cross . . . unless they have more of those monsters on this side already. We need to move. Now."

Within minutes, each of them had shouldered a pack—Emrael prayed that they had enough supplies to last until they reached civilization—and began marching back down the Kingroad toward Lidran to get out of sight of the river. Joral walked under his own power, but Emrael had to walk next to Jaina, supporting her with one arm as she regained her strength.

Soon after the bridge was out of sight, Halrec held up a hand and let out a low whistle. Emrael joined Halrec at the head of the group. His friend crouched, running his hand over a large, worn stone set into the ground next to the road.

Emrael furrowed his brows. "What is it, Hal?"

"If we head that way, we'll find a decent path." He stood and walked briskly into the brush that grew in the cleared area on either side of the Kingroad.

After a moment, Halrec waved Emrael over to him again excitedly. He had found another stone, even bigger than the last, though this one jutted from the ground at a slight angle. "Told you."

Emrael peered farther along the trajectory that his friend was following, and there was indeed a path, overgrown with underbrush and small trees that would keep the path hidden from anyone not looking directly at it from this angle.

"Aren't you even going to ask how I knew?" Halrec seemed slightly deflated.

"I trust that even you know a few useful things."

His friend glared at him.

"Fine. How did you know there would be a path here?"

His friend smiled. "I'm glad you asked! See, in my first assignment, I had a sergeant who had been around a while. You know the type. He practically ran the squad for the first few months until I got the hang of being a Captain Third. Old Sergeant Torman showed me more than a few tricks, but by far the most useful was this."

He pointed to the stone under their feet. "Old paving stone from before the Free Kingdoms even existed. Might even be Ravan. You never know what you'll find when you follow one of the old roads, ruins and the like, but they are almost always the fastest way to cut through the forest. Bandits use them all the time." He smiled triumphantly. "Let's go already."

Emrael rolled his eyes again and started hiking.

⌁

Two days later, the group traipsed through the dense forest. Halrec's path was better than nothing, but they still tripped on deceptive tree roots and trudged through small streams until the late-afternoon rays slanted sharply through the evergreen needles and hardwood leaves. The towering trees cast looming shadows that Emrael's imagination turned into soulbound and Malithii about to attack. He thought he might go crazy trying to watch everything around him constantly. And so it was that he almost ran into a huge, vine-strewn boulder before he noticed it right in his path.

He had noticed this enormous stone like he did any other in the forest but was startled to realize that the path led straight to the moss- and vine-covered boulder. He pulled up short, staring for a time as his friends caught up and gathered behind him.

Had the enormous stone rolled onto the path? Or had he missed a turn? No, the paving stones of the ancient road were clear underfoot and seemed to lead directly to the stone.

"Ah!" Jaina cried, rushing forward. Adoration illuminated her eyes, and her mouth formed the purest, most innocent smile he had ever seen on her face.

Emrael met Halrec's questioning glance with a confused one of his own before he hurried forward to join Jaina, who was carefully removing vines and chunks of moss from the huge stone.

"Hey Jaina?" He kept his voice mild and shared another glance with Halrec. "What are you doing?" They had all been on a knife's edge around Jaina since she had single-handedly demolished the bridge.

She didn't respond, just continued prying at the foliage. Emrael leaned forward to get a better look. The face of the boulder was flat where she had uncovered a section, and he thought dark lines in the stone might be a carving of some sort.

He recoiled in surprise as he felt a small surge of *infusori* from Jaina. The boulder groaned.

Despite himself, he stepped back apprehensively, and felt only slightly better when he saw Halrec do the same. What was Jaina doing now?

The stone continued its deep, disconcerting groan, but Jaina just stood next to it with her same innocent smile. Just as he was beginning to think her mind had cracked, a solid *thud* emanated from the boulder. He squinted. From the tangle of vines and moss, the outline of an opening appeared in the stone, slowly growing more distinct. The thin line soon grew into a doorway as a section of the rock ground its way open.

Why is there a magic doorway set into a boulder in the middle of the forest?

He recovered from his surprise and voiced his confusion in a hushed tone. "What in the name of Fallen Glory is that?"

Jaina finally turned to him. Her innocent smile had turned to one of pure glee, like the smile of a child who's been offered a treat. "It's a temple. A lost temple of my ancestors. Our ancestors, I suppose. I had heard they still exist on this continent, but never thought to find one." She giggled. Jaina actually *giggled*. "In Ordena, only the most senior members of my Order are allowed inside. But here? Well, it opened at my touch, did it not?"

She said that last as if it was supposed to mean something, but Emrael couldn't fathom what.

Before the door had even finished grinding its way open, she darted inside. Halrec immediately followed, hand on his sword hilt, but Emrael paused to take another look at this mysterious boulder-temple. The shapes rounded by centuries' worth of vine and other foliage could have been the peaks and valleys of a structure, but there were no seams, no change in material from walls to roof. He couldn't imagine who would go through the effort of carving a building of solid stone out in the middle of nowhere, ancient path or no.

He turned to look for Elle and met her eye briefly before she followed the rest inside. She brushed past him on her way through the doorway, and the rest of his companions moved forward to do the same.

A shout of triumph came from within the stone. "Ha!"

A steady blue light emanated from the doorway, illuminating those within. He peered inside. The hollow was much larger than he had imagined, and he saw doorways that led to still more rooms. The boulder wasn't nearly large enough to house the space he saw inside, not by a fair margin. What kind of magic was this?

His companions were looking about in wonder at carvings in the stone walls that reflected the light of the *infusori* coil lamp that Jaina held. The lamp was made of a strange, glittering metal the color of copper but somehow deeper, more vibrant. It was the color that copper aspired to be. The metal coil's delicate curves and angles somehow cast the light of a small *infusori* coil throughout the entire interior of the stone temple.

A sharp click and a grinding noise brought his attention back to the doorway where he stood. The stone slab began to inch shut, and he hopped inside to avoid being crushed. As the stone settled into place, pure blue light suddenly emanated from a large circle carved on the inside surface of the door, and from there raced around the room, illuminating the strange script on the walls. It was awe-inspiring and more than a little frightening.

"Jaina?" Emrael called. "Jaina, we can get back out, right?"

Jaina turned off the *infusori* lamp and looked over her shoulder to cast him a withering glance. "Of course we can. Would I just prance in here if I could not get back out? Any adept mage can open them, just like the door in Sarlon's house in Myntar. We are most fortunate to have found this place, Emrael. Very few in our Age have had the pleasure of stepping into a Ravan temple. Isn't it wonderful?"

She spread her arms and gestured all around her at the glimmering carvings in the walls and to open doorways that led to enormous rooms. The rooms appeared furnished with shelves full of odd items, somehow free of the dust that should cover such a forgotten structure.

"The script is angular, as similar to that of the Malithii as Old Ordenan. It is just like Welitan said it would be. I should have believed him," she murmured quietly, voice full of emotion.

Emrael shrugged uncomfortably. "What exactly is a Ravan temple, Jaina? I've heard of the ancient Ravan Empire and their mages but never anything like this."

He noticed out of the corner of his eye that Elle had turned to look at him as well, but he kept his focus on Jaina. The interior size of this place was impossibly huge compared to the exterior dimensions of the stone they had entered. Something about the place felt off to him, but Jaina was clearly ecstatic.

Tears of joy trickled gently from her eyes as she spoke. "The land ruled today by the United Provinces was once the heart of the Ravan Empire, a civilization unlike anything you could imagine. The last of the Ravan mages founded Ordena in an attempt to preserve the Ravan Empire, but even we are but a shadow of their former glory.

"I have dreamed of finding a temple my entire life." She closed her eyes and put her face close to the stone wall, caressing it with her hands.

"Okay . . . but why is it glowing? And what's all that shit on those shelves?" he asked, pointing through the nearest doorway to the racks of objects.

She cast him a withering look. "Temples were always built on *infusori* Wells, a conduit for the earth's pure *infusori*, power that fueled any Crafted device one could build. Works of *A Si'trae—infusori* Craftings—from the greatest minds were brought here for the good of all."

"You mean this place is full of things Crafted by the Ravan ancients, real Ravan mages? And has just been sitting here this whole time?" Emrael paced the room, looking harder into the rooms lined with shelves full of strange objects large and small. His gaze lingered on the rooms sealed by doors of stone like the one that had covered the entrance. "Why hasn't anyone taken these things? Why haven't I heard of people discovering them when digging *infusori* Wells?"

Jaina shook her head sadly. "Emrael, Ravan temples are not so simple as that. Their contents can only be accessed by mages entering properly, as we did. We are no longer in our own world. We are in a Ravan temple, another world entirely from our own." She looked at him with pity in her eyes, as if she were telling a simpleton that *infusori* coils were not magic. "When the structure is destroyed to create a modern Well, they are destroying access to this place, not the place itself. The wonders within are lost but not destroyed. The few accessible temples I know of are all on the isle of Ordena, though I have heard there may be several lost in the ruins of Iraea. The Iraean mages of old forgot the Silent Sisters and much of what their Ravan ancestors were but remembered the worth of the temples."

Emrael felt a tingling sensation flood through him, and he looked around uneasily. "Ah . . . okay. So, let's look to see if we can find food or anything useful that will help us get out of these woods in one piece so we can get Ban back."

He started toward the nearest doorway but pulled up short when Jaina drew in a sharp, hissing breath.

"No!" she said. "Do not touch anything in here, Emrael. Only one who knows the language of the ancients can navigate the devices safely. Even I am only familiar with a very few types of ancient Craftings. We may rest here, but we must touch nothing. Someday I will bring an Imperator Crafter of my Order here to discover the mysteries of this place properly."

Emrael scowled incredulously. "You're telling me that we happened upon a stash of incredible Craftings, devices that could make people fly or bring people back from the dead like the Ravan mages did in the stories, and we are just going leave them here?"

He walked toward the nearest doorway once more. He only took a few resolute paces before Jaina quickly crossed the room to grab his short hair, forcing his head down to look at her. Her eyes were fierce. She was as angry as he had ever seen her.

"No! Some of the devices will be extremely dangerous in such close quarters. These are not simple toys, you foolish boy. They were built for every purpose under the sun. They were tools for everything from warfare to growing food. I would hope that the more dangerous objects would be sealed in the closed chambers, but still, you could fill this room with fire, or water, or sand as easily as find something that will aid us. Your recklessness will get you—and likely all of us—killed."

She shoved him away with a muttered "idiot", leaving him to rub his sore scalp and glare at her sullenly.

"But you traipsed in here and used the lamp," he said defensively.

"Only because I knew precisely what it was, Emrael. I've studied the ancients extensively as part of my training at the Imperial Academy, and still, I'm wary to touch anything in this place." She jabbed a threatening finger at him. "Don't. Touch. Anything."

Emrael put his hands up defensively. "Fine, fine. Mercy, Jaina."

A motion to one side made him glance over to see Elle walking toward him briskly, a serious expression on her face. When she reached him, she stretched her hand towards his head.

He leaned back warily, still rubbing his sore scalp. "Not you too. Had enough of that, thanks."

She gave him an impatient look and leaned in to pull his head forward gently. She examined his head intently, leaving Emrael very confused.

"She didn't pull that hard, Elle. I'll be okay."

She dismissed him with a snort, not pausing her inspection.

Emrael threw yet another confused glance at Halrec, who was smiling openly at his discomfort.

Elle brought her face even closer to his head. Normally, he would have enjoyed the proximity, but she held his head at an awkward angle.

"Does he look odd to you?" she asked suddenly, still studying him.

"Nah, he always looks that way. You'll get used to it after a while," Halrec said with a chuckle.

Elle smiled but continued, "No, his hair. Look at his hair. Does it seem strange to you? Like it's glowing?"

Emrael pulled out of Elle's grip. "What do you mean, *glowing*? It's probably just reflecting the light of the walls."

"Enough, enough," Jaina said, stepping in quickly. "We're all exhausted, and some of us have wounds that need tending to. There should be chambers in the back where we can sleep."

Her excitement had clearly begun to fade, giving way to the exhaustion that had plagued her since setting fire to the bridge back on the Kingroad. She led the way to the only doorway on the right side of the main chamber, turning back to say, "Remember, touch nothing." She disappeared into the chamber with Yerdon, Prilan, and Joral, leaving Elle, Halrec, and Emrael in the main chamber.

After a short moment, Halrec let out a barking laugh. "Your hair does glow, Em."

"It's probably just reflecting the light from the designs on the walls," he repeated defensively.

Elle shook her head. "No, even when I shield it from the light coming from the walls, it glows." She stepped close to him to inspect his hair once more. Her body pressed close to his, warm and firm. He lost himself for a moment just looking at her as she took his head in her hands and inspected his hair again. She smelled of dust and sweat, but he was sure he smelled much worse.

Halrec cleared his throat, and Emrael blushed when he saw the smirk on his friend's face. He did not pull away from Elle, however.

Halrec broke the awkward silence. "Well, I suppose I'll go see what the sleeping quarters look like. I hope they have magic food here, too. I'd even eat it if it glowed. I'm getting sick of travel rations . . ." Halrec trailed off as he followed the rest of the group through the nearby doorway.

Emrael turned his attention back to Elle. She smiled. "Your eyes glow faintly in here as well." She inched closer, her voice firm. "I'm sure it's nothing; you'll be fine. And if it turns into an issue, I'll figure out how to fix it."

He smiled back. "Thank you, Elle. I can't tell you how much your help means to me. I couldn't do this alone, and I was an idiot to try. I've been meaning to tell you: what you did at the bridge was incredibly brave. It was dangerous to get that close to the fighting, and I can't say I like that; but it was brave nonetheless."

Elle took his hand, grasping tightly. "Thank you, Em. Come on, let's get some rest."

Hand in hand, they walked down a short hall and into another large chamber similar to the first one, with seamless stone walls and bright, glowing inscriptions adorning them.

They found that the others had laid their things next to a series of what looked like stone bunks. There must have been at least fifty beds in this chamber alone, and he could see another identical chamber through another archway on the other side of the room. Emrael didn't fancy the idea of spending a night sleeping on stone, but at least they were safe from any pursuers for a night and could all sleep in peace.

Emrael flushed as everyone turned to look at them. He didn't let go of Elle's hand, however.

Halrec gave them a genuine smile, and Jaina favored them with a smirk and raised eyebrows. Prilan glared from where he hid on a corner bunk, of course, though he tried not to let Emrael see. Prilan and Joral had been quiet since the battle at the bridge. Emrael understood; they had watched their entire contingent of Legionmen, their friends, die horribly. And now they were taking orders from those who had been their prisoners. So far, they hadn't caused any trouble, though.

Halrec spoke first. "You have got to come feel this. These bunks feel just like real feather mattresses! Or better!" He pushed on one to demonstrate, and his hand depressed into the material that Emrael had mistaken for stone. "This place is incredible, Em! If there were only food and water in here, we could stay here until those monsters lose interest and go home."

Emrael's smile turned sad. "I can't stay here, Hal. I've got to find my brother. He needs me. Needs us."

Halrec's smile faltered. "Oh. Yeah, I know, Em. I just meant . . ."

"I know what you mean, I want to be rid of those soulbound monsters as much as anyone. It'll be nice to sleep easy for a night, not waiting for those things to jump out of the forest."

He turned to where Jaina was sitting on her bunk. "What do we need to know for next time we fight these things, Jaina? Will there be more?"

"There are always more. We call them *alai'ahn* in Old Ordenan." Her voice, husky and strong, carried throughout the entire room and lent her words a mysterious tone. "The Malithii priests call them their Servants, because they are bound to obey one who wields the master to their binder."

She pulled a bracelet from her coat pocket and twirled it around one finger as she spoke. "Cut off the head or wait for them to bleed dry. They cannot be stopped any other way. But you saw that for yourself."

Emrael recognized the bracelet, an ancient-looking band of dark metal covered in angular runes. Jaina had cut it off the soulbound's arm on the bridge. "Is that a binder, Jaina?"

She nodded. "An *alai*, a soulbinder to you provincials. This is the binder you know from the stories. I've collected many." A few short strands of her straight dark hair fell into her face as she bowed her head slightly, her voice growing oddly quiet. "We—the Sacred Order of Imperators and the Ordenan Imperial Army—fight the Malithii and their armies of soulbound in the Dark Nations. We capture *alai* so the Malithii cannot create more soulbound with them. Though if they've rediscovered the making of binders, our efforts may have been for naught."

"You're telling me that not only are these fairy tales real, you've actually seen them, fought them before? On purpose?" Halrec asked, voice pitching higher and higher.

Jaina smiled sadly. "Soulbound aren't even the worst of it. The Malithii priests force their female slaves to mate with the soulbound in depraved religious ceremonies. Fewer than one in one hundred of the poor women survives the ceremony. Even fewer live to bear their twisted offspring. The result? *Sanja'ahn*, which translates roughly as 'those born in blood'. Their giant bodies are mutated by the evil that twists the soulbound, but they have the cunning of humans. The Malithii raise them to know nothing but bloodlust. Praise the Sisters we didn't encounter any of those on the bridge."

Emrael couldn't imagine having to face anything worse than the soulbound. "And you've fought these things before, too?" he asked.

Jaina nodded. "Every Imperator in the Order fights in the Dark Nations for at least two years. I've fought many soulbound and Malithii but only faced *sanja'ahn* once. It did not go well. We lost many soldiers and even Imperators." She hesitated, then said quietly, "Including my husband, Welitan."

Elle gasped. "You were married?"

Jaina nodded, face a stone mask. "I was. Welitan was an Imperator Mage-Healer, and we served our assignments in the Dark Nations together. We had been married just over a year when he was captured. The Malithii bastards overwhelmed us with *sanja'ahn,* captured him, and put a soulbinder on him before I could get to him. Once a soulbinder is activated, there is no way to recover the victim. The *alai* feed off of the life essence of their hosts, turning them into the half-dead, mindless beasts you saw."

Everyone was silent for a long moment. Jaina's face remained stoic, even as she spun a nonexistent ring around her heart finger.

Halrec broke the silence, speaking softly. "So, how did these soulbinders get here? Do we need to worry about these *sanja'ahn* making their way to the Provinces as well?"

Jaina pursed her lips. "The Malithii try to sneak a ship past the Ordenan fleet every now and then, but they have never made it to Ordena or to the Provincial mainland. Ever. The Ordenan fleet runs on *infusori*-powered engines and can move at double the speed of any other ship known, no matter the winds. The Malithii must have come here another way, and not easily. These soulbound were probably created here on the mainland with soulbinders smuggled into the Provinces. The *mentai*—mindbinders—used at the Citadel are new to me but must have been brought here in similar fashion, or even made here."

Emrael looked at her askance. "What do you mean, new to you? You said that they wouldn't hurt Ban and the others," he asked in a bit of a panic.

Jaina made calming gestures. "I was able to remove the one I found on a Master at the Citadel, with no detrimental effects. The Malithii would not be so stupid as to damage a Crafter. Besides, I've collected my share of *alai,* and they feel different. *Alai* are ancient, an age you can feel. The *mentai,* the mindbinders used at the Citadel, were newly constructed and unwieldy. I believe they were made by hand, which means that there are likely very few of them. Sisters be praised."

Everyone in the room tried not to stare at each other in the awkward silence that followed.

Emrael broke the tension with another question. "Why did the soulbound I fought at the end have black eyes and act differently?"

Her green eyes were deep and mysterious, like she was looking at them but seeing something else. "Somewhere out there, a powerful Malithii mage was controlling that group that attacked us, through their *alai*. I should have felt it sooner, when the Malithii linked itself directly to one of their soulbound." Her lips twisted into a snarl. "But I taught those on the other end a powerful lesson."

No one said much after that, and before long they all found their way to a bunk. Emrael and Elle chose narrow bunks slightly removed from where the others had already set down their things. She motioned at him with one hand. "Take your shirt off. Those stitches should be ready to come out by now."

Emrael complied quietly, still lost in thoughts of Ban and binders. In truth, his stitches could have been removed the morning after Elle had Healed him, but he hadn't had the chance to ask about it.

Elle had just started picking at the stitches—some of which were overgrown with skin and would need to be cut out—when Halrec set his things on the other side of Emrael's bunk.

"Can I bunk with you guys?" Halrec's familiar, innocent grin brought a genuine smile to Emrael's lips as well. Halrec's infectious good spirits had always been able to cheer him up, no matter how dark his mood.

"Of course, Hal. You're always welcome."

"I'll remember that."

After his stitches were out and everyone had settled down, they readied for bed, Elle doing so somewhat abashedly under a blanket. Jaina had none of the same inhibitions, stripping down to her underclothes and revealing surprisingly tan muscles and curves in plain sight of all in the room. Halrec stared as if in a trance.

Trying not to look like he had been staring as well, Emrael took off his boots and climbed onto his own bed fully dressed.

He noticed Halrec still staring wide-eyed at Jaina's impressive form, and Elle glaring pointedly at them both. Emrael shrugged a silent question with as innocent a face as he could manage and pointed at Halrec to make sure she knew it was his fault. Elle just rolled her eyes. Emrael couldn't help but smile as he settled into the strangely soft bunk that the ancients had left in this magical place.

15

Emrael snapped out of sleep into a state of heightened awareness. He could not have said what woke him, nor how much time had passed since he had lain down, but sleep fled from him in an instant.

He swung his legs out of bed, and when his bare feet hit the floor, he was surprised to find it warm to the touch. The lights in the chamber had dimmed, as if the temple itself were aware that its guests slept. This place was creepy as hell.

Even still, he could not help but be curious about the Craftings he had seen earlier in the rooms off of the main entrance chamber. If they offered him a better chance of getting Ban back, he had to take the risk. He was desperate for something, anything that would help him fight his brother's captors. He had to.

He padded on silent feet toward the main chamber and as he did, he noticed that the light coming from the script on the walls was much brighter in the main chamber than it had been. An uneasy sense of wonder filled him as he headed toward the storage rooms.

"Em?" a voice whispered.

Emrael turned quickly back toward the sleeping chambers, but no one was there. A shiver of fear quivered through him.

"Em, can you hear me?"

He looked around again. He could have sworn that was Ban's voice. Gods, he just *had* to follow Jaina into the haunted temple.

"Emrael, if you can hear me, just speak into the pendant I gave you, and be quick. I can't talk too long or the guards will hear me. I've seen others disappear for less. I can't be caught."

"Ban, is that really you?" Emrael asked, clutching the pendant next to his mouth.

"Yes! I managed to finish the pair to your pendant days ago and have been trying to contact you ever since. You must have just come within range. I knew you wouldn't abandon me," Ban whispered back.

Emrael, flooded with hope and relief at hearing his brother's voice, was instantly weighed down by guilt. "Ban . . . I had to leave to find Elle, and then we were arrested . . . I'm in Barros, about to cross into Iraea. I'm trying to find a way to come get you. Can you tell me where you are?"

Ban didn't respond.

Emrael tried again, shaking the pendant. "Ban, where are you? I need to know where you are so I can come get you."

After several more tries, Emrael sank to his knees, all energy sapped from him. Had he imagined the whole thing? Was it some trick of this place? No, that had been Ban; he was sure of it. But why had he stopped responding?

Panic struck him. What if the guards had discovered Ban talking to him? What would happen to him? He tried to convince himself that the damn pendant contraption probably just malfunctioned. Craftings could be finicky.

Finally, he stood and crossed the main hall to the rooms filled with shelves, determined to find out whether this temple had anything he could use to get his brother back. He paused in the first doorway, peering in, not knowing what to expect.

Just like every other room in this place, the storage room was much larger than it appeared at first glance. Row upon row of shelves filled the room, interspersed occasionally with chests, tables and other large containers. The memory of Jaina's strict warning paralyzed him briefly, but his curiosity quickly overcame caution and he stepped inside.

He walked slowly down the rows and rows of *infusori* Craftings. There was no dust in the storage room, but it smelled old, like a deep cave. The metal shelves that held the Craftings had a dull sheen, completely free of rust or blemish.

The Craftings themselves were of all shapes and sizes. Some were mind-bendingly intricate, while others were disappointingly simple, like small blocks of wood or metal. Many caught or reflected the glow of the ever-present blue light emanating from the engravings on the walls, but others seemed to avoid the light, almost hiding in their own shadow. He wished Ban were there to see them.

He wandered aimlessly until a small, leather-bound book caught his eye. All of the other objects had been hopelessly foreign to him, so it was a relief to finally find a familiar item.

He reached for the book, apprehensive about what might happen. When he set his hand on it, however, nothing happened. It felt the same as dozens of other books he had handled in the library back at the Citadel.

He picked up the small volume, undid the clasp that held it

closed, and opened the book to a page near the beginning. A bright light flashed in his eyes, and he fell to one knee, still holding the book open to the same page. Panic filled him briefly but faded as his attention was consumed.

The blinding white that filled his eyes cleared to reveal three figures so resplendent that at first, Emrael thought his vision had stayed white.

As the vision brought the figures into focus, he saw that they were stark white. Not fair-skinned—they shone faintly, as if they were actually *made* of light. Myriad hues of color shimmered through their skin as they moved. Perhaps most interesting to Emrael, they all had pure white hair, though none showed any sign of advanced age.

The three magnificent figures—Beings—stood together at the peak of a tall mountain, huddled together as a massive storm rolled across the pinnacle. Constant flashes of lightning so thick that they seemed to consume the sky blinded Emrael as they arced down from the heavens and struck the earth like crushing footsteps of a mad giant. He could feel the thunder reverberate through him, filling him with visceral panic and fear.

The vision blurred, and Emrael sensed that a great deal of time had passed before the vision cleared again. Everything was much as it had been, except that the mountain had been carved into a massive granite palace. The three Beings stood outside, the two females confronting the lone male. A small cluster of what looked to be ordinary human men and women had gathered behind the male Being, as if for protection.

"This is not a place for such creatures! They are dangerous, Glory!" one of the two female Beings shouted.

"They are *ours*!" the lone male Being cried. "They belong here as much as we do, Justice. Mercy, please, make her see reason!"

"I will sweep them from this world, Glory, and you would be wise to stand clear," Justice said. Mercy stood silent.

As if bidden by the furious Being called Justice, a storm harsher than any Emrael had seen gathered around the mountain palace.

Glory stepped in front of Justice and shouted his defiance as Justice channeled the fury of the storm in an attempt to cast him from their mountain home. Glory stood his ground, but as bolts of lightning and arcs of pure *infusori* struck him, he eventually fell to his knees and began screaming in agony. His form of pure light smoldered to an ashen grey, and the hair was burned from his head. Strange symbols shone in his now-ashen skin, scars burned by the terrible forces the other God wielded.

The two female Gods approached the God of Glory. Justice spoke once more, her face an uncaring mask, her voice mellow as a summer pond. "This is your own doing, Glory." She struck him, knocking him to all fours on the stones of the mountain palace's approach, then tipped his chin upward to stare into his eyes. "Your vanity and love for your creations have been your downfall. You know as well as I that the Accord forbids this. I Bind you to this world, never to leave. Time flows slowly here, so slowly that your mind will rot with the ache of it. And as reward for your love, every Age, one of your pets will we raise up to challenge you. So, Glory begets Glory, and you will reap your Just reward."

Justice turned from him. Glory feebly stretched out a hand toward Mercy, whose face shone wet with tears. But still Mercy stood mute. The Absent Gods wrapped themselves in another storm and, when it passed, were gone.

—◦—

Emrael slowly returned to reality as the book in his hands snapped shut and the vision was cut off. It took him a moment to realize that Elle was standing in front of him in her underclothes, whispering urgently, a worried look on her face.

Her features were hidden in the shadows cast by the odd light coming from the inscriptions in the walls, but her eyes mirrored the muted light beautifully. They were much the same color.

"Em! Emrael, what is the matter with you? Put down that book and say something! Mistress Jaina said these things can be dangerous!"

Emrael blinked, his mind struggling to grasp the implications of what he had just seen. Could he have just witnessed the Fall of Glory? He had never believed in any gods, but what he'd just seen had felt so real. He fingered the symbols on the cover of the book again. They looked an awful lot like those that Justice and Mercy had burned into Fallen Glory in the vision, an awful lot like the runic script on the walls of this temple.

But what did it matter even if the vision was real? What had the Gods ever had to do with him? He put it from his mind as best he could and turned his attention to Elle.

He shook his head, clearing the last of the fog from his mind. "Sorry, Elle. This book . . . it's incredible. I just saw . . . I'm not sure what I saw, but I think I might have just seen the Fall of Glory."

Elle glanced from him to the book and back skeptically. "You aren't making sense, Em. You were just standing there, staring at the wall. You never even blinked."

"It was unbelievable, Elle. When I opened the book, I saw this vision like it was really happening, like I was there, only I wasn't. I was floating above them, and the Gods came down in a huge storm. Glory did something to upset the other two, and they burned him and left him here."

"Huh," she said, wide-eyed with skepticism. "May I see?"

He passed the book to her and waited expectantly. She opened it but immediately fixed him with a reproachful glare.

"Was this some odd joke?"

"What? No, Elle, I swear." He cleared his throat and deepened his voice to a normal level. "I don't know how it works, but I'm not lying to you. I saw it. I think . . . I think it's sort of like a history book but *infusori*-Crafted somehow, or maybe even some other kind of magic . . ."

She pursed her lips, though skepticism had faded from her features. After a moment, she shrugged and handed the book back to him. "There's no such thing as *magic*, Em. But . . . what did they look like?"

"Well, they were like, clear. And really bright. Mercy and Justice had long hair and . . . uh . . . female figures. Just like the Ordenans have claimed about their Silent Sisters. Glory—the Fallen, I guess—was definitely a man, though. Male. Whatever."

"They weren't faceless, then, like the Sentinels claim? Clearly women?"

"I mean, they were different from any woman I ever saw, but yeah, definitely women."

Elle said nothing but clutched the charm on the necklace she wore, two joined circles meant to represent the unknowable Holy Departed. After a moment, she took it off and set it on a nearby shelf.

Emrael tucked the small book into a pocket in his pants and rubbed his hands together.

"So?" he asked awkwardly.

Elle looked down for a moment before looking at him again. She crossed her arms and huddled in on herself slightly, as if suddenly embarrassed at her lack of clothing. "I just heard you get up, and when you didn't come back, I thought I should check on you. You've been out here a long time."

"Oh," he replied lamely. "I couldn't sleep and decided to come see what was out here."

He perked up, remembering his conversation with his brother. "Oh! Ban talked to me through this thing when I was out in the main chamber," he said, showing her the pendant, "then I found the book, and I guess I lost track of time."

Elle raised her eyebrows. "Ban said his Observer would only work within a distance of ten or twenty leagues. We're probably a hundred leagues or more away from the Citadel. He talked to you over all that distance?"

"Only for a moment. He said he had finished my pendant's pairing. He thought we were coming to save him and was afraid he would get caught talking to me. Then he just stopped talking. I didn't even get to ask him where he is."

Rather than looking excited as Emrael had expected, she looked concerned. "Well, it's good you at least got to hear him. We know he's okay now. I can't say the same for my sister."

Emrael bowed his head. "I suppose."

Elle took his hand. "No use moping about it. I'm awake now, so we might as well have a look around."

"But I thought you said they were too dangerous."

"No, I said *Jaina* thinks they are dangerous. *I* am an accomplished Crafter. *I* can do whatever I want." She flashed a mischievous smile and started down the rows.

He stepped quickly to keep pace with her. She stopped every now and then to pick something up and turn it about, a look of concentration on her face. Occasionally she would murmur a long *hmmm*. To Emrael, it seemed as though she was picking them at random.

"What are you looking for, Elle?" he finally asked.

She looked at him in mock surprise. "Can't you feel the Craftings? Some mage you are."

A spike of shame lanced through him, but he smiled anyway. "I can't Craft any better than I could before, Elle. I might have some ability as a mage, apparently, but I've never been good with Craftings. I can't feel anything with these things—I'm not as talented as you are."

She stopped to study him.

"Do you think my father would be a good farmer?" she asked finally.

"Uh . . . what?"

"Do you think my father would make a good farmer?" she repeated. "If we put him in a field right now, do you think he could produce a good harvest?"

"What's this got to do with anything? Were you even listening to what I said?"

"Just answer the question," she said patiently.

He gave her a flat stare. "Fine. No, he would not be a good farmer at all. He's too fat, for one thing, and likely doesn't know the first thing about agriculture."

Elle's lips curved into an amused smile. "Actually, he makes it his business to know many things about agriculture. But you are right, he would not be a very good farmer, at least not at first. Why not?"

He felt at this point that it was very probable that this conversation was a trap of some sort, the kind designed to make him look foolish, or rude. "Because he has never had to actually work to get food?" he said slowly, carefully, waiting for her reaction.

She bared her white teeth in a pleased grin. "Exactly right. And you can't Craft for exactly the same reason. You have never needed to. It's the same reason I'm a much better Crafter than Sami. I want it; I *need* it if I'm going to make something of myself. But you've always planned on a military career, and you've always been so good that you haven't needed to learn Crafting. Sami has her future guaranteed for her, either as governess or as the next Lord Governor's wife, as she chooses, so she has never needed to learn, either. Anyone can learn. Especially you, now that you have the ability to wield *infusori*. I'm sure it is just a simple matter of focus, study, and effort to learn to Craft using that ability."

She took his hand and placed it on a small, round stone vial she had been holding. "What do you feel?"

He paused for a moment, trying to feel. "I don't feel anything, Elle." He shook his head.

"Try harder. Close your eyes. Try to feel it the same way you feel anything else to do with *infusori*. But don't activate it," she warned.

As if he would know how to activate a Crafting he had never seen.

He gripped the smooth, carved-stone vial in his hand and closed his eyes. He tried to project himself, his senses with which he detected *infusori* to the vial, and thought he felt it grow warm. He kept waiting for something more, something like what he had felt when he had done *infusori* exercises with Jaina, but nothing came.

He opened his eyes and looked down sadly at Elle. "I'm sorry, Elle, all I felt was that it got warm. Nothing else, and I could have imagined even that. I don't think I have the talent for it."

She rolled her eyes. "What did you think you were looking for, you great oaf? That warmth is all I feel from Craftings used for healing. It's all anyone feels. You just need to know what to look for. Some Craftings, like ones that aid in healing, give off physical feelings. Yet others give emotional ones. Some don't have any perceptible feeling, though I have a suspicion that one simply needs to learn what to look for, as you just have with healing Craftings."

"Where did you learn all this, Elle? Did Master Yerdon teach this? Why would I have not even heard of it?"

"Because you weren't interested. Did you ever inquire? Do you think it wise for the instructors to be teaching these things to just anybody? The worst idiots are the ones who are too quick to believe that they understand the whole of a thing. I'm only touching the Craftings that I can feel are for healing. The others truly could be dangerous. They could even be activated without touching them or using *infusori*, so only touch the ones I touch."

"You can feel it before you even touch it?"

She nodded nonchalantly.

His eyes narrowed. "I'm going to have a talk with Jaina about why I wasn't told any of this. All this time, I thought I couldn't Craft, when I just didn't know what to look for. Some instructor she is."

Elle bit her lip. "Ah. That may not be such a good idea. It wasn't Yerdon who taught me. It wasn't anyone at the Citadel."

She paused, but he just looked at her impatiently.

"It was your mother."

He must not have heard right. "My mother showed you all of that?"

She nodded slightly.

He clenched his jaw and stood silently, staring at Elle but not really seeing her. His whole world was turning upside down. His brother was being held prisoner, and apparently his mother had trusted others with her true identity—but hadn't trusted him.

"Why?" he asked softly.

Elle's expression was full of sympathy, as if she wanted to comfort him, but she remained where she was. "Because I want to be a healer. Your mother does wonderful things, Em. She is the best healer I have ever met, better by far than Master Yerdon. She can Heal without any healing Craftings, even. Like the Imperators Jaina told us about."

"I know she's a good healer, Elle. First, Jaina tells me she's a mage and a leader of some sort in Ordena; now you tell me she's been teaching you about Craftings all these years. I know I didn't spend much time with her after joining the Junior Legion, but how could I not even know what she is? Who she is? She's my mother, for Mercy's sake."

Elle looked down at her feet and shuffled them a bit. "She taught Ban some things, too. Some of our lessons with her were held together. She made us promise not to tell anyone about what she taught us, and made Ban swear not to tell even you. He wanted to, Em, but she made us promise. It could have gotten her in serious trouble. And you never showed an interest in much outside the Junior Legion."

Emrael put a hand over his eyes. "Am I crazy to think it's odd that she wouldn't tell me all these things about herself, though? Especially when she told you? My own mother?" he asked again.

"I don't know, Em." She placed a warm hand on his upper arm. "Maybe she didn't want your father to know, or perhaps mine. Not everyone is accepting of mages, let alone Imperators, even in our day and age. They might have prosecuted her, wife of the Commander First or no."

He nodded finally and covered her hand with one of his own. "I'll have a good talk with her about it someday, assuming she ever returns from Ordena."

He looked up to find her staring at him. He stared back for a long moment. "You're pretty damn incredible, you know that? I still can't believe it took me so long to realize it."

"You've said that before."

"Yeah, well . . ."

She giggled, squeezing his hand. "I don't mind it." She stood and stepped closer. "Just don't forget it."

She grabbed his head, pulled his face down to her, and stepped close to press her lips to his. Her hair tickled his face as they kissed, but he didn't mind at all.

Some time later—how long, he couldn't have told you—Elle pulled away but kept her face just inches from his. Her breath came fast, her smile mischievous. "Come on. We should get some rest. We can continue this when we've got a little more privacy."

Emrael let her pull him to the main hall. His heart still raced. He couldn't think straight with Elle's warm hand still in his.

As they crossed the hall, his gaze drifted to the stone doors sealing another nearby room. He let go of Elle's hand and walked over to the door. "Give me just a minute. I want to see what they keep behind locked doors."

He ran his hand down the smooth stone of the door and along the edges where it met the wall. There were no detectable hinges or keyholes. Nothing to suggest that this was a door, in fact, except for a slight seam in the rock that was exactly the shape of the doorways in the rest of the temple.

He closed his eyes and concentrated on the stone. It felt almost like some of the Craftings in the storage room had but somehow more compelling. His focus wavered for a moment when he heard Elle approach, but he turned his thoughts immediately back to his task.

When he had opened the tunnel door that led to Sarlon's house, he had felt something, a mechanism that had undoubtedly been built into the door that seemed somehow more receptive to the *infusori* he had wielded. He couldn't have explained it in words, but he remembered the feeling. He started to gather his own *infusori*, his life source, but soon realized that he felt energy all around him—a vast amount of *infusori*, far more than he had felt since being awakened to his ability as a mage. The *infusori* contained in *infusori* coils or even in the life essence of a human was minuscule compared to the power all around him. He did not understand how he had not felt it before. He lost himself for a moment just basking in it, feeling it pulse and course through him as he opened himself to it instinctively.

"Em?" Elle's voice was urgent and trembled with a hint of fear. "What's going on? What are you doing? Your hair is glowing."

He opened his eyes to look at her, and her breath caught. He could see the reflection of his eyes in hers, glowing brightly the same pure, pale blue as the inscriptions in the walls. The color of *infusori*. The color of power.

He smiled and put his hand to the door, knowing nothing could stand in his way. The ecstasy of power ran through him like lifeblood.

He found the actuation point in the door quite easily and wondered why he had experienced so much trouble finding it before. In the next instant, he perceived that the entire door would absorb his *infusori* if he pushed hard enough.

He pushed *infusori* into the countless number of tiny nodes he could now feel in the stone, then jumped back in surprise as the door exploded away from him in a shower of rubble. His ears rang and the cloud of dust—the only dust he had seen in this place—sent him into a fit of coughing. Through the ringing in his ears, he could hear Elle coughing as well and turned to check on her in a panic. She hunched over coughing, but to his great relief, she appeared unharmed.

His hearing had just begun to return when they heard the slaps of bare feet on the floor behind them. They turned to find Halrec, half-dressed, sword in hand and a confused look on his face. Jaina was not far behind, though thankfully she had taken the time to don a shirt instead of padding out in her underclothes. Emrael heard a squeak behind him and turned to find Elle huddled behind him, embarrassed about being in only her night clothes. He chuckled as he tugged his shirt off and handed it to Elle, who pulled it hastily over her head. It only fell midway down her thighs, but it was better than nothing, he supposed. She straightened the shirt, pulled it as low as she could, then stepped confidently up beside him as if nothing were the matter.

The others were gathering groggily behind Jaina, whose expression had turned decidedly flat as she watched the exchange between Emrael and Elle.

"What did you do?" Jaina asked, accusation plain in her tone.

"It's not what it looks like—" Elle began, cutting off as Emrael laid a hand on her shoulder.

Emrael met Jaina's eyes confidently. "I couldn't sleep, so I came to take a look around. Elle came to find me, and when we came to this closed door, I tried to push it open using the *infusori* from the temple." He gestured with one hand at the glowing inscriptions in the walls. "I didn't know what I was doing, and it exploded. I'm sorry, Jaina. The fault is all mine."

Jaina's eyes had widened as he spoke, and her mouth had opened slightly. "You used the *infusori* directly from the Well?" she asked in a quiet voice, almost as if speaking to herself.

Emrael shrugged. "I guess so?"

"Glory take the Sisters," Jaina mumbled, now squinting at him as if seeing him for the first time.

They stared at each other for a long moment until Master Yerdon pushed his way forward from the back of the group. "No one is hurt?" He looked to Elle, who shook her head. "Well, then, that's what's important." The kindly old man looked to Jaina. "Should we get a move on, then? I feel rested enough to continue."

Jaina finally looked away from Emrael and sighed. "Yes, we may as well. Let's eat and gather our things. I'll be there in a minute."

She walked slowly toward Emrael and Elle. Emrael tensed, anticipating an outburst similar to the one the day before. He watched her warily, but she only inspected the rubble for a moment before turning to regard him gravely.

"Show me."

"Uh . . . what?" He had expected a harsh reprimand, not to be asked to repeat his idiocy.

"Show me what you did."

He looked at her warily before stepping up to the next in the row of stone doors in the chamber. He closed his eyes as before, searching for the actuation point in the door, trying to open himself to the power he had felt just moments ago.

He broke into a nervous sweat, acutely aware of Jaina's scrutiny and worried about what her reaction would be to his defacing of her temple.

After an uncomfortably long time, he finally felt the *infusori* from the Well. He forgot his anxiety as he was flooded with its vibrating power. He opened his eyes and could once again see the reflection of his brightly glowing irises in the eyes of the two women. Jaina stared at him with wide eyes for a moment before moving quickly to take his hand, still staring into his eyes.

Just as before, when she had led him through *infusori* exercises in the forest outside Myntar, Emrael opened himself to Jaina, and immediately felt the life essence contained within her, her emotions, everything.

Why would she be excited, nervous? He had expected her to be furious with him.

Jaina's eyes widened as she presumably felt his emotions as well. Could she feel what he felt, the enormous power surging through him, the urge to use it?

Her eyes closed in rapture for a moment, but when they opened, her gaze had hardened.

"You must not use your abilities here, Emrael, and you must not tell anyone about this, not even Sarlon. Not yet. You must learn to control the vast amounts of *infusori* you wield first. Release it," she commanded.

He reacted instinctively to the tone of authority in her voice, the same tone he had obeyed countless times on the practice field. Still, he was slow to release the *infusori*, slow to give up its magnificent power. He finally let it slip away and relaxed to the point that he could no longer feel its beckoning pulse. Once the energy had drained from him, he became extremely self-conscious about what had just happened. He started slowly toward the sleeping chamber, not meeting anyone's eye.

Halrec snorted from across the room. "Em, your hair was as bright as a coil. You've got to show me how to do that."

Emrael looked up to meet his friend's eyes, and his lips tugged upward in a smile. He had been particularly worried about the rift that his newfound ability might create between him and his old friend. Even he was surprised at the relief he felt that nothing had damped his friend's exuberance.

"Yeah, sure, Hal. I don't know much, though. Not yet." He stared at Jaina's back as she passed through the arched doorway into the sleeping chamber. He would learn to use his newfound power, no matter the risk. His brother might depend on it.

16

Several more days of hard hiking carried Emrael and his friends to the Low Road that paralleled the River Stem on the northern edge of the lower Stemwood Forest. Prilan—who had spent the entire trek attempting to regain Elle's attention by walking behind her and making awkward attempts at conversation—grumbled when Emrael didn't call for a halt until well after dark, even after reaching the Low Road. Emrael ignored him. Hearing Ban's voice inside the temple had ignited a fire in Emrael that refused to be damped. He wasn't about to slow down for the likes of Prilan, or anybody else, for that matter.

Emrael and Halrec scouted the bank of the Stem while the others set up camp well away from the road. They stood shoulder to shoulder for several minutes, staring at the far bank. The pale blue light of the full moon shone off the slowly churning water, creating a surreal, dreamlike scene.

Iraea. They had grown up begging stories of their ancestral homeland from their fathers and other older Iraeans, and had invented their own fictional futures in which they became heroes who liberated Iraea from Provincial rule. Halrec's family was very similar to Emrael's own—his grandfather had been one of the seven Lords of Iraea and had sent his family with Emrael's when they sought sanctuary in Barros.

"You think we'll ever actually do it?" Emrael asked quietly.

Halrec grunted. "Do what?"

"Take our grandfathers' titles and lands back. Become Lords Holder. Free Iraea. All the stuff we talked about when we were kids."

Halrec laughed then. "Em, that's crazy. How would we even go about starting something like that? We don't mean anything to those people. Besides, from what I hear, my uncle has a very firm grip on his Holding, and the Sentinels and their Watchers all but rule from Ire's End."

"Yeah, you're right," Emrael replied, even as he remembered his father telling him that the people of Iraea had written to him, asking him to take back the crown. "Not yet," he murmured.

When they returned to find the others, they found Joral and Prilan just outside of camp, sparring with wooden swords cut from tree branches by the bright light of the full moon. Emrael and Halrec shared a predatory look before fashioning their own tree limbs into practice swords and moving to join them. "Justicer, may we join you?"

Joral's eyebrows jumped in feigned surprise. "You boys sure you're up for an ass-kicking?" He chuckled at his own joke. Prilan snickered, obviously misinterpreting the Justicer's humor as genuine bravado.

Halrec flexed the hand that bore the wolf's-head mark and started to say something, but Emrael silenced his friend by laying a restraining hand on his shoulder. "We'd love to try," he said as mildly as he could manage, trying to keep himself from smirking.

They separated, Emrael motioning to Prilan and walking several paces to one side. He turned and waited expectantly.

Prilan sneered but followed, leaving Joral to square off with Halrec.

Emrael drew his half of a dueling square and Prilan finished his own. They turned to each other and saluted crisply. Prilan's eyes glittered as they stalked toward each other.

The two of them came together, and Emrael met Prilan's strikes with a series of neat parries, sliding the blade aside each time, never allowing his opponent's sword near him.

They separated briefly, and a small smile came to Prilan's lips. The poor bastard thought he was doing well.

When they met again at the center of the square, Prilan's strikes came faster than before, faster than Emrael had thought the captain was capable of. Emrael's senses heightened, his body responding to the possibility of defeat.

Deliberate thought fled his mind as he became absorbed in the struggle. He took up the offensive, feinting and weaving, striking and dodging, faster and faster. The rapid *clack* of wood striking wood sang in his ears.

He soon pushed Prilan into a defensive position at the edge of the square. A small, remote part of Emrael's mind was surprised, almost impressed by the skill that Prilan displayed. Perhaps there was more to this pompous ass than he had thought.

In the next exchange, he managed to unbalance the captain

slightly. It was enough. He slipped inside Prilan's blade, secured his weapon arm, and twisted.

He outweighed the captain by a fair amount, though the captain stood several inches taller than he. He used all of that weight advantage to fling Prilan over his hip and to the ground, securing his weapon arm all the while.

Air left Prilan's lungs in a heavy grunt as he hit the ground. Emrael stood over the captain, sword at his throat. The glare from the coughing man was more hateful than ever. He clearly expected some form of further abuse after the loss to Emrael.

Instead of gloating, however, Emrael offered his hand to the man. He almost laughed aloud at the confusion in Prilan's eyes.

Prilan slowly took his hand as if expecting a trick but was soon back on his feet, taking deep breaths and rolling the shoulder that had hit the ground.

Halrec and Joral were still sparring, which surprised Emrael. He would have bet a lot of money—if he had any—on Halrec winning quickly.

As he watched, Halrec gained speed, his practice blade becoming a blur as he moved from one strike to the next.

Joral met each stroke with increasing tension and difficulty. Just as it seemed he would be overcome by Halrec's attack, however, the crafty Justicer dipped out of range from Halrec's sword, throwing Halrec off balance just a hair.

Joral's front foot shot forward and hit Halrec's knee, which had straightened in an attempt to extend his attack.

Halrec's leg buckled, throwing him further off balance. The sparring match ended with Joral's blade resting against Halrec's neck.

Emrael's mouth opened in shock.

Emrael expected Halrec to be upset—he would have been in his place, upset with himself at least—but to his surprise, Halrec let out a short, deep bark of a laugh. "Well done, Joral. I should have expected a few tricks from an old dog like you." He waggled his finger at him as they separated. "It won't happen again," he promised good-naturedly.

Joral flashed a ragged smile. "Young pups like you always think that." He looked toward Prilan, who blushed.

"You man enough for another round?" Emrael asked, throwing a questioning glance toward Prilan, whose mouth twisted like he had tasted something sour even as he nodded. He glared at Emrael as they drew up and saluted once more.

The other man's arrogance sparked something fierce within Emrael, a primal instinct that screamed at him to put this pampered bastard in his place.

Prilan feinted and struck toward Emrael, obviously anticipating a match similar to the last, a game of speed and skill.

Emrael waited until the last moment, goading Prilan into over-extending. When he did, Emrael turned aside, evading the attack, then struck downward onto the other man's practice blade. Hard.

The force of the strike snapped Prilan's practice sword in two, the pieces flying to the ground.

Prilan clutched his sword hand. Emrael knew from painful experience that it would be throbbing unbearably.

Emrael quickly reined in his emotions and again stopped himself from doing anything that Prilan would undoubtedly interpret as ridicule or gloating. He wanted this horse's ass to know his place, not to make a mortal enemy of him, especially since they were going to be sharing a camp for Gods only knew how long.

He nodded to Prilan, and they once again spectated the end of Joral and Halrec's match.

This time, Halrec refused to be drawn into any unwieldy attacks. The contest lasted even longer than the first but ended when Halrec caught Joral parrying a fraction of a second late and made him pay for it with a strike to the arm.

The four of them returned to camp, Halrec, Joral, and Emrael bantering and sharing tips while Prilan traipsed along in sullen silence.

They arrived in camp to find the others sitting around a small campfire dug into a deep pit to avoid detection. They hadn't seen any sign of pursuers, but everyone was quick to exercise caution, the memory of the soulbound fresh in their minds.

"We've only jerky and trail biscuits for supper again," Elle mourned.

Emrael grunted, smiling. "We knew things would get tight, but we'll survive. I hate bad food as much as anybody, but we'll be back to civilization soon. Besides, it might do you good to experience life outside a palace for a few days. My lady," he finished with a mocking bow.

Jaina emerged from the trees as Elle playfully feigned outrage and prepared a retort. She held three large trout threaded on a piece of rope in her hand. "I suppose I should go throw these back in the river, then?"

Elle laughed with joy, and Emrael couldn't help but join her.

"Give them here," he told Jaina. "I've still got some salt in my pack. I should be able to make something of these fish. Pity I don't have any spices to work with. I'd kill to be back in the Citadel kitchens."

"Perhaps it might do you good to experience life outside a palace for a few days," Elle mimicked sarcastically.

Emrael rolled his eyes and started cleaning the fish with his belt knife.

After Emrael had roasted the fish over the fire and everyone had their share on their plates, they settled in around the campfire.

Emrael grinned at Elle around a mouthful of tender fish. It was the best thing he had tasted in a long while. "We should reach a town with a ferry around midafternoon tomorrow, right?"

Elle nodded. "If you've led us due north like you claim to have, it should be about five leagues west. I'll be glad to see a bit of civilization again, even if it is just a small ferry town."

"I'm an excellent navigator, thank you. We'll be warm and well fed tomorrow, then we'll be to Whitehall in no time. But this is likely not the last night we'll spend outside, eating whatever we can catch."

Elle just glared at him.

Emrael chuckled darkly. "It will get a lot worse than this before it gets better."

—

As the fire burned down to coals and the last of the group began seeking their bedrolls, Jaina approached Emrael. "Come with me. Time to train."

"I sparred with the Legionmen earlier. It's late, Jaina."

She punched his shoulder. "You should be ready to train anytime, lazy boy. You still have much to learn. But it is not physical training of which I speak." She strode farther into the forest without another word.

Emrael looked to where Elle had made her bed, but she appeared to be asleep. He had taken to making his bed near hers, but it didn't appear she cared too much about that tonight.

He caught up to Jaina, who stood quietly among the trees, waiting. She stepped up to Emrael. She did not give any instruction, simply offered her hands and closed her eyes. He removed his pendant and took her hands.

He once again felt his senses extend to feel the *infusori* in Jaina through the contact of their hands. He felt the same affinity, the familiarity he had felt when they had connected before.

The experience felt much the same, only neither of them pushed at each other as they had in the woods outside Myntar. Jaina seemed to have a much more rigid wall between him and her emotions this time. He tried to project a feeling of resistance between Jaina and his emotions, his life source. Somehow, he doubted that his was nearly so solid.

After several long moments, his attention began to drift, and he began to wonder why Jaina did nothing. He reached slowly and, without truly thinking about what he was doing, pushed at Jaina's barrier.

All at once, he heard a grunt of surprise from Jaina as a flood of emotions poured through the gap he had created in her mental wall. Prickly irritation, sharp anger, solid determination, and even soft, warm love were present. But what caught his attention were the pulsing emotions that lay beneath them all.

Paralyzing fear and doubt—emotions he never would have associated with her—coursed through his mentor. He opened his eyes and peered into hers, feeling her emotions at the same time. He felt as if he were seeing into her soul—if such a thing existed.

Her eyes were wide, but they narrowed slightly in determined concentration. He felt Jaina push back with her *infusori* senses through their still-clasped hands.

The attack hit him hard, unprepared as he was, and next he knew, he was sprawled backward over a log. He coughed, struggling to catch his breath.

"What in Glory's name was that?" he croaked, still lying on his back.

"Your first lesson. This is dangerous in more ways than you might imagine." He could *hear* the smirk in her voice.

He rolled onto his knees and stood quickly. "Again?"

He was relieved to see her eyes soften as she smiled. If he was going to learn to harness *infusori*, he had best stay on Jaina's good side.

He took her hands again and lowered any barrier to his emotions, hoping that his sincerity would shine through.

Jaina did not retract her hands, nor did she look away from his gaze, but she made no effort toward him with her *infusori* senses, at least that he could tell. He thought she might be blushing.

A thought occurred to him, and he carefully tried to *pull* at her awareness, inviting her to feel his emotions. Her eyes widened again in surprise, but she did not resist. After a moment, she smiled, nodded, and even gave him a short but forceful hug, more affection than she had ever shown him in years of mentorship.

They separated, and Jaina motioned for him to sit. He settled himself on a nearby log.

"That was good, Emrael. You are learning control. Just to keep you humble, I will demonstrate a small portion of what my Order can teach you if you will accompany me to Ordena."

She whipped out a strip of cloth, nothing more than a dust rag. It hung limp from her hand, stirring occasionally in the light breeze that swept through the moonlit trees.

Without warning, the cloth stiffened into a thin, rigid blade shape. She held it out, allowing him to touch the cloth. It still felt like cloth but was as if it had been starched a hundred times over until it was stiff as a board. Emrael tried to bend it, and a small piece broke free.

"Hmm," he grunted in interest. "How did you do that?"

As was her way, her only response was to smile and crack the cloth like a whip, and with a burst of *infusori*, it returned to its original limp state.

Her hand dipped into a pocket to retrieve a small *infusori* coil that dimmed noticeably as she drew *infusori* from it. Dropping the cloth, she held out her hand, palm to the sky. The skin of her palm suddenly burned with an intense pale blue light, illuminating the dark forest. She closed her hand, and he blinked away the burning afterimage.

Just as he regained his sight, Jaina dropped in a crouch to set her fingertips lightly on the cloth she had dropped a moment earlier.

As soon as her fingertips came in contact with the cloth, it burst into flame.

Emrael realized his mouth was hanging open and closed it.

He looked back to Jaina just as she drew her belt knife and laid it flat on her open palm. He peered at it, not sure what to expect. He almost didn't believe it when Jaina's body jolted backward slightly and the knife shot forward, sinking to the hilt in a tree not far from where Emrael sat. His stared at her wide-eyed, frozen in place in surprise.

"Absent Gods," he breathed, looking from the smoldering pile of ash to the knife planted in the tree.

Emrael stalked over to the tree to inspect the knife. He gave it a tug, but it didn't budge. He took a firm grip on the leather-wrapped handle, braced his other arm on the tree and heaved with all his might. It still didn't move.

He swore as he desisted from trying to pull the knife from the tree. He stared over his shoulder at his mentor in disbelief. How had she thrown the knife with such force, without even moving her arm? She had been too far away for him to feel much other than a great deal of *infusori* being used.

Jaina paced easily to the tree, drew *infusori* until her coil went dull, and wrenched the blade free with one quick jerk.

This time, he had been close enough to feel more of what she had done. As she had pulled, she had also released energy that seemed to pulse through her entire body instead of just from her hand.

"Absent Gods," he repeated, stunned. "You've got to show me how to do that."

Her tinkling laugh echoed through the moonlit forest. "You truly believe that I can teach this safely in one evening? Adorable. Learning these skills safely is a long, controlled process. All in due time, my young mageling. All in due time."

Emrael shook his head in frustration. There was so much he needed to learn, and he had little patience for Jaina's rules. If he knew how to use that kind of power, he might be able to break Ban out of Whitehall or the Citadel on his own.

"Jaina?"

"Yes?"

"Will I ever earn a Master's Mark from you?"

Jaina pulled up her sleeve to show her tattooed Mark earned as a Master of War, though the Mark she had received in her native Ordena differed significantly from those given at the Citadel. The detailed tattoo covered a large portion of her right forearm, two crossed swords inscribed inside a circle of runes. Runes that he now recognized as being quite similar to those that had circumscribed the walls inside the Ravan temple.

"I think you are nearly deserving of a Mark from a Master of the Citadel, Emrael. But this Mark, it is so much more than the Mark of a mercenary you would have received at the Citadel. It is the Mark of an Imperator and is the only Mark I will give you. In time. It will be a symbol of your power, your mastery of the Art, as mine is. You have no need for a Mark from the Citadel any longer."

She patted him on the shoulder and stalked back to the camp, leaving him to stew in his thoughts. His whole life, he had wanted to earn a Mark from the Citadel like his father had. But what she had just shown him, that *magic* . . . that was his life now. He still had a long way to go.

Jaina had already wrapped her blanket around herself when he made it back to camp. Everyone else lay sleeping except Halrec, who was still on watch out near the road.

Emrael didn't feel like sleeping just yet, so he sat next to the fire, now just heaps of glowing coals. He picked up a nearby stick and fiddled with it as he thought. How would he light something on fire as Jaina had done?

Curious, he drew *infusori* from within himself and began pouring it into the stick, in a similar fashion to what he had done to the stone door in the temple. The stick grew warm but nowhere near warm enough to ignite.

Perplexed, he looked down at the stick in his hands. He concentrated on infusing as much energy as he could into the small piece of wood but met with little success. He only managed to elicit small wisps of smoke before he had leached enough *infusori* out of himself that he began to feel light-headed and sick to his stomach.

A deep breath and a few muttered curses helped calm his frustration, and he sat staring blankly into the coals for a time. *Why can I blow down stone doors but can't even light a simple flame?*

He remembered the sensation of opening himself to the power around him, delving into the stone slab door, feeling its internal structure on a level he had previously been unable to comprehend.

He opened himself similarly to the embers popping with heat before him. Not just to the heat emanating from the burning wood, but to the wood itself.

Something was happening to the wood in conjunction with the release of heat as it burned. He had seen wood burn so many times that he had taken the process for granted, but now he could *feel* it happening.

He had been trying to force *infusori* into the entire mass of wood at once, but fire only burned a small portion of the wood at one time. The *infusori* transfer needed to be concentrated in order to release the energy stored within the wood.

His attention snapped back to the present, and he concentrated on the stick once more.

Instead of trying to focus his *infusori* on the stick as a whole, he touched his finger to the branch and focused on a small spot, pushing what little *infusori* he had left into a point smaller than his fingertip, just on the surface of the branch's rough bark.

Tongues of flame flared from the pine branch, turning it into a short-lived torch. Emrael jerked his hand back with a startled cry.

The putrid stench of burned hair filled the air as he smiled triumphantly, watching the small branch burn.

17

They entered the small town called Ben's Crossing after a long day of walking the river road, watching the occasional boat drift down the broad, deep blue ribbon of water—when they weren't busy nervously scanning the woods around them.

The small town sat between the Low Road and the river, with two ferries moored at weathered wooden docks. Several dozen sprawling houses and half as many shops surrounded a vastly over-grown farmhouse that served as an inn. The smell of wet wood and half-rotten fish permeated the air.

Two young girls skipped through the grass beside the dirt road in front of the inn as Emrael and the group approached. They teased and poked at a boy who seemed torn between embarrassment and eagerness at playing with the two girls. Every few moments, laughter would erupt from the girls and the boy would halfheartedly attempt to chase one or both of them, smiling sheepishly all the while.

The scene reminded Emrael of when he and Ban had been that age, playing in the Legion compound and palace grounds in Naeran with Halrec, Elle, and Sami. Now Ban was likely locked up like an animal, forced to build Crafted weapons for Corrande and his armies.

Despair chilled his mood, but he steeled himself quickly. No matter the odds, he couldn't leave Ban in the hands of the Watchers and their Sentinel priests, not to mention the Malithii bastards. He couldn't leave anyone to that fate.

They arrived at the inn, which looked comically slapped together but well kept and inviting nonetheless. He smelled worse than a pair of rancid boots and urgently needed a bath. And a hot meal. For all his teasing of Elle, he was tired of hard trail biscuits and salted meat too. Maybe whoever passed for a cook there would even let him prepare something himself. That would be a treat—for him and likely for everyone else.

Emrael and the others stamped their way through the free-swinging double front doors of the sprawling inn, and immediately the smell of roasting meat and baking bread made his mouth water.

Counting his meager funds through the thin leather of his coin purse brought him back to reality quickly. He could feel a few marks and several smaller pennies. Likely all gold, iron, or silver. He couldn't remember the last time he had even seen a copper mark, much less a full copper round. One day.

As he was contemplating using the last of his money for a decent meal, Elle stepped up to the husky, middle-aged man behind the bar. "The best food you've got for everyone who came with me. Laundry and baths as well. One room for the other lady and me, two for the men to share. This should cover it, and a meal in the morning as well."

Emrael heard the clicking of metal on wood and almost swallowed his own tongue when he saw three copper marks on the well-oiled bartop. The innkeeper just nodded and swiped the money into his palm. Emrael wasn't even sure if Elle had just been swindled or not. He'd never had that much money at one time.

He smiled his gratitude at her, but his pride stopped him from thanking Elle out loud. *I'll do something extra nice for her soon to make up for it.*

As hungry as he was—you couldn't beat good food, especially after the dismal fare on which they had been subsisting—he wanted a bath even more. They were shown to the bath houses in the yard behind the inn, and after shaving and taking a bath so long and hot he almost fell asleep, they placed their things in their cramped rooms and gathered in the common room for a meal. Only a quarter of the tables in the room were filled, so Emrael and his party had no trouble securing a large table in a corner of the room.

A kindly-looking woman brought them plates filled with thick cuts of roasted meat—pork, judging by the color and smell—bright green beans, and fried tubers. Large loaves of dark bread were set on the table along with a crock of butter and pitchers of a light amber ale.

"Fallen take me if this isn't the best thing I've ever seen," Halrec murmured fervently. Joral chuckled his agreement, and even Prilan smiled.

One by one, they each ate their limit and leaned back into their wooden chairs with a contented sigh. Yerdon mumbled something about bed and left the table to trudge down the hallway to their rooms, and Joral voiced his agreement. "I've never been one to turn down a good bed when it's available."

Prilan followed the Justicer without a word to the others, as had become his habit.

Emrael continued eating undaunted, calling for a second plate. He wasn't about to let good food go to waste.

At last, he decided that if he called for a third plate, he would make himself ill. He took his turn settling back into his chair and sipped his jar of ale. Halrec sat beside him in a similar state of food-induced contentment. Jaina and Elle sat across from them, murmuring softly over cups of wine.

Halrec turned to look at Emrael, a sly grin lighting his face, then glanced at Jaina before taking a long swallow of ale and bouncing from his chair.

Emrael rolled his eyes as Halrec swaggered over to an area that had been cleared of tables and chairs, likely for the occasional musician, though judging by the sparse crowd and the dilapidated state of most of the little town, Emrael wondered how long it had been since they had seen enough patronage to pay for a decent musician.

Halrec reached the clear space and turned to face the room, eyes closed, head tilted up slightly.

Emrael groaned. "Here we go . . ."

Halrec began to sing, and every head in the room turned.

> *There once*
> *Was a fool*
> *Who thought he could rule*
> *Fought war after war*
> *But never could contain*
> *The war within, the never-ending pain*

On he sang, his voice soaring and waning expertly, holding everyone in the room captive.

> *. . . the last, most bitter kiss, I give.*

Halrec held the last note, his sweet voice fading theatrically. The room stayed silent long after the sound of his voice had faded.

Emrael had known what was coming but despite himself had gotten caught up in Halrec's song just like everyone else. Halrec had a surprisingly gentle soul for a soldier, and a singing voice as good as any Emrael had ever heard. Pity he only used it to get attention from women.

He turned and was surprised to see a tear fall from Jaina's eye as she eyed Halrec as if seeing him for the first time. Emrael had seen many girls look at Halrec that way after one of his performances but hadn't thought to ever see Jaina be one of them. Just great.

The room slowly revived, and Halrec made his way back to the table. Emrael punched him as he sank into his seat. "Show-off."

Halrec laughed but glanced several times at Jaina, who was pointedly not looking anywhere but into her wine glass.

Elle caught Emrael's eye and smiled. "I thought it was lovely, Halrec. You really should have been a musician. Your talent is wasted on the sword."

Halrec blushed but thanked her.

Elle turned to Emrael. "Would you care to join me for a stroll? Sunsets are lovely on the river."

Emrael's stomach roiled with nervous excitement. He had not been able to spend any time alone with her since their kiss at the temple, and though it had only been a few days, she had occupied his thoughts often.

Emrael smiled and hopped to his feet, his scabbarded sword banging the chair loudly. "Of course," he said, ducking his head slightly to hide his embarrassment.

Elle's bright lips blossomed in a crooked, amused smile, but she took his arm without comment.

"Bosy, Jaim, Tori, come in for supper!" the innkeeper's wife called from the front door as Emrael and Elle walked past the three playing children. The children broke off their game and raced inside.

Elle breathed a small chuckle as she watched them push at each other to get in the door first. She looked back at Emrael and grabbed his hand. Her hand was warm, soft.

"Do you think life will be ever that simple for us again?"

Emrael pursed his lips. "Not for quite a while, if ever, Elle. That doesn't mean it has to be all bad, though." He squeezed her hand gently.

"We haven't had a moment alone in days. I thought we should talk," she said, looking up at him. She wasn't much shorter than he was.

"I've hardly been out of your sight." Playing nonchalant was awfully difficult with the setting sun lighting her honey-gold curls. And she smelled good, like some sort of flowery soap. He hardly thought that was fair. He had been given just a lump of lard with questionable amounts of lye for soap. It had left his skin feeling oily, but anything was an improvement over how he had smelled.

Elle glared but still clasped his hand as they walked. "You know what I mean, Em. You've been with Jaina or Halrec every spare moment we haven't been walking," she said, snuggling in close.

"You didn't seem to mind filling your time with Prilan instead."

Elle stopped and pulled away to hit him this time. "What I do with my time is none of your concern, you buffoon. He's been nothing but courteous, and I've made it clear I'm not interested in him. Besides, you've been more interested in your conversations with Jaina than in me. What have you two been doing?"

He grasped her forearm and smiled with excitement. "I've been training, Elle. She's finally showing me how to control *infusori*. I need to learn everything I can if I'm going to have a chance at rescuing Ban."

Elle pursed her lips but nodded. Some somber thought darkened her eyes. "Yes, that is good. Very good. Learn all you can. You may need it." She leaned in and kissed him on the cheek before asking, "Have you learned anything interesting?"

"Yes, actually. I think I could repeat that trick with the door if I had to, and I lit something on fire for the first time last night. That's it so far. Jaina can do a lot more. Though there are some things she can't do at all. Did you know Jaina can't Heal anything at all, not even a scratch?"

Elle looked surprised. "Really? She makes such a big deal about being an Imperator of her Sacred Order. You'd think they'd have included that in their training, especially for a warrior."

Emrael shrugged, and they walked hand in hand for a time without talking. They passed vacant market stalls and oddly spaced houses that composed this village that stood at the top of a small rise near the river.

"Elle?"

"Hmm?" She turned from looking west toward the sun, which was halfway below the horizon and casting its last dying rays into the sky, painting the water of the river the color of blood.

"How do you think this will all turn out?"

She hesitated before responding. "I don't know, Em. I can only hope. I hope that Ban and Sami are okay. I hope that my father will do something about Corrande and the traitorous Watchers, and whoever sent these Malithii and their beasts. I hope that he *can*, and that he's not involved. These next few years will likely be hard, ugly. I don't know what will happen. But if I could pick anyone to be

fighting next to, it'd be you. For your stubbornness, if nothing else."
She leaned her head into the hollow under his chin, and he wrapped
his arms around her tightly, pressing her to him.

"Thank you, Elle. I'm just bouncing from one thing to the next,
trying not to screw up too badly. I'll need you around to keep a level
head and help me figure out how to navigate this mess."

She laughed. "I point, you fight."

"I don't know that I'd go that far—"

The sound of horses galloping into the small town from the road
disrupted their moment.

This town might plausibly see a decent amount of traffic, as it
seemed to be the only ferry crossing for many leagues in either direction. But why so late and in such a hurry?

Nervous energy crept into his limbs as he stared back across the
town in the fading light. He still had one arm around Elle but let it
slide down to her hip. He started to lead her back towards the inn,
still with all of his attention on the new arrivals. It was hard to tell
at this distance, but it appeared that several men on horseback were
escorting a large enclosed wagon that was just pulling up to the
inn. Emrael and Elle jogged to one of the houses near the inn and
crouched behind it, peering around the corner.

The town's houses were all locked up for the night by now, small
windows lit with candlelight, small streams of smoke rising from
chimneys to join the darkening clouds in the sky.

"What . . ." Elle began, but Emrael motioned for silence as they
crept to the fence that surrounded the inn.

He put a finger to his mouth and whispered, "Quiet. Just in case."

They watched as the wagon pulled around back. Before it had
even stopped moving, nearly a dozen grey-skinned soulbound
spilled from the wagon like maggots bursting from a carcass.

Emrael sank behind the chest-high wooden fence that enclosed
the inn's yard, heart pounding. He pulled Elle slowly back toward the
nearest house, keeping his eyes on the milling soulbound and the
horsemen he assumed to be their Malithii masters. Ice-cold fear
froze his insides and set his heart to thudding as he waited for the
Malithii to spot the two of them. He sank lower as they crept back
toward the small house.

Luckily, the Malithii and their soulbound slaves were focused on
the inn and did not see or hear them as they crawled through the tall
grass to the nearest house.

"Stay hidden," Emrael whispered to Elle. "Scream if you need me."

Elle just nodded and sank farther into the shadows. Emrael could hear the soulbound kick open the back door of the inn with a crash. A surprised shout sounded somewhere inside the building. Screams followed.

As quietly as he could, Emrael sprinted, leaping the low picket fence enclosing the inn, almost falling as his boot snagged on one of the slats. As he rounded the bathhouse, the last of the soulbound were filing into the inn, hampered by the relatively small doorway.

He sought out the Malithii who had accompanied the grey-skinned creatures, and spotted a short, hooded man standing in the shadow of the building, not far from the doorway that the soulbound were squeezing through.

Emrael had always been quick, and he sprinted now for all he was worth, wresting his sword from its scabbard as he ran.

The Malithii started at the sudden clomp of rushing boots across the dry dirt of the yard and spun just as Emrael bore down on him. The Malithii brought his sword up to block Emrael's overhand swing, but Emrael had a great deal of momentum behind his heavy sword. His strike knocked the upraised blade aside easily, and his blade bit through the Malithii's skull with a dull *crunch*.

He wrested his sword from the wreckage of what had been the Malithii's head and nearly retched when its hood fell back to reveal long auburn hair and a female face, pretty behind her tattoos except for the gaping hole in the top of her head.

He shuddered as he tore his gaze away to hurry through the doorway, sword at the ready. The hallway inside was empty. Smoke and the foul smell of burned food saturated the air.

The sound of steel on steel echoed down the hall from the direction of the common room. He stepped quickly, sword poised to strike, eyes darting to take in every detail of his surroundings.

An inhuman bellow of rage shook the walls of the wooden building, and Emrael increased his pace. As he rounded the corner to the common room, a scene to sicken even the Fallen greeted him. His senses sharpened, taking in information so quickly that time seemed to slow.

Master Yerdon lay in the corridor that led from the kitchens to the common room, motionless but breathing. A gash in his side soaked his clothing and the floor around him in dark crimson blood. His eyes were wide, but he stayed silent, clutching his wound.

Multiple soulbound and Malithii lay gutted or decapitated on the floor, along with several rent bodies of patrons and serving men and women. The swarthy innkeeper himself lay facedown in a pool of his own blood on the bar.

Jaina, Joral, and Prilan fought in varying states of undress in the common room, obviously having been disturbed as they prepared for bed. They dodged chairs and tables as they fought the crazed soulbound, doing their best to keep them from two scared-looking serving women huddled in the corner.

Jaina didn't seem bothered by the tight, cluttered room as she hacked, slashed, and tumbled in a deathly struggle with one of the mindless soulbound in front of her. It went down quickly, but another two that had just charged in the front door quickly filled its place. There must have been even more Malithii and soulbound at the front of the inn besides the ones he had seen rushing in the back door. It would be a miracle if they survived the attack.

The two Legionmen were faring worse in the tight quarters, though they only faced one between them. The soulbound they fought threw a bench at Prilan, and he went down in a tangle of limbs and furniture.

Joral's quick bladework was all that saved Prilan from being crushed by a mean swipe of an axe, and the heavy bench still trapped the younger Legionman. The soulbound lurched toward Prilan again, forcing Joral aside with a broad, powerful sweep of its weapon.

Emrael surged forward to meet the soulbound's attack with a growl, and Joral swept the grey man's head from its shoulders as Emrael pinned the soulbound's ax with his sword. The veteran soldier motioned and shouted, "We can handle it here, boy! To the back! Help them in the kitchens!"

Emrael ran toward the kitchens but pulled up short just in time to see Halrec hurtle from the side hallway that led to the rooms, blade red with blood. His friend's face was rigid with concentration as he engaged one of the Malithii priests, fighting desperately within the confines of the narrow hallway.

Emrael took a step toward them to join the fight but heard a cry from the back of the inn. He reluctantly turned away from helping his friend to stalk quickly toward the kitchens. He peered around the doorframe into the spacious kitchen, saving himself from running headlong into a melee.

A man stood facing Emrael perhaps ten paces into the kitchen, a medium-length sword held at the ready as he faced two soulbound alone. The innkeeper's wife and her two small girls cowered in the open pantry behind the man.

Surprisingly, one dead creature already lay on the floor, dismembered. This man, likely a patron with the simple poor luck of being there at the wrong time, seemed to be holding his own against the remaining two soulbound. Soulbound that had their backs to Emrael and did not seem to notice that he had entered the kitchen.

Impressed by the lazy quickness with which the stranger kept the two creatures at bay, Emrael rushed around a worktable and swung hard at the unsuspecting soulbound nearest him.

Emrael's ugly sword bit deep into the shoulder and torso of the grey man and it dropped, twitching uncontrollably as the blade severed its spine.

Emrael stepped past the creature he had just felled to stick his sword through the heart of the second beast. The tip of the other man's blade sprouted from the back of the soulbound at almost the same instant. It shuddered with a disturbingly human groan and slumped forward.

Emrael met the man's eye and nodded in respect. "Emrael," he introduced himself, panting from the effort and battle joy of the fight.

The man nodded back. "Toravin."

Emrael had already started back to help Halrec and the others as Toravin checked on the sobbing woman and her girls. He told them to stay in the pantry, then started toward the front room with Emrael, where the sounds of battle still rang.

Before they took two steps, however, the door leading from the kitchen to the inn's yard exploded inward once more. Four more grey men plowed through the door, bestial rage in their eyes.

Emrael recovered quickly and struck, chopping deep into the knee of the closest soulbound with a sweep of his blade. He pivoted, using the momentum of the strike, and planted a kick square in the midsection of the next grey man as he parried the clumsy but powerful swing of its sword.

The soulbound fell back into the two immediately behind it, but Emrael's ankle popped painfully with the impact of the kick. He limped backward, two of the soulbound following hungrily.

Emrael flicked a glance at Toravin, who confronted the remaining grey man as well as the one Emrael had hobbled. He held his own but wasn't going to be helping Emrael anytime soon.

Emrael snatched a rag from the counter and used it to shield his hand as he grabbed a pot of boiling water from the stove, likely meant for an evening coffee or tea. He hurled it at the two grey men shambling toward him.

They screamed as the water scalded their faces and torsos, but as ever, they did not slow. These things were a damn lot of trouble to kill.

He lashed out quickly with a thrust at the chest of the closest grey man, but it used the forearm of its off hand to deflect the blow, ignoring the long slice down its arm. Blood ran to the floor in rivulets, but the grey man attacked unabated, swinging its sword recklessly as its companion jabbed at Emrael with what looked to be a Legion-issue infantry spear.

Emrael cursed as they forced him to retreat to the corner of the kitchen. Out of room to run, he set his feet and feinted, causing the two soulbound to swing their own weapons clumsily. It was the opening he had been hoping for.

Three successive, brutal strikes knocked the sword from the first soulbound's hand. His next strike severed its arm at the elbow. Blood sprayed the floor as the soulbound still continued forward. Emrael gave it a shove and it crashed into the far wall, though it wasted no time in scrambling back to its feet. Absent Gods, what did he have to do to kill these things?

As he turned to face the soulbound with the spear, a scream emanated from the pantry to Emrael's right where he had just thrown the wounded grey man. He had forgotten the innkeeper's wife and children hidden within. The woman stood at the broken pantry door, her children huddled behind her.

Emrael's stomach lurched as the wounded soulbound raised a knife in its remaining hand.

With a cry of defiance and desperation, he leapt, sword streaking toward the scabrous, veiny hand of the soulbound.

Something grabbed his injured ankle mid-leap. Pain shot up his leg as he slammed to the floor, just short of striking the grey man that threatened the woman and children. The soulbound with the spear raised its weapon to strike.

He attempted to roll, desperately trying to tug his leg away from one of the soulbound that he had assumed dead. He pulled free and scrambled on all fours to leap again, finally sinking his blade into the neck of the soulbound that threatened the woman and her children.

At the same moment he struck, he felt an immense pressure in his back, just below his rib cage. He tried to push himself up to confront the last, spear-wielding soulbound, but his muscles spasmed and he collapsed in a heap.

He looked down in shock at the bloody point of a spear protruding from his side and almost retched. He needed to do something about the steel stuck in his abdomen but could only stare at it.

A sudden jerk of the spear lodged in him brought shuddering, nauseating pain, leaving him gasping, barely clinging to consciousness. The wet sound of a sword striking home preceded the *thud* of a body hitting the floor behind him, and the spear was blessedly still.

Some small rational part of him noted that his clear breathing indicated that the spear had missed his lungs. Jaina would be so proud.

"Ah, lad."

Emrael turned his head to see the remaining soulbound dead. Toravin stood over him. Pity shone in his eyes. "That was a brave thing you did, boy. Stupid, but brave."

"Yerdon. Elle," Emrael groaned.

"Are those your friends? I'm going to help them now, lad. Just you rest easy. I'll come back for you soon as I can." The look in Toravin's eyes scared Emrael. The pity, the complete lack of hope. He could feel warm blood pooling under him, the cold of death seeping into his legs and hands.

A gasp came from somewhere behind him.

"Ma'am, are you all well?" Toravin asked.

"Y . . . yes, thank you. Oh, dear, there's so much blood," said a shaky female voice.

Someone pressed a cold hand to the side of his neck, then probed his back carefully. "Children, help me hold these to the wounds," the innkeeper's wife commanded in a soft voice. Her children came into Emrael's view with kitchen rags in their hands, which they pressed hesitantly around the protruding spearhead. The innkeeper's wife tore and wound a long cloth around him, holding the makeshift bandages in place.

Toravin pursed his lips sadly before hurrying to the common room. He had seen men take a wound to the midsection before, likely.

Emrael grew tired and rested his head on the cold floor as he contemplated the ugly death that was likely to greet him if he was lucky enough to survive the next few minutes. Or unlucky. Unless . . . unless Elle could figure out a way to Heal him. But how, in this Fallen-damned backwater where there likely wasn't a single *infusori* coil to be found?

Quick footsteps approached.

Toravin walked briskly back into the kitchen, followed by Jaina,

Halrec, and Joral, who were carefully carrying the injured Yerdon between them. They set Yerdon next to Emrael.

Jaina knelt next to the two injured men and caressed Emrael's head briefly. Pity and fear shone in her emerald eyes when she looked at him. "We need to find Elle to tend to the both of you. I have no skill with Healing. Emrael, where is Elle?"

"Outside," he grunted painfully. He pointed his thumb toward the back of the inn.

Toravin left immediately, sword still held at the ready. He began calling Elle's name loudly.

Halrec and Joral took up positions at either door to the kitchen. Halrec limped slightly and Joral bled down one arm, but otherwise they both appeared unharmed. Prilan finally dragged himself in and sat heavily against one wall.

Jaina bent down next to Emrael. She ran a hand softly through his short white hair, which was slick with sweat and blood from the fight. "Oh, Emrael. They will never forgive me if I let you die. Damn my lack of Healing ability," she muttered fiercely to herself. Emrael would have laughed if he had the energy. He felt tired. So tired.

Shoes slapping rapidly on the wood floors announced Elle's arrival, Toravin shadowing her with heavy booted steps.

"Em!" she cried upon seeing him. "Master Yerdon! You'll be all right, I promise. I promise." She came to kneel between him and Yerdon, concern warring with determination on her dirt-smudged face.

She lay a hand on him, and he felt a burning sensation around his wound, which had begun to throb with mind-numbing pain. A pathetic moan sneaked past his lips.

The pain in his back and midsection faded some as she moved over to Yerdon's still form. Emrael closed his eyes, concentrating on breathing softly so as not to jar the spear. He heard Yerdon begin to mumble frantically as Elle laid a hand on him.

"It was me!" the old healer gasped.

"I know, I know Master Yerdon, you did well. I'll have you back on your feet in no time," Elle whispered convincingly.

Emrael opened his eyes and appraised the ugly hole in the man's side again. He likely would not live out the hour. He made a mental note not to trust Elle when she made promises to Heal him, should he make it through this.

"No!" Yerdon growled. "They made me . . . The Citadel. I helped them follow, with this." He held out his arm, shaking it gently so that the sleeve of his shirt fell back, revealing a slender bracelet, so thin that it resembled a fine chain. A piece of jewelry that, while not exactly common for a man, would not have occasioned mention.

"Binder," Emrael growled softly.

Elle and Jaina turned to look at him quizzically but turned back to Yerdon as he nodded sadly.

"Had to. My family. My family." Tears flowed freely from his eyes. He reached his hand across to Emrael, sobbing. "My family. Please. My family."

He clutched at Emrael's shirt, tugging at it painfully as he stared into Emrael's eyes, pleading over and over, "my family."

"What . . ." began Elle.

"Family," Emrael cut in with a painful grunt. He had an idea of what would cause a good man like Yerdon to cooperate with the Watchers. He nodded to Master Yerdon, and the old man smiled, then reached up to grab Elle's hand.

"Heal him," Yerdon breathed, barely audible. For some reason, the blood drained from Elle's face as she looked down at her mentor. Tears tumbled down her cheeks.

Emrael didn't know what was going on, but he was too tired to care anymore. He let his eyelids slide closed once more. The pain in his side grew more tolerable as he drifted toward sleep.

⚬⟿

Elle felt frantically at Emrael's neck, searching for a pulse as his eyes closed. She took a deep breath, trying to slow the tears wetting her face. She nearly sobbed with relief when she found his pulse.

She calmed herself with another deep breath, swept her hair out of her eyes, and looked back down at Master Yerdon. He still held her right hand in both of his, smiling his kindly smile. Could he really have caused all of this? Let those men into the Citadel and led these monsters to them? Even still, could she do what he asked? How did he know she could Heal with mage skills?

Every healer at the Citadel knew that all living beings possessed a life essence composed of a special kind of *infusori*. She had studied the art and science of restoring balance to this life essence there for years, though Master Yerdon and the others at the Citadel had depended on *infusori*-Crafted devices to facilitate the process.

Maira Ire had introduced her, in the years before she had gone to the Citadel, to a different, more direct form of Healing, manipulating *infusori* to aid and manipulate the body's natural healing mechanisms directly. A form of Healing seen as heresy and witchcraft throughout the Provinces.

Could Yerdon have known about her ability all along? Heeding Maira's warning, she had revealed it to no one, had never practiced it at the Citadel, even on the most desperate of patients. Though, she realized, Yerdon must have suspected by now, after she had already Healed Emrael once without any Craftings.

But she did not know if she could do what Yerdon was asking, or whether it was even possible. To take life essence from her kindly old mentor, even to Heal Emrael, felt wrong. Even with what he had confessed. She felt dirty just thinking about it.

She looked down at Emrael once more. Her hand moved of its own accord to stroke his silvery-white hair, wet with sweat, pink with blood. She shuddered to look at the bloody spear point sticking out from his side and the pool of blood gathering beneath him.

She looked up to Halrec, who had a haunted look in his eyes as he stared down at his oldest friend.

"Halrec," she said quietly.

He didn't look up.

"Halrec!"

He looked up, dazed, his bloody blade forgotten in one hand.

"Come here. You too, Jaina," she commanded, her voice sounding much stronger than she felt. She was almost surprised when they obeyed, kneeling next to Emrael.

She gripped Yerdon's hand tightly, and he squeezed back. His eyes were closed, but he still had a peaceful smile on his face.

Tears blurred her vision. Better to lose just one of them than both.

She lay her other hand on Emrael, pressing into the ribs around his wound.

She looked to Halrec and Jaina. "Halrec, you will pull the spear from him when I say *now*. You understand?"

She waited for his grim nod and looked to Jaina. "You will try to keep the wound from bleeding as the spear is removed. The bleeding could kill him before I can do anything."

He may die anyway.

She put that thought out of her head and closed her eyes, concentrating on the life sources of her two patients. The *infusori* that comprised the very essence of each injured man was weak, turbulent, but still present, thank the Gods.

"Now." Her voice sounded calm, detached, like someone else speaking from her mouth—a skill she'd developed over years of treating dying patients.

She felt Em's body spasm as Halrec tore the spear from his side with one powerful pull. Em's life energy pulsed with his body, a reaction to the pain. She heard him gasp.

Ignoring the panicked shuffling that followed as Jaina and Halrec worked to stem the flow of Emrael's blood, Elle tore the *infusori* from Yerdon's body. She could think of no kinder word for it. Death was death. She fought down a surge of bile rising in her throat.

The *infusori* from Yerdon filled her. It felt similar to when she had worked with the *infusori* from infused coils with Maira, but somehow different, harder to control. More alive.

She pushed the living *infusori* into Emrael, calming and balancing his life essence, urging his body to close its wounds. She pushed and pushed, but still his body needed more. The spear had severely wounded him, even worse than she had feared. She'd never Healed a wound nearly this grave before. Not successfully.

Even when Yerdon's life essence ran out, she kept going, doing her best to balance, coax, and bolster Emrael's life essence with *infusori* she drew from herself. She began to sway with the effort and opened her eyes, breaking her connection before she too lost consciousness.

Emrael lay in a pool of blood, his face pale and sickly, but his breathing was strong and regular, as was his heartbeat. She leaned forward unsteadily, pushing Jaina's hands away from where she still held bandages to Emrael's side. Elle peeled the bandages away, hoping to see healed skin.

An ugly, red, puckered scar just under Emrael's ribs and a matching one in his back stared up at her when she rolled him enough to peek. It was nowhere near as large as it had been, no more than the size of a Provincial round, but it was still there. She could only hope that the internal damage had been healed and that the superficial remnant was the only lingering effect of the wound

Even Lady Ire couldn't heal every wound, she consoled herself. At least Emrael seemed to be healed to the point that he would live.

"Clean and bandage it just in case," she instructed wearily. "It may pain him for a time, but he should be back to normal within a week or two. We'll have to watch him over the next few days to make sure his pulse and breathing stay strong. Make sure he eats and drinks as soon as he can."

She sank to sit on the floor and turned to her mentor, Master Yerdon, knowing what she would find. She had felt the life drain from him. She had felt the power of his life essence—his soul—flow through her hands as she used it to bolster Emrael's body as it healed itself.

She pressed her fingertips to the hollow of Yerdon's neck but snatched them back as if burned by a fire. Not only did he not have a pulse, but his skin was cold, stiff. Like a side of pork.

Her teacher's kindly, self-sacrificing smile now seemed twisted, accusatory. She shuddered and drew herself to her feet.

"We will need to bury him," she said, staring blankly at the wall. She snapped her attention back to the room, full of gore and dead soulbound. "But not with those monsters. I don't care what he said just now. He was a good man!"

She realized she was yelling and looked around with tear-filled eyes at the others, who regarded her with surprise.

"I'm sorry. I'm just tired, and . . . I'm just tired. Please bury Yerdon properly and see Emrael to a bed. I need to lie down."

To her surprise, Jaina stepped forward to slip an arm under her shoulder, concern and respect plain on her face. Halrec picked Emrael up gently and followed as she tottered toward a bed.

18

A Watcher in blue stood in the doorway, club in hand, as Ban entered what had been a Master of the Citadel's study. He walked forward hesitantly to hand his latest Crafting to the elderly dark-robed priest seated behind the desk. The priest turned the Crafting over in his pale, tattoo-laced hands.

"What does this do?" the old man asked in a heavily accented voice.

"It is an incendiary device, sir."

The priest's face scrunched in confusion. "In . . . cendiary?" he said awkwardly.

"It will create fire. Quite a lot of fire, actually, paired with the proper medium. I can likely put it on a rough sort of timer as well, to give a proper delay before igniting."

The old man smiled, revealing large, yellowing teeth beneath his wrinkled lips. "Excellent! I tell you, my young one, this is good. Very good. Even the Ordenan dogs"—he paused to spit to the side in disgust—"they would be pleased to have such a thing."

He continued beaming. Ban tried to smile back, though he wanted to sob with relief. The student before him had been taken out of the room blank-eyed, a binder on his wrist, with Watchers shouting about readying him for transport to Whitehall. Apparently, the boy had not pleased the old priest. Ban had delivered a working device, but it was far from the best he was capable of. He wasn't about to hand this Fallen lot of bastards anything more than he had to. But when he had seen his fellow Crafter hauled out like a crate of rotted food, he had immediately regretted his decision to hold back.

The smile slipped from the old priest's lips when Ban failed to respond. "Yes, well. You will return to your station. Bring me something even *better* next time, eh?"

He slapped his hand on the desk and shooed Ban from the room.

Ban shuffled out as quickly as he could, already looking forward to the chance to fiddle with his Observer as he pretended to be starting his next project. The short conversation he'd managed with Emrael several days before had left him desperate to reach his brother again. He needed to know that Em was out there, that he had a plan to get him out of this horrid prison.

~

Emrael woke, confused by the gentle rocking motion of the wagon he occupied. Where had they come by a wagon? A moment later, he was significantly more worried by the sharp pain in his side when he sat up. Memory hit him like a hammer as he tenderly felt at the wound.

The soulbound and Malithii.

Fighting side by side with a man named Toravin.

The spear jutting from his side.

He had only been sitting up for a moment before Elle spotted him. Her face brightened with a smile as she dismounted her horse—apparently, everyone had acquired horses as well—and ran to him on light feet. She jumped into the wagon and embraced him gently. "Em! I'm so glad to finally see you awake. How do you feel?"

Emrael smiled, his eyes locked on hers. "I'm well, all things considered. The last thing I remember is a spear sticking out of my side. So, I feel better than that, at least."

He looked around and seeing everyone astride a horse save for Yerdon, asked, "Where is Master Yerdon? You Healed him as well, right?"

At that, Elle's face fell. "Em . . . Yerdon's gone. I . . . I used his life source to Heal you. I had no choice."

She bowed her head to hide her tears. His eyes filled with tears to match hers. "Elle, I'm so sorry."

He put a hand on her arm while she cried. After several minutes, she took a few deep breaths to calm herself. "It's what he wanted." She lifted her reddened eyes to meet his gaze. "And I think we will need you," she whispered.

Emrael nodded and leaned over to kiss her forehead. "Thank you," he murmured.

Elle filled him in on what had happened during the day or so he had been unconscious. Jaina had bought horses for everyone, and the wagon for Emrael, once they had crossed the river by ferry. She hadn't dared stay in Ben's Crossing for fear of further pursuit by the Malithii and their soulbound monsters.

He was surprised to hear that Toravin had joined their party, and even more surprised that Jaina had allowed it.

"What do we know about him?" Emrael asked quietly.

Elle sniffed, trying to control her emotions. "He says he's an Iraean trader or some such, just over in the Barros Province to trade furs, but Jaina suspects he's a criminal of some sort. Probably one of the Iraean bandits the Barros Legionmen were telling us about. He'll only travel with us the few days it will take to get to Whitehall."

Emrael studied the man circumspectly. "Traders don't fight like he did back at that inn. The man is damn good with a blade; I'll be glad to have him around if those soulbound show up again."

"Jaina checked him—and all of us, you included—for mindbinders after finding one on Yerdon. He doesn't have a binder on him, at the very least."

Emrael smiled sadly. "Yes, but how far can we trust a stranger even so?"

<hr />

Two slow days of travel later, they started to pass more and more villages and towns built on the outskirts of Whitehall. Emrael itched to get out of the wagon to ride with the rest of the group, but it wasn't worth the fight with Elle. No matter that the pain in his side was no more than a twinge by now. He'd sneaked out to walk behind the wagon the day before, and she'd been angrier with him than he'd ever seen her. He supposed he owed it to her for sacrificing her longtime mentor and friend to save his life yet again.

Emrael leaned back, trying to nap the hours away, but snapped his eyes open at a shout from Halrec. "Look, Em, it's the bridge! It's just like our fathers said it was."

Emrael twisted around to look ahead. Sure enough, an enormous grey stone bridge was just visible up ahead, arcing high over the River Stem to connect the highway they traveled on the Iraean side of the river to Gadford, a large walled town that straddled the Low Road on the Barros side of the river.

Forangerr, a town about half the size of Gadford, sat at the foot of the bridge on the Iraean side. According to Elle, an ancient Ravan city had encompassed modern-day Whitehall and Forangerr both. Ancient ruins could still be found for leagues and leagues in the surrounding forest, and throughout most of the forgotten wilds of Iraea. This enormous bridge was a prominent reminder that the Provinces were far from the first—or the most advanced—civilization to occupy these lands. Emrael wondered now whether any of the lost ruins might actually be Ravan temples like the one Jaina had found in the Stemwood.

As they drew closer, numerous statues lining the bank near the landing of the bridge came into view. Most were weather-worn or broken to the point of being unrecognizable as statues, but others still had a great deal of detail.

"Who are they supposed to be?" Emrael wondered aloud.

Toravin turned to him. "They are great mages, pagan heroes from centuries past. The Iraeans used to worship them as demigods. Many still do, when the Sentinels aren't around. A band of mage worshippers still lives in the ruins of Trylla, despite the Watcher's attempts to keep them out."

"It's likely that many of those statues were erected for your Ire ancestors," Elle chimed in.

Toravin whipped around in his saddle. "Did you say 'Ire'? As in Janrael Ire?"

"Janrael was my father," Emrael said carefully, aware that Toravin was now looking at him very intensely. Elle looked like she had swallowed a bug as she realized she had probably said too much.

"Is that a problem?" Emrael challenged quietly.

Toravin still stared at him as if he was seeing a ghost. "Ah. No, no. Not a problem."

"Did you know him?"

Toravin laughed then. "Know him? No, can't say I did. Men like him don't associate with the likes of me."

Emrael grunted as Toravin turned back to watch the road, then turned to fumble through his pack for his waterskin. As he was putting it back after slaking his thirst, he felt a bulge in one of the deep pockets. He rooted around, frustrated that he could not seem to locate whatever was in his pack. Finally, he found a tear in the lining of his pack, reached inside, and pulled out the small leather-bound book from the temple. He had forgotten about it with everything that had happened since.

He set it on his lap carefully and undid the copper buckle from the front, squinting at the book. He pried the pages open slowly, further on in the book than last time.

⌒

A blur of light obscured his vision, startling him even though he had some idea of what to expect.

The scene that filled his vision was similar to the last he had seen, in that he seemed to be watching from a distance, as if he were a bird high in the sky.

It was dark, sometime in the late evening. He floated just outside the walls of a large, sprawling compound, three pyramids of dirty grey stone, one much larger than the rest, and many smaller rectangular buildings, all surrounded by large stone walls. The parapets that ran along the top of the large walls glowed brightly with the blue light of *infusori*, though Emrael couldn't see any *infusori* lamps, or even coils being used as an energy source.

His field of vision drew closer to the walled compound. The walls were tall enough for a city, though the structure itself was no larger than a large Legion compound. Some sort of castle or military installation, then?

He blinked as he realized what created the strong blue glow that emanated from the walls—bands of metal ran along the parapets, glowing and casting the bright blue light. It was eerily similar to the glowing script on the walls of the Ravan temple, though here the glowing metal stretched in a simple band across the parapet, enough to clearly illuminate the wall and many paces to either side.

A loosely organized group of several dozen people creeping through the tall grass outside the walls drew Emrael's attention. They moved so stealthily that he almost passed his gaze right over them. They wore tight, light grey clothing. Only one among them stood out; he had long flowing hair the same stark white as Emrael's.

The men dragged a pair of ragged-looking men, bound hand and foot, gags in their mouths. Tattoos covering their visible skin identified them as Malithii. Their heads drooped and their feet dragged limply across the ground as the grey-clad men towed them in their wake.

No one seemed to be keeping watch on the wall other than two robed men standing stiffly near the single gate Emrael could see. The group dressed in ash grey reached the wall and one of them stood, pulling a copper dagger from his belt. The man drove the small blade into a space between the stones of the wall and held on to the hilt, then leaned down to touch the struggling Malithii prisoners. The Malithii withered and collapsed as the man touched each in turn.

Emrael watched for a moment, not sure what to expect.

Crrrmmmp!

An entire section of wall exploded inward, carrying the gate and its two guardsmen screaming with it.

The grey-clad men and women—they must have been mages of some sort—rushed forward through the breach in the wall, engaging

Malithii guards that charged from smaller stone buildings that surrounded the pyramids.

The white-haired man stepped calmly past the small grey-clad
man who had blown the hole in the wall, who still stood at the scene
of incredible destruction, leaning wearily against the breached wall.
The two Malithii prisoners lay lifeless at his feet, twisted and stiff
as if they had been corpses for days. Several grey-clad warriors followed closely, as if they were the white-haired man's personal guard.

A few Malithii challenged the small group and were killed immediately. One tattooed priest who made it to the white-haired man
himself crumpled as the man released an enormous pulse of *infusori*.

More and more Malithii rushed from buildings, only to be cut
down swiftly by the grey-clad mages, who were impossibly quick
with copper-colored short swords that glowed with the light of *infusori*. Blood gathered in thick pools on the cobblestones of the compound yard.

A deep, vibrating scream of rage cut through the pandemonium.
A monstrous, bald figure emerged from the largest pyramid. The
being was at least twice as large as any of the humans fighting in
the courtyard.

Emrael recoiled in shock as he recognized the ashen skin, glowing with angular script. It was the Fallen God of Glory, just as he
had seen in the last vision.

All hell broke loose.

A wave of monsters with white skin, long hair, and close to half
again as tall as a man—though still much smaller than the Fallen—
erupted from the smaller pyramids, swarming toward the grey-clad
mage warriors. Mages and pale monsters died, and still the white-
haired man and his guard surged forward to meet the Fallen.

The white-haired mage and the Fallen circled each other, weap-
onless. The mage darted forward suddenly, touching the Fallen and
releasing another incredible blast of *infusori*. The script in the Fall-
en's skin flared brighter, and the God paused as if frozen for a brief
moment, but otherwise the Fallen was unaffected. The God threw
back his head to roar an impossibly deep laugh.

All the while, the mages that had accompanied the white-haired
man were evenly matched at best with the Malithii and white
skinned monsters they fought. Bodies littered the ground, with
more falling every second amid flashes of *infusori* and splashes of
blood.

The white-haired mage moved to strike again, but the Fallen

grabbed him around the neck with one huge hand and lifted him from the ground. The Fallen's script flared once again as the mage struck with *infusori*, brighter this time, but the God paid it no mind. His lips moved as he spoke to the mage in his grasp, but Emrael couldn't hear what was said.

With a jerk of its enormous fist, the Fallen crushed the mage's neck and set his limp form to the ground gently, as if handling a baby. The Fallen looked almost sad but did nothing to stop the slaughter all around him.

Emrael blinked in confusion as he was jolted from the vision by someone shaking him.

"Damn it, Em, what's wrong?" Halrec was all but yelling at him from beside the halted wagon. The rest of the group gathered around, peering at him in worry.

Emrael blinked in momentary confusion as his friend continued to shake his shoulder forcefully. Nervous energy still pulsed through his veins as the memories of the battle he had seen in the book lingered. Why had the white-haired mage thought he could defeat the Fallen single-handedly? Did the vision mean that the Fallen God was still alive in this world?

Elle knew exactly what had happened, and it showed plainly in her calm demeanor. Jaina squinted suspiciously, looking from Emrael to Elle, then back to the small book still in Emrael's hand.

Emrael blinked once more at his friends, who were still staring at him, waiting for a response. "I fell asleep reading is all. I've been very tired."

Jaina arched an eyebrow, clearly not convinced. Elle chuckled. "She knows something happened, Em. Just tell her."

Halrec's eyebrows drew down as he looked sidelong at Elle in confusion. "Knows what? What the hell is going on?"

Jaina continued to stare at him, obviously expecting a full answer.

Emrael gave in. "Fine. I took this book from the Ravan temple. When I open it, I see visions. I think they're of the past. The story of the Fallen—"

"The Fallen?" Jaina cut in quickly. "What of the Fallen?"

"Well," Emrael started hesitantly. "The first time, I saw Justice and Mercy cast the Fallen out of a castle carved into a mountain. Just now I saw a mage with long white hair attack the Fallen and a bunch of Malithii at a pyramid."

Jaina's stare had gone from skeptical to amazed. "You *saw* all of that? May I see?"

Emrael handed the book to her and she flipped from page to page quickly, obviously frustrated.

"Is this a joke? How did you know those stories? Did your mother tell you?"

Emrael raised his hands in protest when she glared at him. "No! Elle couldn't see them either. I'm telling the truth; I see real visions like I'm floating in the sky watching them happen, and the different visions are on different pages."

Jaina still regarded him skeptically but nodded grudgingly after a time. "What you describe resembles passages in the Holy Book of Ages preserved from the time of the Ravan Empire, though you have some details wrong." She fingered the pages again. "The script is not Old Ordenan. It may be the same we found on the walls of the temple, likely true ancient Ravan. You must tell me about any other visions you see in this book. Who knows what marvels such a book from a temple could contain."

Emrael shrugged. "Fine. I didn't ask for them, and as far as I can tell, they don't mean much. I'll tell you about anything else I see."

Jaina nodded again. "Thank you, Emrael."

Halrec still looked at both of them like they were insane. "Just warn me next time, okay, Em? I about shit myself seeing you like that, eyes wide open but dead to the world."

He shook his head in frustration and pointed in the direction they were riding. "Oh, by the way. We're here."

19

Emrael stood in the wagon, stretching carefully. His side twinged, but not horribly. He stared at the city of Whitehall in dismay. Ban could be anywhere in that enormous jumble of buildings and people.

The Whitehall Keep, so named for the large white blocks of stone from which it had been constructed, stood hundreds of feet above them between the mouths of two diverging canyons. Behind a large, guarded gate to the north side of Whitehall, a paved road wound its way up a small, steep canyon that held the series of *infusori* Wells that were the lifeblood of this region.

On the southern side of the large keep, the broad highway they traveled cut through the city to follow a wide natural pass in the mountain range on its way to the Corrande Province. A second keep, much smaller than Whitehall but still large enough to house thousands of soldiers, sat on a hill on the southern side of the pass, connected to Whitehall by a grand bridge spanning the entirety of the highway pass, hundreds of paces above a heavy gate.

The flag of the Holy Provincial Legion, four black bars on a field of blue, snapped in the wind over the keep. It was a visual reminder to all that Iraean Lord Holders may still govern their Holding lands, but the United Provinces—with the Sentinels as their agents and the Watchers as their military force—ruled the Lords Holder.

Below the keeps lay the sprawling city of Whitehall. Large estates, mansions, factories, and warehouses filled the space immediately surrounding the Whitehall Keep. These likely supported the wealthy merchants, *infusori* Crafters, *infusori* traffickers, old nobility, and the like.

Smaller, increasingly ramshackle dwellings, shops, and markets sprawled outward from there, past the highway and down the river's edge, filling many square leagues of gently sloping terrain in the large mountain valley.

The river itself rushed from multitudes of mountain lakes high in the heart of the Duskan Mountains, through a deep vertical stone chasm until it emptied over a small cliff just above the Whitehall valley. There, next to the city, the gentle slope of the valley floor created a small natural lake where dozens of docks ventured out into the water like spindly fingers. Ships large and small moored there, ready to take *infusori* and other goods down the large river channel to Naeran and beyond.

Emrael finally climbed down from the wagon, stamping his feet to test his ankle. Elle fixed him with a concerned stare, which he ignored. He was fine.

He looked to Jaina. "Okay, how do we figure out where they have Ban?"

Jaina pursed her lips. "My best guess puts them either in Whitehall Keep itself or somewhere up the canyon that holds the *infusori* Wells, as the Wells will have the strictest security. Perhaps the Watcher keep across the highway. But they truly could be anywhere, assuming Darmon was even telling the truth."

Emrael growled in frustration. "He was telling the truth. I could feel it. But he didn't know for sure. I'll search this city house by house, room by room if I have to."

Jaina pursed her lips. "I may have a few contacts in the city who deal in information. I'll seek them out as soon as we are settled."

Toravin pitched in. "I am somewhat familiar with this place and some of the . . . less visible people that run things. If your friends are here, they will at least have heard something."

Emrael nodded. "Thank you, Toravin. I'll owe you anything within my power to grant, if you help me find my brother."

Toravin winked and shrugged off the offer. "If I can help, I'll help. No guarantees."

Emrael turned back to Jaina and the rest of the party. "My thanks to all of you. Let's find somewhere to stay, then Elle and I will try to talk to Lord Holder Norta at Whitehall Keep while you find your contacts. I have to think he'll grant Elle an audience as a matter of course."

Jaina raised one eyebrow and frowned at Emrael. "You're just going to walk in and ask for your brother back? How do you see that working?"

Emrael pursed his lips, thinking through his options before answering. "Even if Norta is working with Corrande, he won't dare do anything to Elle."

Jaina stared at him with the same expression, clearly unimpressed. "He'll recognize you, Emrael. Even if he leaves Elle be, you'll be arrested or worse. What can you hope to learn from him that is worth putting yourself in prison?"

Emrael smiled tentatively. "If I can do what I did in the temple, I don't think being imprisoned will be all that bad. I have to try, Jaina. If he thinks Elle will bring the might of the Barros Province down on him, he might be willing to give Ban up, if he's here. From what my father used to tell me, most Iraeans are hesitant allies to Corrande at best. I have to try."

Jaina looked like she wanted to say more but shrugged her reluctant acceptance instead. "Fine. Just don't expect me to risk my life to save you this time."

A few hours later, their things stowed at an older but serviceable inn and their draft horses traded for mounts more suitable for riding, Emrael and Elle set off for Whitehall.

"Should we name them?" Elle asked, patting her horse. "I haven't named a horse since I was a child."

Emrael chuckled. "Don't get too attached. Like as not, we'll have to sell or abandon them again before this is over. Lord Holder Norta wouldn't have retained his Holding unless he was in league with Corrande. He could try to detain us, or worse. It might not be an easy thing to leave Whitehall freely after speaking with him."

"So, why go at all? Why not just search the city and avoid the Lord Holder?" Elle asked.

Emrael clutched at the pendant hanging from his neck, keeping it near his ear anxiously, hoping to hear his brother's voice confirm that they were close. "I have to risk it. Ban can't wait that long, Elle. You should have heard him when he contacted me in the temple. He was scared. If he's here, I need to know now, no matter the risk. The Lord Holder will know where any important prisoners are being held. Besides, I think I can get us out fairly easily if he detains us. I just have to remember how to crush stone like I did with that door."

Elle didn't look convinced. "What if they decide to just stick a spear in you, Em? There has to be a smarter way to go about this. Ban still hasn't responded to you via the amulet since we arrived?"

"No, but we can't know for sure what that means. He could have lost or broken his. Or they could have done something to him."

Sobered, Elle nodded resolutely and they picked up the pace. They soon slowed again, however, when they encountered masses of people clogging the roadways as they came nearer Whitehall Keep. Trade must have been booming, because both the road leading to the *infusori* mines and the road leading to the Corrande Province seemed to be attracting more travelers than they could handle. Their mounts soon became a liability, restricting their mobility in the increasingly dense pack of people, carts, and animals.

Emrael shouted into the din of the crowds to get Elle's attention before turning onto a small side street that seemed relatively clear. He jumped from the saddle to lead his horse quickly down the much calmer side street. He tied his horse to a hitching post outside a tavern on the next corner and turned back to look for Elle just in time to see someone in dark clothing leading her mount into an alleyway. Several more people followed, surrounding her horse and trapping her on horseback as she shouted for help.

He held his sword belt with one hand as he sprinted across the street, the uneven cobblestones catching at his boots and threatening to trip him. He pressed on, stumbling as he turned the corner where Elle had disappeared just moments before.

Panic gripped him as he searched the alleyway and could not find Elle or the group of men. He was about to sprint to the other end of the alley, where it let out into another bustling street, but heard a high-pitched yelp from nearby. He spun about and noticed a gate leading to a high-fenced wagon yard. He rushed through the gate without a second thought.

Two large men dressed in faded black clothing pulled Elle from her horse just as he entered the yard. A third, also clothed in black but of much finer quality, held her horse's bridle. They didn't notice Emrael pushing through the gate until his sword whispered as it left its scabbard.

"Put the lady down. I'll give you to the count of five before I gut you." The confidence in his voice surprised even him, and the two larger men who held Elle paused with their swords half-drawn, casting a doubtful look at the well-groomed man, obviously the leader of this little gang.

The refined man's most prominent feature was a fine, dark, beard oiled into a point just below his narrow chin. The amount and quality of hair on his face almost made up for the man's completely bald head. His expensive clothes would normally have marked him as either a noble or well-to-do merchant, but the muscular frame beneath his fine clothes spoke of frequent physical activity.

Emrael didn't care if he was the Fallen himself.

The man smiled, showing large, straight white teeth. "Ah, excellent, the boy followed. He will be a nice bonus to the price the girl will fetch. Go get him." He waved a hand nonchalantly toward Emrael and turned back to Elle.

The two big men stalked forward with weapons drawn, and out of the corner of one eye, Emrael saw another man enter through the gate behind him, this one smaller, weasel-faced. He pretended not to notice the man behind him, backing up as far as he dared without protecting himself.

When he judged he was within reach, he spun without warning, whipping his sword in a lightning-quick arc. The tip passed through the throat of the weasel-faced man that had been trying to sneak up on him from behind. A spray of blood spattered against the weathered wooden fence. The man fell to his knees, blood bubbling through his fingers as he tried in vain to stop the flow of blood from his neck.

Emrael took several quick steps forward to press the attack on his remaining foes, slamming his sword into that of the large man to the right. He struck hard near the hilt, and the man swore as the impact jarred his hand. Emrael stepped farther to the right as the man backed off. The man who had been at his left stepped forward slowly, fear painted on his face. Emrael almost felt pity for the man.

Almost.

"Enough!" the man in the fine suit growled loudly. The two large men backed away gratefully, and Emrael looked up to see the bald man with Elle's hair gripped in one fist. The edge of his blade rested against her neck.

Emrael's heart turned to ice.

"I'll kill her if I have to," the man in black said in a rich baritone. "They are offering a great deal for her alive and you dead, but I know others who will pay almost as much for her head. And now that you've killed Simma there, I'd kill you both for free. Or you can leave now, the girl lives to see her family again, and everyone will be happy."

Emrael did not take a step forward for fear that he would goad the man into harming Elle, but neither did he lower his weapon or retreat. He stared into the man's dark eyes with as much calm as he could muster.

The man stared back for a long moment. "Gah!" He swept the sword away from Elle's neck and stalked forward.

"Watch the girl!" he snapped to his two large, shabby companions. "I'll do for him myself."

Emrael stepped forward and met the man in a rush of carefully placed footsteps and sword strikes. He imagined the sneer of effort on the man's face matched his own as they each sought to spill the other's blood. They locked swords briefly, then pushed away and circled each other slowly. The man must have had extensive training—he was excellent with a blade.

Things grew dire as Emrael began to fatigue. He hadn't healed fully from the wound he'd taken at the inn, and it affected him more than he thought it would.

His opponent, who had joined the fight late, showed few signs of tiring. To make matters worse, one of the large, shabby men edged away from where his friend held Elle and crept around the outside of the fight, weapon ready. Emrael was in trouble.

Emrael stepped back, pulled his boot knife, and hurled it at the larger man before he could get near. The man's brutish features froze in surprise, and he cried out as the knife struck his shoulder. Unfortunately, instead of sinking into his shoulder, the knife glanced off. It left a long gash that would bleed profusely, but that wouldn't slow the man for several minutes. By that time, Emrael would likely be lying lifeless in a ditch.

Absent Gods, if you exist, help me now.

He defended himself desperately as the man in the fine black suit took advantage of Emrael's diverted attention and pressed the attack. Emrael parried, then feinted and changed the direction of his blade mid-attack, gambling as he tried to catch his opponent off guard. He put all of the power of his strong frame into the blow.

Emrael caught the man in black by surprise as he had hoped, but it wasn't enough. His opponent danced back just in time, deflecting the point of Emrael's sword enough that it only grazed the man before it struck the ground, hard.

Emrael pulled back from the man's counterstrike, but too slow. He caught a full swing from the other man just above the hilt of his own sword, and the blade was knocked from Emrael's hand.

He backpedaled, staying just outside of the reach of the two men now stalking him like forest lions stalking wounded prey.

His back hit something hard. The fence.

Panic gripped him, and his eyes darted, trying to find a way to keep from ending up with a sword through him.

The man in black smiled and hefted his sword as he moved forward. The other man had stopped advancing, turning his attention to stemming the flow of blood from his shoulder now that Emrael was little threat.

Emrael's body tensed and he stared at the smiling man, waiting for the momentary tension that would precede the final attack.

In the fractions of a second he waited, he saw from the corner of his eye another large man enter through the gate, this one carrying a staff. Yet another lackey, no doubt. He couldn't afford to look away from the man in black for even a moment. Though part of him knew he was going to die, the larger part was determined to go down fighting.

The sword flashed toward him finally, and Emrael dove frantically to the side. He managed to evade the strike, taking only a shallow cut across his left arm. He was still alive.

The man's expression turned from a pitiless smile to a sneer of rage. He stepped forward to slash at Emrael again but, just before striking, turned his head at the sound of a scuffle behind him.

Unlike the other three men that had accompanied the black-suited man, the latest arrival had a head of hair and beard that made him look remarkably like a bear. What Emrael had taken for an ordinary staff he now saw to be a copper alloy rod. It was Sarlon.

Sarlon had already knocked the man holding Elle senseless with his staff and now stalked toward Emrael and the two men that had cornered him. As soon as he was within striking distance, he exploded into a whirlwind of violence.

Sarlon felled the wounded man first, a blow to the neck that sent him flopping to the ground like a hooked fish. The encounter with the black-suited man took somewhat longer.

The whirling staff sought purchase on that black suit, but the man danced just enough to avoid being struck. Emrael watched, dumbfounded as he realized just how skilled the swordsman was.

The man in black lashed out with an attack of his own, his blade meeting the whirring staff with a screeching clang of metal on metal. An instant later, their weapons still touching, a loud clap erupted, blue light flashed, and the sword flew. Sarlon whipped his staff immediately and connected with the bald man's head, crunching with a wet, sickly sound.

Emrael dropped to one knee, exhausted and overwhelmed with relief at being alive. Sarlon planted his staff on the ground, breathing heavily through his thick beard.

"Well? Don't just stand there, boy; get the girl. And wrap that arm of yours before you bleed out. Do I have to do everything for you?"

"Sarlon, I can't believe it's you," Emrael breathed, lurching to his feet.

"Who else?" Sarlon grunted harshly.

"But what are you doing here? Thank you for saving us, but how did you find us?"

"Tracked you with a Crafting," he said simply. "I wouldn't have had to save you if you'd had some sense in you. That whole lopsided fight, you never once thought to use *infusori*? I've a door back in Myntar says you could have done a lot more than be bested by some headhunter, no matter how good with a blade. Someone needs to teach you what Jaina obviously has not."

Sarlon seemed much surlier than the last time they had met.

Elle walked over as Emrael gathered his sword. He looked at the now-dead headhunter's sword and decided to take it instead. It was much finer than the beater he had been using since the battle at the bridge. The double-edged blade had good balance and weighting, and was about the size Emrael preferred.

"Take his purse, too," Sarlon grunted, watching impassively. Emrael complied and was rewarded with a purse fatter than any he had ever owned. After some consideration, Emrael tugged the fine black boots off the bald man as well and put them on. He wriggled his toes happily. Though it was a bit disconcerting to put on warm boots looted from a dead man, boots this nice were expensive, and these fit Emrael surprisingly well. It had been years since he had a pair that fit right and had no holes in them.

Elle laid a hand on Sarlon's arm. Tight muscle showed through the material. The man had lost a significant amount of weight in the short weeks since they had seen him.

"Sarlon, where is Yamara?" Elle asked, looking about.

Sarlon's brow furrowed and his lips pursed beneath his thick beard. To Emrael's surprise, a tear streaked from one eye. "She's gone, lass. Not long after you left, she took a turn for the worse, and the healers said that bastard Gerlan would not allow them to help her any longer. Then the Watchers showed up, and I knew it was high time to be gone, so I left, thinking to take Yamara to a healer elsewhere. But then the bridge was burned out, and she . . ." His voice broke, and he went silent, tears flowing freely. He breathed hard but said no more.

"Oh, Sarlon, I'm so sorry. We should have stayed, should have insisted you come with us," Elle said, catching him up in a hug.

The big man closed his eyes and rested his head on hers for a moment, but soon pushed away. When he opened his eyes, they were dark, cold. Emrael suppressed the urge to shiver.

"No need for that, lass. What's done is done; it's nobody's fault but mine—and those that wronged her. Justice will grant me my revenge. We had best be running before the Watchers find us here with these bodies. They crawl in this town like maggots in a dung heap. Where are we headed?"

"Whitehall Keep," Emrael said grimly.

20

Emrael hesitated in the large square just outside the steps that ascended to Whitehall Keep, clutching his pendant and calling Ban's name for what must have been the hundredth time, still with no response. They would just have to find out the hard way whether Ban was in the city.

It wouldn't be a cordial visit—they were about to risk their lives to openly accuse the Lord Holder of enslaving *infusori* Crafters. Well, he would be risking his life. Elle would be relatively safe as the daughter of Lord Governor Barros.

He briefly reconsidered just searching the city themselves after all, or relying on Jaina and Toravin's secret contacts in the underbelly of the city. How likely would a bunch of thieves and foreigners be to know the secret dealings of the Watchers and a Lord Holder?

No, he decided—the Lord Holder was the fastest way to find out whether any captives were being held there, and it was time someone confronted the people behind all this. He almost hoped it came to a fight.

The large double-door timber gates that guarded the sweeping white stone steps stood open, a steady stream of people coming and going. Most of them looked wealthy and important, mostly merchants from the Corrande Province, judging by their clothing. Elle might have been able to move among them without eliciting comment, even dressed in shabbier garb than she normally wore, but he and Sarlon stood out like wolves among sheep with their rough garb and well-used weapons.

The number of Sentinels and Watchers hanging about the place made him wary as well. Luckily, none of them seemed to be very interested in him. Word must not have been sent this far to keep an eye out for a white-haired man and a blond girl. Or maybe everyone assumed they were dead after finding the carnage at the bridge on the Barros Kingroad.

"We are just going to stroll in there and demand your brother back? That's your plan?" Sarlon grumbled, looking at Emrael as if he were a horse-kicked simpleton.

Emrael shrugged defensively. "I didn't say it was a *good* plan. But the alternative is searching this city brick by brick. We don't have that kind of time. Elle's with us, so at worst, they'll throw us in a cell for a while, which shouldn't be much of an issue, especially now that you're with us. You don't have to come with us, but we're going in."

Sarlon shrugged. "I haven't much to lose."

The Watchers and the Lord Holder's guards still paid them no mind as they climbed the stairs, entered Whitehall, and made their way to the desk outside the main audience hall.

The clerk at the desk didn't look up from shuffling papers when Emrael spoke. "Emrael Ire and Arielle Barros to see the Lord Holder."

"Mmm?" the clerk responded, still not looking up.

"Emrael Ire. Arielle Barros. Here to speak with Lord Holder Norta."

The clerk slowly looked up from his paper, eyes widening with surprise as he processed what he'd just heard. "Oh. Ire . . . Barros? Uh. Y-yes. G-give me just a moment," he stuttered, nearly tipping his chair over in his hurry to stand. He all but ran into the main hall, and reappeared quickly. "Yes; he'll see you now." He shooed them through the doors.

The Lord Holder's guards lined the hall, one posted on either side of each of the columns that supported the structure. Several Sentinel priests and a few Watcher officers were in the room as well, in a loose group in one corner behind the Lord Holder's chair. These watched Emrael intently.

The Lord Holder, a thin old man with filmy eyes, addressed them as they drew near. "What's this, then?" he crowed in a warbling tenor voice. "A little Ire come back to his homeland at last, has he? And he's brought a governor's daughter with him to boot, eh?"

Emrael paused a moment before responding. "Lord Holder Norta, you obviously know who I am, and I think you know why I'm here."

Norta cackled so hard, he could hardly speak. "Yes, yes! I expect you are here to reclaim the throne that the Corrandes washed with your grandfather's blood. Well, boy, one ruler is much like the next. Corrande treats Whitehall plenty well as long as we pay his tribute. We have no need of you here."

Emrael shook his head in confusion. "What? No, I'm here for my brother, Norta. Tell me where you've put the prisoners Corrande sent you," he demanded, putting a hand to his sword hilt.

Norta's laughter cut short. He drew himself up in his large

wooden seat, clipping his words angrily as he responded. "My business with Lord Governor Corrande is none of your concern. I had thought to do this cordially, but the Lord Governor will be very pleased with me no matter what happens to you."

Elle stepped forward. "Lord Holder, you obviously know who I am. Harming me would be foolish enough, but how will your people respond if you act against the rightful king of Iraea?"

Norta snorted. "Is that what you think, girl? That boy, a king? Ha! He is nothing, not even a Lord Holder of Iraea unless the six of us that remain say he is. Seven, I suppose, if you count that weasel Marol. And even if we wanted to—and we don't—you see those fellows in the corner?" He pointed with a crooked finger at where the Watchers mingled with Sentinel priests. "There are Sentinel priests and thousands of their Watcher dogs crawling all over our kingdom. Province, yes, my mistake. It's safe to say they aren't in favor of any Ires in Iraea. Not alive, anyway."

Norta made a sharp gesture and a dozen of his guards stalked forward menacingly, spears and swords ready. Emrael bared half of his blade in the space of a heartbeat, and Sarlon stood ready with his staff held in front of him. Elle, however, stood unarmed. She was regal, ready for whatever would come, but would be a major liability in a fight. One look at her, and Emrael slammed his sword back into its scabbard with a growl.

"We'll go peacefully," he called out.

A short, fat Sentinel shouted, "Be sure you search them for any Crafted devices. They studied at the Citadel—who knows what kind of mischief they could be planning!"

Norta nodded in agreement. "Search them. Put them in a cell here in the keep. I want them close," he barked to his soldiers.

The guards approached carefully, but Emrael and Sarlon surrendered without incident. Their weapons were confiscated and hands secured forcefully behind their backs, but they were otherwise unharmed.

After descending several flights of increasingly narrow stairs and passing through as many iron security doors, they placed Sarlon and Emrael in a cell together, while Elle occupied the one next to them.

When the guards had gone, Sarlon turned to Emrael. "Well, boy, that was a fantastic plan. We've got them right where we want them," he said sarcastically.

Emrael had hoped the walls of the cells they would be taken to would be constructed at least partially of stone, but each of the cells were iron bars from floor to ceiling. Only the floors, ceilings, and what Emrael assumed was the exterior wall of the keep were stone. It wouldn't do much good to create a hole in the outside wall only to find themselves a hundred paces above the ground.

"Can't you just . . . do something?" Emrael asked Sarlon, waving toward the bars of the cell.

Sarlon muttered something that sounded a lot like *Fucking idiot*, then said louder, "I'm a simple warrior, a Battle-Mage, not a materialist. Not every mage can just whip up any magic you can dream of. Besides, those bars would just drain you of any *infusori* you could throw at it. You're on your own, kid."

Emrael rolled his eyes at Sarlon, muttering, "Lot of good you are."

He knelt, ignoring Sarlon's irritated grunt behind him and Elle's silent, judging stare from the cell next to theirs. He ran his hand along the intersection of iron bar and stone floor, trying to recall what he had done to the stone door in the temple. He opened himself to the stone, felt its structure, its composition. He drew from the *infusori* within himself until he felt cold and sick to his stomach, then pushed it into the nodes of the rock. The stone popped audibly, turning to rubble and dust where the bar was anchored at the bottom.

He pushed and pulled the bar back and forth until it moved several inches either way through the broken rock. He scraped with his hands, clearing as much of the rubble from the newly created hole as he could, then stood back, breathing hard. He looked to Sarlon, who lounged against the far wall. "You mind helping me out here?"

Sarlon sauntered over and inspected the loose stone. "What in Glory's rotten scrote did you do?"

Emrael shrugged. "I used *infusori* to break the stone apart. The bar should be free. I think."

Sarlon squinted at him for a minute. "Huh" was all he said, and he sat to grasp the bar, bracing his feet on the bars to either side. He pulled with a mighty grunt, and the iron bent free of the stone.

Sarlon fell back, breathing heavily after the effort, but Emrael was already inspecting the bent bar. "I think I can squeeze through here. Help me through before one of the guards comes back."

Elle squawked something about being able to pick the lock on her cell, but Emrael already had his head through the gap Sarlon had created. He panicked when his shoulders caught, but Sarlon gave him a shove from behind and he soon wriggled free, then rolled to his feet, smiling triumphantly.

Elle and Sarlon stared at him from the other side of the bars. Sarlon barked a laugh. "My ass will not fit through that hole."

Elle chimed in. "I tried to tell you, I think I can pick this lock, given enough time. They didn't search me. I still have pins in my hair. Unless you plan on doing that again and bending the bar yourself this time, you must be planning to leave me behind."

Emrael raised his hands in a placating gesture. "Absent Gods, calm down, would you two? I'm not exactly helpless. I'll go find the keys and be back before you two can think up another reason to ridicule me."

He stalked down the hall in the direction the guards had gone, past rows of empty cells. Light poured from an open doorway at the end of the hall, next to a narrow stone staircase. He stopped a pace away from the doorway to listen.

". . . the poor bastard had no chance, he did. The blue boys were on him with clubs just as soon as he come up to that gate. I wonder what they are doing up in that canyon . . ."

". . . who knows, Jeb? Best to stay far away from any business of theirs . . ."

It sounded like there were only two of them, probably relaxing between walking the halls. Doable.

He took a deep breath and set himself next to the door. As the jailers continued their conversation, Emrael sprang into action. He sprinted through the doorway, letting his peripheral vision show him the room.

There were three Norta guardsmen, not two as he had guessed. Two sat at a small square table, backs to the door. A third sat in a chair off to the side, polishing a pair of boots.

Emrael dashed at that guard first and caught him with a kick to the face just as he looked up in surprise. The man tumbled backward over his chair, and Emrael pivoted to the other two.

The guardsman nearest him had just looked up from watching his friend tumble to the floor when Emrael's fist caught him on the side of the head. He fell facedown on the table, limp, making a terrible rasping noise.

The third guard proved to be a problem. Emrael's assault on the other two had given this guard time to draw a hand-length blade from his belt. Worse, he handled it like he knew what he was doing.

Emrael didn't have time or space to find a weapon of his own, and the guard didn't waste any time in coming at him, blade at the ready. Emrael pushed a chair at the man to buy himself some time, then waited for the man's next slash. It came, just a bit too hard. Emrael stepped to the side and into the man's charge, securing the guard's sleeve while positioning his hip under the man's center of mass.

Emrael twisted and pulled, throwing the guard onto his head, blade-bearing hand secured behind his back via the sleeve of his uniform. The guard tried to pull his arm free and struggle to his feet, so Emrael twisted the man's arm until he felt it pop.

The guard dropped the knife and screamed, twisting and kicking in an attempt to free himself. Emrael secured the knife and in one smooth, powerful motion slammed the hilt into the guard's temple, knocking him senseless.

Emrael sank back against the wall, his chest heaving, heart pounding. Maybe he should have waited to see whether Elle could pick the locks after all.

Luckily, there was no noise out in the hall. He silently thanked whatever gods might be listening and lurched to his feet.

He found a key ring on one of the guards. His sword and Sarlon's staff were harder to find, but after a short search, he discovered them locked in a weapons cabinet in the corner.

After belting his sword around his waist, he rushed down the hallway to find the door of Elle's cell open. He couldn't help but chuckle as Elle stood in the open door, arms crossed and a haughty look of victory on her face.

"I told you I could open it, you dolt. You just *had* to go get in another fight all by yourself, didn't you?"

Emrael could only shrug uncomfortably. "It turned out well enough."

"This time."

Sarlon came to stand next to the still-locked door of his cell. "Are you two going to flirt all day, or would you mind freeing me already?"

Emrael fumbled with the keys for a moment before finding the right one. The big man snatched his staff from Emrael as he exited. "Okay, now how do we get out of here, boy?" he asked, butting his staff on the floor.

Elle nodded, arcing her eyebrow at Emrael. "That's an excellent question. Where now, fearless warrior?"

Emrael ignored their sarcasm and pursed his lips, thinking. Neither end of their long hallway seemed promising. He had no idea where the far end of the hall led, but he certainly didn't like the idea of having to make their way up the narrow staircases and through the locked iron doors that separated each level. He started toward the far end of the hall, motioning for the others to follow.

He whirled around in surprise as a deep, rasping voice emanated from the darkness as he passed what he had thought was an empty corner cell. "Wait. I can help you."

Emrael, Sarlon, and Elle all inched closer to the cell to get a look at the man. He stood of a height with Sarlon—about a head taller than Emrael—but had a thin frame. His clothes might have once been fine, but were soiled and tattered. His long hair twisted in snarls, and his beard had not seen a blade in a very long time. He looked like he had been rotting in this cell for years.

Emrael approached him. "Why should I believe you can help us? You'd say anything to get out of that cell, and will likely just get us all caught or killed."

The man shrugged. "Fair point. Any man in my position would promise the same. But I assure you, I know this place well. They don't keep just anybody in this row of cells, you know. I can get us out; I just need the key to this blasted door. How did you get out, if you don't mind telling me?" he asked in a raspy voice with a strong Iraean lilt. He didn't sound desperate, as Emrael would have expected—he was simply curious. What an odd man.

Emrael liked the man already. "How we got out will have to remain a mystery for now. We'll let you out, but I should warn you that Sarlon here won't hesitate to crush your skull if you turn out to be more trouble than you are worth."

The man backed away from the cell door smoothly to fold himself into a bow. "Fair enough. I count myself indebted to you all the same, young man. Let's get going before the guards change their shift, shall we?"

"What are you in here for?" Elle asked as Emrael fiddled with the lock. It hadn't been opened in some time and the key did not turn easily.

The man laughed softly. "I don't know what the official charge was, or if they even made one. For all I know, there is no record that I'm even down here. If they had to put a charge to me, I suppose it'd likely be tax evasion. Or maybe illegal trafficking of goods. Lack of respect for my betters. Rebellion. Who knows. I also hurt a few

Watchers pretty bad when they came for me; might have even killed some. They didn't like that much."

Emrael finally turned the key in the lock and stepped clear of the door as he opened it. "Sounds like we are in good company, then. Listen, we're here looking for my brother and other *infusori* Crafters that the Lord Holder might be holding captive for Corrande. Do you have any idea where they might be held?"

The prisoner shook his head. "This floor is for the ones they don't intend to let out for a very long time. There's a chance that they are being held elsewhere in Whitehall Keep, but you'll have to go through dozens of guards and as many Watchers to search for him. What's your brother done to upset Corrande?"

"My brother's done nothing but be a genius Crafter. Corrande attacked the Citadel and imprisoned *infusori* Crafters to build weapons for him."

The prisoner whistled through his beard. "If they have anything to do with *infusori* Crafting, they'll likely be up in the manufactory buildings near the *infusori* Wells themselves. But there's no way up there that doesn't entail going through scores of Norta guardsmen and Watchers at the gate."

"Damn them," Emrael swore. "Well, you said you know the way out of here. Lead on."

True to his word, the man seemed to know exactly where he was going. They followed him down the dark hallway, through a series of doors, vacant storerooms, and small, quiet passageways. At times, he'd have them stop and wait in the shadows as Norta guardsmen and others passed by in adjacent hallways.

Just as Emrael was wondering whether it had been wise to follow a man they had just met—who had obviously been in solitary imprisonment for quite some time and was quite possibly cracked in the head—they arrived at a dusty storeroom with a large door set in the exterior stone wall. This door was strapped with iron and obviously sized for large items to pass through but just as obviously hadn't been used in quite some time.

"This is it," the prisoner said. "The door will be locked but lets out right in front of the canyon gate that leads up to the *infusori* Wells. The guards at the gate will certainly see us, so once we exit, we'd better be moving quickly."

Emrael found the right key and turned it in the several locks built into the door. Before he could jerk the door open, however, the prisoner put his hand on Emrael's shoulder. Emrael's gut instinct was to lash out violently, but he restrained himself after only a twitch. Fallen take him, he was getting jumpy.

"I won't be staying with you once we are out there," their fellow escapee said, offering his hand. "I can't risk being caught, and I have a much better chance on my own. But I'll leave first and draw the guards off. If you do make it, I'll repay you, I swear it. What's your name, lad?"

Emrael shook the man's proffered hand. "Ire. Emrael Ire."

"Is that so?" he asked, sucking air through his teeth in surprise.

"It is."

"Hmm," the man said, stroking his beard.

"And yours?" Elle asked, stepping up beside Emrael.

"Dorae Norta."

"Any relation to Lord Holder Norta?"

Dorae smiled. "I'm his most beloved son. He loves me so much, he wanted to keep me real close, you see?"

Elle didn't return his smile. "What did you do to get your own father to imprison you in the deepest level of his keep?"

Dorae squinted at her as he replied, all traces of his smile gone. "I tried to steal his Holding. His people starve under the burden of Corrande's taxes while he profits more than ever from kissing Corrande's feet. I . . . didn't exactly follow in his footsteps."

Emrael nodded approvingly as he recalled his father mentioning a rebellion led by the Norta heir. A rebellion Janrael had been asked to join but had declined. He wondered whether Dorae held any ill will toward his father. Or toward him.

Though the man seemed to be eyeing him with respect and curiosity more than anything, Emrael watched Dorae carefully and turned to Elle and Sarlon. "Ready?"

They both nodded. He jerked the door open. The doorway was carved into the base of Whitehall Keep where it met the canyon roadway, about fifty paces from the gate leading up to the *infusori* Wells.

Dorae sprinted out immediately, crossing the large square that surrounded Whitehall and heading down the roadway toward the city as fast as he could. He ran well for a man who had obviously spent considerable time locked in a small cell. Shouts echoed down from the gate, and Emrael stuck out a hand to stop Elle from exiting the doorway.

Several guardsmen on horseback burst from the gate, galloping after Dorae, who turned abruptly into a side street. Emrael sincerely hoped he made it, but he was glad the man had created a diversion for them nonetheless.

He waited for the gate to close and to make sure no more riders emerged, then exited the doorway at a run, Elle and Sarlon immediately behind him.

21

Hours later, they crashed into the common room of their inn near the river to find Toravin, Halrec, and Jaina sitting at an isolated table in one corner, talking intensely but discreetly.

Joral and Prilan sat a few tables away, quiet but watchful as they hovered over tankards, ensuring no one came close enough to hear what was being discussed. Prilan glared openly at Emrael but seemed content to keep it at that.

Emrael clapped Joral on the shoulder as he walked by their table, then planted his fists on the corner table next to Toravin. Before he could say anything, however, Jaina jumped up with a gasp.

"Sarlon! How did you get here? Where is Yamara?" she exclaimed, looking around.

Sarlon approached the table, shaking his head silently, unable to speak. It was Jaina's turn to envelop the big man in a hug. "Oh, Sarlon, I'm so sorry. The Sisters will watch over her in the Halls above."

Sarlon separated himself from her and took a deep, shuddering breath. "I know they will. She feels no more pain or sorrow. Now, enough about me. We have matters to tend to."

Emrael cleared his throat, drawing the group's eyes. "Ban may be up near the *infusori* Wells." He told them about the Lord Holder, and about meeting Dorae in the dungeon beneath the keep.

Toravin interrupted him there. "Dorae? You are certain of the name?"

Emrael, Elle, and Sarlon all nodded.

Toravin's face broke into a wide smile. "I knew that shifty bastard wouldn't go down so easily. I'm glad to hear he's alive."

"He was alive last we saw him, at any rate. Norta guards were on his heels." Emrael looked from Toravin to Jaina and back. "Did either of you learn anything from your contacts in the city? What do they know of captives being held here?"

Jaina shook her head. "None of my people know any more than we do. Our sources across the Provinces have gone silent in the wake of Corrande's declaration of war. The Sentinels and their Watchers have been hunting for Ordenans."

Emrael pounded a fist into the table, shaking the tankards enough to spill some ale. "Absent Gods take them. I need *something*."

Toravin cleared his throat. "Several acquaintances that I talked to said that wagons loaded with people have indeed gone up the canyon that holds the *infusori* Wells. As only the Watchers and Corrande's own men have been allowed up the canyon since they arrived, my people don't know much more than that."

Emrael's gut fluttered with nervous anticipation. His brother might be in this city after all. "Will any of your friends help us? We need to get in there as quickly as possible."

Toravin shook his head. "Not much chance of that, I'm afraid. Together, the bands that run the darker side of this city would likely be enough to overwhelm the Lord Holder's guards and the Watcher garrison. Most of them have military training of one sort or another, and they hate the Lord Holder and his Corrande masters more than most. But they hate each other almost as much as they hate the Lord Holder. They'll never work together."

Emrael pounded his fist on the table again. "Can you think of any way we can get into that canyon and bring the captives out by ourselves? Any of you?" He looked around the table, only to see a chorus of shaking heads. "Maybe we can force their hands, then. Would these criminal lords fight if the Watchers attacked them?"

Toravin's brows drew down pensively. "How do you mean?"

"Dorae said something about hating his father's taxes. I'd imagine it's a sore spot with your friends and the people of the city as well?"

"It is . . . Most blame the Lord Holder for playing nice with them, but the real oppressors are the boys in blue. They're the ones that gather the tax money these days, and deal harshly with dissent." Toravin said, steel in his voice, "You should know, Ire. They were the ones that kicked your family off the throne at the end of the War of Unification."

Emrael nodded, baring his teeth in a vicious smile. "I'd imagine that said taxes are gathered and held for a time in Watcher garrisons before being transferred to a more secure vault in their keep?"

"I'd imagine so."

"What do you suppose might happen if a few Watcher patrols in the rougher parts of town, say, the areas where these gangs control things, were to be attacked and the taxes taken back?"

Toravin's face was blank as he stared at Emrael for a tense moment.

Then he smiled, a wide, mean smile. "I like it. We plant the money with the gang leaders only, though. Then nobody gets hurt but those that deserve it and can fight back. What's more, if I can find Dorae, he'll join us in a heartbeat. He'll know which Watcher guard houses hold money, and he's well regarded by less savory folk, high and low. They'll follow his lead once things turn ugly, and they will keep the Watchers and the Lord Holder's guards busy while you hit the *infusori* Wells."

Emrael smiled back. "Perfect."

Halrec shook his head from where he sat next to Jaina. "Innocent people are going to get hurt, Em. What you're talking about isn't an isolated conflict between Watchers, guards, and these street toughs. Ordinary folk will become involved—you know they will. Fathers, grandfathers, women, even children will be killed. Hundreds, thousands of them."

Guilt pricked Emrael, but he replied hotly. "Do you have a better idea, then, Halrec? Glory, Hal, we're talking about fighting a man who treats his entire Holding like dogs, and Watchers who took my own brother as a literal slave. I bet there are plenty of towns just like this one, all suffering at Norta's or some other Lord Holder's hand, at Corrande's. I don't like it either, but we don't have another choice."

Halrec's demeanor darkened. "You are sacrificing all those people to save one person—your brother. I understand, Em, I do. But how is that just? What do you think Corrande and the Watchers will do to these people once the dust settles? Things will be much worse for the regular people, just like after the last ill-fated rebellion. You are the only one who wins with this scheme."

Emrael slammed his hand down on the table a third time, hard enough to knock Toravin's drink over. "Fallen take you, Hal, how is this any different from anything you've done in the Barros Legion? The people you're sent off to fight—Iraeans, mostly, unless I miss my guess—would probably prefer to be left alone. Besides, we are just encouraging a conflict that is likely to happen anyway. The Iraean people are all prisoners; they just haven't had a real chance to fight free. They want this, and I might be able to give it to them."

His friend looked uncomfortable now, conflicted. "Some want this, sure. But do they know what this could turn into? Do you? This could spark a war that could last years, could cost hundreds of thousands of lives. Lives you can choose to save, Em. In the Legion, I didn't get to choose. But now we do. *You* do."

Emrael paused, throat tight with emotion. He knew his friend was right, but it didn't change what he had to do. This felt right, no matter the cost. "I have to, Hal. I can't let my brother die in chains. If this Dorae and other Iraeans are willing to help me, I'll help them. I'll pay the price with them." He paused again and looked at his friend sadly. "You don't have to help. You're free to leave anytime you'd like."

Halrec took a deep breath, his expression deflating as anger turned to defeat. "Perhaps that's exactly what I should do. I left my post, and there will likely be a warrant out for my arrest as soon as it's discovered we survived the ambush at the bridge. I'll be in deep shit, but better I face it willingly than be brought in like a common criminal."

Elle chimed in. "I'll go with you, Halrec. You only left your post to help us, and I can vouch for you with my father and his Commanders. Besides, if Ban and Sami aren't here, we're likely to need my father's help to rescue them from the Citadel. But let's go after we help Emrael here."

Emrael's anger and guilt now warred with disappointment that Halrec and Elle were willing to leave him. He looked from his oldest friend to Elle and back before nodding, jaw clenched. "Okay. I understand. If you are going, it might be safe to leave now, before the fighting starts."

Both Halrec and Elle shook their heads.

"I may not agree with it," Halrec said, one hand raised in protest, "but I am not going to leave before seeing whether Ban and Sami are here."

"You're a Fallen idiot if you think I'll leave without knowing, either," Elle said hotly.

Emrael raised his hands in mock defeat. "Okay, okay. Mercy, I don't know what you want. You want Ban and the others free but you don't want to start the battle that will free them. Make up your minds."

Halrec glared at him, but less balefully than before. "I may not like it, but I'm not going to leave you here to do this by yourself, either. Someone has to keep you from getting yourself—and everybody else—killed. At least for the next day or two."

Emrael gripped his friend's shoulder and smiled sadly. "Thank you, Hal. I truly appreciate that."

He turned back to Toravin. "How quickly can you find Dorae and have the attacks on the guard houses arranged?"

Toravin shrugged. "Midnight?"

"Do it."

—••—

Crossbows twanged, quarrels flew.

A full squad of Watchers crashed onto the dirt road, bleeding and gasping for their last taste of air. Tough men in rough clothing moved in quickly with assorted weapons, silencing the wounded. In moments, the Watcher mounts that survived had been led from the street and ten men pulled on bloodstained Watcher uniforms.

Dorae smiled. He'd been waiting for this moment for a very, very long time. Who'd have thought it would come today? He rubbed his hand over his now clean-shaven face. It was odd to not have a tangled mass of beard after so many years locked away in his father's dungeon.

The men following him were a mixture of off-duty soldiers from his father's guard and friends he had made over the years in less-reputable circles. No matter their background, one and all knew what Dorae was about and were willing to fight for him, especially if it meant opposing the Lord Holder and his Provincial masters.

Dorae gathered them quickly, pointing at several of them who had less blood on their blue uniforms. "You four enter the guard-house as soon as we arrive. The rest of us will be just a step behind you. Start killing as soon as somebody realizes you aren't Watchers. After tonight, we'll have these blue bastards out of our city for good. And we'll get our money back while we're at it."

His boys gave a quiet cheer before falling in line behind him.

The nearest Watcher guardhouse big enough to hold levied money was only two streets away. They flaunted their wealth and superiority over their inferiors; large, expensive blue *infusori* coils lit the exterior of the building, making it visible from a block away.

They trotted up to the building, and the four men he had picked slipped through the doors. Dorae counted slowly to three, then waved the others through. Shouts, screams, and the screeching of metal on metal severed the silence of the night. He strode in to find several Watchers bleeding out on the floor, and two more being led from the back in their underclothes, wild-eyed, arms tied tight behind their backs. Only one of his men was wounded. He was carried away by his friends, clutching the wound in his side.

Dorae clapped, and his soldiers joined in slowly. "Tonight," he shouted, "we throw off the shackles of Provincial bondage! We have suffered since the war of our grandfathers. Tonight, we are free Iraeans again!"

22

"That was fast," Emrael murmured in Toravin's direction. They hid in an alley off the *infusori* Well canyon highway, near where the canyon gate funneled into the vast square that surrounded Whitehall Keep. From their vantage at the edge of the square, dozens of fires could be seen blazing throughout the city. Most were Watcher outposts, but not all. In more than one place in the city, entire neighborhoods looked to be burning. He could only hope that the residents had escaped the violence.

One particularly large blaze illuminated the square in front of the Watcher compound across the bridge. The sounds of intense battle sang sweet in the night air. He had hoped for a diversion but had started a war. One that the Iraeans looked likely to win, at least tonight.

Toravin smiled in the darkness. "Freeing Dorae was the smartest thing you've ever done, Ire. He knows his business. He would have fought his father again sooner rather than later. You just accelerated the timeline."

As they spoke, the creaking of the canyon gate preceded five squads of Watchers leaving on horseback, weapons drawn, riding toward the battle raging across the overpass bridge.

Emrael tapped Halrec and Jaina on the shoulder. "Now is as good a time as any. Those five squads are likely to be the bulk of the men they had stationed in the canyon."

Nervous energy coursed through him as they left Toravin, Sarlon, Joral, Prilan, and Elle in the alleyway. He wasn't happy about Elle joining them, but she had insisted, and Jaina had agreed that a healer might be needed. He wasn't happy about Prilan being there, either, but wasn't about to let him out of his sight.

They skirted the square in front of the canyon gate quietly, staying in the shadows cast by the coils mounted atop the wall and gate. When they arrived at the point where the wall met the natural rock of the canyon, Emrael laced his fingers together, boosting first Jaina, then Halrec up the wall to find their first handhold.

Emrael scrambled after them, making the top of the wall just after the other two. Hands stinging, breathing heavily, he crouched with Halrec in the shadows to watch as Jaina swiftly stalked the only guard in sight. The Watcher stood on the rampart above the canyon gate, peering toward the fighting across the bridge when Jaina's knife opened his throat. She kicked him to squirm helplessly in the corner between the stone floor and the waist-high crenelated wall, then waved to Halrec and Emrael.

Emrael stared a moment, impressed and slightly stunned by the sudden lethal violence. It was easy to forget how dangerous Jaina really was, how accustomed to real combat. They weren't mock-fighting in a training yard any longer.

He shook it off quickly, and the three of them moved to the door of the guardhouse that served as the only entry point to the keep from the top of the gate wall. Jaina grabbed the handle and looked to Emrael. He drew his sword and nodded.

She jerked the door open, and Emrael charged through, Halrec close on his heels. The guardhouse was empty.

Emrael looked around carefully, then straightened from his fight-ready stance. He met Halrec's puzzled look with one of his own. Jaina entered and shook her head. "Idiots. They leave their station unguarded at the first sign of trouble."

Halrec snorted. "Isn't this what we were hoping for? Emrael's plan is working, for better or worse."

Jaina just shook her head again. "Idiots."

Emrael moved quickly to the door leading to the stairwell that would let out onto the highway on the canyon side of the gate.

Before he could open it, the door swung open. Four Norta guardsmen and one Watcher rushed through the doorway. They took several steps inside before registering that Emrael, Halrec, and Jaina were standing there, weapons drawn.

As the men went for their weapons, shouting in alarm, Emrael put his sword through the Watcher's chest. He twisted his blade as he pulled it free in a spray of blood. Halrec's blade found the throat of one of the guardsmen, and Jaina met blades with another who pulled his weapon free just in time to save himself from a decapitating blow.

"Yield!" Halrec shouted, but the guardsman he now fought either didn't hear him or didn't care. Each of them had an even fight now, and Jaina's opponent was slowing visibly, barely able to keep his blade up after taking several wounds in rapid succession.

Emrael feinted, knocked his opponent's blade aside, and followed with a sweeping stroke that nearly took the man's arm off at the elbow. He screamed, and Emrael clubbed him in the side of the head with the pommel of his sword.

He took stock of the situation around him. Jaina's foe was down, but Halrec still fought the last Norta guardsman.

"Yield!" Halrec shouted again. "We aren't here for you!"

The guardsman ignored him, pressing the attack.

Emrael stepped forward and drove his blade into the guardsman's back, straight through the heart. He jerked the blade out of the man and stepped back to let him fall.

"Sad," Halrec panted, shaking his head. "He's an Iraean, just like us. It's not his fault Norta and the Watchers are assholes."

Emrael grimaced. "My brother doesn't have time for us to debate everyone who tries to kill us tonight. They are on the wrong side of this fight, and that's that."

Jaina strode forward, giving them both a gentle shove. "No time for this, either, boys. Let's go."

Emrael broke his gaze from Halrec's and slipped through the doorway. They did not encounter anyone in the stairwell, but a lone Watcher had been left to mind the gate itself.

The Watcher looked over in surprise when the three of them sprinted out of the stairwell. Jaina threw a knife just as the Watcher tried to cry out in warning. The blade took him in the chest, turning his shout into a squeaking wheeze.

Emrael ran to the gate's *infusori*-powered crank mechanism and depressed the lever actuator for a few seconds, opening one side of the gate just enough for their friends to fit through.

Almost immediately, he heard boots pounding across the cobbled square outside. Toravin was the first through, Sarlon the last. The big man had to turn sideways to fit through, which he did with a muttered curse directed at Emrael.

Once they were all through, Emrael closed the gate and gathered them quickly. "Double file on me. Stay quiet."

Jaina paused long enough to liberate the now-dead guard lying by the gate of his crossbow while Elle stared at the dead man in horror, then fell in next to Emrael at the front of the column. They trotted up the road that had been carved through the mountain in places where the natural landscape would have made a road this wide impractical. Emrael's anxiety spiked each time they traversed one of these tight passes. If prisoners were being held up there, the

Watchers would have kept at least a small force with them, and if a Watcher patrol happened to be coming down the canyon, Emrael and his friends were in trouble. Most of them were armed, but they had no shields and only one crossbow between them.

They did not have to go far, but the quick pace and the steep slope of the canyon had most of them breathing heavily and wiping their brows as they approached a complex of several buildings that occupied a large, flat area where the canyon opened into a bowl.

The largest building was a Watcher outpost, judging by the *infusori* coils mounted on the exterior and the detached stable large enough to house dozens of horses. The other buildings likely housed equipment and coils coming to and from the Wells. Three smaller roads led from this bowl up smaller canyons, presumably to *infusori* Wells.

They stopped well short of the large building, as Emrael could see a sentry posted next to the door.

"There's no way we can clear the whole building if there is even a stripped contingent of Watchers in there," Emrael whispered.

Jaina hefted her crossbow to one shoulder and pushed him out of the way with a curt "Stay quiet."

Sarlon chuckled darkly as Jaina crept forward in the shadows until she was a mere hundred paces or so from the outpost. "Get ready, kids. She'll have it clear in no time."

A sharp snap of a crossbow string echoed through the little valley, and the sentry crumpled. Jaina's lithe form darted to the downed sentry, stabbed him for good measure, drew his weapon, and approached the building. She did a quick circuit of the building, peering through the windows carefully, ensuring that Watchers were the only occupants.

When she was satisfied, she snuck back to the door, snagging an *infusori* coil from a sconce on the way.

Emrael stood and ran a few steps toward her, worried that she would try to fight an entire building full of Watchers by herself. Instead, she jammed the stolen weapon into the doorframe and placed her hand on the wooden door. The entire door burst into flame at once.

"Holy shit," Emrael said. Elle gasped behind him, and several of the others murmured in surprise. Emrael and the rest ran toward Jaina as she retreated twenty paces to reload her crossbow.

The entire building was in flames within moments. The walls

were made of stone, but the door, window casings, and roof were made of wood and were apparently very, very flammable. Screams and confused shouts emanated from the building.

Emrael grabbed Jaina's arm in a panic. "You made sure there are only Watchers in the building? You're sure my brother isn't in there?"

Jaina nodded confidently. "I am sure, Emrael. I had a good view of the inside; it is only one big room and holds only Watchers in uniform."

A window broke, and Jaina calmly turned to put a quarrel through the man who tried to climb out of it.

Emrael turned to Elle, touched her shoulder gently. "You okay?" he asked softly. She nodded but gagged a little as the smoke reached them, smelling of burning hair and meat.

He was going to be sick himself if he stayed there much longer. He backed up a step to take everyone in. "Toravin and Halrec, you take the north road. Jaina and Sarlon, take the middle road. Elle and I will take the south road. Joral, Prilan, search these warehouses here. Meet back here with anyone we find. Get me immediately if you find Ban. All good?"

Everyone nodded and set out. Joral was already kicking down warehouse doors while Prilan moped along behind him, but Emrael paused, looking up at the long canyon road in front of them.

"Wait here," Emrael told Elle. He raced back to the compound, swerving wide around the still-burning building and into the stable. Emrael found a horse with saddle already on—likely kept ready for messengers—and led it from the stables.

He swung into the saddle and trotted quickly back to Elle. "Elle, are you sure you want to be part of this? You can stay here with Joral and Prilan, I can take this canyon myself."

She growled her displeasure and climbed into the saddle, forcing Emrael to slide back to sit behind her. "You wouldn't last a minute without me."

The road up to the Wells was more of a cart path than a road, and their horse cautiously picked its way up the rocky path in the dark.

Emrael felt it before he saw it. A pulsing, vibrating power beckoning to him, almost like he'd felt in the temple. Though this was muted, more distant than it had been in that mysterious place. He opened himself to it but couldn't flood himself with the *infusori*, no matter how hard he tried.

The Well came into view as they rounded a curve. It was a massive pit carved into the rock, big enough to swallow a small house whole. Dozens of coils hung on posts around the Well and along a path carved into the outside edge of the pit, spiraling downward. The coils pulsed brighter, then dimmer, in cadence with the ebb and flow of *infusori* Emrael could feel emanating from the Well.

As interesting as it was for Emrael to see this *infusori* Well—control of a Well was worth several fortunes, even a relatively small one like this—his attention was on the large stone building perched next to it. He hopped down from where he sat behind the saddle, snagged a glowing coil from one of the posts, drew his sword, and strode to the door.

He kicked in the wooden door in with a shower of splinters and rolled the coil into the building, blade held at the ready.

He gasped. He had expected to find at least one guard, had hoped to find some captives, but was not prepared for what he found.

The stench hit him first. The building smelled like a barn that hadn't been mucked for weeks. Rows of steel-barred cages lined each side of the building, with several dirty, scared people staring at him from each. There must have been thirty of them in the building, each shackled to a worktable within their cage. They cowered from the light of the coil. None of them said a word, though several wept quietly.

Picking the coil up quickly, he checked the building just to be sure no guards or Malithii were hiding in the shadows. When he was sure it was clear, he called to Elle, and she searched frantically for a key as he inspected the cages. He approached every cell, shining the light in to make sure none of them were Ban. His stomach sank as he searched the last cell and didn't find his brother. He recognized some of the prisoners as fellow Citadel students, though he couldn't remember any of their names. He hadn't made many close friends at the Citadel, especially among the Crafters.

"Elle?" a tremulous voice called softly, the first noise they'd heard out of any of the caged Crafters. Elle and Emrael both spun around, staring. A girl in a dirty dress approached the front of her cage, pointing at Elle. "It *is* you! Oh, Elle, get us out, get us out! They've been so horrible to us. They make us work on their Craftings all day, and hardly feed us or let us wash."

At that, the rest of the captives clamored and wailed to be let out of their cages as well. Emrael shouted to try to assure them that they were doing their best, but the captive students wouldn't listen, and the din grew louder.

Emrael desisted looking for a key to the locked cells and stalked outside angrily. He wrenched one of the coil-bearing steel poles out of the ground and hurried back inside. He sucked *infusori* from the coil until it was dull gold and his hair shone with blue fury.

He tossed the coil and stopped in front of the first cage.

"Get back." He jammed the steel pole into a gap near the lock mechanism of the door and pulled the pole with all the force he could muster.

The lock broke almost immediately, and Emrael ended up in a heap on the floor. Elle even giggled a bit despite the circumstances. Grumbling as he picked himself up, he approached the next cell and broke that lock. The Watchers must not have been too worried about these people breaking free—these locks were terrible.

When the cells were all open, he looked to where Elle was tending to the worst of the captives in the middle of the large building. Many of the captives had stayed in their cells, apparently still too frightened to exit, though all seemed healthy enough to walk.

Emrael shook his head. He didn't have time or patience to deal with this. "If you want to live, follow us. We'll get you out of here. Or you can stay and work for the Watchers."

That got them moving.

Emrael strode through the crowd of freed captives, shepherding Elle before him. She stopped him at the door, a hand on his chest. "Em, these people can't move very fast. None of them are injured badly, but they're confused and on the brink of panic. You yelling at them won't help."

"Elle, we really don't have time for this. Especially after that fire Jaina set, we could have Watchers down our throats at any minute. We move now, and I'm going to keep yelling."

Elle's eyes darkened and she drew herself up, ready to argue, but sighed instead. "You're right," she said sourly.

Emrael nodded, nonchalant. "Get them moving however you can. And ask them if they've seen Ban or Sami."

He retrieved the horse and helped Elle boost two of the younger girls into the saddle. In short order, Elle had checked with each of the prisoners and reported that none of them had seen Ban or Sami since leaving the Citadel, and that they were as ready to move as they'd ever be. They started down the canyon, Elle leading the horse at the front, Emrael bringing up the rear of the loose, stumbling group of freed captives.

His instincts made him duck as he caught a flash of motion out of the corner of his eye as he passed the ramp down into the *infusori*

Well. He watched in horror as a quarrel sank into the side of the boy—Ban's age—who had been walking next to him. The boy fell, squirming and coughing blood.

Emrael's chest tightened as he turned from the dying boy, his imagination turning the boy momentarily into Ban. His vision went white at the edges as his shock quickly turned to rage. Breath coming in ragged pants, he whipped his sword from its scabbard as he stalked in the direction from which the quarrel had come.

A Malithii priest emerged from the Well and tossed an *infusori*-Crafted crossbow to the side. He unhooked a metallic coil from his belt, just like the ones the Malithii had used on the road outside Lidran. Unlike those priests who had relied solely on the cable, however, this one drew a short sword with his other hand and approached Emrael at an arrogant, purposeful walk.

Emrael paused, suddenly unsure of himself despite the anger surging through him, spurring him on. To hear Jaina tell it, these Malithii could be extremely dangerous. He had caught the few he'd fought by surprise, and he couldn't count on getting that lucky with this one.

If he waited much longer, however, the priest would exit the ring of light cast by the *infusori* coils, and Emrael would have a hell of a time keeping track of the black-clad priest then. The kids they had just freed would be slaughtered. Mind made up, he screamed in Elle's direction, "Run, Elle! Get them down to the compound. Tell Jaina there's a Malithii up here. I'll hold him as long as I can. Run!"

He didn't wait to see whether Elle obeyed. He jogged to meet the dark priest, anger and fear fueling him in equal measure. The Malithii stopped, waiting calmly to meet Emrael.

Emrael didn't like the confidence with which his opponent waited for him, so he slowed, circling the priest instead of rushing him.

Like all Malithii he had seen, both in real life and his book-vision, extensive tattoos covered his pale skin. While intimidating, what really concerned Emrael were the man's eyes. They showed no fear, no hatred, no emotion; the man simply studied him. His eyes flicked down to the pendant around Emrael's neck and back to his face. He knew about the Observer.

I might be in trouble, Emrael thought.

As they circled, the Malithii reached out to nonchalantly pluck an *infusori* coil from where it hung from a steel post, drawing the *infusori* into himself in the space of a breath. The light around them dimmed and the Malithii's eyes glowed blue.

Emrael would have been content to keep circling the Malithii, distracting him from the rest of the captives and giving Jaina a chance to help him.

The Malithii had other plans. He whipped the metallic coil at Emrael's head.

Emrael jerked backward, stumbling in his haste to avoid the attack. He felt the cable snap, grazing the skin just below his right eye.

The Malithii pressed the advantage. Emrael desperately deflected a thrust of the priest's sword. He kicked at the priest's knee to force him backward, then launched an attack of his own.

They traded several blows, each of them narrowly avoiding being skewered by the other.

The Malithii smiled suddenly. He whipped the metal cable much faster than before, latching it on to Emrael's left forearm. A look of concentration flitted across the priest's face as he encountered the impedance of Ban's amulet, then Emrael's world turned to agony. He cringed, desperately resisting the Malithii's *infusori* attack while keeping his sword up in a feeble attempt to counter any physical attack.

Emrael straightened slowly, rebuffing the unseen attack until the pain subsided. Both men stood still, eyes locked, continuing their invisible struggle for several long moments. Emrael threw every ounce of determination and will that he could summon into the struggle.

Rather than count on his newfound and unreliable talent with *infusori*, Emrael decided to play to his strengths.

He heaved his left arm back with all his strength, hauling on the cable and nearly pulling the Malithii off his feet.

The priest's strike came as Emrael expected. He parried the priest's blade and planted a kick squarely in the priest's midsection as momentum carried him into Emrael. He felt bones snap through his boot, and the Malithii crashed to the ground, coughing and struggling to breathe. A broken rib must have punctured a lung.

Emrael freed his arm from the cable and approached carefully. The priest still held on to his blade, so Emrael planted the tip of his sword in the priest's forearm, pinning it to the ground while he kicked his foe's blade away.

Emrael rolled the Malithii over roughly. "Where's my brother?" he asked roughly.

The priest laughed softly, blood bubbling at his lips. "You'll not learn from me, mageling."

"Where is my brother?" Emrael shouted this time, stabbing the priest in the leg for emphasis. The priest screamed hoarsely and cursed in a harsh foreign tongue but said nothing Emrael could understand.

Emrael rammed his sword into the man's gut, screaming, "Give me my brother!"

The priest doubled over, blood dripping from his mouth, painting his teeth red as he grinned through his pain.

Emrael stabbed him over and over, rage drowning rational thought. His hands and arms were covered in blood.

He stopped, fell silent, and watched as the priest choked his last breaths. When the priest had fallen still, Emrael kicked the body one last time before dragging it to the edge of the Well. He picked it up and heaved it into the pit, spitting after it. He never heard it hit bottom.

As he trudged away from the pit, exhausted, the Malithii's copper cable caught his eye. He picked it up and was about to jog down the canyon after Elle and the others, but something else caught his eye; the body of the boy that had been hit by the quarrel meant for him.

He knelt next to the boy, placed a hand on his still-warm shoulder. Hot tears pooled in his eyes, then streamed down his face. A sob croaked from his lips as crippling panic gripped him. He could hardly bear the thought that Ban may have shared this boy's fate at the hands of the Watchers and their Malithii allies. He would kill them, every single person involved, if anything happened to Ban.

He took a deep breath to calm himself, steeling himself mentally against what would come. He wiped the tears and blood from his face with the inside of his shirt, then closed the boy's eyelids gently before rising to trot down the canyon.

Emrael arrived at the main compound just as Jaina and Sarlon did. They had several freed captives in tow, though none were Ban or Sami. Emrael threw the Malithii metal-cable weapon near Jaina's feet as she drew near. "There was a Malithii priest hiding in the Well up there."

Jaina's eyebrows climbed her forehead, but she said nothing as she eyed his bloodstained hands and arms. Sarlon clapped him on the shoulder. "Good on you, lad. About time you made yourself useful."

Proud of Sarlon's compliment but trying not to show it, he walked over to where Elle, Halrec, Toravin, Prilan, and Joral waited near the warehouses, talking to the prisoners that had been freed. Hope surged in Emrael as he realized that there were more there than Elle had led down the canyon. He checked each of the prisoners frantically, desperate to find Ban among them, but to no avail. Ban wasn't there.

He gripped his intricate hourglass-shaped pendant tightly once more, holding it up to his ear to listen for any contact from his brother. Nothing.

Please, Absent Gods, let him be alive. He's got to be at the Citadel. He's got to be.

Emrael turned to his friends, anxiety roiling his gut. "You are sure you got all of them, you checked everywhere?"

They all nodded, and Halrec stepped forward to put a hand on Emrael's shoulder. "We checked everywhere there was to check, twice. There isn't anybody else here, Em."

Emrael hurried over to the prisoners, addressing the ones who looked the most coherent. "Do you know where Ban Ire is? My brother, looks about like me but taller with brown hair?"

The liberated prisoners shook their heads slowly. A black-haired girl broke down sobbing, tears streaming from her eyes. "I . . . I haven't seen him since we left the Citadel. They . . . they brought us here because we weren't very good at Crafting."

Emrael punched the side of a nearby warehouse, cracking the wood exterior. Pain lanced through his hand. He didn't care. "Fallen take these bastards!" he screamed.

His last hope was that Darmon hadn't been lying, that Ban was still at the Citadel.

He jerked his sword from its scabbard and led the way back down to the gate, not looking behind to see who followed. *Infusori* surged within him as his emotions ran wild. He almost hoped Watchers or Norta guardsmen would give him a fight, regardless of the odds. It was probably for the best that the road remained empty.

The gate adjacent to Whitehall Keep still stood unmanned but for the dead guardsman. Emrael scanned his surroundings as he approached the gate, unable to believe that more guardsmen or Watchers hadn't discovered the open gate and their downed comrades. He heard the sounds of heavy fighting from somewhere outside and opened the gate to find Norta guardsmen and townsfolk fighting a squad of Watchers in the square. He watched, stunned, as the Watchers were overwhelmed one by one.

The guardsmen and armed townsfolk ran toward the gate as soon as the Watchers went down. Emrael leapt for the gate mechanism with a strangled curse.

The men outside arrived at the gate just before it shut completely, and one of them jammed a wooden stave into the gap. Several *thud*s and a great deal of grunting and shouting announced more bodies throwing their weight against the gate. The men outside jabbed spears and swords blindly through the small gap, though who they hoped to stab was beyond him. Blue light flashed as the *infusori*-powered gate mechanism groaned, struggling to shut the gate against the force of the men pushing outside.

Then Toravin was there, shouting at the men outside the gate. "Boys, boys, it's Toravin. We're with you, you shit-brains!"

The shouting and the struggling against the gate stopped, and a baritone voice called out. "Tor? Why'd you shut the gate on us?"

Toravin looked at Emrael with one eyebrow raised as he responded. "What would you do with a bunch of armed ruffians running your way in the dark?"

"Hey," another voice complained from the other side of the gate, "we ain't ruffians. We's freedom fighters."

Toravin laughed. "So you are." He reached past Emrael to throw the lever that opened the gate. "How's the fight been?"

The baritone voice answered again as they waited for the gate to open. "Oh, just about the way Dorae said it would be. Didn't expect most of the city guard to join in with us, that they didn't. Them blue boys is all just about done for or run out of the city. Dorae's sent us to get into the keep the back way while he keeps his dear ol' dad busy out front. Didn't know he sent you, too."

Toravin laughed. "He didn't. We sent him. Come on in; the way into the keep should be clear."

After the men had filtered through the gate and into one of the open doors to the keep, Emrael slipped out the gate and into the square. His friends followed quickly.

Bodies littered the square in front of Whitehall Keep. Men in ordinary garb lay next to men in the uniforms of the Norta guardsmen at the foot of the steps to the keep. Some sported quarrels and arrows jutting from their corpses. Others had been cut down with a blade, with horrendous rents in their flesh.

Nearer the keep, dead Watchers and more guardsmen adorned the steps in haphazard heaps. Here and there men still fought, guardsman against guardsman, street tough against Watcher, but from the look of it, the fighting had already made it through the front doors of Whitehall itself.

Emrael pulled up short and his friends gathered around him, still shepherding the freed captives.

"Absent Gods," he said quietly. "They took the city."

Halrec stepped up next to him and pointed across the bridge to the Watchers' keep, where columns of smoke now rose in several places. "I told you it wouldn't just be a small distraction, Em. There may be hundreds or even thousands dead tonight. What do you think will happen when the Watchers come for them? We aren't ready for this, not even close. They aren't ready."

Anger surged in Emrael again, even though he knew his friend was right. He shook his head resignedly. "These people obviously wanted this, Hal. Glory, you saw how quickly things escalated. We didn't force that on them. We just gave them an opportunity."

Halrec sighed, then nodded. "Just be ready. I know Elle hopes her father will join you, but it's just as likely that he stays neutral while Sagmyn and Corrande join forces against you, like happened in the War of Unification. If you're going to stand a chance, you're going to need to recruit the entire Iraean kingdom, not just those loyal to Whitehall. Even then, you'll be outmatched in supplies, weaponry, and trained soldiers. I hope you have a plan for what comes next."

Emrael met his friend's stare with a serious one of his own. "I have an idea. They will come if we lead them, Halrec. Just look at them." He waved his hand at the byproducts of the just-finished battle all around them. "The Iraeans are obviously willing to pay the price for their freedom, and I'll pay it with them."

23

Emrael sent the others to get the freed captives safely back to their inn while he and Toravin approached the front steps of Whitehall Keep. Most of the fighting had subsided, but here and there, the sound of metal on metal and the screams of men drifted down to them.

The light of numerous *infusori* coils bathed the entire keep and surrounding areas in their beautiful blue light. The precious resource came cheaply to the Lord of Whitehall.

Emrael put a hand to his sword hilt as they neared the doors to the keep, but Toravin stopped him with a sharp look. "Do you want to get us killed?" he asked sarcastically. "Because that's a good way to get us killed."

Emrael glared back but left the sword in its scabbard. They proceeded through the doors and found a group of rough men with bare blades talking quietly in front of the closed doors to the audience chamber.

The men looked over sharply as they entered. Three of them approached, hefting their weapons menacingly. Toravin immediately showed his empty hands, and Emrael followed suit.

Toravin addressed the men calmly. "Dorae will want to see me. Tell him that Toravin is here."

All three of the men pulled up immediately when they heard Toravin's name. The man in the lead studied them for a moment before nodding and saying, "Wait here, sir."

The man slipped into the audience chamber and returned almost immediately, waving them inside. Sounds of laughter and shouting hit them as they entered the room.

Dorae, now in much better clothing, sat in his father's vacated chair. A few dozen men, obviously fighting men, lounged about the hall. Emrael was surprised to see that many of them were Norta guardsmen, and that they were obviously friendly with the street toughs.

The most surprising sight, however, was an old man in bedclothes sitting in a large cage in the middle of the audience chamber. As

Emrael passed the cage, he saw that the old man was in fact Lord Holder Norta. The former Lord Holder Norta, he supposed.

He and Toravin stopped just short of where Dorae sat with one leg hung over the arm of the large, ornate chair.

Dorae smiled, waving one hand at them. "What do you think? I quite liked this plan of yours, Toravin. We finally did it." He laughed, turning his attention to Emrael. "And you. I have to thank you for freeing me, Emrael Ire."

Emrael nodded, then gestured toward where Lord Holder Norta sat in his cage. "I'm surprised you left him alive, Dorae. The Holding passes to you with him gone, does it not?"

Dorae sobered. "Death is too good for that man, young Emrael. His suffering would be done in moments, when I spent years languishing in that filthy cell, and years before that living in hiding, fearing for my life and the lives of those I loved. No, I have nothing to fear from that old man anymore, and I like him just where he is. Whitehall is mine. Let everyone see what has become of the man who bled his own people—and his own son!—for his Corrande overlords."

Emrael shrugged. "Suit yourself. What now? Corrande and the other Governors—not to mention the Watchers—will be down your throat in a matter of weeks."

Dorae threw back his head and laughed, a deep, genuine laugh. "I thought to ask you the same thing, Ire! This was your plan, after all. Did you find your brother?"

Emrael clenched his fists. "No. Your father had dozens of captives up near the *infusori* Wells, but my brother was not among them. He must be at our old school, the Citadel in Myntar. I'll be heading back there tomorrow."

"By yourself?"

"I'll have a few friends with me."

Dorae's rubbed his face thoughtfully. "It's not going to be enough. You could try to sneak into your Citadel, but it won't work. You'll run into someone eventually, if the Watchers hold it. They know their business. You need an army." He held his arms out in a grand gesture. "And it just so happens that I've just acquired one, ragtag though they might be. I pay my debts, Emrael, and I'll help you."

Emrael tried not to show the excitement he felt. He wasn't even going to have to talk Dorae into giving him men for his attack on the Citadel.

Toravin chuckled. "You'll save your own skin by sending Emrael to turn the Provinces' attention elsewhere, you mean."

Dorae grinned. "Well, there's that. The Ire boy gets what he wants, I have a fighting chance at keeping my throat un-slit for a little while longer. Everybody is happy in the short term."

Emrael smiled. "I'll take your army, Dorae, but I'm not going to stop there. I'm getting my brother back, but make no mistake—we have a war on our hands, and I mean to win it. Give me an army and we'll take the Provinces for ourselves. Just as soon as I've got my brother."

Dorae stood abruptly and walked over to stare into Emrael's eyes, uncomfortably close. "You looking to be a king, put your family above us again, are you boy?" he asked quietly.

Emrael stepped even closer, until their foreheads almost touched, meeting his gaze without flinching. "I want what you want. Freedom. If I have to be a king to get it, so be it."

Dorae surprised him by smiling suddenly and pulling him into a fierce hug. "Well! We'll see about that when there's a kingdom to be had. But I like you, boy. I hope you don't die before we can give it a try. Maybe you can fill the shoes that your father never would."

He kept his close grip and pitched his voice so only Emrael could hear. "I know you're a mage, Emrael Ire. That's the only way you could have broken out of that cell so quickly, and why those Ordenans follow you like tame lions. I had my men check the cell you were in, and the stone around the iron bars is destroyed. As if a team had taken a hammer and chisel to it, they said. My father would have killed you, but I hold to the old ways. And once our people hear that there is an Ire come back to Iraea, and a mage to boot? The cry of *Mage King* may well be raised again."

Dorae pulled back and called to one of his men. "Commander, come here. I want you to meet someone."

A short boulder of a man with long, mostly grey hair and a square beard approached them, eying Emrael quizzically. Bulk covered every inch of his frame. He moved in deliberate, powerful motions, like a squat oak swaying in a heavy wind. Most intimidating of all were his eyes—hard, dark eyes that reflected the dancing light of the torches as they sized Emrael up.

Emrael peered at the man, sure he had seen him somewhere before.

Dorae put his hand on the man's shoulder. "The Commander here is the reason we are sitting in Whitehall tonight. He's a very old friend of mine, and he knew my father for the fool he was, despite being the Commander Second of his guard. I trust him with my life and more. He knows war, and he knows the Iraean people. More importantly, every fighting man within a hundred leagues will come running when they hear he's leading our army."

Dorae turned to gesture at Toravin and Emrael. "Voran, you'll remember Toravin from the old rebellion—I've *almost* forgiven him for leaving me in that cell these three long years while he roamed free. His friend here is Emrael Ire, but I'd guess that you already knew that. We have him to thank for our freedom—or I do, at any rate. He might just be our ticket to getting out of this mess with our heads still attached to our necks. The crazy bastard is going to attack the Citadel in Myntar, and we're going with him. And by *we* I mean *you*."

"Is that so?" the Commander asked, lips pressed together in a frown.

At the sound of his voice, memory of this man burst into Emrael's mind. Voran Loire had aged a great deal in the short years since Emrael had last seen him, and his appearance was very different due to the hair and beard, but Emrael was sure it was the same man who had been with him—and had saved him—the day his father had disappeared.

"Voran Loire," Emrael said suddenly. "You're the one who carried me back across the river when my father died."

Voran continued to eye Emrael darkly. "Aye, it was me. Boy, I know your history better than most, but if you think that your blood entitles you to play god with my people, you had best think harder."

Emrael laughed, taken aback. "Play god? There are no gods left in this world, Voran. After tonight, my plan might be the only thing that saves you and your people from the shit storm that's coming. This city will burn, and every man, woman and child with it. I will give you a fighting chance at freedom."

Voran's expression grew darker.

"We fight," Emrael continued, pitching his voice so every man in the crowded hall would hear him. "You have grievances? Settle them with the sword. You want rights? Earn them with the sword. You want freedom? Free yourselves with the sword. I march for Myntar, and I *will* take any who are willing with me."

"You look here, you little bastard—" Voran began, before Toravin cut in, putting a hand on Voran's arm.

"I'm going with him," Toravin said, meeting Voran's stare for a long moment.

"You are, are you?" Voran asked in a surprised, quiet voice. "And just what could make you, of all people, trust this boy? Many men will follow him if we let them—for his name, if nothing else. They are scared, tired of Corrande's taxes, tired of the Sentinels' preaching and the Watchers' ready clubs. They will all die, Toravin, every single one of them, if we follow this boy. This lad knows nothing of real war, or of caring for a people."

"He will if we help him, Voran. Especially if *you* help him. I watched the lad take a spear for a woman and children he owed nothing. Which of us would do that? The people want a king, and who're we to keep one from them? He has the blood right, the same as Dorae here does to Whitehall."

Voran laughed. "He has no blood right left—his family forfeited blood right when they fled Iraea after the war, as did mine for following them. Even the meanest beggar in Iraea has better claim to the Ire Holding, much less the throne."

"I know that. You know that. But the people don't, or don't care. Laws won't save us. The Lords of Iraea won't save us, hiding in their keeps as they have all these years. This boy and his name, his blood, his stupid courage have the chance to save our people. I'm taking that chance, blood right or no."

Voran again stared at Toravin for quite some time. "I'll do what I can. But Justice help me, Toravin. If you are leading us on a fool's chase, you will both envy the Fallen God's fate before I'm done with you."

Toravin chuckled darkly, and Emrael allowed himself a relieved smile. A smile he hoped hid his uncertainty.

Voran's icy glare turned to Emrael. "I'll raise you an army, but the responsibility is yours." His voice broke slightly, grew quieter, harder. "I will hold you accountable for every life lost."

~~~

The next day, Emrael stood at a dock with Halrec, Elle, Jaina, Joral, and Prilan. They had found a boat setting off downriver despite the unrest in the city—or perhaps because of it. They would be in Naeran within a few days, faster if the wind held right.

Joral shook Emrael's hand and with a silent nod joined Prilan on the boat.

Elle embraced Emrael carefully. "I can't promise anything, Emrael. I'll do everything I can to convince my father, but plan for the worst. I'll be back if I can. Good luck, Em. Be safe, please." She planted a kiss on his stubble-covered cheek as she withdrew to allow the others their chance to say goodbye.

Jaina was less reserved. She touched his arm and said bluntly, "You will fail without Ordenan Imperators, if significant numbers of Malithii are involved. I will sail for my homeland and return with as many as I can convince my Order to give me. You would be wise to wait for me."

Emrael smiled. "Hurry back, then. I can't wait any longer than it will take to gather the Iraeans, but I'll welcome any help you can muster."

He was stunned when Jaina pulled him into a rough, quick embrace, then held him by the shoulders at arm's length. "Just don't do anything too stupid, Emrael. Remember, if you're going to assault the city before I get there, you'll have to take the city before the Sagmynans can recall the rest of their Legion from the surrounding area. Gates first, then walls, then the Citadel. Quickly, and in that order. Offer quarter to the Sagmynans if you want them to work with you afterward."

Emrael nodded sagely. "Makes sense. Thank you, Jaina. For everything."

She nodded and turned finally, boarding the small ship.

Halrec approached him last, putting a hand on his shoulder. "Take care, Emrael."

Emrael grasped his friend's shoulder in return. "You too, Hal. You don't have to go back, you know. I could use your help. Your family is old Iraean nobility too—you can help me win these people over. We could even send word to your uncle. His Holding isn't too far from here . . ."

Halrec shook his head sadly. "My uncle doesn't recognize me or my parents as family, or as anything, really. It would do no good, Em. Besides, I need to see to my obligations to the Legion. I can't have that hanging over my head. Elle can help me clear my name, and I'll make my way back here to see what I can do to keep you out of trouble. I might even be able to help Elle convince the governor to send men to help."

Emrael smiled sadly, knowing that help from Barros wasn't likely, and neither was his friend's return if he rejoined the Barros Legion. "Sure, Hal. See you soon."

Emrael stayed on the dock for a long while after his friends sailed out of sight, wondering whether he'd ever see them again.

24

Ban took a deep breath, trying to calm his shaking hands. He barely recognized the hands as his own, they were so blackened from nonstop *infusori* Crafting. He hadn't eaten for over a day, and if he made another mistake on the wiring of this Crafting, he would not receive today's rations, either.

A commotion in the hall outside the tiny room in which they kept him made him start. He didn't dare look toward the door. He'd seen his friends disappear for less—he was the last left of his original group of four, and he had no idea where his friends had gone. Any mistake, lack of production, or disrespect shown to the Watchers guarding them resulted in starvation, beatings, and disappearances.

"Out of my way, idiot!" screamed a voice from just outside the door. Seconds later, Darmon Corrande burst past the Watcher guarding Ban and into the room. Darmon looked just as he had when the Citadel had been a place of learning instead of the prison it was now— save for one arm that ended in a pinned sleeve instead of a hand.

Despite his better judgment, Ban looked up and met Darmon's eyes. Panic coursing through him, he kept his eyes on Darmon while his hand went behind his back to snag his Observer from the desk. He slipped it into a secret pocket inside his waistband.

The Observer he had made to match Emrael's had been complete for weeks, but he couldn't figure out why it wouldn't transmit. He had talked to his brother only briefly that one time, and it hadn't worked since, though he would have bet his life on the design being correct. It was his only chance to contact Em and get out of this Fallen-cursed place, so he fiddled with it any chance he had away from the prying eyes of the Watchers and the dark-robed priests that prowled the Citadel. He might lose his sanity if it were lost or destroyed now.

Darmon pointed at him, rage widening his eyes and twisting his face into a snarl. "You!"

He kicked a chair out of his way and fell upon Ban, knocking him to the floor and striking with his fist and feet.

Ban had taken several minor beatings in the weeks he had been living in this hell—they came frequently whether one invited them or not. He thought he'd become accustomed to the punishment, but this was personal. Darmon screamed as he flailed, something about his arm and Emrael.

Ban must have blacked out, because the next he knew, he was curled up on his side, spitting blood. He looked up and saw someone restraining a still-thrashing Darmon. "Let go of me! My father will have your head for this!"

The man in Watcher blue securing Darmon did not respond. He just pushed Darmon roughly toward the door and motioned to the other Watcher standing there. "No one hurts this boy again. See that Darmon is escorted to the palace. He will not access this room."

The Watcher who rescued him reentered the room and picked Ban up off of the floor. "Can you walk?" he asked.

Ban climbed slowly to his feet and lost his voice when he saw his rescuer was Corlas. "Ye-yes," Ban stuttered. "Thank you, Corlas."

Corlas didn't answer. He took Ban by the arm and escorted him down the hall to a room occupied by a small man seated behind a plain desk. This man wore a blue Watcher uniform with a big white patch on the shoulder.

"Make sure he gets cleaned up, then put him back to work," Corlas commanded, then strode out of the room.

The small man looked at Ban. "Ah. I'll wrap you up and then back to it, eh? We have something special for you."

The man nodded toward the door. Ban looked back and found a dark-robed priest with a tattoo-covered face entering the room, a slim binder in his hand.

"NO!" Ban screamed. He'd seen what happened to those fitted with binders that looked like that. Rather, he'd seen them led blank-faced into wagons in the Citadel courtyard, never to be seen again.

Pain exploded in his side as he stood up in a rush, knocking the chair to the ground and backing up until he hit the wall. "He said I'm to be put back to work! I'm working on Craftings for the Commander himself! I'm your best producer—you can check the records. I'm supposed to stay here!"

The small man tilted his head as if thinking. "He's right," he said reluctantly, just as the robed man grabbed Ban's left elbow. "Release him. I'll tend to him—this time. Take a seat. I'll see to you in a moment."

Janrael Ire lifted his head from the cold, dirty stone floor to the sound of booted footsteps pounding toward him. His hands clenched into fists. Nobody ever came for him during the night. Each morning, he was hauled from his windowless cell just before the sun came up for a full day of backbreaking labor outside the small mountain keep. Each night, he was thrown back in his cell as the sun sank behind the mountains in the west. Every day, every night was the same.

The cell, so small that he could not fully extend even when lying corner to corner, had been his home for long enough that he didn't even dare to guess at how many years it had been. Ten? Five? He would drive himself mad—more than he already had—trying to guess. And in the end, it didn't matter. The only thing that mattered was today, staying alive to seize his opportunity to escape. It would come.

The boots stopped at his door. The blue light of an *infusori* coil shone through the space between the door and the floor. A key turned in the lock, revealing three men. A tall, lithe man with the tattoos and dark robes of the odd priests who had brought him to this place motioned, and the other two, much burlier priests, moved forward to grab Janrael by each arm.

The two strong-arm priests forced him to his knees and held one of his arms out for the more heavily tattooed priest who seemed to be their leader. Janrael was too weak, too tired to resist. The lithe priest leaned down to stare into Janrael's eyes as he extended a thin bracelet.

The bracelet clamped around Janrael's wrist. Cold, searing pain tore through him. He tried to open his mouth to scream, but no sound came out. His jaw wouldn't even move.

The priest murmured something in his harshly musical language, still staring into Janrael's eyes. One of his assistants handed him a sword belt—Janrael's old sword belt. They had kept it all this time? Why would they give his sword back to him now?

The tattooed man buckled the sword belt around Janrael's waist and smiled, patting him on the cheek. He straightened and said in halting Provincial Common, "You will see your sons now."

25

Two weeks later, Emrael paced the length of the Whitehall meeting chamber. Voran and Toravin sat at a long table, poring over papers. Sarlon sat in one corner, picking at his fingernails with a small dagger.

"You said you could raise an army, Tor. A more appropriate term would have been *build an army*. Glory, can we do anything to speed this up?"

Toravin gave him a level look. "These are farmers and tradesmen, Emrael. Most don't have a weapon to their name, let alone a shield. If you want an army large enough to take a city like Myntar, you will have to wait until our smiths and armorers can outfit them properly. Or would you have them charge the city walls with pitchforks and spades? You should be grateful Dorae agreed to arm them. His treasury will be light after this."

"I'm just frustrated," Emrael admitted. "Ban has been a prisoner for too long, and I'm his only hope."

"You can't let the life of one man take precedence over those of thousands of others, even if he is your brother," Voran said from his seat, looking up from his stack of papers containing figures on supplies, soldiers and livestock. "You claim to be a king, you had better act like one for *all* of your people, not just your brother."

"I haven't claimed to be anything."

"You didn't discourage it, either, and most of the men signing up in the camps have word of an Iraean Mage King on their lips. You *are* a king to those that join us, Emrael." Voran turned his attention back to his papers.

Emrael lowered his brows. "I'm willing to fight for them, same as you."

Voran peered up once more and nodded. "Just you remember that when the killing starts, and the dying. This isn't a game or a story. Your attack on Myntar is a declaration of war on all the Provinces. This will be war, ugly and true."

Emrael stood. "I have seen my father fall to bandits, friends fall to men and monsters. I know what I'm asking of them."

"Ah. But do they?"

"Iraeans have a long and bloody history. My father said that every Iraean is born a warrior."

Voran chuckled. "Most of those that have seen battle are old and weathered like me. A number came from Legion ranks like Toravin and me, or from a Lord Holder's Guard. But for most of these men, the days of every Iraean being a blooded warrior are just stories told around the fire. They need training, leadership."

Emrael nodded. "Good thing we've got you, then, eh?"

Voran just grunted, but Toravin laughed.

Emrael turned to Sarlon. "And you, my surly friend. We need a plan for taking Myntar. You know the city. Can you get a few of us in to hold the gates for the rest of the army?"

Sarlon's lips retracted in a snarl. "I'll come with you on one condition. I have another two-man job I need to see to before we go. A certain acquaintance in Lidran is due a visit."

Emrael hesitated before nodding. "We have time. Voran and Toravin can finish the preparations here."

He looked to Voran and Toravin. "We will meet you and our army in the woods between Gadford and the Pass. One week. Sarlon and I will leave for Lidran this afternoon."

Voran nodded and turned back to his papers.

Sarlon smiled, teeth bared in a grin, but his dead eyes revealed the festering wound deep in his soul. Losing his wife had crushed him.

Emrael pitied Captain Gerlan when this man found him.

⁂

Emrael crouched beside the wall of Lidran in the chilly early-summer night. His feet were cold, and the hilt of his sword jabbed into his side.

The wall towered over him, the off-white color of the stone catching the faint blue glow of the current moon. They had approached the city from the woods to the south, where the torches of the Legion guards were spaced farther apart than they would be near the gates or Legion compound.

Emrael and Sarlon huddled in the deepest dark directly between those torches, invisible to the fire-blind eyes of the guards on the wall. Emrael shook his head, unable to believe that the Barros Legion could have grown so inept in the few short years since his father's death. As Commander First, he had never allowed his men to be so lax. But it suited their purposes well enough tonight.

They had been crouching in the same spot for over half an hour. He ran his hands along the roughhewn stone for what felt like the hundredth time. He could feel the grain with his fingers as well as with his newfound *infusori* mage senses. He could feel how the tiny parts that made up the stone fit together, and how just the right amount of *infusori* exerted just so should reduce the wall to dust.

Only, he couldn't make it work.

Sarlon had been explaining that mages typically gravitated toward a few certain skills. He was confident that given Emrael's past manifestations involving the stone door at Sarlon's house in Myntar, the door in the Ravan temple, and the stone in the cell at Whitehall, he should have no trouble creating a space in the wall for them to enter Lidran.

Or, rather, Sarlon *had* been confident half an hour before. After the first five minutes, he cursed and complained at Emrael in a constant rumble.

Emrael kicked the wall in frustration, stubbing his toe in the process. He reached for another gold coil and angrily drew as much *infusori* as he could. He pulled up the hood on his jacket to hide the glow of his hair and made sure to keep his glowing eyes cast down.

Sarlon spoke softly. "Easy now, lad. Just break an opening, soft-like. Don't bring the wall down on top of us." He stood at a safe distance behind Emrael, and even so was coiled like a spring, ready to jump to safety should anything go wrong. It was very comforting.

"Yeah, easy for you to say. You can't do this, and you have had decades to practice. Many decades."

Sarlon grunted sourly, and Emrael chuckled at the memory of Sarlon trying in vain to learn to break a stone at camp the night before. He closed his eyes and placed his hands on the wall again.

He lost himself in his task once more, finding just the right spots to push *infusori* so that a small hole would open without bringing the wall down.

A loud *crrrrmmmmp* rumbled beneath his hand and a jagged hole in the wall about a pace high and a pace wide erupted away from him violently. So much for keeping quiet.

"Damn." He had been sure it wouldn't explode this time.

Sarlon was at his shoulder immediately. "Best get moving, boy. We've got guards coming."

Sure enough, the torches that had been several hundred paces to either side of them already bobbed closer. Shouts sounded in the dark.

Sarlon shoved him through the hole and the two of them had sprinted several blocks into the depths of the city by the time the Barros Legion guards would have reached their hole.

They made their way quickly through the modest parts of Lidran, comprised of square, closely packed dwellings and craftsmen's shops. Most were dark at this time of night, but candles burned in windows here and there. The sour smell of too many people living in too little space reminded him of nights spent wandering about the poorer tiers of Myntar.

The smell improved, the dwellings grew, and more windows were lit by blue *infusori* instead of the orange flicker of candles as they stalked closer to the Legion compound. Several people roamed the streets despite the late hour, too busy doing their own skulking to pay any attention to the two of them.

They strolled down the main avenue, walking right past the main gate of the Legion compound. Once out of earshot, Sarlon spoke in a low, cold voice.

"The good captain's quarters are lit. Seems to be enjoying some late company. Or reading, perhaps. What do you say we join his little party?"

Emrael couldn't see his face but was sure that a humorless smile was painted on his lips. Sarlon's emotionless tone chilled Emrael, until he remembered Yamara's twinkling eyes and easy laugh. Gerlan deserved what was coming to him.

They skirted the compound, coming finally to a garbage-strewn alleyway between buildings that backed on the Legion compound walls.

"Up and over?" Emrael asked hopefully.

Sarlon did not answer, just stood silently in the dark.

"Fine," Emrael muttered darkly. The gold coil still warmed his left pocket but wasn't nearly as warm as it had been. It was running low. He thought he might have enough *infusori* for this one hole. He hoped.

He drew the *infusori* from the gold coil, discarded it in a pile of trash, and placed his right hand on the wall. He closed his eyes. Again—more quickly this time—the stone whispered its secrets to him. He held his breath, then pushed *infusori* gently into what he thought were the right veins of stone, veins harder and more crystalline than the softer stone around them.

Nothing happened. He opened his eyes and exhaled slowly.

"Why, why, why . . ." he muttered to himself.

His brows furrowed as he ran his hand over the stone. Dust and small pieces of stone fell away as he passed his hand over the wall.

He peered at his hand and smiled, took a step back, and gave the wall a solid kick. A portion of the wall under his boot gave way slightly.

He kept kicking, and in a few moments, he stood breathing heavily over a pile of sand in front of a hole in the wall, again about a pace around. He bowed with a flourish.

Sarlon hefted his heavy metal staff with a grunt and ducked through the opening. Emrael passed through behind him, eyes darting about, looking for motion. He knew that the Legion would react instantly and lethally upon finding any intruders, particularly at night.

They placed their feet carefully, avoiding patrols as they slipped from building to building. Halfway through the compound, they stumbled upon two guards playing cards quietly on an old barrel next to a barracks. These had been nearly silent, as they were also avoiding the attention of their fellow on-duty guards.

The two gambling guards looked up in surprise, guilt and fear on their faces. Before they had time to realize that Sarlon and Emrael were not fellow Legionmen, Sarlon had dropped them both with quick swipes of his staff. Just for good measure, Emrael knifed each of the downed soldiers below the ear to make sure they wouldn't wake up anytime soon, then rolled them into the shadows next to the barracks. With any luck, they wouldn't be found until morning.

They hurried on through the compound, taking much more care to peer around each building instead of relying primarily on sound.

They barely slowed as they reached the command building. It would have guards posted, one pair outside and one pair inside every door, per Legion protocol. As Sarlon struck the first pair outside a small service door, Emrael rushed to the door, depressed the latch, and kicked it open as hard as he could. The dull *thud* of the door striking flesh harmonized with a cry of pain, and Emrael stepped in from the night, sword in one hand, knife in the other.

One guard picked himself up off the ground, clutching his arm where the door had hit him. His companion was ready, however, and almost took Emrael's head off as he strode through the doorway. Only the fact that Emrael had his sword up in the right position saved his life.

Emrael swept past as he parried and delivered a kick to the head of the man struggling to his feet. That man crumpled, and Emrael's full attention was back to the other guard.

The remaining guard flicked his eyes from Emrael to the open door. Emrael clearly heard Sarlon dispatching the other guards outside.

The guard took a deep breath and opened his mouth, undoubtedly to bellow a warning to his fellow Legionmen. Before he could make a sound, however, Emrael threw his knife underhand.

The knife sank into the man's abdomen with a wet sound. He hunched over violently, sinking to his knees. He put a hand to the knife and choked out a whimper.

Emrael had to resist the temptation to go to the man's aid. This Legionman was likely no different from any number with whom Emrael had been friends growing up. Except that now fate put this man on the wrong side of Emrael's war. He steeled himself and moved to finish the man, sinking his sword into the man's chest and jerking it out quickly. He retrieved his knife and cleaned it on the Legionman's uniform quickly before sheathing it.

Sarlon dragged the bodies of the two men he had killed into the building and rammed a knife from one of the Legionman's belts between the door and its frame, jamming it shut. They swept quietly through the house and by some miracle encountered no one as they crept up the stairs to the captain's quarters. Placing their feet carefully, they moved up to crouch beside the double doors to Gerlan's suite. Blue light still spilled beneath the doors, a scratching pen the only noise in the quiet of the night.

Sarlon tested the doors. They creaked slightly but didn't move. The scratching of the pen never slowed.

Sarlon rose slowly, careful not to make the floor creak. His eyes began to glow faintly as he drew *infusori* from his own coil.

Sarlon struck the doors with his staff and a surge of *infusori*. They splintered and blew from their hinges, flying into the room with a thundering crash.

Sarlon's eyes glowed more fiercely as he continued to draw *infusori*, making his longhaired and bearded figure even more imposing than usual. Emrael stood in the shadows next to the doorway as Sarlon entered the room.

Captain Gerlan sat frozen at his writing desk on the far side of the room, his eyes wide with shock.

A young woman hid beneath the bedcovers and squeaked in terror as Sarlon stalked into the room.

"Make sure the girl stays quiet," Sarlon called to Emrael, voice grim. He walked calmly toward Gerlan, who stood up from his chair. Sarlon set aside his staff as he walked.

Gerlan knew what was coming and leapt with a grunt of effort for the sword belt hanging foot of the bed. It was too late.

Sarlon's large, meaty hands snatched Gerlan from the air like a child catching a doll. The Captain First hung several inches off the ground, flailing and kicking at Sarlon, trying desperately to loosen the large man's grip on his arms.

Sarlon smiled and tightened his hold as he jerked his arms violently. Bones popped, and Gerlan screamed.

The young girl chose that moment to scream shrilly and bolt for the doorway. She wore nothing and tried to cover herself with the sheet as she ran, but the sheets stuck in the bed and pulled the girl off her feet. Poor girl.

Emrael stepped from the shadows next to the door and secured the girl from behind, covering her mouth with his hand and stifling her screams.

"Shhh, we won't hurt you. I just need you to—Ah!" Emrael growled as the girl bit his hand and tried to scream again. Emrael shifted his arm to rest under her chin and restricted her airflow enough that she could not scream. Her clawing and kicking intensified, however.

He growled again and tightened his hold, cutting off blood flow to the girl's brain until she stopped struggling. He eased her to the floor and checked her. When he was sure she was merely unconscious, he quickly gagged her, bound her hands and feet, moved her into a closet, and shut the doors after covering her as best he could with the sheet she had pulled free.

He looked to the bed and found Sarlon gripping Gerlan's neck with one hand, pinning him to the bed and silencing him. The other hand rained down bone-crushing blows to Gerlan's face, stomach, and rib cage. Blood and spittle streamed from Gerlan's mouth, and his arms hung broken and useless at his sides.

Sarlon worked himself into a frenzy but finally released Gerlan's neck. Gerlan tried to lurch to his feet, but Sarlon stomped hard on his extended knee, breaking the joint backward with a sick, popping sound. Emrael was taken aback by the sheer violence but made no attempt to stop Sarlon.

Emrael stepped out of the room and to the stairs. He couldn't believe no one had come to investigate the noise, though it occurred to him that a man like Gerlan might well have ordered the guards not to disturb him while his mistress was there. The man's own pride had been the end of him. Or had at least made Sarlon and Emrael's job easier.

As if his musing had been a signal, someone began shouting downstairs. Undoubtedly, the guards at the rear entryway had been discovered.

"Sarlon, time to go!" Emrael said as he strode back into the room. Gerlan was either unconscious or dead, his body a bloody, crumpled mess, his face unrecognizable.

Sarlon looked up at Emrael, breathing hard, wild rage in his eyes. Slowly, the feral look drained from his face as he regained his senses. He drew his belt knife and sank it to the hilt in Gerlan's forehead with a wet *thud*. He snapped the knife blade off in Gerlan's skull with a savage twist and discarded the hilt as he strode from the room, snatching his metal staff as he exited.

Emrael turned and led the way, pulling an *infusori* coil from a sconce as he passed. Their boots pounded the stone floors as they descended the stairs, jumping three or four at a time. They hit the bottom landing just as a group of eight or so Legion guards rushed into the foyer from the front of the building. Two of the Legionmen were Justicers with blue armbands, the hulking type Gerlan liked.

Emrael drew his sword calmly and consumed the *infusori* from a coil he had stolen from Gerlan's rooms.

"He's a demon! Look at his eyes," one of the oversized Justicers exclaimed.

Emrael smiled and stalked forward, ready to engage whichever guard came at him first. Before he could, however, Sarlon threw himself into the huddled group of guards, staff spinning in tight, powerful arcs. *Infusori* burst from his weapon wherever it made contact, tearing through weapons and Legionmen alike. When the first three Legionmen hit the ground, the rest fled, shouting at the top of their lungs for reinforcements.

Absent Gods, I need to learn that, Emrael thought.

Sarlon stopped, barely breathing harder than normal, and headed toward the backdoor.

"Not that way," Emrael said. "They will be waiting for us to exit there."

Remembering the large windows in the captain's ground-floor office, he darted into that room. As he had hoped, the windows were well-oiled. After breaking the latch and lock, Emrael swung one open and they dropped easily to the ground and into the quiet darkness behind the building.

As they skulked their way back to the hole in the compound wall, the image of Gerlan's crumpled and torn body stuck in Emrael's mind. He looked at Sarlon, who jogged just in front of him. The Ordenan mage was not a man to trifle with.

26

"They should be here by now," Emrael raged, pacing back and forth in the clearing where they had made their camp. "It's been weeks!"

"Armies take a long time to move. Supplies, formations, scouts, all that." Sarlon had been quiet since they had snuck out of Lidran. Emrael thought about how he must feel, empty and hurting even after avenging his wife. Still, it did nothing to temper Emrael's mood. He was desperate to rescue his brother. Rescue. Not avenge.

Emrael continued to pace. They had agreed on this exact spot with Voran and Toravin, he was sure. "Could they be lost?"

"They know this forest better than you, boy. They will be here. Give them a few days."

Emrael growled in response.

Sarlon just chuckled. "That Voran knows his business, and they have no choice but to meet us. Corrande and the Watchers will have their heads if they dally or try to change their minds, and they know it. Their only hope is to follow your plan. Dumb bastards."

"It's a solid plan. You said so yourself."

"Aye, it's solid and simple, as it should be. Doesn't mean it will work. Just takes one wise guard to raise the right alarm, or one slow battalion of farmers to give up the advantage of surprise. And who can say what happens even if we take the city?" Sarlon said drowsily. He was sitting with his back resting up against a large tree trunk, eyes closed, bearded face pointed toward the sun. "Fighting in cities can get ugly fast, especially if the Malithii get involved. You'd be wise to wait for Jaina and her Imperators."

"Hmm," Emrael grunted worriedly. "I have no way to know where Jaina is or who she managed to convert to our cause. We can't afford to wait for her. Once we have the Iraeans here, we need to move before we are discovered and word travels. Best we can do is make sure the plan is simple and everyone knows their job. It will work. I'll make it work."

"If you say so."

"I do. Now show me how to use *infusori* when I fight. Can I do with my sword what you do with your staff?"

Sarlon kept his eyes closed. "If you are good enough, yes. But a mage weapon will typically be made of a copper alloy or have a copper alloy melded into it to ease transmission of *infusori*. Go fetch your sword and we'll see what you can do."

They spent the next several days training. At least, Sarlon claimed it was training. Emrael grasped one end of Sarlon's copper alloy staff while Sarlon held the other, still half-asleep on the ground. When Sarlon grunted, "Now!" Emrael attempted to send a quick surge of *infusori* through the weapon before Sarlon could do the same to him.

Sometimes, Emrael sent his surge of *infusori* as quickly as Sarlon did, and the copper staff rang like a gong. Sarlon would grunt in appreciation, then say, "Again."

The other times—most times—Emrael was knocked on his ass by the burst of *infusori* he had been too slow to counteract, and his arm would be numb for several minutes.

Sarlon was consumed by a fit of giggles every single time. "Training idiots is fun."

Emrael awoke in the middle of the night, sure that something had woken him but not knowing what. He looked around the moonlit clearing, straining to see what it might have been.

"Em!" A voice spoke out of thin air, as if someone had whispered right next to him. "Emrael, can you hear me?"

Emrael almost laughed for joy as he dug his hourglass amulet out from under his shirt. The soft glow of *infusori* emanated from it as Ban spoke again.

"Please, Em, are you there?"

"I'm here," Emrael said, tears forming in his eyes. "Absent Gods, Ban, it's good to hear you again. Are you okay? Where are you?"

"I'm okay for now. I'm at the Citadel. Corlas and Darmon are here. Please come get me. Please please please please please," Ban pled.

"I'm coming, I promise. Just hold on. It will be a day, maybe two before I can get you. Just hold on."

Ban sobbed, then the Observer was silent. Emrael pounded a fist into the ground.

It took another day and a half of nervous pacing and constantly checking his amulet, but Voran and Toravin finally arrived at the appointed spot.

Emrael whistled to signal them. "Where is our army?" he asked impatiently as they approached.

Voran stopped to look at Emrael. "Keeping to the woods. One doesn't hide an army of nearly twenty thousand easily, but I think we've managed so far. We had to cross the river on a flotilla north of Gadford. The first companies are no more than a few hundred paces behind us."

Emrael peered into the forest, surprised. "Really? You were able to gather than many? I don't see any of them."

"Living with absurd taxes and under constant threat of death for skirting those taxes has given us plenty of practice hiding in the woods, Emrael. That may be the one thing they're good at."

"Oh. Right. Do you need time to rest before we begin the assault?"

"We've just moved an army across half a province in under a week without using major roads. Yes, some time to rest and organize would be prudent."

Emrael gave him a hard stare, not amused by the sarcasm. "See that the men are ready to move by tomorrow. I want fifty of your best fighting men with Barros Legion armor to report at my tent as soon as possible. I'll go over the attack on the pass."

Voran took a deep breath but nodded. Toravin looked around and said, "Where's lunch?"

The night's chill warmed into a pleasant early-summer morning as Emrael and Toravin rode at the head of a column of five squads of Iraean townsfolk and woodsmen garbed in old Barros Legion armor. They climbed the Kingroad through tree-covered foothills and finally up to the pass that led into the Sagmyn Province.

Emrael wore the stolen armor of a Barros Legion Captain Second. The breastplate dug painfully into his shoulders and the helmet was a bit too big. Luckily, he wouldn't be wearing it for long.

Toravin called for a halt as they reached the first set of gates that real Barros Legionmen guarded. Four of them stood guard, one pair to either side of the open gates. A fifth soldier ran to the command buildings that sat behind the gates on the south side of the narrow canyon.

"Captain First Lurima, bound for Myntar on orders of the governor," Toravin said with an air of authority, pulling a sheet of paper from his satchel and waving it in the air. "Send your Captain to me immediately."

The Barros Legionman nearest Toravin and Emrael shuffled nervously. "Ah . . . he'll be on his way, Captain. Just a moment, please, sir."

Toravin nodded without responding, and they waited in silence.

Almost ten minutes later, an overweight man in ill-fitting armor bustled out of the command building, followed by two nervous clerks and the Legionman who had fetched them.

The red-faced officer blustered as he came to a halt behind his men at the gate. "What's this about a Captain First wanting through? I've had no word to expect anyone! We have a procedure for this!" He peered at Toravin, inspecting the three steel straps of a Captain First riveted to the left shoulder of his armor.

Toravin tossed the folded-up paper at the man, who fumbled with it but finally snatched it out of the air. "A personal missive from the governor. I'm on urgent business, and I'll see to it that the governor and Commander First hear about it if we're delayed any longer. I've already been sitting here for half the morning, man! Get your lazy ass moving and open this gate!"

The fat officer—a Captain Second, judging by his armor decorations—glared at the supposed missive from the governor a moment longer. Sarlon had forged all of the appropriate documents, confident that they'd pass any inspection. Apparently, forgery of all types of documents had been common practice for Sarlon as a merchant, but Emrael still sweated anxiously. Having to fight their way through the Barros gate could ruin all of their plans. One rider from the Sagmyn side could alert the guard at Myntar and turn their surprise attack into a siege, and Ban would not be kept alive for long during a siege. Glory, Emrael and his ragtag army wouldn't stay alive long either if it came to a siege. They were effectively declaring war on all three of the United Provinces and couldn't afford to be caught out in the open.

Finally, the officer licked his lips nervously and thrust the papers at one of his clerks, who handed them back to Toravin. He mumbled "Let them run off if they want; I'm not paid to keep people in" and then addressed Toravin directly. "Sir, does this have anything to do with the trouble in Lidran? We've not received official word, but travelers speak of something bad at the Legion compound."

Toravin shook his head. "Don't know anything about it. We came from the south."

The fat man grunted. "Let them through!" he shouted as he waddled back to the command building.

Toravin and Emrael trotted their column through the gate quickly once it opened. They waited only long enough for the gate to be closed behind the last of them before giving the signal. At a long, steady whistle from Toravin, a squad of their men broke from the column and disappeared into the command building. Another detachment ran to secure the barracks while their companions at the back of the column secured the gate guards at sword point. There was some shouting and cursing, but in a remarkably short amount of time, Emrael and Toravin were in command of the Barros guard station.

Now for the tricky part.

"On me!" Emrael shouted. He kicked his horse to a gallop, and three squads followed suit. Toravin rode directly behind him and the rest arrayed themselves in a loose double column.

They drew near the center gate, which was always kept open but blocked by two pairs of guards, one pair from each province.

"Clear the way! Urgent business of the governor!" Emrael shouted at the top of his lungs, praying that the guards would not lower their lances. Luckily, the guards from both the Barros and Sagmyn Provinces either trusted the Legion-issue armor or did not wish to contend with over thirty charging Legionmen.

As before, the group charged past, the last squad peeling off to confront the guards at the gate. Emrael had to trust that they would get their job done while he did his.

His attention was now on the Sagmyn Legion guardhouse at the eastern mouth of the canyon, built snug up against the towering rock canyon face. As he reined in his horse just outside the door, he counted three, maybe four guardsmen within but was sure it housed at least a squad. The Sagmyn guards at the last gate some fifty paces farther down the Pass turned to look at the commotion but thankfully stayed at their posts.

He vaulted from the saddle, drew his sword with one hand, secured an *infusori* coil in the other, and swept through the door.

There were five Sagmyn Legionmen and three clerks at desks full of papers and ledger books.

He took two quick steps into the room, careful to keep a wall at his back. He rested the tip of his sword on the chest of the nearest Legionman and addressed the room.

"Put your hands on your desks! Stay where you are and no one will be harmed," Emrael barked, looking the stunned men in the eyes as his Iraeans filed in behind him.

The Sagmyn men slowly complied as they realized they were far outnumbered. "What's the meaning of this?" one of them demanded. None of the Iraeans bothered to answer as they moved quickly with shackles in hand to chain their prisoners. One of the Sagmyn officers pulled a belt knife as the Iraeans attempted to secure his arms. The end result was a deep gash in the arm of a grey-haired Iraean, and a much deeper hole in the chest of the Sagmyn officer who had pulled the knife.

Emrael had known it would come to this, but he stared at the first blood spilled for a moment while his men bound the stunned Sagmyn guards in chains. Thank Glory none of the Sagmyn Legionmen were men he knew. He thought about them, and the others in Myntar that had been his friends. His war with the Provinces had begun in earnest, and more likely than not, there would be friends among those who died tonight.

But this had to be done. The unfortunate Sagmyn officer happened to be defending the people who took Ban and who knew how many others as slaves. The Sagmyn Legion stood in the way of Emrael's freedom, and that of all Iraeans, who had been ruthlessly oppressed and bled dry for generations at the hands of the Provinces. Blood must be spilled.

An Iraean officer Emrael did not know approached him from outside. Gods, he didn't know any of them. "All gates are ours, Lord Ire. None escaped. Two killed at the Sagmyn Gate and one more in here, looks like. Three of ours injured, none dead."

Emrael nodded. "Thank you, Captain. See that the wounded find their way to healers and send the signal to Voran."

The soldier nodded. "As you say, m'lord," he said with a half-hearted salute, then ducked out the door.

Emrael stepped out from the guard post into the late afternoon sun just as Sarlon arrived with a small wagon pulled by two sad-looking, mouse-colored horses.

"Get your gear off and get over here," Sarlon growled. "If we don't make the city before dark, we're all dead."

Emrael jogged over to the cart and began stripping his armor. "We'll make it. Are you sure you'll be able to fight with your hand like that?"

Even more than a week after the excursion into Lidran, Sarlon's right hand was discolored and swollen from punching Gerlan to death. The big man flexed his hand without so much as a grimace and stared right at Emrael. "It's not me I'm worried about. You're the figurehead these people look to right now. You're good, but I could find a soldier or two who will be almost as good in a fight. You should stay here, guide the main force."

Emrael spat to the side to show what he thought of that. "How many soldiers could you find that can put holes in a stone wall? This is my fight. I go in first and come out last."

Sarlon nodded as if he had expected that answer.

Emrael turned to stow his sword among the goods placed in the small wagon. When he was sure it was well hidden, he turned to Voran and Toravin, who had just arrived with the bulk of their army. "You know the plan. March hard through the woods and wait for our signal. No roads, no lights. Supply wagons stay here with a company of men to hold the pass. Hit Myntar's west gates when you see the three torches lit and thrown above the walls. If we don't light any torches, hit at midnight no matter what. You can't get caught out in the open."

Voran and Toravin nodded, though with a measure of exasperation. They knew their business.

"One more thing," Emrael said, turning to face the Iraeans. "I will hang any man found intentionally harming civilians. I will kill them myself, Voran. No killing, no rape, no pillage, nothing. And any Legionmen who surrender are to be granted quarter. We are here to liberate and assimilate, not to destroy. We need these people."

Voran saluted silently, and Toravin looked offended that Emrael had felt it necessary to give such orders. He wasn't about to take any chances, however. The Iraeans had been under the cruel thumb of the Provinces for a very long time.

Emrael hopped up onto the wagon bench beside Sarlon, now dressed like a common merchant. "Away we go."

⌐◦

"Yeah, they really won't recognize you now," Emrael said sarcastically.

Sarlon glared at him from underneath a wide-brimmed hat. His appearance was otherwise unchanged save for the significant weight he had lost in the past month or two. Emrael had covered his only recognizable feature, his white hair, with a cloth tied about his head, as travelers often did.

"They won't know me," he promised. "I never did handle the goods in person. I paid people to do the work. I just handled the business."

Emrael didn't blink. "Even still, you can bet after raiding your place the night we left, the Watchers and Sagmyn Legion will have given your description to their gate guards and put a bounty on you. You're huge, obviously Ordenan, and nobody normal keeps a beard like that anywhere as hot as the Sagmyn Province. It has to go."

Sarlon threw the reins to Emrael, jerked his belt knife from its sheath dramatically, and began hacking at his large, burly beard. Huge chunks of dark hair fell to the ground.

"There. You happy, your highness?" Sarlon gestured at his face wildly with his knife.

Emrael burst out laughing, though he watched the knife as he did. "You look like a leprous bear. Have you never shaved before?"

Sarlon glared but pulled a pair of scissors from a pack behind him. "I didn't pack a shave kit," he said scathingly. "These are the best we've got."

He thrust the scissors at Emrael, who took them and quickly did his best to even out Sarlon's short beard. As he leaned over Sarlon, he noticed the man's tattoo on his neck, the same two hollow circles intersecting a fully black circle that Jaina and his mother had. Absent Gods, he wished Jaina had made it back to the Provinces in time for this attack.

"Aren't we cute?" Sarlon grumbled as Emrael finished and they pulled back out onto the road. "Just wasted a perfectly good beard. I tell you true, nobody will know me from the Fallen."

Finally, the wall of Myntar came into view. The large cluster of inns, markets, and dwellings that invariably sprang up around the gates of any major city bustled with activity. A small line of carts and riders waited for admittance into the city, but they had plenty of time to get inside the walls before the sun dipped below the mountains and the gates were locked for the night.

After a brief wait and a cursory search of their goods and more forged documents, they were through the gate. Emrael noticed that a squad of ten Watchers had taken up positions just inside the wall, watching those coming through the gates much more intently than the Sagmyn guards who checked papers and goods perfunctorily. Emrael tried not to meet their eyes as his stomach roiled with a mixture of fear and anger.

He breathed a little easier once they were a few hundred paces from the gate. He looked at Sarlon, who winked at him but maintained a passive face.

It was time. His legs were weak with anxiety.

Time to fight. He felt sick to his stomach.

Time to free Ban. He smiled.

Finally.

27

O ne of them is following us." Sarlon pitched his deep voice just
loud enough for Emrael to hear.

Emrael ducked his head and turned slightly toward Sarlon to
sneak a look behind them. The street was still fairly busy with people
wrapping up their business for the day. All he caught was a flash of
blue uniform, but it was enough. "Watcher," he growled.

Sarlon whipped the reins, and they turned several corners fast
enough that the goods in the cart that weren't tied down tumbled
into the cobbled roads. The cart itself creaked under the strain of
turning so sharply. Emrael was forced to secure his seat by holding on to the wagon bench beneath him with both hands. Sarlon
seemed to keep his seat with ease, both hands still on the reins.

During a longer stretch without a turn, Emrael reached back and
grabbed his sword. Sarlon already had his staff across his knees.

They rounded another hard corner. Sarlon pointed ahead at a se-
cluded alleyway to their left and shoved at Emrael's shoulder. They
jumped from the moving cart and darted for the alleyway.

No more than half a minute passed before a man in the blue
uniform of the Watchers stopped next to the alleyway to peer at the
now-driverless cart horses that had slowed to a halt several paces
ahead. He was of average height and build, and without the uniform
could have passed as anyone else out on the street. But something
about the man kindled Emrael's emotions to a slow-burning rage.

The Watcher was so busy peering in confusion at the abandoned
wagon that he never saw Emrael and Sarlon coming.

Sarlon crushed the man's knee from the side with a swing of his
staff. Before the man could scream in pain and surprise, Emrael
darted forward and slammed a fist into the man's gut. Nothing but
a retching gurgle came from the man as they dragged him into the
alley.

No one from the street had raised a cry of any sort beyond a
nervous murmur, but just in case, they hoisted the man between
them to traverse several narrow alleys and dusty back lanes until

they came to a suitably deserted corner. Eventually, someone would tell the Watchers that one of their men had been attacked.

They threw the Watcher to the ground roughly. Emrael started toward the man, drawing his belt knife, but Sarlon laid a firm hand on his shoulder. "This is my job."

The Watcher, lying on his back in the dirt, looked at the giant man as if seeing the Fallen in the flesh.

Sarlon rested the butt of his staff on the poor man's ruined knee and rested his weight on it. The Watcher tried to scream but only managed a pathetic, raspy wail.

"This will go much better for you if I know what I want to know very quickly. You understand?" Sarlon pulled his staff from the man's knee.

The Watcher stopped trying to scream and nodded frantically.

"Good. Now, why were you following us?"

"I . . ." the man rasped, then doubled over in a fit of coughing. Sarlon pulled his waterskin from his belt and handed it to the man, who drank gratefully.

"I recognized you," he panted, having regained his voice. "We were told to watch for a large man that looks like you, only with a beard. A merchant who is in league with the Ordenan devils. The Commander has a right nice bounty on you, he does." The man stopped and looked hopefully from Sarlon to Emrael. "But I won't say nothin'. Not about either of ya."

Sarlon turned his head slightly to give Emrael a sidelong glare. He rubbed at his now closely cropped beard.

"Recognized me, did you? And nothing about this ugly lad behind me sparked your interest?"

The man's eyes widened slightly, and he began darting his gaze back and forth between them as he realized that he was once again expected to answer.

"Uh . . . you see . . . ahhhhh!" The man screamed, louder this time, as Sarlon ground the butt of his staff into the man's twisted leg.

"Answer me quickly and clearly, and it will be better for you. I told you that."

The man half-panted, half-whimpered on the ground. Sweat ran in rivulets down his now-filthy face, leaving streaks of mud. The man looked to be on the verge of passing out. "Yeah, yeah, I saw him, too. He's the one with the real money on his head. We . . ." He cut off, his head beginning to nod forward.

"We?" Sarlon asked.

Just then, they heard a faint shout and the distant clop of boots pounding the dirt-surfaced alleyways.

"Time to go," Emrael said.

Sarlon turned and without looking or changing expressions, jerked his staff backward to crush the Watcher's forehead.

⌁

The last rays of light bled their life out onto the stones of the city wall. Emrael, disguised in a hat and stolen workman's clothing, watched the gates close with feigned disinterest.

He and Sarlon, similarly disguised, squatted just far enough away not to arouse suspicions. They had slipped a few coins to the foreman of a crew repairing cobblestones—always done at night to avoid disturbing traffic—to let them loiter about the job site while the others worked.

As the Legionmen and Watchers up on the wall began to light torches, Emrael and Sarlon picked up their canvas-wrapped weapons and slowly sauntered down the street towards the gate. Emrael left his sword and scabbard in the canvas wrapping but belted it around his waist to free his hands.

On his other side he carried a satchel retrieved from the cart. It contained half of all the *infusori* coils they had been able to sneak into the city with them. Sarlon had the other half in a bag of his own.

The two of them turned down a side street and stopped just behind the building that housed the Watchers and Legionmen responsible for this gate. They leaned against the wall, out of sight of the soldiers guarding the gate. Emrael placed one hand in his satchel to access the *infusori* held in the coils and placed his other hand on the stone wall of the building.

He had studied the building from their vantage point as much as possible, and he thought he had identified the correct points of the structure to soften. If he just weakened the joints of the reinforced exterior walls that supported the roof of the building and the floors above, the stone's weight should do the rest.

He closed his eyes, trusting Sarlon to watch for danger.

After what seemed hours but was likely only a few minutes, Emrael opened his eyes and looked around in consternation. He was sure he'd done exactly what he had intended, softening the building stones at the joints to the point of being almost sand. Why couldn't he ever just make his powers work like they were supposed to? He pursed his lips and drew on more *infusori* from the coils in his bag, ready to exhaust his precious stored energy. The wall in front of him dully reflected the glow coming from his own hair and the irises of his eyes.

He took a deep breath, in and out. As he exhaled heavily, he noticed dust blowing from the stones at the corner of the building just to his left. He should have known, after nearly the same thing had happened with the Legion compound wall in Lidran.

He pushed the *infusori* back into the coil he held in his left hand, then threw his shoulder against the wall. The wall teetered, and sand that had been stone just moments before cascaded to the ground. Emrael was thrown off balance and fell forward into the pile of sand, sinking his arms in up to the shoulders. More sand continued to pour from the wall above him and threatened to bury him.

Sarlon hauled him backward by the belt and they sprinted a safe distance back down the side street. The first wall of the building fell inward as Emrael was shaking sand out of his hair. Men within cried out in alarm, but the roar of the entire building collapsing soon drowned them out. More and more of the structure tumbled into the heap, until the wreckage piled against the city wall and spilled into the street.

Emrael felt an odd combination of satisfaction at having achieved such a marvelous feat and horror at having just crushed a full company of men within the collapsed building, despite the fact that he was there to kill them in order to capture the gate. He tried not to think about any merchants and other civilians that had been standing in the street who had likely been crushed as well.

Sarlon just grinned with dark delight. Crazy bastard.

The large man let out a growl, almost a purr, and ran around the corner to sprint down the main avenue and climb the stairs next to the pile of rubble to the top of the wall in long-legged leaps. Emrael's battle anger rekindled at the sound, and he hurried to join Sarlon atop the wall, though on the other side of the gate.

The first five or six guards that rushed to the scene of the destroyed building from their stations atop the wall were completely unprepared for an attack from within the city walls. They fell from the wall quickly, bones crushed by Sarlon's staff, or run through with Emrael's sword.

The next several Legionmen were more prepared, but not enough. They too fell from the battlements of the wall to hit the ground with wet crunches.

"Light them," Sarlon called.

Emrael tore three torches from his pack, lit them on one of the torches in a bracket on the battlements, and threw them as high in the air as he could, one after the other. There was no way the Iraeans could miss the signal, and the torches served a dual purpose, as Emrael aimed for wooden structures within the walls that would hopefully light and add to the confusion.

Just as Emrael threw the last torch in a high arc, Sarlon wrenched the huge lock pin from the top of the city gate and actuated the large *infusori*-driven pulley wheel on that side to open the gate fully. Rubble from the remains of the Legion guard buildings partially blocked Emrael's side of the gate, so he didn't bother trying to open it farther.

A crossbow quarrel hit the stone battlement just in front of Emrael's face, spraying him with a shower of stone chips. He flinched as the stone chips drew blood, but turned immediately, primal aggression filling him.

A Watcher stood on the wall with a Sagmyn Legionman, fifty paces from him. The Watcher fumbled a spare quarrel from a small quiver at his belt. Emrael drew his sword again and began running. With every step, he drew more *infusori* from the coil in his off hand.

Emrael crashed into the two men just as the Watcher raised his crossbow to shoot again. The Legionman with the Watcher lost his sword hand to Emrael's blade and fell backward into the Watcher, sending his second shot sailing into the city. Emrael reversed his grip on his blade, putting all his weight behind the sword as its point plunged through leather armor and bone to skewer both men. He twisted and wrenched the blade as he jerked it back. Both men shuddered and groaned weakly as they died in a growing pool of blood.

Emrael crouched with his back to the battlements to catch his breath and scan his surroundings. Several Legionmen attempted to gain access to the wall and the mechanism to shut the gate, but Sarlon seemed to be keeping that group pinned on the stairs for now. He occasionally sent one of the soldiers who grew too brave hurtling from the wall with powerful strikes of his staff. He didn't appear to notice the three Legionmen rushing toward the bottom of the stairs with bows in hand, however.

Emrael went to his knees to snatch the *infusori*-Crafted crossbow from the Watcher he had stabbed. He checked that the actuator was primed with *infusori*, loaded a quarrel, and took aim. The first bowman crumpled with a quarrel to the chest.

Emrael rushed to reload the crossbow with a trembling hand.

The remaining bowmen had spotted him and turned his way. One stood behind the other as they aimed. The first loosed, his arrow falling a few feet short of Emrael and skidding on the stone walkway. The first Legionman paused to re-nock, and the second man raised his bow to shoot.

Emrael brought his crossbow up, set the aiming pin on the man's chest, and loosed. Emrael watched his quarrel hit his target in the center of the chest even as the last Legionman's arrow took a small chunk of skin from the side of Emrael's neck.

Calm now, he drew another quarrel from the small leather pouch—still attached to the dead Watcher—and loaded the crossbow again without taking his eyes from the last archer, who had made the fatal mistake of checking on his fallen friend before taking aim at Emrael.

Emrael loosed another quarrel, instinctively infusing an extra bit of power into the shot. It soared high, disappearing into the man's neck with a small spurt of blood. The man flopped to the ground instantly, his spine likely severed by the quarrel.

Emrael came out of his focused state and realized that his army had finally arrived. The first battalion of one thousand Iraean soldiers now streamed through the partially blocked gates, Toravin at their head. They took swipes at the Sagmyn Legionmen within easy reach as they galloped past on their way to secure the two other main gates in other quadrants of the city and numerous smaller gates along the outer wall. Everything hinged on their taking the city and holding it against the rest of the Sagmyn Legion, most of which was stationed outside the city in other parts of the small province.

Toravin looked back just as Emrael rose to his feet on top of the wall. The rangy Iraean raised his sword in salute. Emrael returned the gesture and watched as company after company of his men flowed into the city. The Sagmyn Legionmen plaguing Sarlon soon realized their hopeless situation and threw down their weapons, calling for mercy.

With the immediate danger and excitement passed, weariness washed through Emrael. He could feel blood seeping slowly from the gash on the side of his neck, wetting the collar of his shirt. It would have killed him had it hit just an inch nearer its mark.

He pushed the thought out of his mind and turned to look northward at the Citadel. It dominated the city, even next to the governor's palace. The opulent glow of thousands of *infusori* coils illuminated them both. Once a shining beacon of hope, the Citadel now represented a menacing objective that might cost him his life.

His grip tightened on the hilt of his sword, the sword he had taken from his would-be captor in Whitehall. Determination overcame his weariness. He would free Ban tonight. He wasn't going to let anything stand in his way. He smiled, thinking of his brother.

"The hell is wrong with you, Ire? Staring off smiling like that in the middle of a battle gives a man the shivers." Voran had climbed onto the wall, accompanied by Sarlon, who was splattered in gore from his battle on the stairs.

Emrael's smile melted from his face as he was reminded of his surroundings. Men dead, dying, screaming. "It worked, Voran. We're in. Now all we have to do is fight. Are my men ready?"

"Hold on, man—there's plenty of coordinating to be done. We haven't gotten half the lads through the gate and you want to begin the assault on the Citadel already?"

Emrael slammed his sword into its scabbard. "Get them through and begin the assault, Voran! We have to get up there before the Watchers figure out what's going on. The assault starts in one hour, just like we planned. Sarlon, let's round up our company and get over to your old house. It's time to pay the Watchers a visit."

28

When Elle and Halrec arrived in Naeran a few days after leaving Whitehall, Elle led the way directly from their riverboat to the palace, where she sent for the captain of her personal guard to vouch for her and let her in.

Joral and Prilan accompanied them to the palace gates but left almost immediately to report to the Legion compound. The older Legionman bowed to Elle and offered his hand to Halrec. "I'll cover for you best I can, boy. I can't say the same for that lad, though. He don't like you or Ire much," he said, pointing a thumb back at Prilan, who glared at them from several paces away. "Best you keep an eye out for that one."

Halrec thanked him and the Legionmen departed. He had changed into plainer garb purchased in Whitehall before they'd left and stashed his sword among Elle's things. There was surely a warrant out for his arrest. If anyone from the Legion recognized him, he likely wouldn't have time for Elle to secure a pardon before he was arrested, tried, and hung.

Elle grabbed Halrec's arm as the captain of her guard arrived to escort them to her rooms. "Just stay in my rooms. I'll tell Father about you and get a writ of excusal from him tonight."

Halrec smiled over at her and said quietly, "Thank you, Elle. But won't it look odd for me to be seen in your rooms? Plus, I mean, you and Em seem to . . ."

Elle snorted and rolled her eyes. "Oh, stop your blathering. No one will see you, and Emrael doesn't own me. We kissed a few times, nothing more. Not that there will be anything between you and me, you understand. I'll see that you get your own chambers and a position in my personal guard, unless you'd rather go free."

"I go where you go, for now. Do you think you'll be able to convince your father to join Em?"

She shook her head, trying not to let her anxiety overwhelm her. "I don't know, Halrec. I want to believe that my father will believe me, that he'll value Samille's freedom over the Treaty of the Provinces. But I just don't know."

Halrec's face sobered, and his voice dropped even lower. "What if he doesn't?"

"Then we find a way out of here as soon as we can and head up-river to help Emrael raise an army."

⚓

Elle's white dress sparkled in the blue light of the *infusori* coils lining the hallway. For a moment, she felt a pang of regret at the thought of giving up such luxuries. She wouldn't have any of that if she decided to leave to help Emrael. Still, maybe she could take a few dresses with her if she left. They might fetch a good price in a pinch.

Her slippered feet whispered on the marble floors as she marched confidently to the arched double doors of her family's private dining chamber. Her breath seized momentarily when she saw a uniformed Watcher standing at attention with the Barros Legionmen. The Watcher paid her no more mind than the two Legionmen holding the doors for her, however, so she strode in with as much confidence as she could muster.

It appeared just as she remembered it, for the most part. Flames licked the air in the large hearth, warming the space nicely. The large rectangular table had not moved an inch since she last stood there over a year and a half before, and even the wall hangings appeared unchanged.

Her family sat in their usual places. Her vastly overweight father dominated the head of the table near the far wall in a comically over-sized chair designed to contain his bulk. Her mother, still auburn-haired and beautiful even in late middle age, sat at his right hand.

Elle froze in shock at seeing Samille sitting at her father's left hand. A slim bracelet graced her sister's wrist, but she looked up at Elle, smiling as if nothing were out of the ordinary. Elle had seen its twin on Yerdon's wrist, however. The Fallen-damned Malithii had gotten to her.

Samille had always been a slightly mischievous combination of clever and ambitious but not evil. Elle refused to believe that her sister would willingly join the cause of enslaving other Citadel students, and the binder on Sami's wrist confirmed her suspicions. But what could she do but put herself in danger by revealing her knowledge of the binder? She had no idea how to remove the thing, and there was undoubtedly a Malithii nearby if Sami had a mindbinder on her wrist.

Elle swept into the room and toward the chair next to her sister, her family rising to greet her with smiles. She greeted them briefly and sat but did not move toward the food, though her stomach rumbled at the smell of roasted meat and vegetables. Instead, she met her father's gaze.

"When did Samille arrive? I want to know what the Watchers have told you, because I saw them attack the school with my own eyes. I barely escaped with my life!"

Her father drew in a deep breath, the smile melting from his face. Typically, when out of public view, his manner softened. Elle remembered him as often jovial, but he was visibly irritated now.

"Elle, my dear. I love you, but I don't know where you have been for weeks. What you are saying is at odds with every report I have received from multiple sources—from the representative I had in Myntar, and from Captain First Gerlan, who reported you to be in the questionable company of Emrael Ire in Lidran. I've had no reports of any conflicts at the Citadel, including from your sister. She only came home because you went missing. I wondered what story you would bring to me when I heard you had reappeared out of nowhere, with only a Legion deserter for a companion. I am awfully glad to see you, my dear girl, but I fear you may have been misled by that Ire boy. My own fault, really, for allowing my precious daughters to attend that infernal school without proper oversight. The Ire boy isn't the one you have squirreled away in your rooms, is he? I'll fish him out soon enough."

"No, Emrael is elsewhere. Halrec is a Barros Legionman who took it on himself to see me safely here. And Father, I—"

"Enough!" the governor barked. He fixed Elle with a hard stare but soon buried his face in his hands. "I want to believe you, my sweet. But I don't, I can't. Besides, it doesn't matter what either of us believe. Corrande and his Watchers have men everywhere. They have 'counselors' with all of the southern Lord Holders. I've been threatened—courteously, of course—with a revolt if I don't play along with Corrande, and he—along with everyone but you—says Emrael Ire is a criminal. So, he's a criminal."

Elle glared daggers at her father, tears of frustration forming in her eyes. "I'm telling the truth, what I saw with my own eyes. Samille sits and says nothing—" She cut off suddenly as her father threw his drink in a rage. A splash of wine hit her in the face, startling her into silence.

"I'll hear no more of it!" He roared. "I won't hear another word of it, or I swear to whatever gods are left to us, I will beat stripes into your hide and lock you in your apartments until you come to your senses and start acting like the daughter of a governor! You have disgraced our family and I'll hear not a single fabrication more from you. Just be decent until I can find a proper match for you, one willing to overlook this little dalliance with peasant outlaws."

Elle wiped her face dry and stared at him in icy silence. She saw no more point in arguing.

Elle's mother had pity and compassion painted all over her face, but as usual, she kept quiet.

What was not normal, however, was Sami's silence. Elle stifled her frustration with her father and gave her sister a sidelong glance. If Sami was not jumping into the argument, something was definitely wrong. Could no one else see it?

—◆—

Elle reflected on the evening as she walked down the wide, marble-tiled hall to her rooms.

The rest of the meal had been quiet. Elle had stopped arguing, trying to give the impression that she had accepted her father's admonition. Her mind had been on Halrec the entire time, worried about whether guards had been sent to retrieve him from her rooms.

She couldn't just get up and leave without further angering her father, however, so she had tried—several times—to strike up simple conversations with her sister. Each time, the conversation had fizzled out after a few short answers, which was very unlike Sami. The binder had surely affected her.

Finally, the meal had ended when her father fell asleep in his chair, and she scurried to get back to her rooms.

She unlocked her door and entered her quarters, already mentally running through what she needed to do to escape. Halrec rose from a chair in the corner of her sitting room, silent as a ghost.

Elle started. He had been so still when she entered and her mind had been so occupied that she had momentarily forgotten to expect him.

"Gods, Hal, you startled me. I'm glad to see you here safe and sound."

His lips twitched into a slight smile. "How did it go?"

She made a noise somewhere between a growl and a sigh. "It went about as poorly as it could have. My father is being simultaneously fed misinformation and threatened, and so he is playing along like a good little puppet. He shouted me down rather than even listen to me. My mother keeps quiet, and my sister is here, with a mind-binder like the one Yerdon wore. The Watchers must have brought her here almost immediately after the attack on the Citadel." She bit her lip and paced as she talked. "I'm sorry, but I don't have your writ of pardon. You are still a criminal, I am going to be little better than a prisoner, and we have no army to help Emrael."

He nodded. "That's okay, Elle. Emrael may have a small force of his own by now, and I'm not sure staying in the Barros Province was the best idea for me, anyhow. I've got my things ready and a bag laid out for you, just in case. I didn't want to . . . ah . . . handle your personal items, so you'll have to pack for yourself."

She blushed a little. "Thank you. Well. I haven't seen anyone following me, and I don't think my father thinks enough of me to deem it necessary, but I don't think that the Watchers will be as lax. I'd wager that someone is already on their way here to see about apprehending you. At the least, I would wager that they are watching for us at the gates. We need to find a way out tonight. Right now."

He grimaced. "If we're caught, it will be obvious that we were looking to run, and they'll likely kill me on sight. But I suppose we don't have much choice."

Elle smiled. "Just as well, then, that I happen to know all of the little-used side doors and entrances. We'll be out of here and catch up to Em in no time."

Halrec smiled in return, but it looked forced. "Sure thing."

"Go!" Elle urged in a hushed voice.

One of the benefits of having grown up a curious child in an ancient castle was that she knew of passageways that no one else did. She had never actually sneaked out in her youth but had enjoyed fantasizing about it. It was coming in handy now.

Halrec's sword remained in its scabbard, a hand-length dagger in his hand instead as he darted through the small, rusted service gate ahead of Elle.

She followed closely, closing the gate slowly. She cringed at every squeal of the rusted iron hinges, but the night stayed silent as she replaced the broken locks.

She tapped Halrec's shoulder. "Okay, let's go."

They each carried a small travel pack stuffed with clothing, food, a few stolen *infusori* coils, and other necessities. She had also given Halrec charge of a sizable purse of coins, trusting that anyone wanting to relieve them of their coins would be less inclined to do so to Halrec.

What they didn't have, however, was a mode of transportation. She hadn't figured out how they were going to catch a boat at this time of night without attracting attention.

They walked quietly down side alleys and small streets until they were a league or more away from the palace.

Elle grabbed Halrec's sleeve. "Well, I got us out. Now we need a boat upriver. Your turn."

Halrec raised his eyebrows and guffawed. "I know a place at the harbor, but plenty of Legionmen know about it too. I suggest we leave via the river gate and buy our passage at one of the trading towns just outside Naeran," he said, jingling the heavy coin purse. "But it might take all the coin you've got to get a decent riverboat to leave at this time of night."

"Do you have an alternate plan?"

Halrec shrugged. "No."

"Then let's get moving; we've got a boat to catch."

29

Emrael, Sarlon, and their company of one hundred Iraean soldiers—the best close-quarters fighters, according to Toravin—encountered only occasional resistance from small bands of Sagmyn Legionmen as they marched through the dark, deserted streets. Toravin must have been doing his job of clearing the city well.

Emrael could feel the eyes of the residents of Myntar on him as they rode through the streets, however. He hoped that they would be smart enough to stay out of the way.

When they arrived at Sarlon's old house in the second tier, Emrael's burly friend let out an emotional sigh before he kicked the boarded-up door in. He and Emrael entered with weapons ready, but the place was deserted. It had been partially burned and ransacked, besides. Absolutely nothing of the lavish copper furnishings remained, and the place smelled as if it had often housed transients in the weeks it had sat abandoned.

"Smells like shit," Sarlon growled softly.

"Yeah, I had really hoped that a few weeks without you here would freshen the place up."

Sarlon punched him in the arm, quite hard, but chuckled. The pain was worth lightening his friend's mood. It couldn't be easy to come back to the home he had shared with Yamara.

They stomped through the house, and their company of men crowded in behind them. The doorway to the tunnel that led to the Citadel dungeons still looked like a wall with no visible seams or hinges. Sarlon put a hand on the wall, and with a brief burst of *infusori* that likely only Emrael felt, the door creaked open.

"*That's* how you open this door," Sarlon said pointedly.

"Yeah, yeah. I almost fell asleep waiting for that thing to open."

Sarlon shook his head and ducked through the doorway. Emrael turned to the Iraean troops and whispered, "Quiet and no lights. Pass it back." He followed Sarlon, using the sound of the big man to keep pace. His excitement to free Ban made it difficult not to sprint the length of the hallway.

He almost tripped as he exited the tunnel and entered the less-stale air of the Citadel dungeons. He hadn't even heard Sarlon opening the door.

"Sarlon?"

"Shh, quiet, boy; they'll hear you!" Sarlon's voice drifted back as a near-silent hiss. Metallic clinking came from just in front of him.

Emrael shuffled forward carefully, probing the air with his hands until he felt the cold iron bars of the cell. "What's wrong?" he whispered.

"They locked the damn things. They've never locked them before. Should have thought of that," came the breathed reply. "Can't get it. Never was good with these things."

"Move over—let me try."

Emrael sidled over, fumbling his way across the iron bars until he found the lock to the cell door. He drew *infusori* from one of the remaining coils in his satchel and sank his senses into the metal.

He had never attempted to manipulate metal and was astonished at the completely different feel of it compared to stone. The cold took his breath away, and the metal diffused any attempt at manipulating it with *infusori*. He stubbornly set his will and poured *infusori* into where he thought the locking mechanism was.

He depleted an entire coil and drew on another. Sweat dripped down his forehead and into his eyes. He leaned heavily against the cell door but continued to infuse energy into the metal.

He almost fell when the lock pins finally melted and the door swung open suddenly. He regained his balance and exclaimed triumphantly, "Ha!"

"Damn idiot," came Sarlon's low growl. "What if they are patrolling down here? Any Malithii could easily have felt that much *infusori* from a dozen paces away. And how did you get that open, anyway?"

Emrael was too embarrassed to answer, so he just said, "Come on."

He swung the gate open slowly, and he heard Sarlon pad his way out into the hall and continue on. Emrael turned back toward the tunnel opening and called softly, "On me, double file."

He turned back to the hallway. Even having spent several minutes adjusting to the darkness, his surroundings only appeared as shadows and darker shadows. "Sarlon?" he called softly.

"Here," came the terse reply from up ahead.

Emrael followed the sound of his voice, then the sound of footsteps as Sarlon led the way out of the depths of the Citadel. As they

crept onward, the darkness faded to the point that he could at least
see Sarlon's outline. All the cells they passed were empty.

Sarlon stopped a few paces from another intersection of hallways
and raised his closed fist in the air without turning around. Emrael
and the rest of their company behind them halted. Sarlon crept forward silently to peer either way down the hall in front of them.

He was at it long enough that Emrael was about to join him to
ask what was wrong, but just as he lifted his foot to step forward,
a faint light became perceptible from the right side of the hallway.
Soon, a low murmuring of voices accompanied the increasingly
bright light.

Sarlon motioned for everyone to hug the wall and take a knee,
and they did so with an alarmingly loud shuffle of feet. The light
and voices didn't react, luckily. The light was strong now, the voices
clearly audible. It sounded like a small group of bored, tired soldiers
on a routine patrol in the small hours of the night. Sarlon kept his
hand raised, signaling the men to keep still.

The first pair of soldiers—Watchers—came into view. One carried an *infusori* coil set in a sconce designed for carrying like a torch.
Too busy chatting—about the poor quality of the food they were
being given, from what Emrael could gather—they failed to notice
the hundred or so men hiding in the hallway next to them. The next
pair were somewhat more observant.

When the second set of Watchers came into view, one of them
glanced to his left. He stopped, squinted, and looked harder. His
eyes widened with fear, and he took a step backward.

"Now!" Sarlon roared, even as he jumped forward, metal staff
whirling. Emrael followed, slamming his sword viciously through
the chest of the Watcher nearest to him. He pushed the hilt hard
against the gasping man's chest before wrenching his sword out
with a growl, relishing the chance to finally fight those who took his
brother from him.

He quickly flicked his eyes to either side to make sure he would not
be taken by surprise. As he had guessed from the deafening sounds
of weapons and men shouting, the Iraeans had engaged the Watchers
to his right. He was free to engage the remaining Watcher in front
of him, who looked as if he couldn't decide whether he wanted to
avenge his friend's death or flee from the horde of intruders.

Emrael didn't allow him any choice, darting forward with blade
raised. This Watcher's grizzled face grew determined, fear draining
from his eyes to be replaced by forlorn resolve. This was no raw

recruit. Still, Emrael wasn't going to let any Watcher stand between him and saving Ban.

He feinted left, and the Watcher shifted his balance perfectly. Emrael feinted again, then carefully tested the man with his blade. Steel rang on steel, and Emrael realized that the only remaining sounds of fighting were between him and this lone remaining Watcher.

They exchanged blows several more times, pressing each other harder and harder. Emrael grinned. The Watcher returned a snarl.

From out of nowhere, Sarlon's staff whirled in and crushed the back of the Watcher's head, sending him pitching forward into a motionless heap, sword skittering away across the stone floor.

Emrael leaned down and wiped the worst of the blood and gore from his blade on the blue jacket of the downed Watcher, then fell in with Sarlon.

They took a few more twists and turns before they came to a part of the Citadel's underground he recognized: the cold-storage cellars just below the kitchens where he had worked for years.

Large, incredibly pure *infusori* coils sat locked into hinge-lidded copper wire receptacle baskets that sat on top of large metal boxes— the Craftings that made the cellars extra cold—fixed to the walls. The coils glowed fiercely, casting a steady blue light on the food stores—hams, cheeses, vegetables, and things even Emrael could not name set in rows.

Emrael's breath became fog in the cold air as he stepped into the storeroom. He smiled. He had dreamed about the money he could get from the sale of one of these coils. The assurance from the head chef that anyone allowed access to the rooms would be searched carefully and quarantined should one of the coils go missing had always damped his temptations. He wasn't one to steal, but with such potential wealth sitting in front of your nose, it was hard not to think about.

He had no such reservations now. He strode to one of the boxes, put a finger to the intensely glowing coil and a finger of the other hand to the locking mechanism that trapped the coil within the thick wire basket. His smile slipped when the copper wire whisked away every bit of energy he poured into it. He scowled. He should have known copper would conduct even better than steel.

"Fine, we'll do this the hard way," he grumbled.

He went down the line of soldiers to inspect the weapons they carried. Emrael stopped to peer up at an incredibly large man who carried what he wanted.

"May I borrow your axe?"

The soldier's eyebrows lifted in surprise at the request, but he held the enormous axe out to Emrael with a nod. It was a menacing axe, plain by design but obviously intended for war, with its large half-moon blade and metal-banded haft.

"Thank you. I'll have it back in a moment, and I'll grind any damage out myself." The giant's expression grew concerned at that, but Emrael turned and hurried back with the axe before he could raise any objections.

As Emrael reentered the room, he found Sarlon trying to pry one of the baskets open with a large belt knife, to no avail.

Sarlon heard him approach and said, "These would be damn useful when we get above ground, but I can't get the Fallen-cursed things open."

"Let me have a try," Emrael said casually, resting the enormous axe on one shoulder.

Sarlon looked over his shoulder and guffawed when he saw the weapon. "Sure you can handle that all by yourself?"

"Just stand back."

Emrael rolled his shoulders, set his feet, and swung at the lock holding the basket closed. The axe bit deep into the copper wire and passed all the way through to the metal box beneath, exposing all sorts of copper, silver and gold wires. In any other time, he would have been scrambling to gather up all of the precious copper he could, and maybe even some of the less-precious silver and gold if he was desperate.

What he needed now was the *infusori* in these coils, particularly since he had drained much of what he had brought with him opening the dungeon cell door.

He ripped open the copper basket and plucked out the *infusori* coil. The energy within was incredibly intense, concentrated. He didn't know whether he could even hold all of the *infusori* contained in just one of these supercoils.

He handed the coil to Sarlon, who accepted it with a nod. He then hurried to the next cold box and smashed the next coil free.

In just a few minutes, Emrael had put a few gouges in the large axe but had five supercoils to replace those he had depleted. He could feel their power pulsing in the satchel at his hip. He longed to draw on the *infusori*, to feel the power coursing through him, to bring the roof of this place down on whoever had taken his brother. The only problem was that his brother was probably still in the Citadel somewhere. Time to remedy that.

He quickly returned the axe to the giant of an Iraean, then motioned to Sarlon, who now had several giant coils of his own.

Emrael took the lead up the small staircase, as he knew his way around these kitchens as well as he knew the way around his childhood home.

Emrael lifted the black iron latch on the rough wooden door and stepped through, scanning the dark rooms with wide eyes. The ovens, roasting racks, and worktables full of pots made frightening shapes in the darkness, but he didn't see anything move and so continued through the seating area of the cafeteria. Sarlon and the hundred Iraean soldiers crept along behind him.

They came to the large arched opening into one of the main common areas of the Citadel, and Emrael motioned for a halt. The large, dark open area worried him. Anything could be hiding just out of sight. He reached a hand into the satchel and drew on the *infusori* in one of the coils, as much for comfort as to ready himself. He knew the glow would give him away in the darkness, but he didn't care.

Soft footfalls announced Sarlon arriving at his shoulder. "What in Glory's name are you doing, boy? They'll see us from a mile away with you glowing like that."

"Something doesn't feel right," he said without taking his eyes from the large foyer. "We haven't seen a single person. There's *always* somebody in the kitchens, and they've taken down all the lighting coils from this hall. We saw the lights outside—they obviously aren't hurting for coils."

"Mmm," Sarlon grunted. "Turn back, then?"

Emrael paused. "No. But let me go first and take a look around."

"Suit yourself."

Emrael slipped around the corner, still glowing. He followed the wall, just grazing the cool stone with his shoulder.

His gaze swept constantly across the expanse of the foyer as he tried in vain to peer into dark hallways. He stopped and pursed his lips, then reached into the satchel for one of the smaller spent coils. It began to glow softly as he poured a small amount of *infusori* back into it.

He tossed the coil down the nearest hallway quickly, well aware that if there were anyone in sight and his glowing hair and eyes hadn't given him away, throwing a glowing coil to clink down the hallway certainly would.

The coil clinked and clanked its way slowly down the hallway. Empty.

He made his way round the room, slinking beneath the protruding upper-level balcony, clearing each hallway with one of the previously spent coils. All empty.

Backing up a few paces, he peered through the darkness at the next floor up. The student quarters were up on that level—those students that could afford lavish apartments, that is. There *had* to be people up there, even if they had chased all of the students out. He was out of spent coils but saw nothing, heard nothing. It still made him uneasy, but the area was clear, as were the stairs leading upward.

He drew in even more *infusori* from the coils, more than he had ever held before. His fear began to dissipate. He felt invincible. Even his fingernails began to glow, and trailed lines of soft blue light through the darkness as he beckoned Sarlon and the others forward.

As soon as Sarlon's footsteps grew close, Emrael turned and took the center hallway, the one that would lead to the main staircase which in turn led to the Masters' quarters on the very top floor of the Citadel. Judging by what he knew of Darmon, that was where the Corrandes and any important henchmen like the High Sentinel and Corlas would be staying. Revenge was so close, he could taste it. Ban would be free before dawn.

As they moved forward, the sound of a hundred footsteps on the stone slab floors thundered through the silence.

Emrael again called a halt when they reached the end of the hallway. The grand staircase opened up in front of him, wide enough to fit twenty men abreast. It spiraled gently one revolution to the second floor, where the students' apartments were, then completed another revolution to arrive at the third and top floor. The Masters' quarters.

"Tight formation, five across, shields on the outer columns," he called back softly.

He motioned them forward and allowed the formation to envelop him, as he didn't have a shield. He ended up in the third rank beside Sarlon.

Sarlon grunted. "Shit, boy, how are you even breathing? That much *infusori* should kill you in seconds."

Emrael shrugged, and together they shuffled up the stairs, by-passing the second floor after a perfunctory glance and continuing to the top floor, which held the larger quarters.

Emrael figured the people he wanted wouldn't be in the first rows of suites where more junior Masters and Mistresses like Jaina had been housed, back before the Citadel had been befouled by the taint of Corrande's ambition. Still, he ordered teams of five to break down each door on his signal, while he marched straight to the large suites at the far end of the floor that had belonged to the Headmasters.

"Too quiet," Sarlon grumbled as they eyed a door.

"Mm," Emrael grunted his agreement.

The squad of ten men left around him shuffled their feet and peered about as they stood in front of the largest door in the hallway. Each of them, Emrael included, had hoped to catch the Watchers unawares, but never did they think to get this far after only fighting through one small patrol in the basement.

Something isn't right.

"Can't stand here all night, kid. Open it." Sarlon motioned, and the giant of a man with the axe blew the door to bits with one brutal swing.

His squad wasted no time. A man slipped past the ruined door before Emrael could dart through, but he was right on the man's heels.

"Fallen take them!" he said as soon as he entered the luxurious quarters. They were empty. The rest of his squad filed in behind him, quiet and confused. The massive bed was rumpled, the blankets thrown about. The wardrobe doors had been left open, and several small decorative items had been knocked over.

"Left in a hurry," Sarlon said at his shoulder.

"Shit," Emrael cursed again.

Loud crashes announced other doors being knocked in all down the hallway. He turned on his heel and strode back into the hallway, sword in hand, eyes blazing.

One man from each squad came running. "All clear!" said the first to reach him. The runners behind him nodded and chorused "All clear!"

"Absent Gods damn them! Where *are* they?"

He stalked down the hallway, his boots' harsh fall on the stone floors echoing his displeasure.

"Sir!" someone shouted from the end of the hallway, way down near the main stairs. "Lights, lots of them!"

Emrael broke into a run, skidding to a halt where the men stood on the landing of the staircase.

Quickly arriving lights—fire torches and light coils both—brightly lit all three hallways leading to the stairway below on the first floor. The click and jingle of boots and armor announced the arrival of armed men. A lot of armed men.

"They knew we were coming," Emrael said softly.

"Lord Ire, sir?"

"They knew," he stated again, louder this time. His voice sounded flat, even in his own ears. "They knew right where we'd be."

As he finished speaking, Watchers in blue uniforms poured from the hallways, all marching in step. Hundreds of them filled the first-floor landing in a matter of seconds.

For an instant that seemed to drag on for quite a long time, Emrael stared down at them, and they stared up at the Iraeans in tense silence.

A tall man with dark hair winged with white at the temples and dressed in white-enameled armor marched into the room below from the hallway on the right. Watchers parted for him like seawater before the bow of a ship.

Emrael felt a shiver of cold emotion run through him. Fear. Determination. Anger. "Corlas," he said.

"Take them!" Corlas barked. The Watchers sprang to action in a cacophony of clanging armor and weapons as they trotted up the stairs.

Emrael turned, scanning his men quickly for a ranged weapon. While not as good as the crossbow he had hoped for, a soldier near him clung to a medium-length bow with thick staves. Emrael pulled the weapon from his grip, and the man hurriedly handed over the quiver as well.

Emrael ignored the Iraeans running to form a shield wall to meet the Watchers on the top landing. He stepped up to the balustrade that edged the terraced landing and drew an arrow to his ear. He focused on the white-enameled figure of Corlas, who stood arrogantly at the bottom of the first staircase, still shouting orders to his Watchers.

Emrael instinctually wove *infusori* into the wood of the bow to stiffen it as he drew, aimed for the small opening above the chest plate of Corlas' armor, and loosed the arrow. The bow twanged loudly and the string snapped a burning line across his unprotected wrist, but he kept his attention on his target.

If the Absent Gods existed, they must have hated Emrael, because Corlas stepped back slightly just as Emrael released. Emrael cursed even before the arrow hit Corlas's chest plate with a metallic *thud,* audible even over the sound of the marching Watchers who had reached the second set of stairs.

White enamel turned to fine powder and sprayed in a cloud around Corlas, who toppled backward with a crash due to the unexpected force of impact. The arrow remained lodged in the chest plate, sticking up like a flagpole. For a moment, Emrael hoped that the arrow had penetrated Corlas's armor deep enough to kill him.

Alas, Corlas flailed and was lifted to his feet almost immediately by his personal guard, who moved into a tight circle around him to shield him from any further attacks. Corlas's face reddened with anger, not injury. Emrael just could not catch a break when it came to shooting Corlas.

Corlas pointed up to where Emrael still stood with bow in hand and began yelling once more. A squad of Watchers with *infusori*-Crafted crossbows hurried forward. Emrael didn't stick around to give them an easy target. Quarrels flew overhead to ricochet from the ceiling in small showers of stone chips no more than a second after Emrael dove backward out of view.

He stayed where he was for a moment, crouched, surveying the battle raging no more than twenty paces away at the top of the stairs. His men held their own despite being outnumbered, largely due to having high ground against Watchers who had to force their way up stairs. Still, he felt a surge of pride. Men who had likely been craftsmen and artisans a few weeks before stood toe-to-toe with professional soldiers and bested them. For the most part.

Emrael's pride turned to horror as five of his men on the flank nearest the balustrade fell, quarrels riddling their shoddily armored bodies. Bright red blood leaked onto the smooth stone floors.

He growled wordlessly and scrambled sideways until he pressed against the wall farthest from the battle. He stayed low as he crept toward the edge of the landing until he was as close as he could be to the edge without being an easy target for a crossbowman.

Flicking a glance at the ceiling above him, he reached one hand into his satchel to access his *infusori* coils. He pressed the other to the cold stones of the wall next to him and closed his eyes.

Sweat ran down his face within moments as he emptied all of his *infusori* into the stone. He focused on spreading the power outward as much as possible and was successful, though he could not seem to direct his *infusori* in a particular direction as he had hoped to do. Rather, the *infusori* spread in a rough circle from his hand, degrading the elemental structure of the stone all around him.

Crashes of armored bodies hitting the stone floor and the cries of the mortally wounded behind him told him that more of his men were dying.

Emrael stopped when he became light-headed and feared he would lose consciousness. A few deep breaths later, he put his hand back to the wall. Instead of sending a steady flow into the stone, this time he sent a powerful pulse of *infusori* through the wall he had just degraded.

Bits of rubble and sand exploded from the wall in a huge circle. Almost immediately, enormous stones began falling from the ceiling.

"Clear the landing!" Emrael shouted. He followed his own advice, sprinting back into the hallway. "Back to the hallway," he screamed over the deafening crash of the crumbling ceiling.

Large chunks of stone continued falling for several moments. Soldiers—Iraean and Watcher alike—abandoned the furious battle to seek cover. A few Watchers even tried to fight their way into the hallway for cover as the Iraeans retreated but were quickly cut down.

After a moment, a chorus of men choking on thick, swirling dust was the only sound in the hallway. Emrael stared into the dust from between narrowed eyelids, trying to see how effective he had been.

A great rent had opened to his left where the wall had collapsed into a heap of sand and rubble, bringing a sizable portion of the roof and support structures down with it. A steady breeze blew into the Citadel through the new hole, clearing the dust rapidly. As the dust cleared, the stars and pale blue moon shone bright in the large patch of night sky visible through the jagged opening.

Holy shit. It worked.

Twice in one day, he had brought an enormous structure down on the heads of his enemies. He needed to diversify his arsenal of mage skills, but for now he was content to gloat briefly to himself over his accomplishments—the foremost of which was still being alive. He walked on legs unsteady with exhaustion to the edge of the rubble-strewn balcony to look at the levels below.

The stairs had withstood the impact of several large building stones and countless heaps of smaller ones, though some had left rather dubious-looking craters that he wouldn't want to be the first to walk near.

Emrael was glad to see that there did not appear to be many more

Iraeans lying beneath fallen stone than had already fallen in battle. The Watchers that had crowded the stairs had not fared so well, however. Scattered bunches of men lay motionless or feebly squirming in futile attempts to free themselves from large piles of stone. The few who had been lucky enough to survive looked lost, most of them crouching and looking around for cover.

The Watchers who had been on the bottom floor had fared even worse. The roof over the stairs and balconies had stayed more or less intact, with only small portions of the roof tumbling down to crush those below. The bottom floor was directly below a section of roof that had collapsed completely.

Bits and pieces of men remained visible in between enormous building stones. A blue-clad arm here, a crushed helmet there. It was difficult to tell how many of the Watchers had been caught in the foyer below, but from the looks of it, relatively few had managed to crowd back into the hallways. Unfortunately, Corlas and his guards were likely among those who had escaped, as Emrael could see no evidence of their bodies anywhere.

Emrael turned to his men, who still coughed and looked around with wild, confused eyes. "This is our only chance, boys. They are trapped down there for now, but they'll find a way to get to us before long. We need to get out of here and to the front gate, right now. Let's pray Voran made it through. Otherwise, we'll have to take the Citadel ourselves if we want to live." His men all nodded slowly, understanding their odds. They knew that their latest reports said there were several thousand Watchers there in the Citadel compound. At least.

Sarlon, blood-spattered and covered in dust like the rest, pushed his way to the front. "And where do you propose we go? Back stairway is caved in," he said.

Emrael smiled despite his weariness. "I know the way."

He took a deep breath and started toward the main stairs. There were several ways to the front courtyard from the second level, and he could probably even find his way back to the cellars with enough time.

No sooner had he stepped on to the stairs, however, than the boulders and pile of rubble blocking the hallways two floors below began to shudder.

They can't possibly be trying to move them already.

"Form up on me. Let's move quick," he called to his men. Perhaps eight of his squads had survived and now trotted down the hallway to stand behind him. Several carried wounded comrades.

The room exploded below him.

His ears rang and he wavered on his feet as he hunched against the wall and looked down at the main floor.

The boulders that had blocked the hallways were gone. Where they had been, hooded Malithii stood in each entrance to the main foyer. Behind them stood dozens of giant figures, half again as tall as a normal man.

At first, Emrael thought it was a horde of impossibly large soulbound. But then he noticed the hair. All of the soulbound he had seen had been almost completely hairless, but these had long, raven-black hair. And now that he took a harder look, he could see that these giants had pale white skin beneath red and black warpaint, not the ashen-grey skin of the Bound.

"What in Glory's name?" he asked no one in particular. A cold icicle of fear slid through his belly. These creatures didn't have the crazed, confused eyes of the soulbound. Their eyes shone with intelligence and glittered with malevolence.

Sarlon stepped up beside him. "Filthy Fallen-spawn," he spat.

"What are they?" Emrael asked. The creatures below started to clamber over the boulder-strewn floor toward the stairs. Now that they emerged from the shadows, he could see that they had what looked like binders around their necks, not their wrists.

"They are *sanja'ahn*," Sarlon said with wonder. Or maybe fear. "There is no chance for us to outrun them. We must defeat them here or die."

"Great," Emrael murmured, remembering Jaina's description of the beasts. He hurt in more places than he wanted to count, and his last feat with *infusori* had left him tired enough to sleep for several days straight.

He grumbled but stepped to the edge of the stairs. He rested the point of his sword on the rubble-strewn ground to rest his shoulder. It would be aching soon enough.

Almost immediately, his men formed on him. Emrael felt a fierce pride stir deep within him, balanced by the heavy weight of responsibility for these men who were likely about to die for him.

The *sanja'ahn* were close and coming fast, but there were not so many as he had thought. Fewer than thirty long-haired *sanja'ahn* marched up the stairs. Even with casualties, the Iraeans outnumbered them by more than two to one and held the high ground besides. They had a chance, but he knew there were bound to be many more Watchers on their way, not to mention the Malithii mages that had destroyed the boulders to let these *sanja'ahn* through. They would have to move quickly once these monsters were dealt with.

"Hold until they reach us, then punch through hard in a wedge," Emrael shouted to be heard by his men over the thundering footsteps of the oncoming giants. The first wave was just starting up the last set of stairs. "Follow me once on the lower level!" His shout became a scream as the demons neared.

It was immediately evident to Emrael that Sarlon had been right to fear the *sanja'ahn*. Despite what Jaina had told him about these *sanja'ahn*, Emrael had been hoping for the clumsy strength of the soulbound. Instead of rushing forward and relying solely on brute strength and aggression, however, the giant *sanja'ahn* warriors feinted and struck with surprising agility as they covered the last steps. Despite fighting with shields while the giants had none, at least half of the first line of Iraeans fell screaming, but only a handful of *sanja'ahn* fell in the first clash.

Emrael didn't have a shield like most of his men and thus fought with just his sword. He only narrowly avoided being one of those who fell in the first clash. A *sanja'ahn* redirected its blade at the last instant toward his face instead of his chest, and Emrael barely deflected it enough to take a long, burning cut above one ear instead of being decapitated.

He flinched but ignored the searing pain as best he could. With a flick of his wrist, he slid his sword down the length of the *sanja'ahn*'s weapon, knocking aside the crosspiece to sever several of the giant's fingers. It screamed and snarled but simply switched its blade to the other hand as it retreated. These monsters reacted to pain and injury, at least.

Emrael took a step back to rest, one of his soldiers filling his place as another giant jumped forward immediately.

Emrael and the Iraeans had all been stunned by the attack, but not Sarlon. The bearded Ordenan launched himself into the fray with a wordless shout, copper staff whirring and glowing with blue *infusori*. Where the staff struck, bodies convulsed and weapons flew from numb fingers. The group of giants thinned where he had entered their ranks.

With what felt like the last bit of strength Emrael had in him, he gathered the last of his *infusori* and prepared to feed as much as he could into his sword.

"On me!" Emrael roared, jumping back into the fight beside Sarlon. The soft blue glow around Emrael's blade was fainter than that around Sarlon's staff but still gave the advantage he needed. He used hard, sweeping strokes in conjunction with pulses of *infusori* to knock weapons from giant hands. Blood and flesh sprayed wherever he struck.

He heard more than saw his soldiers following him to form a wedge, pressing the advantage that Sarlon and Emrael created with their *infusori*-charged weapons. The twenty or so surviving *sanja'ahn* retreated, backing down the stairs while holding their ranks.

Emrael simply focused on keeping up with Sarlon. He took one blind step after another, not allowing himself to slow though his shoulders burned with a deep ache.

He almost didn't realize it when he reached the landing on the second floor and stumbled slightly upon encountering level ground where he had expected another step. The giants took advantage of that single faltering step.

Emrael screamed in pain and fell to one knee as his leg buckled suddenly. He looked down and found a long spear with a barbed head protruding from his left calf. The *sanja'ahn* on the other end of the spear jerked it back with a shout of triumph.

Pain made Emrael's vision go white as he was dragged along the floor by the weapon, which had caught on the bone of his leg. He lifted his sword and lunged futilely at the giant's sneering face. It avoided the strike easily and sneered as it drew a sword from its belt.

Instead of another sad attempt at fighting the giant, Emrael swung frantically at the haft of the spear in his leg. It cut cleanly with a *snap* and another jolt of nauseating pain. Emrael scurried backward as quickly as he could, smearing blood in a wide trail across the floor.

The *sanja'ahn* followed at a leisurely pace.

Where are my soldiers? Where is Sarlon?

The giant raised its sword.

Emrael raised his, though from his seated position, he would not have the leverage to stop a hard swing, especially from the thickly muscled giant.

The *sanja'ahn*'s arm flexed, its weight shifted.

Emrael braced himself, sword hilt gripped in his right hand and flat of the blade resting in his left palm. He stared straight at the oncoming blade.

Emrael watched the blade whip downward. A dull *crunch* sound registered somewhere in his mind, but all of his attention was on stopping the blade that rushed to spill his lifeblood.

His shoulders were set to absorb a powerful blow from the *sanja'ahn*'s short sword, but when he caught the blade on his own, the giant's weapon bounced right off.

The *sanja'ahn* fell beside him, scaring him so badly that he nearly screamed. He looked down at the giant in bewilderment and found the back of its head bashed in.

He looked up to see Sarlon spinning his copper staff in a whirlwind of destruction. Where he struck, *sanja'ahn* blades slammed to the ground, limbs broke, heads crushed.

Emrael watched it all as if in a dream. His leg had gone numb, which some barely coherent part of him knew was a bad sign. A frighteningly large pool of blood already soaked the stones beneath him, and still more seeped from where the spearhead still jutted out of his leg.

Where are my soldiers?

He dropped his sword and expended what seemed like a great effort to tear the sleeve from his shirt and tie it around his leg, trying—and mostly succeeding—to stop the bleeding.

His head swam as he turned to look back up the stairs. A battle still raged, a dozen *sanja'ahn* holding their own against more than double the number of Iraeans. Though greatly outnumbered, the *sanja'ahn* had butchered scores of his men and had stopped their charge down the stairs. He and Sarlon were the only humans alive there on the landing among another handful of *sanja'ahn*.

His stomach twisted into a knot of fear and shame. Panicked thoughts tumbled through his blood-deprived brain.

We're going to die. I failed them. Failed Ban. How did they know we would be here? Why hasn't Voran come in through the main gates yet? He should be here.

He began to shiver, starting with a small tremor and escalating quickly to a body-wracking shake. He felt cold, numb.

He looked up.

Sarlon no longer whirled his staff in a vortex of destruction. Though he continued to get the best of the giants left fighting around him, he now leaned heavily on the staff between exchanges.

As Emrael watched, another *sanja'ahn* took a swing at Sarlon. Again, the big man disarmed his opponent with a small flash of light and an audible *crack* of *infusori*.

How could Sarlon still be wielding so much *infusori*? His stores had to have long since run dry.

A *sanja'ahn* giant screamed a surprisingly human scream and scuttled away after clashing with Sarlon, nursing an undoubtedly broken arm. Sarlon followed up with a quick surge of *infusori*-fueled violence, stabbing the end of his staff into the giant's skull, crushing it in an eruption of gore.

Sarlon never saw the other *sanja'ahn* behind him.

Emrael opened his mouth as he noticed a giant twitch while lying prone next to several of his dead, mangled brethren. It had been hiding in plain sight, playing dead for an opportunity to strike unseen.

The giant on the ground gathered its legs beneath it and drew a long knife. Emrael opened his mouth to shout a warning to Sarlon, but it came out raspy, weak, barely audible.

Sarlon turned just as the *sanja'ahn* leapt. They collided, and Sarlon grunted in surprise. A knife hilt protruded from the Imperator's midsection, several inches below his rib cage on his left side. His eyes opened wide in shock and confusion.

Blood frothed at Sarlon's lips as he exhaled a quick, whistling breath when the giant jerked the blade out of him. The giant kicked Sarlon in the midsection, sending his body flying to land limply on a pile of dead *sanja'ahn*.

The *sanja'ahn* warrior turned to Emrael with a smile on its ghostly pale face. White teeth shone out from between cherry-red lips. Sarlon's lifeblood dripped from the knife still in its fist.

Emrael fought to clear his thoughts. Muscles in his shoulder and good leg tensed as he readied himself to make a sudden last effort at killing the giant approaching him.

When he judged that the giant had drawn close enough, Emrael twisted from his seated position and lunged, thrusting his sword at the *sanja'ahn* with as much speed and strength as he could muster.

The giant intercepted his thrust with its own blade at the last moment, turning it aside. Even still, Emrael's sword bit into one of the creature's enormous arms. It didn't even blink. It just continued walking calmly toward its now-unarmed prey. Emrael dragged himself back toward the balcony's railing but slowed as he realized it was the end.

A sudden shout came from somewhere to his left, and three Iraeans charged the *sanja'ahn*. Two long blades and an axe finished the giant in a matter of seconds, though the huge axe-wielding Iraean took a long cut across his chest and one shoulder.

All of the *sanja'ahn* were dead, the Malithii priests that had accompanied them nowhere to be seen. How could that be? Where were the rest of the Watchers?

One man tended to his large friend, and the other hurried over to Emrael. Other Iraeans began to shuffle down the stairs. All had injuries of some sort. Blood stained their plain clothing and mismatched armor, and some had to be helped down the stairs. They looked tired but determined.

Emrael just felt tired.

"My leg . . ." he mumbled to the soldier with light brown hair and narrow face who knelt beside him. Emrael had trouble keeping his eyes open.

"I see it, Lord. Just take it easy. I'll try to keep you from losing more blood."

"Mmm," Emrael mumbled.

The soldier lifted Emrael's leg gently, and Emrael grunted with pain. He began shivering again.

"Hu-hurts," he chattered.

"I know, Lord, I know," the mousy-looking man said, grimacing as he inspected the wound on Emrael's leg. "This gonna hurt some, just so you know."

Emrael couldn't have responded coherently if he'd wanted to. He was so cold and felt light-headed and sick to his stomach but didn't even have the energy to retch.

This is what dying feels like, he thought.

Then his leg was ripped off, just below the knee. Or at least he was pretty sure that's what had happened until he managed to look down to see his soldier wrapping a makeshift bandage tightly around his leg wound, now free of the spear.

This time, he did find the energy to retch, and ended up choking as vomit flowed down the front of his shirt. All of the remaining soldiers gathered around him with somber faces.

"He gonna make it?"

"Depends on how fast we get to a healer," the small man replied. "I'm just wrapping this so it don't bleed. Dunno what else to do."

"How we gonna get out?"

"Why you keep askin' me all these Fallen questions? How'm I supposed to know? I'm just praying more of those monsters don't show up."

"We was supposed to open the front gates."

The narrow-face man looked at Emrael with serious eyes, then said, "That was before all but us few got killed and our lord here decided to get himself speared. But I suppose we can't go back the way we came, neither. Boss said they knew we was here. So, front's as good a place as any. Voran and the rest shoulda knocked down that front gate by now. He won't have left us here alone."

The giant of a man, now patched up, nodded but said nothing.

The small, rodent-featured man stood up. "Cleive, you cut up too bad to carry him? He ain't walkin'."

Instead of answering, Cleive the giant handed his axe to one of the few soldiers who remained relatively unharmed—enough to walk and carry an extra weapon, anyway—and picked Emrael up with only a minor grunt of effort.

Emrael thought he might have been better off left for dead as he bounced along in Cleive's arms like a child. Each time his injured leg bumped something, he had to clench his jaw to keep from vomiting again.

He had taken serious injuries before—like the spear through the ribs only a few weeks earlier—but always before he had been healed soon after, before the pain had fully set in.

An eternity later, they arrived at the grand entrance to the Citadel. It too was eerily empty.

A small part of Emrael's brain that had remained rational screamed at him, telling him something was wrong.

Unfortunately, Emrael was fighting just to stay conscious, and the rational part of his brain was thoroughly ignored.

Cleive stopped, panting slightly. "Do we just go out the front doors? Where is everybody?"

"I don't know," answered the small soldier. "Nowhere else to go."

Emrael watched with heavy eyes as the little man opened one large door cautiously, stuck his head out briefly, then pulled back inside.

"It's all dark," he said, shaking his head. "Can't see any lights or nothin'. But that gate's still there and closed, that's for damn sure. I don't even hear fighting."

He closed his eyes, his face scrunched up with obvious consternation. "Shit. We can't keep wandering around, waiting to find another detail of Watchers and those giants. Maybe they all went home." He chuckled as if trying to convince himself, then sighed. "I guess the front gates are as good as any, being dark like they are. Don't know as I like crossing that open courtyard, but we've got to get out somehow. Let's go. Quiet, now."

He pushed the door open and held it for everyone to pass through, then let it close softly and started down the steps. They were so close to the front gates. Emrael felt a glimmer of hope squirm its way into his heart.

As the door shut with a faint noise behind them, the courtyard was flooded with sudden, bright blue light. All of them froze.

Emrael looked around groggily. Multitudes of coils now lit the entire outdoor area, where darkness had reigned just moments before. How had they done that?

Watchers ringed the courtyard. *Infusori*-Crafted crossbows rose. Strings *cracked*.

Emrael felt Cleive's body jerk as several quarrels struck him in the back when he turned to shield Emrael. He fell from the large man's grasp, and the darkness finally took him as he hit the stone stairs.

30

E mrael blinked himself awake.

Where am I? Am I dead? Maybe it was a dream.

He blinked and squinted some more to clear his eyes. He was in a large, dark, circular room. It was empty save for him.

Not a dream.

He was on his back; his bare shoulder blades, buttocks, and legs rested on a smooth, hard surface. It was too warm to be stone or metal. Wood, then.

Why am I on a wood table?

He shifted his arms and legs, and found them tied to the table with soft rope. He pulled at the restraints, and the rope cut into his arm. He looked more closely and found sparkling strands of metal wire woven through the rope.

At least I'm not dead. But where am I?

He looked around again, trying to remember everything that had led him to be in a strange circular room, with no doors that he could see. He couldn't twist his head enough to see behind him, though, so there might be a door back there.

Memories of the battle in the Citadel and the crushing defeat pierced him suddenly, like a knife in the gut.

Tears came to his eyes as he remembered the battle with the giants. His wound. Sarlon. His men falling to a volley of crossbow quarrels.

He flexed his leg hesitantly and, to his surprise, felt no pain. He worked the leg more enthusiastically, just to make sure. It was completely healed.

Who heals someone, then ties him to a table in an empty room?

He rocked back and forth a bit to explore his range of motion, then pulled at his restraints to test their strength again. Unfortunately, whoever had tied them used knots so tight and complex that Emrael had no hope of undoing them.

At some point, he drifted off to sleep again, only to be startled awake by the sound of footsteps behind him.

His eyes opened wide. His heart beat faster as the soft footsteps approached. The footsteps were odd, perfectly regular. Most people's footsteps were slightly irregular, a pause here, a stumble there. But these footsteps came like the beating of a drum: soft, slow, methodical.

Emrael tensed and craned his head to look when the footsteps halted. He could only see an unkempt mane of black-and-grey hair that partially covered a wrinkled, weathered forehead.

The person with disheveled hair stood there for several moments, making strange noises, almost like groans or whimpers. Emrael became more confused by the moment, his tension and anxiety growing.

Maybe they are keeping me alive to ransom me. Assuming Toravin managed to take the city.

This circular room could easily be one of the towers of the Citadel. Perhaps the Watchers had pulled back for a last stand. He hoped he was still in the Citadel, or even still in Myntar for that matter.

He broke the silence. "So, how long can you hold me here before my men come to free me? I assume I wouldn't be alive unless you need me for something, and since I don't have any information you would want, I think you are hoping to trade my life for yours."

The figure standing ominously behind him said nothing but finally stepped into Emrael's field of vision.

A man with a dirty, harshly weathered face stared at him intensely. His hair fell in snarled waves over his shoulders and down his back. It was difficult to tell where tangled hair ended and ragged beard began, but they framed a pair of eyes that Emrael would never forget.

Tears from red-rimmed, forest-green eyes traced wrinkles in the man's weathered cheeks, then disappeared into a forest of greying beard. Something familiar in those eyes tugged at Emrael, which made the mad light burning in them even more disturbing.

Emrael hadn't been prepared for his captor to be crying. The crazed look in the man's eyes wasn't helping him keep his calm, either.

A rational captor would keep Emrael alive, even in good health in a ploy to trade for his own life. A madman was unpredictable. Emrael's blood ran cold.

The old man paced closer with the oddly mechanical steps Emrael had heard earlier.

He tracked the man's movements warily, though it seemed unlikely that the man would make any sudden moves. Not that he could do anything to stop the man if he did.

The old man stopped beside him and prodded at his leg like a farmer prodding a cow. Emrael suffered the attention in silence.

More footsteps behind him announced two more visitors— tattooed Malithii in their traditional dark, cowled robes. Emrael's heart beat a little faster.

The first Malithii priest, a large man, single-handedly carried a table that looked like it might be a twin to the one Emrael occupied. From what he could see of the frame of the table, the tabletop appeared able to rotate on its base.

The second Malithii dragged a semi-conscious, blood-soaked man with him. Emrael recognized him as one of the Iraean soldiers who had saved him on the raid into the Citadel. He didn't know the man's name but recognized his narrow face and mouse-brown hair.

The two priests set the second table directly in front of Emrael and strapped the obviously suffering Iraean to it roughly. Blood soaked the soldier's clothing in several places; he had obviously not received Healing like Emrael had.

"If you hurt that man any further, I will kill you," Emrael promised groggily.

He met the Malithii's eyes and tried to look menacing, but the priests just laughed. The large one said something in a sharp, clipped language, and they both left the room, chuckling.

The ragged old man remained in the room. For a time, he simply stood next to Emrael's table, staring at the wall.

Emrael looked to the Iraean opposite him. "Hey," he whispered. "You all right?"

The Iraean lifted his head and focused on Emrael for a moment. The man opened his mouth to speak but coughed instead, bringing up red-tinged spittle. The wound in the man's side was the likely culprit. He would die soon without proper attention, and there was nothing Emrael could do about it.

He jerked harder at his restraints. The rope dug into his wrists, but he didn't care. He kept pulling.

Something gave with a loud *pop*, and agony radiated from his shoulder. He groaned as he choked back a scream and sagged onto the table. He breathed haltingly until the pain waned, then looked up. The man strapped to the other table had dropped into unconsciousness.

A dark smile touched Emrael's lips. He reached out and touched the old man, intending to draw the life source from him, but found he couldn't. Something in the cord that bound him to the table blocked him from accessing the man's *infusori*.

He growled and drew anger-fueled *infusori* from within himself. He would get free and help the Iraean man or die trying. To his delight, whatever impeded his ability to draw *infusori* from the old man did not stop him from drawing on his own life essence, bolstered by the anger, frustration, and fear roiling through him.

He pushed the *infusori* into the rope binding him to the table, with the aim of lighting it on fire. Instead of bursting into flame and releasing him, however, the *infusori* flowed smoothly into the rope with no effect.

Emrael blinked away tears of frustration and stared at the rope in confusion. The rope should have burst into flame instantly, just like wood or any non-conductive material should have. Even the metal wire woven into the rope, thin as it was, shouldn't have been much of a conduit. He had burned through the lock on a jail cell door, for Glory's sake. But the strands of metal in the rope restraints somehow wicked away the enormous burst of *infusori* as if it had been nothing. Not even the purest copper would have been able to channel that much *infusori* through such small strands.

He lay his head back against the table, closed his eyes, and tried to calm his breathing.

He had almost succeeded when the old man moved nearer.

Emrael opened his eyes and peered warily at the old man, who now had a small knife in his hand that appeared to be made from pure copper.

He flinched as the old man set the knife next to him on the table. The old man shambled over to Emrael's other side.

Without warning, the man seized the arm he had injured trying to pull free of his restraints and pulled with surprising force.

Emrael groaned loudly but kept himself from screaming as his shoulder popped back into place. He panted and worked the stiffness out of his clenched jaw, and only noticed the old man again when he felt a cold band encircle his left wrist.

He tried to jerk away, but too late. A thin band of the same dark metal that was woven through his restraints was now locked to his wrist. He looked on in stunned silence as a similar band was fastened around the soldier on the table across from him.

Then the cutting began.

The old man recovered the copper knife and began carving intricate designs—into Emrael's *leg*. He tried to thrash and push against his restraints, but his muscles were completely unresponsive below his neck.

He was so focused on the insane torturer carving his skin with a knife that it took Emrael some time to notice the soldier across from him squirming and groaning in pain as well. Blood spread across the soldier's pant leg, as much blood as was flowing from the cuts inflicted on Emrael.

The knife cut, and blood flowed. Emrael screamed until his voice gave out, then settled for hoarse groaning.

The soldier woke.

It was clear from the panic in his eyes that he did not know where he was or why he was in continually increasing pain. His protests began as whimpers but quickly rose to full throated screams.

Emrael could feel every slice in his leg, but he was forced to watch helplessly, still rendered immobile by the odd Crafting. He was completely powerless to help the soldier or himself.

"No!" Emrael screamed in a hoarse voice.

Power welled within him as he drew on more *infusori* from within himself, now bolstered by fear and panic.

Instead of sending a surge of energy into the rope restraints again, he waited patiently until the old man placed the tip of the copper blade in his flesh. He released as much power as he was able, sent it coursing up the copper blade and into the cruel old man.

Cold so intense it seemed to burn Emrael's skin emanated from the Crafting—undoubtedly a mindbinder of some kind—on his left wrist. The old man did not even blink, though Emrael thought he saw a flash of light in the man's green eyes. A mage, then, though he had none of the Malithii's tattoos.

The old man just kept tracing oddly complex patterns into Emrael's skin, like those tattooed into the Malithii priests' skin but more angular, more complex. Like the patterns Emrael had seen on the Fallen in his book visions.

After draining his spare life essence for escape attempts twice, Emrael could do no more. He closed his eyes and tried not to focus on the pain of the knife carving its way up his leg. The faces of the people dearest to him cycled through his mind: Ban, Elle, Halrec, his parents, and, somewhat surprisingly, Jaina and Sarlon.

Accept the pain.

An uncontrollable sob betrayed him.

31

Emrael had long since stopped trying to tell how long he had been in the stone-walled circular room. It could have been days. It could have been weeks. The only frame of reference he had was pain.

The shabby old man in dirty black robes now sobbed incomprehensibly as he carved his designs on both of Emrael's legs and midsection, and had just finished with his right arm. Three Iraean soldiers had bled to death in the process, screaming and writhing as the designs carved into Emrael were duplicated on their bodies.

Emrael was not so lucky.

As each soldier screeched his last breath, a bored-looking Malithii priest was brought in to Heal Emrael before he could die as well.

The Healing was the worst part. Instead of the relatively gentle Healing Elle had administered, it felt as though his skin were being torn from his entire body each time. Buckets of water were tossed on him to wash away accumulated blood and filth, and the dark priest left Emrael alone with his torturer.

After several such episodes he became delirious, and didn't even bother to look up as they brought yet another victim and strapped him to the opposite table. Burning lines grew on his left hand as the old man started in on one of the few areas not already covered in intricately carved wounds.

He had grown accustomed to the pain, more than he would have thought possible. It was the helplessness of someone taking a knife to his paralyzed flesh that threatened his sanity.

He could feel the cold madness burrowing into his mind with each stroke of the knife.

After a few more scars had been added to his growing collection, Emrael lifted his head.

The old man continued his grim work, silent save for the occasional mad sobbing and blubbering. Emrael no longer cared why the bastard cried.

He tried to ignore the cutting and the new man screaming, so he cast his mind somewhere—anywhere—else.

Each new face placed before him hurt, another man who would die for his mistakes, his ignorance, his pride. He hadn't even been able to look at the last two. He hadn't been able to ignore their screams, however.

He steeled himself and let his gaze drift past his torturer and to the new victim.

His eyes had trouble focusing, but the first thing that he noticed was that the man in front of him wasn't wearing the typical workman's garb the Iraeans had worn.

Emrael looked more closely at the man across from him. His clothes could have been any color, once, but were now a faded black from so many smudges of dirt or soot.

The man himself wasn't much cleaner. Soot stained his slim hands and hollow face worse than it did his clothes.

The man looked familiar. He peered closer, past the tangled hair, sunken cheeks and black-stained skin.

Ban.

It was Ban.

A wave of frustration, guilt, and overwhelming anger rushed through him, eradicating all rational thought as it did. He snapped into a berserk rage. He managed to jerk his arms despite the paralyzing binder on his wrist. It just made him angrier.

He bellowed so loud, he thought his vocal cords would snap, and opened himself once more to the *infusori* that comprised his life essence.

He didn't stop there.

An odd buzzing now surrounded him, similar to what he had felt in the Ravan temple. He reached without thinking toward the ambient buzz of power, instinctively burning his internal *infusori* to amplify his ability to access the power around him.

He could feel his body growing cold with the effort, but he cast his awareness out farther still.

He again felt the life essence of his torturer and seized it. Nothing happened. The old man continued his torture.

Now operating on a primal level, Emrael passed over the familiar life essence of his brother and searched farther still.

This isn't possible. Have I gone insane?

He ignored the thought and fixed his focus on the buzzing,

humming power he felt in the air around him. In *everything* around him. He could feel the *infusori* thrumming through the stones, even through the wooden table, though that was fainter.

He pushed on desperately, until he felt so weak, he was sure that his body would not have energy to keep his heart beating.

Dimly, he realized that the old man had carved all the way up his left arm, and that at least half of his face was now covered in swirling lines of fire.

The pulsing of *infusori* all around him grew stronger and stronger, but he couldn't seem to find the source. If he'd had the freedom to, he would have slammed his fist on the table in frustration.

His lips stretched in a hard smile as the memory of harnessing the *infusori* at the Ravan temple flashed in his mind. He shifted his mental reach from an arrow-like projection to something more like a net, drawing from all of his surroundings as he had done in the temple. Carefully excluding Ban's life essence, he tapped into all of the pulsing power around him, sending his awareness as deep into the ground as he could reach.

Power such as he had never felt rushed into him until he knew that if he drew any more, he would be burned to nothingness.

He opened his eyes and saw that they glowed so fiercely that the light shining from the irises of his eyes cast distinct, overlapping rings of light wherever he looked. He grinned, murder in his heart.

His eyes snapped to those of the old, shuffling madman who had tortured him nearly to death several times.

The old man's eyes widened with momentary surprise. Then the man smiled. Not a malicious smile, but a smile so innocent, it almost seemed that the man was genuinely happy.

It just made Emrael angrier.

The binder melted from Emrael's wrist as he lashed out with an immense amount of *infusori*, leaving an angry black burn in a ring around his wrist. With a jerk of his arms and legs accompanied by a flash of *infusori*, he burst free of his bonds and rolled off of the table and to his feet.

Rather, he tried to land on his feet.

Despite the seemingly boundless supply of *infusori* he drew and the strength it made him feel, his body was still weak from blood loss and from his time strapped to the table without food or water. He sank to one knee, his eyes never breaking from those of the torturer.

Emrael forced himself to his feet with a sharp grunt of effort and seized the unkempt old man roughly with his right hand.

The insane old man smiled again and did not struggle. Emrael locked eyes with his captor as he drew the life essence from him in a flash, killing the old man in an instant. He cast the lifeless body to the floor with a howl of triumph.

His satisfaction at having exacted his revenge on the man who had nearly broken him was short-lived. His brother still lay bound and moaning in semi-coherent pain.

He rushed to Ban's side and quickly tore away the grimy, ragged sleeve that covered his brother's bleeding arm.

"It's going to be okay, Ban. I'm here. I've got you."

Emrael continued to murmur soothingly to his brother even as his own panic grew. His brother bled badly from the deep, swirling wounds inscribed on his left arm and half of his face that mirrored Emrael's own. Ban must have been severely weakened by the conditions of his captivity, because he seemed to be in much worse shape than Emrael despite having similar wounds.

He tried several times to Heal Ban but could not make it work no matter how hard he tried. No amount of *infusori* would help him do something he didn't know how to do. He gave up with a frustrated snarl and looked to stem the slow ooze of blood but had nothing with which to bind the wounds and stop the bleeding, as he himself was naked.

He scrambled about the circular room, looking for a clean piece of cloth, anything that would keep his brother from losing too much blood. With all of his other options exhausted, he knelt beside the body of the old torturer.

He pulled aside the none-too-clean robes gingerly. If the smell of the man was any indication, using the old man's robe to wrap Ban's wounds would be counterproductive.

Luckily, the old man had a somewhat clean length of black cloth in one of the interior pockets of his robing. Emrael snatched it and turned to tend to his brother. His hand brushed against something as he did. A sword.

Not just any sword, he realized, but his father's sword. Emrael would have recognized its rune-engraved hilt anywhere. This old, twisted torturer carried his father's sword. How was this possible? His father's body—and sword—had never been recovered.

Emrael then spotted a binder on the old man's left wrist, and a cold, sick feeling swept through him. He lurched forward and caught the corpse's face in his hand.

It was a face worn not just with age but with extreme exposure, as if the man had spent years in the out-of-doors and his body had adapted to survive by thickening the exposed skin.

The face was almost unbelievably gaunt, as if the man had been starved continually for years on end. And now that the blank, semi-insane expression that had occupied the face in life had faded, Emrael finally had a baseline from which to interpret the man's facial expressions.

The torturer had been in pain. The sobs and twisted facial expressions had been displays of sorrow and agony.

The smile on the old man's face suddenly made sense. The man had been a prisoner, forced to torture against his will. And now that he stopped to think rationally, that smiling face was astonishingly familiar in his mind's eye.

The man was his father.

How? How can this be my father?

Emrael had killed him. He had consumed his father's life as callously as a horse eats an apple.

Emrael sobbed uncontrollably, now clutching his father's lifeless body to him.

"No. No no no no no. Father. I'm so sorry."

As Emrael clutched his father's robes, his finger caught in a chain in one of the pockets. It was the amulet Ban had made for him. Emrael held it in his hand, sobbing over his father's body.

A groan from behind him tore him from his grief, and he stumbled over to help Ban. Emrael clasped the amulet around his brother's neck, and immediately the binder on his wrist came free.

When Ban's arm and face were bandaged as well as he could manage—Emrael's own left hand and arm were cut quite badly; he could barely use them—he wiped some blood that was beginning to run into his left eye and knelt next to his father.

Gently, almost reverently, Emrael removed the sword and belt from around his father's wasted body and buckled it about his own waist. Emrael knew that the workmanship was unsurpassed, the balance perfect, and that the ancient runes that decorated the hilt extended down the blade. It was his father's, and had been his father's before him, handed down from generation to generation for as long as there had been an Iraea. The sword of the Mage Kings of House Ire.

Emrael stood, the power within him burning even stronger with his uncontrollable sorrow. He drew *infusori* from the stones, the earth, and everything around him. It was easier now that his bare feet were in contact with the ground.

Ban had never been heavy, though he was taller than Emrael. Now, though, his emaciated frame hardly seemed to weigh anything at all as Emrael lifted him onto his relatively uninjured right shoulder.

Ban squirmed a bit, then was frighteningly quiet. Emrael froze, only moving again after he felt his brother's beating heart and slow, shallow breathing.

Emrael turned to leave through the only doorway but paused as he passed his father's ragged form. He stared for a moment, then squatted down and laid a hand on the body, concentrating.

Finally, with a massive surge of *infusori*, he set the entire body alight instantaneously with an intense blue fire.

He stumbled with fatigue as he backed away from his father's burning body, then set off down the sloped hallway, his brother draped over one shoulder.

32

Jaina shielded her eyes as she watched the sun rise over the rolling surface of the sea. Dawn was her favorite time of day. She took a deep breath and marveled at how refreshing the stiff, salty breeze was, even after more than a week at sea. The freedom she felt standing on the bows of an Ordenan warship was beyond compare.

The ship the Ordenan Council of Imperators had allowed them, an impressive *infusori*-powered cruiser, cut through the water at more than double the speed of the sail-driven ships in which the Provincials still scuttled about.

Jaina's lip lifted in a smirk, though she was careful not to let Maira see it. The older Imperator had a soft spot for Provincial heathens, had even married one—though that had been on orders from the Council of Imperators, she'd heard.

Maira was more than just a senior Imperator. She sat on the Council of Imperators, half of the ruling body of Ordena. The only individuals with higher rank in all of Ordena—and thus the world—were the two High Judges, one elected from the Council of Imperators and one from the Council of Citizens.

"Quaint, aren't they?" Maira said with a small smile as they watched several of the archaic sail-driven ships approaching the Ladeska harbor ahead of them.

"The heathens are limited by their backward beliefs," Jaina said. She couldn't help it.

"Hmmm. You are that sure of the purity of your beliefs, are you?"

Jaina could hear as much as see the smug half-smile on Maira's face. "I am," she retorted heatedly. "Look at what their persecution of mages has earned them. The Iraeans revered mages—misguided pagans though they were—but the Provincials tore even them down. Now they languish in darkness and filth. Outside the Citadel, they don't even have running water!"

Maira's high, light laugh filled the air. "I won't argue for their technological capabilities. But the pagans you so lightly dismiss? The Iraean mages were powerful, the Ire kings in particular. Some say they retained knowledge from the Ancients that we did not. You yourself found a Ravan temple here in the Provinces that had been lost for millennia. Why do you think I was instructed to get close to their bloodline?"

Jaina smirked again. "Got a little too close, didn't you?"

Maira's laugh died away, but she continued to smile, eyes flashing. "Do not mistake my kindness for vulnerability, girl. My marriage to Janrael was the crowning success of my life and a great victory for the Order. I have not forgotten your failure with my son. If you had protected my boys and extricated them as the Council instructed, we would not be in this mess. My sweet Banron would not be a prisoner in the hands of our enemies. Emrael would not be leading a suicidal attack to rescue him. My mercy only extends as far as your usefulness, and Sisters help you if either of my boys has been harmed."

Maira's smile never faltered, but her eyes were as hard as steel and glowed with uncontrolled *infusori*. Jaina had heard stories about Maira but had never put much stock in them until now. Judging by the fierce glow in her eyes, she could wield a very large amount of *infusori*. And without a coil to draw on.

Jaina was accustomed to being the best at everything, even among fellow Imperators, but she was suddenly sure that this woman could—and would—destroy her in an instant if she so desired.

She was taken aback and more than a little scared, a rare feeling for her. "Councilor Maira . . ." she protested quickly, looking at the ground. "I did all I could. Emrael is not easily convinced of anything—"

Maira snorted. "I'm sure a clever girl like you will manage. You must gain his trust, or my entire life's work will be for naught. This is bigger than you, just like my marriage to Janrael was bigger than me. The Holy Ordenan Empire needs more resources, more citizens, more soldiers, or we will be overrun by the forces of the Fallen. My sons are the key to taking the Provinces, starting with Iraea. If my sons still live, I trust you will not fail us again."

Jaina clenched her fists but did not look up. "I believe I have Emrael's trust, but Elle may be a threat. He's quite enamored with her and is likely to let his emotions for that girl guide him more than my counsel."

Maira grunted softly. "Hmm. I am quite fond of the girl. I mentored her closely during my years with Janrael in Naeran. Disposing of her is not the option I prefer. She is very talented, and in a position of potential influence besides. We must gain her trust as well."

The older woman's fingers beneath Jaina's chin forced her to look up.

"We can't lose them. Not now," Maira said. "This is who we are and what we must do. We must succeed or the Fallen will have this Age."

Jaina blushed in embarrassment at being lectured, but nodded, finally relaxing her hands. "I will not fail."

⚊⚊

Despite having marched a full day and well into the night after landing on the Sagmynan coast west of Ladeska, Jaina rose well before the sun, intending to be the first one up. She stepped carefully through the sleeping figures of the five squads of Imperators—including a few Mage-Healers, Sisters be praised—on her way to relieve herself.

Maira had not been able to convince the other members of the Council of Imperators to pull significant numbers of troops from heavy engagements with the Malithii in the Dark Nations on the other side of the Aerwyn Ocean. They had been unable to look past the ages-old fear that if they allowed the Malithii control of the Dark Coast, the fight would soon be brought to the shores of Ordena and the unsuspecting mainland. Not all believed the Ire family to be as important as Maira did. Not all believed that the Malithii had already landed in the Provinces.

So, there they were, with a mere five squads of young Imperators. Most looked like they were fresh out of the academy, though she knew that the Order would not allow them to wear the overlapping scale armor nor carry the copper-alloy weapons of an Imperator if they hadn't done their time fighting in the Dark Nations.

"Jaina," Maira's voice called softly from the predawn darkness.

Trying to look as if she hadn't nearly pissed down her leg, Jaina turned toward the sound of Maira's voice. The older woman stood perhaps fifty paces away at the top of a small hill, barely outlined in the dim light.

Jaina moved as quietly as she could through the trees to reach the Councilor. Maira said nothing for a time, and they stood with shoulders touching, looking north and east toward the large wall of Myntar. Flames were clearly visible in several places throughout the city, fires that had not been there the day before.

Finally, Maira drew in a deep breath. "It seems that Emrael has arrived before us."

Jaina grunted softly. "Could the fires be something else? He can't be daft enough to have tried to take the city by himself. He can't have raised enough Iraeans to defeat the Sagmyn Legion, let alone the Watchers in the Province."

Maira chuckled softly. "Yes, but does *he* know that? I have heard stories of you when you first graduated the Academy. And you have spirit, but Emrael . . . he started those fires, or I'm the Fallen himself." Her voice trembled and she paused. "Sisters, I hope he's okay. My eldest son cares a great deal for his brother and is capable of great things, terrible things. His passion amplifies his natural capability but clouds his judgement."

She pointed toward campfires already dotting the countryside outside the city walls. "The Sagmyn Legion is already here. We must get to the city as quickly as possible. We make for the west gate. Rouse the others."

Jaina nodded and walked quickly back to camp, clapping her hands and calling, "Up up up, lazy ones! The hour of Justice has arrived! We move in one quarter hour!"

<hr />

"Fallen-blind fool of a boy," Jaina muttered under her breath.

Jaina and Maira stood several hundred paces from the west gate, hiding in the trees on the side of the highway. Their five squads of Imperators crouched in the trees behind them.

The gate in front of them was propped half open and hung askew. An entire city block's worth of stone lay in a pile across the road in the broken gate's path.

Armed men milled about the rubble, trying to clear the stones and repair the gate. But they weren't Sagmyn Legionmen—not Legionmen at all, as far as Jaina could tell.

Jaina barked a short laugh and turned to Maira. "Emrael's aim when I left was to recruit Iraean fighting men from Whitehall. Most of them are likely jumped-up craftsmen, and I'm willing to bet that those men speak with an Iraean lilt. The new Lord Holder in Whitehall sent a man named Voran with Emrael to lead them. He seemed to know your son."

Maira stood without explanation and strode toward the gate, leaving Jaina and the other Imperators to hurry after her.

Jaina drew on her *infusori* coil, ready to stiffen her clothing into armor as they approached the gate. One bow after another aimed in their direction, and the men laboring at the gate drew their swords.

Maira raised empty hands and called loudly, "My name is Maira Ire. We are looking for my son, Emrael."

The reaction from the soldiers at the gate was immediate. Bows and swords were lowered and the men looked at each other with eyebrows raised. A man indistinguishable from the others stepped forward, and sure enough, he spoke with an Iraean accent.

"With respect, ma'am, none of us here would recognize Lord Ire's mother, and I can't allow an armed group to pass this gate. Please wait here while I send for Commander Second Toravin or Commander First Voran."

Jaina heard the baritone voice before she saw the swarthy man with grey hair stride through the gate. Voran, the man she had seen with Emrael at Whitehall just a few weeks before. A nasty purple bruise decorated one cheekbone.

"I'm here. I vouch for her."

Maira smiled warmly. "Voran. Commander First? You've come a long way from your days in my husband's guard."

Voran chuckled. "Ah, Lady Ire. But I'd gladly have those days back if I could."

Jaina could not see Maira's face, but the pause before speaking and the small catch in the older woman's voice told her all she needed to know. "So would I, Voran. So would I," Maira said quietly. "Voran, is Emrael with you? Do you truly have the city?"

Voran's face was grim as he replied. "Aye, Lady, we have the city. Your son led a valiant assault, and we have control of it for now, though the bulk of the Sagmyn Legion is approaching quickly from the valley. We have just half a Legion's worth of men, enough to hold the walls for now but not indefinitely."

"And where is Emrael now? Has he found his brother?"

Voran shook his head. "Lady . . . Lord Emrael and that man Sarlon led our best men into the Citadel by a back entrance, but we were unable to take the gates to aid their attack. They haven't been seen since they went in before dawn yesterday."

Maira's head sagged slightly. Voran made to step toward her before retreating awkwardly.

Jaina stepped forward to put a hand on Maira's shoulder. "Let's get inside the walls."

⚓

Jaina leaned against the inside of the doorway of the commandeered inn and looked out at the square that surrounded the governor's palace and the Citadel, hardly able to believe that she was just a few hundred paces from the main gate of the Citadel, where she had spent the last several years of her life. She had eaten often at the restaurant two buildings down, one of the few in the city to offer traditional Ordenan cuisine. It was dark, silent now.

The city had been taken quickly but not easily. Even there in the first tier of the city, in the square that surrounded the Citadel itself, corpses lay strewn about in haphazard groups. The bloody bodies of plainly dressed Iraeans mingled with uniformed Watchers and Sagmynan Legionmen, most still lying where they had fallen, though the Iraeans were currently working to move their fallen brethren and foes alike out of the way so wagons and men could get through to the giant square. Trails of blood like gruesome strokes of a giant paintbrush crisscrossed the cobbles where they dragged the bodies out of the streets.

As bad as it was, however, Jaina was grateful for those who weren't counted among the dead. Memories of past battles from the wars in the Dark Lands weighed heavy in her mind. Ordinary men struck down in the midst of trying to live a normal life. Women, children dead in the streets, or worse. The Iraeans had somehow kept the civilians out of the worst of the fighting, a commendable feat when storming an entire city like they had.

Many buildings there near the Citadel that had been beautiful homes, inns, or upscale shops just weeks before were now smoking shells and piles of rubble that spilled into the road. Voran said that most of the damage had been caused by the defenders themselves, burning and pulling down structures in an attempt to slow the Iraean advance through the city. Most of the Watchers had retreated to the Citadel compound when the Iraeans had attacked the city, if Voran was to be believed.

At a table in the room behind her, Maira conversed with an overly relaxed Voran. Something about the man bothered Jaina. He hadn't been happy about accompanying Emrael there, from what she had seen before she left Whitehall. Now he didn't seem to care a whit that Emrael was missing, likely dead or in enemy hands. At the least, she would have expected him to be at attention, with an army of Watchers gathered on the other side of the Citadel compound wall, nearly within range of a Crafted crossbow. His men outside in the square appeared vigilant, however, so she had to credit him somewhat.

The inn they had commandeered was relatively untouched by the recent battle—other than the absence of any patrons or staff. Everyone left in the city was shut away in their homes, those whose homes were still standing. Jaina didn't blame them. The keeper of the inn—a large man with unusually thick black hair that covered every visible part of his body besides the top of his head—hunched nervously behind the counter of the bar, ready to attend any of the various Iraean soldiers rushing in and out of the building. Voran had probably dragged the poor man from the cellar to wait on him.

Several Ordenan Imperators occupied the common room as well. The rest were busy scouting the Citadel compound. The Imperators hid their emotions well, but a foot tapping here and a fidget of a hand there told her that they were almost as anxious to be fighting as she was. Though she had done all she could to guide the stubborn boy, she still felt responsible for getting Emrael out of the Citadel. Sisters knew Maira was going to hold her to account.

Jaina concentrated on the conversation in the room behind her, hoping to hear a command to finally move on the Citadel.

"What do you mean, 'We can't afford to assault the Citadel'?" she heard Maira ask incredulously. "That's what you're here for, isn't it? Your leader, my son, is inside. Likely *both* of my sons. I have five full squads of mages, and you have at least five battalions sitting idle. There can't possibly be enough men inside to stop us. Knock down the gate and be done with it."

Voran did not straighten from his reclined slouch, he simply shook his head. "You don't understand, Lady Ire. There are thousands of Watchers in there, perhaps even more than the forces I have here in the square. We would lose hundreds of men trying to take the Citadel walls, thousands. If we pull the soldiers we need from the fight for the walls, we'll lose the city before we can even capture the Citadel. There are still many pockets of Sagmyn Legionmen fighting in the city. Our best option is to capture the city, then starve them out of Citadel."

"My sons may not have that long. At the very least, they will be the first to starve," Maira grated.

Voran's face crinkled slightly in sympathy. "Lady, I cannot in good conscience order away the lives of twenty thousand men for a fool's chance at saving two, whoever they may be. Any sane leader would agree with me. We *cannot* lose the outer walls, or we are all as good as dead."

Maira opened her mouth to speak, but an Iraean soldier in plain civilian clothing and an Ordenan Imperator in full metal-scale battle gear interrupted as they raced through the door.

The Iraean opened his mouth, but the Ordenan spoke over him. "Lady Ire, a girl claiming to be Arielle Barros just arrived at the west gate. Rode up to it bold as a bear. She has several thousand peasants with her."

The Iraean glared at the Ordenan and shouldered him aside. "They are our *families*, not peasants, you fancy-ass pirate. Voran, more people from Whitehall are here. They say they were chased out of Whitehall, that Dorae sent them to us because he couldn't help them and fight off Corrande at the same time. They're in bad shape, Voran."

Voran's boots thumped hard on the rough wooden floor as he sprang to his feet. "Thank you, Seten. Are they coming down the main avenue?"

The Iraean man nodded. "Maybe ten minutes behind us. We ran ahead."

Voran grunted approval. "Find the nearest Captain First and tell him to organize shelter for them. Then go tell the healers to be ready to care for even more sick and wounded. And Fallen strike me, don't let them unload here! Take them back to the crossroad square in the second tier."

He strode from the room with his scout, Maira, and Jaina close on his heels. True to the Iraean soldier's word, a large group of wagons escorted by a mere hundred or so armed Iraeans was just visible rolling its way up the main avenue toward the first-tier square. Voran and his men ran toward them, waving them back toward the second tier, but a few of the lead wagons continued on toward the first tier, where Jaina and the others waited with thousands of Iraean soldiers.

As the few wagons drew closer, Jaina saw that the soldiers guarding the large caravan were in bad shape. Blood-soaked bandages adorned nearly every person with a weapon and even some of the civilians riding with the wagons. Worn clothes, dirty faces, and sunken eyes showed that the battle for Whitehall was hard-fought.

A woman shouted and hopped down from one of the lead wagons as they reached the square. An armed man followed her closely. The man's bearing made it obvious he was no Iraean workman, but it took several moments for the two figures to draw close enough for Jaina to recognize them as Elle and Halrec.

"Oh, Maira," Elle panted with a hint of a sob as she stumbled to a halt, Halrec a half-step behind her. "Maira, Jaina, thank the Gods. Please help them. We returned to Whitehall and found it a burning mess. The Watchers retaliated, and much of the city burned before Dorae could push them out again. These people have nothing, and nowhere to go."

Tears welled in Elle's eyes but she did not look away. The girl had some steel in her spine after all.

Maira stepped forward to wrap the blond girl in a tight embrace. "Shh, child, you are safe. My, how you've grown. We will help as much as we can. Bring the most gravely injured to this inn behind us; I'll see that a few of my Mage-Healers tend to them. I'm afraid that's all I can spare. The others will have to wait until I get my sons back."

Elle's head lifted sharply. "Where is Emrael? Why isn't he with Voran? He's supposed to be here."

Jaina spoke up. "He was here. Or still is, I suppose. The Watchers still hold the Citadel compound, and Emrael has not been seen since he and Sarlon led an attack through the tunnel sometime last night."

"Why are we all standing here, then?" Elle demanded.

Maira smiled fiercely. "As much as I share your sentiment, dear girl, Voran assures me that the Citadel gate is securely held by thousands of Watchers. We are looking for alternate entry as we speak. We'll find a way in, or I'll have some choice words with my Imperators—"

The sudden, deafening sound of stone tearing and crashing to the earth drowned out Maira's words. A cloud of dust and airborne rubble washed over Jaina like an ocean swell, almost knocking her from her feet.

Coughing and choking, she stumbled toward where she had last seen Maira. She bumped into someone that looked vaguely like her in the dim dust cloud, but it turned out to be Elle.

The clamor of people calling frantically for their friends calmed as the dust settled. Within moments, Jaina found all of her companions unharmed. They were still trying to get their bearings when Halrec pointed toward the Citadel, which just then became visible in the slowly thinning haze of dust in the air.

Half of the Citadel was gone. Half of the main wing nearest the compound wall, anyway. The tower that held the Headmasters' offices no longer existed, and the huge rectangular structure of the south wing that had supported it had partially collapsed. Large blocks of stone with which the Citadel had been constructed now lay in a swath of destruction that had knocked down most of the wall that surrounded the Citadel. The enormous steel-clad gate itself lay twisted on the ground, pulled down by the weight of the crushed wall.

A bright blue light emanated from the top floor of the now open-sided building. Jaina had never seen anything like it.

"Fallen Glory, what could do that?" Halrec exclaimed, hand on the hilt of his sword.

The blue light began to descend from the top floor of the Citadel, moving slowly down the rubble of the wreckage as everyone in the square watched in stunned silence.

Everyone but Maira. "Imperators! Form on me!" she shouted.

Imperators that had been stationed all around the Citadel came running to stand in perfect formation within moments. Even some of the nearby Iraean soldiers hurried to gather in a loose group to one side of the Imperators' orderly ranks.

Voran wasn't far behind in roaring commands to his own troops, though his commands included a great deal more cursing. Shouting relayed down the streets, and a steady stream of men soon poured into the square in front of the twisted and fallen Citadel gate.

"Oh, perfect," Halrec grumbled from beside Jaina.

She was about to ask Halrec what he was muttering about when she noticed row upon row of Watchers gathering on the other side of the Citadel compound's wall, in the large open square between the Citadel and the Governor's Palace. Though the wreckage of the Citadel and the wall stood between them, the Watchers and Iraeans now stood a mere thousand or two paces apart. Battle was imminent.

She was dismayed and disgusted to see soulbound and their Malithii masters gathering near the rear of the enemy formation. Soulbound continued to file from crude encampments erected on the Citadel grounds, dark-robed Malithii spurring and corralling them into milling, anxious clusters that left little open space between the two enormous buildings.

The Watchers now stood in well-organized groups and kept some distance from the soulbound, as if even they could not stomach the mindless beasts that had once been human. Perhaps the alliance between the Malithii and the Watchers was not so comfortable, after all.

A small knot of men in dark armor—or at least they appeared to be men at first glance—stood apart from the gathering soulbound.

When Jaina noticed several small figures among them, her breath caught in her throat. The smaller figures were, in fact, full-grown men—Malithii in black robes. They looked like children next to the armored giants.

"*Sanja'ahn*," she growled.

"The monsters you told us about that are even worse than soulbound? Great," Halrec said without looking away from the growing mass of enemy soldiers. He sounded resigned, wearied by the prospect of the coming fight. Perhaps the boy was learning.

Anger and seething hatred for the Malithii and their evil creations swelled within Jaina. *Infusori* flowed to her from the gold coils in her pouch until she buzzed with its power. She took an involuntary step forward.

Elle gasped. "Emrael!" And with that, the girl sprinted toward the blue light that had just reached the bottom of the pile of crushed stone and rubble that had spilled into the square outside the gate, near where the Iraeans had formed up to meet the Watchers who formed their own ranks a few thousand paces away.

Jaina stared at Elle's retreating back in confusion, then looked more closely at the mysterious blue light. It *did* look like a person. Could it be?

She drew her sword and ran after Elle, vaguely aware of Halrec just behind her. Maira barked orders once more, though Jaina was too distracted to comprehend what she said.

As they drew close to the glowing blue personage, she could see that it was indeed a man. A man naked above the waist, covered in blood and fiercely glowing scars. The blue light seemingly came directly from the patterned scars in his skin. He struggled to carry an unconscious form on his shoulders, a thin, dirty man with bloody patterns of his own on his face and one arm.

Emrael. He was safe. Her charge yet lived. She would have another chance.

33

Emrael nearly wept when he saw Elle, Halrec, and Jaina running toward him as he staggered across the rubble-strewn courtyard. Exhausted as he was, he hadn't thought he would make it to where the Iraeans had lined up in battle ranks outside the Citadel gate before the Watchers and soulbound in the Citadel courtyard charged him. He could hear their bestial cries, the stamp of feet, the metallic ringing of weapons and armor.

But his friends were somehow—miraculously—there. As Elle reached him, he pled, "Heal him. Please. I can't. You'll need to take the pendant off of him."

Elle stared at him mutely, pity in her eyes.

He tried again. "It's Ban, Elle. I found him. Help him!"

Halrec and Jaina took Ban gently from Emrael's arms and ran immediately back toward where the Iraeans were gathered.

Elle still said nothing. Despite the enemy army nearby, she just looked at him, staring at his face but not quite meeting his eyes.

The scars.

He knew his scars glowed because he could see it on his arms and chest but had no idea what he must look like. Was his face disfigured? The knife had never seemed to stop.

An arrow whistled and clanked into the paving stones just paces from their feet. The Watchers and their twisted allies had begun a slow march toward where they stood in the square just outside the now-crushed Citadel wall.

"Elle, we have to move!"

Finally, Elle's large blue eyes snapped to his. He snagged her hand and limped more than ran toward the Iraean shield wall as the army of soulbound, *sanja'ahn* and Watchers behind them continued to volley arrows at them. Thankfully, they did not give chase, likely because the Iraean army waited near the wall with bows of their own.

As they reached the Iraean ranks, he felt the eyes of every soldier turn to him.

He raised his fist as he limped through their ranks, covered in scars and glowing like the moon herself. "Iraea!" he called hoarsely.

A brief silence followed, quickly succeeded by a thunderous roar that startled him with its ferocity. "Ire! Ire!"

His arms tingled with goosebumps as the men who had followed him to this battle chanted, and he felt a knot of emotion form in his throat.

When they came to the rear of the Iraean formation, Elle helped him sit on the paving stones beside where Jaina and Halrec had set Ban. He closed his eyes for a moment, but the memory of his father's smile—even as Emrael had drawn the life from him—immediately haunted him. When he looked up, his mother was there.

Emrael watched through a veil of exhausted shock as his mother addressed Jaina while working on Ban's inert form. "Jaina, lead the Imperators. The Watchers are about to cross the wall. Watch for the Malithii and any *sanja'ahn*. Neutralize them first. Go now."

Jaina ran immediately to where a group of oddly dressed soldiers—Imperators, he assumed—stood to one side of the massed Iraeans, already calling out orders. He'd never seen her obey anyone like that.

His mother's voice chimed again. "Elle, fetch me the healing kit and the best coils you can find. Halrec, dear, make sure Emrael is not gravely injured. I'll see to him in a moment."

Emrael sat in an exhausted stupor for the next long while. He was dimly aware of his surroundings: The clash of weapons and screams from several hundred paces up the square, at the broken gate where the two forces battled. His mother bustling about his brother. Halrec pressing something to his arm and trying to get his attention.

Despite the dire nature of the situation, he no longer felt any sense of urgency. He was not sure when, but he had stopped drawing *infusori* from his surroundings and had let what he held dissipate. Now his head felt as though it was pumped full of air. His limbs were leaden and resisted movement. He knew he should pay attention to the battle in front of him, should care about *something*, but he couldn't seem to focus.

Then Halrec hit him. Hard.

Emrael's face was already carved up, so the slap hurt badly. He staggered to his feet and shook his head, instinctively filling himself with the pulsing power of *infusori* that now came so easily to him there near the Citadel.

Before he could react further, his mother said, "Good."

Her hands gripped either side of his head. She pulled him to her so that he was staring into her eyes. Now that the *infusori* rushed through him, he felt his head clearing, power infusing his body once more.

"I need you to hold onto this *infusori* you've accessed. No matter what, Em. This is going to hurt, but hold on to it. Do you understand, Emrael?" His mother's voice was simultaneously commanding and comforting, just as he remembered from when he was a child. He responded with a simple nod, his eyes still locked to hers. "Yes."

She nodded once. Worry was plain in the wrinkles on her forehead and around her eyes, but even with the renewed vigor from the *infusori*, he was too tired and had gone through too much in the last several days to care.

His world was consumed by fire.

An ankle he had twisted badly seethed with agony as it knit back together, and the newly carved wounds in his skin felt like they were being carved anew, all at once. He screamed until his voice gave out, then drew a breath and screamed hoarsely once more. It was worse than when the Malithii mage had Healed him. Much worse.

Then it was over. He looked around wildly. Sweat beaded on his forehead and rolled into his eyes.

His mother sagged back to sit on the ground next to where Ban lay sleeping. His brother still had his eyes closed, but his face was no longer pale, and blood had stopped seeping from his arm and face.

Emrael turned to look up at the fallen walls of the Citadel, startled by the nearly deafening sounds of battle. His heart raced from the flood of *infusori* and the agony of his mother's Healing, and his focus was now razor-sharp, heightening his senses and slowing his perception of time.

He watched the clash of shields and exchange of blows between several large groups of soldiers scattered about the square. An Iraean took a sword to the neck and fell, thrashing. A distant scream reached him as an arrow impaled a Watcher. Cries of desperate struggle rose wherever a *sanja'ahn* joined the fray. Sharp *crack*s of *infusori*-charged weapons marked where an Ordenan Imperator sought out one of the Malithii that peppered the enemy ranks. Already the scene smelled like a slaughterhouse, a pungent stew of sweat, metallic blood, and shit.

And well behind the battle lines, still in the courtyard that separated the Citadel and Governor's Palace, stood a man in blue,
watching calmly.

Corlas.

Several dark-robed Malithii stood near him within a double ring
of blue-coated Watchers. They stood with shields, spears and swords
at the ready.

All thought flew from Emrael's mind as rage consumed him. Fear,
fatigue, and rational thought were gone, supplanted by a boundless
thirst for blood.

He drew more *infusori* into him in a flood of power and noted absently that while his scars had diminished with his mother's Healing, they still glowed brightly when he was full of *infusori*.

He drew his father's sword and stalked forward, eyes locked on
Corlas across the battlefield.

"Emrael!" his mother barked at almost the same time that Elle
cried, "Em, no!"

He paid them no mind. He began to jog as the energy within
him howled to be released. Halrec cursed, then appeared at his left
elbow.

"Jaina! Protect Emrael!" his mother shouted from somewhere behind him.

None of it mattered. None of them were Corlas. Nothing could
stop him.

Emrael shouldered his way into a knot of Iraeans locked in an
exhausted struggle with Watchers that had fought their way past the
wall and formed a tight half-circle, spears jutting out from between
shields. He pushed as much *infusori* as he could into his weapon
and laid about him with long, powerful strokes. Shields exploded
beneath his blade and Watchers fell lifeless, thrown to the ground
by violent bursts of *infusori* as his sword bit through their shields and
into their flesh.

The Watchers broke, panic clear on their faces. Emrael felt only
the thrill of battle and satisfaction at being a step closer to killing
Corlas, the man who had betrayed him, his brother, and his father.
The man who had broken him.

Another group of Watchers moved from the wall to intercept
them, these without shields, and Emrael hit them like a hammer.
Halrec was a blur of sharp steel and spurts of blood on his left, and
even Emrael in his fury was impressed at the incredible violence
meted out by Jaina on his right. At least half a dozen blue-clad sol-

diers lay motionless on the paving stones within moments. The Iraeans who had been fighting nearby and several Imperators who had
followed Jaina swarmed the rest, killing or taking them prisoner in
moments.

Emrael continued unabated toward Corlas. He could see the
man's face clearly now across the battlefield.

Corlas looked as regal as ever, his stark features confident as he
surveyed the battlefield from a hundred paces behind his own front
line. He had good reason to be confident, as his soldiers occupied
the high ground, had superior numbers, and were better trained and
better equipped than the Iraeans—half the Iraeans didn't even have
a shield, for Mercy's sake. The soulbound and *sanja'ahn* that Corlas's
Malithii allies commanded were a dagger to the heart of Emrael's
army. The Watchers had almost pushed the entire battle line past
the broken wall.

Almost.

Emrael scaled the remnants of the broken wall at a sprint, kicked
a shield aside, and sank his sword into the chest of a Watcher with a
graceful lunge. Blood sprayed him as he shoved the man backward
onto the other Watchers defending the pile of rubble, scattering
their formation and giving Emrael the opening he needed.

He jumped down after the dying enemy and followed with a wide
swing of his sword that connected with the leg of another of the
astonished Watchers, further widening the gap in their wall of overlapped shields.

The crunch of gravel to either side of him announced the arrival
of Halrec and Jaina.

Emrael blocked a blade intended for Halrec and just managed to
dodge a thrust aimed at his own gut before elbowing the man in the
nose. He followed the man closely as he reeled, ending him with a
quick sword thrust to the throat.

The fury of battle continued, Emrael hacking at Watcher after
Watcher, *infusori* and rage driving him forward in a furious attack,
Halrec and Jaina following closely to keep enemies from his back.

Swing, duck, kick, swing. Screams of the dying filled his ears.

He straightened as he suddenly found himself without anyone
else to kill. The Watchers had broken and were running back into
the compound to regroup. The Iraeans had followed his charge
and now poured over the wall behind Emrael, chasing the fleeing
Watchers.

Halrec panted loudly, and even in his *infusori*-fueled state,

Emrael's lungs burned. Just as he sank to one knee to rest, however, he caught sight of a large group of Watchers farther up the hill preparing to shoot their crossbows. They would loose their volley as soon as sufficient distance opened between the retreating Watchers and Emrael's soldiers. He and all of his men would be massacred.

Shouting hoarsely, Emrael raised his sword and sprinted after the Watchers, cutting one of the slowest down from behind as he ran. He hoped his soldiers would follow him. They were about to become pincushions if not.

Each step carried him closer to Corlas. The fleeing Watchers began to slow and form with shields overlapped as they reached the soldiers gathered about their commander—human, Malithii, and *sanja'ahn*.

Emrael slowed as well. No amount of *infusori* coursing through his veins would help him if he ended up on the end of one of the long spears protruding from the enemy line.

He felt a moment of panic as he pulled up and saw the group of Watcher crossbowmen readying to shoot. He had no shield or even armor to protect himself; he was wearing nothing but the breeches and boots he had pulled from a Watcher he had killed during his escape from the Citadel.

As he slowed, a small group of shield-bearing soldiers in a tight wedge formation caught up to and flowed around him to attack the line of Watchers before they could loose a volley. He froze in shock, not understanding who had come to save him.

He had hoped that the Iraeans fighting outside the Citadel walls would follow him into the courtyard, but these soldiers were not wearing the rough clothing of his people. They wore dark grey and silver uniforms under well-crafted infantry armor made from overlapping metal scales. Copper-alloy weapons worth a small fortune broke shields and *crack*ed as they encountered flesh and steel, pushing aside the spears and breaking through the shields of the Watchers in an instant.

Imperators. They must have been.

A euphoric rush of relief spread through him, and he quickly joined the melee. He stepped over a still-twitching *sanja'ahn* and cleaved the arm from a Watcher who had just stuck a short sword into the unguarded back of one of the Imperators.

He ignored the Watcher's screams and danced forward to meet a charging *sanja'ahn*, checking the creature's attack with a powerful swing of his own weapon. His sword reverberated so hard, he almost dropped it, but he ducked the *sanja'ahn's* next strike and pivoted, sweeping his blade in a wide arc, releasing a burst of *infusori* through it as he did. A surge of satisfaction filled him as his sword encountered resistance, shearing through the monster's leg just below the knee.

Hot, viscous blood splattered across his hands, chest, and face as the *sanja'ahn* fell with a shout of pain.

The smell of iron filled Emrael's nostrils. He screamed his defiance as battle joy flooded him.

He defended against another wild swing from the crippled monster before striking a killing blow with a quick thrust under the *sanja'ahn's* rib cage.

Infusori raged through him as he fought farther up the gentle slope of the Citadel courtyard. Corlas stood just paces away, staring at him. No emotion showed on the man's face.

"Corlas, you bastard!" Emrael screamed.

Corlas's eye twitched, but he merely bowed his head slightly and drew his sword. Two Malithii priests stepped wide, one to either side of the Watcher Commander, shaking loose their copper cable weapons.

Emrael flourished his own sword and flexed the muscles in his arms as he drew in more and more *infusori* from the Well beneath him, until he and his weapon glowed with a fierce light.

"I'll have you all!" he shouted, and rushed forward, completely ignoring the chaos of the battle around him.

He chopped at Corlas with all his might, as if he were trying to fell a tree in one stroke. *Infusori* flashed. Corlas managed to block the blow, though he staggered backward and fell at the burst of *infusori*, eyes wide with surprise.

Emrael bellowed once more, charging forward with his sword raised for another strike, trying to finish Corlas before the Malithii could come to his aid.

Pain flared in his left wrist and he was jerked off balance as something pulled at his arm. He glanced to that side. One of the Malithii priests held one end of his sinuous copper cable with both hands—the other end was wrapped tightly around Emrael's left wrist.

Emrael stumbled, righted himself, and tried again to charge at Corlas, who was just regaining his feet. Again he was jerked aside painfully by the wrist. He set his feet and pulled with all of his *infusori*-enhanced strength.

The priest's lips curled in a grimace of effort that revealed teeth so yellow, they verged on brown. He stumbled and fell to one knee but did not release the cable.

Corlas had regained his feet and paced forward, sword poised to strike.

Emrael frantically parried Corlas's expert attacks while straining against the dark priest attached to his left arm. He pulled in more and more *infusori*, more than he could have imagined possible. His body vibrated with it until he could hardly contain the energy.

A close exchange with Corlas left Emrael bleeding from a small gash above his right eye. Soon, he could not see properly from that eye but dared not use his sword hand to wipe the blood from his brow.

Panicked, he poured *infusori* into the copper cable attached to his wrist.

The Malithii on the other end of the cable glowed momentarily as he tried to absorb the *infusori*, then screamed as he was burned by the rapid influx of energy. The stench of burning meat filled the air. But to Emrael's surprise, the madman wrapped the cable quickly around both forearms as he burned to death so that Emrael could not shake it free from his ruined hands.

Without warning, a second cable snapped around Emrael's neck and pulled him backward. The second Malithii priest must have walked a wide circle around the fight and out of Emrael's view.

Glory take them!

Emrael roared with rage and flooded both copper cables with even more *infusori*. Screams from both priests tickled his ears, but still they pulled at him, weighed him down.

Corlas darted in, blade flashing. Emrael swung awkwardly, horribly off balance, and managed to deflect the attack enough that he took a burning slice along his hip instead of being run through the gut. He paid Corlas back with a kick to the throat.

He laughed at the older man's rasping choke, then launched himself backward and swung his sword wildly at where he thought the second Malithii must be.

His sword encountered nothing but air, and Emrael fell. He cursed, spinning about on one knee, trapping his left arm against his body and further tightening the coil around his neck. His head pulsed. His vision began to fade.

Eyes locked on Corlas, Emrael staggered quickly to his feet and jerked against the cables once more. The two dying Malithii lurched with him, but he was trapped, weighed down by their bodies.

Corlas's eyes gleamed as he started forward once more. Emrael was practically defenseless, and Corlas knew it.

Corlas studied him for a moment, then knocked Emrael's sword to the ground with three strikes in rapid succession. Emrael was powerless to counter the attack, encumbered as he was.

Frustration and fear welled in Emrael. His body still thrummed with the immense power of *infusori* he drew from the Well beneath the Citadel, but he was as helpless as a lamb trussed for slaughter. He tensed his body and growled, waiting to feel the cold steel of his enemy slide through his body. He was determined to take Corlas with him, even if he had to take a sword through the gut to get close enough to suck the life out of him.

The sound of Emrael's sword clattering to the ground had not even faded, however, when a whirring knife thrown from somewhere behind Emrael planted itself hilt-deep in Corlas's chest, cutting through his breastplate as if it had been made of paper. Corlas stumbled, dropped his sword, and fell to his knees.

"No," Emrael growled hoarsely, staring at Corlas, who convulsed as he choked on his last breaths.

Halrec appeared on his left to finish off the Malithii still tangled in the cord attached to Emrael's left wrist.

Dark hair twined in scalp-tight braids and a flashing short sword were all Emrael saw of Jaina as she gutted the other dying Malithii, who had been strangling him. She quickly unwound the copper cable from his neck, and he sucked in a ragged breath.

"No!" Emrael growled, regaining his feet and shaking himself free of the now-inert copper coils. "He was *mine!*" he screamed with irrational rage and despair, kneeling down to tear the knife from Corlas's chest.

Emrael turned to brandish the bloody knife at Halrec. Halrec gave him a wary look and took a few small steps backward, sword at the ready. "Em. He's dead. We have Ban. The Citadel is ours. Your charge broke them. Put the knife down."

"Emrael," Jaina said from beside him. Her short sword already rested in its sheath. "Emrael, I threw it. He would have killed you had I not. Do not make me hurt you."

She approached him slowly, then stopped when he made no move to put the knife down.

Emrael stared at her for a moment, breathing heavily, still overcome by irrational rage and the pulsing energy supplied by the *infusori*. He finally threw the knife to the ground with a growl and

stalked past them without a word, limping badly due to the wound
he had taken on his hip. He snatched his sword from the ground and
sheathed it, then continued stalking back to where Imperators and
some of his Iraeans still fought the last small group of Watchers who
stood their ground at the far end of the courtyard.

Halrec and Jaina caught up to him a moment later. Jaina jogged
in front of him and turned to confront him.

"Stop, Emrael. You are bleeding, and the *infusori* is clouding your
mind. I've never felt anyone hold so much. You are pushing your
body and mind too far. Let it go. Let us help you."

Emrael stopped and stared at his former mentor for a moment.
He was furious, mostly at his own failure to exact revenge, but he
knew she was right. With a deep breath, he let go of the *infusori*.

His injured leg buckled immediately as he was overcome with
fatigue. He knelt on one knee, head bowed, trying not to vomit. As
his strength left, his rage settled to merely a simmering anger.

Halrec helped him to his feet and ducked under his shoulder to
help support his weight. Emrael grasped his oldest friend's shoulder
as they made their way back to the breach in the Citadel wall.

Only now did it even occur to Emrael that he should have been
paying attention to the battle raging around him and not just his
personal quest for vengeance.

Some leader I am.

Maimed bodies and injured soldiers covered the wide square between the Citadel and the governor's palace. The paving stones were
slick with dark blood. Iraean soldiers roamed about, checking the
bodies for any of their friends that still breathed. Imperators stalked
the courtyard, dispatching any soulbound, *sanja'ahn*, or Malithii
still breathing. Groups of Watchers who had surrendered were being stripped of their weapons and herded like cattle.

They arrived at the gates, or rather where the gates had stood before the wall had been toppled. Emrael limped along with Halrec's
help until he caught sight of his mother and Elle tending to rows
and rows of injured Iraeans. Their moans and cries of pain riddled
him with guilt.

His brother had woken up and was sitting with his back to the
wall of a building not far from the other injured. All sign of the
wounds inflicted by the torturer—their father—were gone, save for
faint scars on his left arm and face that matched Emrael's own.

Something tickled his cheek. When had he started crying?

"Take me to Ban," Emrael rasped. His voice did not work properly.

Jaina appeared at his other shoulder, and she and Halrec helped him over to his brother.

As he eased down to sit next to Ban, his brother said, "Did you get him?"

Emrael looked at his brother quizzically. "Corlas? Jaina did. He's dead," he said quietly.

Ban shook his head slightly and looked up at Emrael with sunken, haunted eyes. "No. The man who hurt you." He reached out with a gentle finger to trace the scars on Emrael's arm, less visible now that they weren't glowing. "Did you get him?"

Emrael stared at Ban for a long moment, trying to find the right words, trying to speak through his tears.

"Yeah, I got him," Emrael whispered finally, putting his head on his brother's shoulder. He closed his eyes, not able to stop crying. "I got him," he sobbed.

EPILOGUE

Emrael sat cross-legged on the cold stone floor of the circular room where he had been tortured, spinning a dagger on the blackened stones where he had burned his father's body. He wrinkled his nose. Though the room had been scrubbed repeatedly, Emrael swore he could still smell the char.

It was dark, but he had no idea what time it was, as he'd had all of the windows covered to keep the tower chamber black, to suit his mood. He had been coming there each night when he couldn't sleep. He couldn't remember the last time he had slept more than a few hours in a night. Every time he closed his eyes, his father's ragged, smiling face filled his vision. It seemed no matter what he did, every door he opened revealed more secrets, more mysteries. Nothing was as it seemed. Who could he trust?

The whir of the spinning blade was hypnotic, and for a time he simply stared, letting emotions and memories wash through him unfettered.

Footsteps pounded up the stairs, accompanied by the blue light of an *infusori* coil. Elle stepped into the room a moment later, Ban just a few steps behind her. She regarded him with sympathy in her eyes, her curly honey-blond hair swaying as she regarded him and shook her head softly.

"Emrael! It's nearly midmorning. No one could find you. Halrec is convinced you were abducted and is out in the city looking for you. What are you doing up here?"

Emrael looked at her, then looked away and spun the knife again. "Couldn't sleep. Needed to think."

Elle's voice softened. "About what, Em? I wish you'd talk to me, to somebody. You've been . . . distant. All you've done for days is train with Jaina and brood."

"It's not you, Elle."

"Then what?"

Ban stepped forward to put a hand on Elle's shoulder before settling on the floor next to Emrael. "It was bad, Elle," he said quietly.

Elle looked to him. "I know, but—"

"No. You don't," Ban cut in. He still spoke softly, but the emotion in his voice quieted her. "You don't know; you can't. Even I was only there for a small part, the end of their cutting, and I can't sleep either. He needs time."

Emrael leaned on his brother's shoulder, tears wetting his cheeks. He had been avoiding Ban—everyone, really—since the rescue and subsequent battle five days before. Every time he saw his brother, he became a sobbing mess—not something Emrael was comfortable with. He couldn't help it now. Ban put an arm around his shoulder.

Elle sat on Emrael's other side and put a hand on his knee. "I'm so sorry, Em. I want to help, and I will help any way I can. But we need you to lead us again, help us rebuild. We will all die if you don't do something. We are still at war."

Emrael laughed, a deep, rasping laugh. "Lead? Rebuild? All I do is destroy, kill. People around me die—friends as well as enemies. Yerdon. Sarlon. Thousands of Iraeans. I do not know how to build."

Elle reached out to hold his hand. "Emrael, Corrande could be at our doorstep tomorrow with another nightmare army, and the Sagmyn Legion has the city surrounded. These people need you to maintain hope. Sometimes, the sword needs to clear the way for the trowel."

Emrael picked up the dagger and inspected the blade. "What is it you think I can do, Elle? Do you think your father will ally with us?"

Elle's face hardened. "No. He is Corrande's puppet now. If anything, he might fight against us."

He looked up at her. Mercy, she was beautiful. He still felt hollow inside, but she was right. Everything they had fought for would crumble if he didn't pull himself together. He could hide the pain.

"Thank you," he said finally.

"For what?" she asked.

"For believing in me, for choosing me, us, over your family."

"I'm just doing what my heart tells me is right. I couldn't let them have Ban, and I couldn't let you fight them alone. What they are doing is wrong."

Emrael ran his hand over the scorched stones one last time, then stood and helped Elle to her feet. He looked down to meet her gaze and was surprised when she pulled him in for a quick kiss on the lips.

She smiled as they parted, and he couldn't help the smile that appeared on his lips. He looked to Ban and was relieved to get an encouraging smile from his brother. He felt better than he had in ages.

"Let's go see about that Sagmyn Legion," he said, still gripping the dagger. "Where's the Lord Governor?"

⸻

Emrael tugged the chain he held, causing the trepidatious Lord Governor Steffan of Sagmyn to lurch onto the steps leading up to the top of the city wall. "Come now, Governor. Either you play along, or I will gut you and hang you by your entrails over the wall."

After the battle for the Citadel, the Lord Governor Sagmyn had been holed up in his palace, surrounded by several Malithii and their *sanja'ahn* soldiers. Scores of Iraeans had been killed in the initial assault, and the Lord Governor had held his palace for a day or so.

Then Jaina and the Ordenan Imperators had stormed the palace. She was rather upset about Sarlon's death—though they still hadn't recovered his body—and had jumped at the chance to lead the attack.

Within an hour, the *sanja'ahn* and Malithii lay dead, and Lord Governor Sagmyn was escorted in chains to where the majority of the Iraeans were camped in the large courtyard near the Citadel. The Lord Governor had not had a good time of things in the few days since.

The Lord Governor Steffan Sagmyn—*former* Lord Governor, Emrael thought with a grim smile—looked at Emrael with wide, fearful eyes. An intense blue glow emanated from the closed satchel where Emrael carried several of the gold coils from the Citadel cellars. He needed the coils, as he was only able to draw *infusori* directly from his surroundings inside the Citadel compound—the *infusori* Well was concentrated there, it seemed.

Emrael tugged again on the chains and continued up the steps, pulling the wretch behind him. He felt no sympathy. The man had cooperated with Corlas and the Malithii in killing, enslaving, and even turning people into soulbound. He deserved worse than death.

Toravin watched with hard eyes from where the flight of steps let onto the battlements of the city wall. He had been there since they had taken the city, fighting back the Sagmyn Legion's periodic attempts to breach the wall.

When Emrael reached the top of the wall, he tugged on the chain sharply. Governor Sagmyn sprawled to his knees and struggled to regain his feet. Voran, who led the squad of Iraeans accompanying Emrael, shoved their captive back down to his knees. "You'll stay there until Lord Ire tells you differently."

Emrael nodded to Voran brusquely, though in his head he continued to question the man. How had Corlas known right where Emrael and the Iraeans would be? Why had Voran not attacked the gates as they had planned? Emrael would get to the bottom of it soon, but for now, there were pressing matters to attend to.

Whatever his faults, Voran understood Emrael's plan today and agreed with it. Jaina, who had followed him as he left the Citadel, did not. As she gained the top of the wall with several Imperators accompanying her, she stomped over to him. "Emrael, I would know what you plan here. Why do you have those coils in your bag, and why do you expose yourself to the army down there?"

Emrael smiled. "The risk is worth the reward, dear Jaina. The warriors of this province need to understand their situation. We can't continue under this siege, hiding like a turtle in its shell."

He turned to survey the valley below. Sagmyn Legionmen in the tens of thousands camped all around the city, cutting off the flow of supplies and preventing Emrael from guarding the passes on the east and west—much less the harbor at Ladeska. Emrael might have the manpower to fight the Sagmyn Legion and win from his position behind the wall, but he would be a sitting duck for anyone who marched on him thereafter.

Emrael motioned to Voran, who hauled the governor to his feet and pushed him forward by the back of the neck. Emrael took an *infusori*-Crafted speaking cone from another Iraean soldier and addressed the camps below, where a large group of Sagmyn soldiers had gathered to see what was happening on the wall. The low murmur of their conversations ceased when Emrael began speaking.

"Sagmyn Legionmen! I am Emrael Ire, leader of those who now own this city. I have declared war on your governor for crimes against my family and the families of all those who had attended the Citadel. He sold them to Governor Corrande, enslaved them, and allowed unspeakable things to happen to them—and to many other citizens of your own province!

"I'm given to understand, however, that many of your officers feel a lasting allegiance to this man, this criminal. They feel a need to waste your lives trying to save his. I'm here to put an end to this nonsense."

Emrael handed the speaking cone to the soldier at his side and drew his sword. In one smooth motion, he gripped the blubbering Governor Sagmyn's hair and severed his head from his neck with a powerful chop of his sword.

The headless corpse buckled and flopped to the ground. Blood pooled on the stones of the wall. The soldiers below shouted in surprise, anger, and dismay but soon quieted.

"I am not here to play games! I am not here to wage a war on your people. I am here to free all of us from the tyranny of men like him."

Emrael raised the former governor's head in the air, then heaved it from the wall toward the gathered soldiers below.

He cleaned his bloody weapon on the body, then sheathed it and put his hand into his satchel, drawing every bit of *infusori* from the huge coils. The inscribed lines of scars on his bare hands and arms began to glow brightly even in the full light of day, and he knew his eyes must be shining even brighter. He took the cone once more.

"All those who wish to join me may come to the south gate for admittance to the city and enrollment in my Legion. A bounty of land and copper will be given to all who join me willingly. Those who continue to oppose me will suffer the same fate as this man."

Emrael hefted the governor's headless body and let *infusori* surge through him. The body burst into flames as Emrael hurled it from the gate to land with a wet sound, right in front of the astonished Sagmyn Legionmen below. They scrambled to keep their distance from the burning corpse.

Massive amounts of *infusori* still coursed through him, goading him to jump from the wall and destroy the opposing army himself, but he refrained. He needed them, and he knew that the *infusori* clouded his judgement. So, he stayed on the wall for a short time, making sure the soldiers below had a good opportunity to show their friends the man who glowed with power. None took up a crossbow to attempt a shot at him. Just as he had suspected.

After a few minutes, Halrec appeared at his shoulder, breathing heavily and scowling. "Elle didn't know where you had gone, Em. I had to look all over the damn city to find you. One of Jaina's Imperators just returned from the pass to report that Barros is gathering his Legion near Lidran. They appear to be preparing to attack Whitehall but could easily travel this way instead."

Emrael considered the news. They would not be able to defend the city for long if Barros joined the remnants of the Sagmyn Legion in an assault, and he'd never get the Sagmyn Legionmen to join him if they thought they'd have help from Barros.

Whitehall falling to an attack from Barros would be nearly as bad. Without Dorae and his men in Iraea, Corrande and Barros would be free to bring their full might to bear on Emrael and his fledgling Legion. Besides, many of those who had followed him here still had loved ones in Whitehall and wouldn't follow him for long if he left their families to die. He needed them most of all.

He needed these Sagmynan soldiers in his army, and quickly. He clapped Halrec on the shoulder and reached for the speaking cone again.

"You have until sundown to claim your bounty, soldiers of Sagmyn! Those who join me will fight for the freedom of all men, not for the riches of a Lord Governor. Do not waste this opportunity."

With that, Emrael went to one knee and placed his hand on the stone of the wall. He let *infusori* flow from him in a rush. Instead of concentrating the energy to destroy a section of stone, he allowed it to dissipate freely over a large area, through the stone of the wall and into the ground itself. The earth pulled at the *infusori* hungrily, soaking up all Emrael gave it.

A groaning sound emanated from the ground almost immediately, and the earth trembled violently. Even the city wall shook, and Emrael began to fear he had overdone it. Shingles and bricks crashed into the streets behind him, and he could see tents collapsing in the Sagmyn camps nearest the wall.

When the shaking subsided, Emrael stood again. The men around him and those in the camp below slowly regained their feet.

Emrael raised the speaking cone once more, his voice thundering over the bewildered crowd. "Sundown! Choose wisely."

A spring storm crashed against the mountains west of the city as Lord Governor Bortisse Corrande's coach approached his palace. A flash of lightning and a roll of thunder preceded cascading hail, his favorite type of storm.

Bortisse stepped out of the coach and into the storm. A large fire in the distance caught his eye. It appeared large enough to be one of the forts that dotted the highway that connected his province with the Ithan kingdoms. He motioned to the captain of his guard. "Find out what is burning out there. Send a battalion if you have to."

The captain saluted and ran to find the head of the palace guard.

Bortisse turned back to the open coach. "Well, Priest? Aren't you coming?"

His long legs carried him quickly up the steps to the seat of his power. He had been forced to leave Myntar hurriedly when that Ire boy had surprised him, attacking first at Whitehall and then suddenly in Myntar. No matter. He had a surprise waiting for that peasant.

Bortisse couldn't help the smile that bared his teeth. Quite a surprise indeed. Funny, how easily he found agents among his rivals, supposed men of values who so easily succumbed to the enticements of small fortunes in copper.

The Provinces would be united before the year was out, and he would be their emperor—to lead them to glory against the meddlesome Ordenans, and then against the insolent Ithans and Freemen to the east. Not even the ancient Ravans had controlled so much territory as he soon would. His name would be known for all of history.

He entered the foyer of his castle and shed his cloak on the floor. Footsteps behind him told him that his Malithii advisor followed, prisoner in tow. Why the man he knew only as "Priest" cared so much about this particular prisoner, Bortisse didn't know or care. He just wanted a hot bath and an hour alone with his wife. It had been a long, hurried journey.

As he crossed the audience room, however, he noticed that Priest still followed him. He turned, a rebuke ready on his lips. The rebuke was forgotten when he found Priest and his prisoner—a great bear of a man rendered placid by a mindbinder—kneeling prostrate.

"What—" he began, before a deep, booming laugh coming from the Ruler's Chair surprised him. Bortisse narrowed his eyes and ground his teeth. Why were the torches on the dais out? He'd have his steward's ears for this!

"I don't know who you think you are, but I'll have your head for sitting on my throne!"

The deep, vibrant laugh continued. Bortisse drew his sword and gathered himself to storm up to the throne. He stopped when he noticed two eyes glowing blue in the darkness.

"A throne, now, is it?" The lightly accented baritone rumble seemed to vibrate its way through Bortisse's body. "Perhaps a throne, indeed. I haven't decided yet, but this city is very nice. I particularly enjoy the storms that break over the castle. Quite lovely, invigorating."

"Who are you?" Bortisse asked, considerably less fire in his voice now. Something wasn't right. Where were his guards?

The figure sitting on the throne rose from the shadows, revealing a tall, sharp-faced man with long black hair and a clean-shaven face. He had the typical Malithii tattoos covering the skin of his hands and presumably the rest of his body—they even covered every inch of his face. A broad smile revealed square, bone-white teeth.

"Me? I am called the Prophet by my people, like your little priest there. But you may call me Lord Savian. I'm here to see that my plans are executed correctly—the plans given me by the Returned God. Were my wishes executed at the Citadel?"

Bortisse stood confused, suddenly afraid to answer. He had the distinct feeling that this man could end his life with the flick of a finger. He'd have to make sure this new priest was killed quickly.

He watched the glowing eyes warily as he responded. "Ah . . . the Citadel is lost, and those monsters of yours were left along with the Watcher Commander and some of my best men to cover our escape. I am not pleased to have lost them, I'll have you know. I agreed to use your money and your *men* to help unify the Provinces and fight the Ordenans. I didn't sign up for undead monsters or uninvited guests!"

"Hmm," Savian murmured. "And what of the Ire boy?"

"The Ire boy escaped."

"Did you hurt him?"

Bortisse stared, perplexed. Priest, still kneeling beside him, responded without looking up. "Yes, Lord. He was given the marks of Glory as you instructed. By his father. All went according to plan."

Bortisse looked down in bewilderment at Priest. "According to plan? I lost everything! My top commander, my soldiers . . . We barely escaped with our lives!"

Priest was silent.

"Answer me, insolent dog! Do you know what it has cost me to get you and your filth into the Provinces? And you serve me with tricks and lies?"

The Prophet, Savian, still standing on the dais, giggled happily. He ignored Bortisse, addressing Priest. "Ah, yes. Well done my child. Splendid. The Returned God will be most pleased when they meet; he has been planning this for so many years. And who is this, wearing one of my creations?"

"The man known as Sarlon, Lord."

"Ah!" Savian shrieked happily. "I know of him. I shall enjoy becoming acquainted."

The large, hairy man didn't respond. Nor should he, with that dreadful mindbinder on his wrist.

Savian spoke again. "Bortisse, my dear fellow, I've taken your chambers—as well as your Province—but your lovely wife awaits you in the best guest chambers. I trust you understand?"

Bortisse looked around once more, noting now the complete absence of his guards. Only now did he notice several of the Malithii's giant pet monsters—the priests called them *sanja'ahn*—lurking in the corners of the room. Those pale beasts scared him shitless.

Savian's eyes glowed brighter.

Bortisse dropped his sword. "Who are you?" he asked again, softly this time.

Savian smiled again, white teeth beneath radiantly shining eyes. "I told you, my dear fellow. I am Savian, the Prophet of the Returned God of Glory. You know Him as the Fallen."

ACKNOWLEDGMENTS

I have many to thank for helping me on my writing journey, and many who should be thanked but remain unknown even to me. Still, it's worth a shot.

My wife, Kailey, who put up with a lot of shit so this book could happen. I've been working on this story for nearly ten years as of this writing. She's been there for me every step of the way, reading drafts, encouraging me, helping me create time to write. I love writing, and I love this book. But most of all, I love her for putting up with me and my crazy plans. Without her, this book wouldn't exist, and I would be a lesser human.

My dear child, who often watches over my shoulder as I write, offering to help. I hope that one day she will be as proud of me as I am of her.

My mom, for always believing in me. Words can't describe my debt to her.

My dad, for opening my eyes to the joys of fabricated worlds.

My brothers and best friends, Hunter, Taylor, and Harrison. They read more drafts than anyone should ever have to.

My agent, Matt Bialer, for taking a chance on me, spending many, many hours helping me build this book into what it is today. He is simply a wonderful human being.

My editor, Jen Gunnels, a fierce but unfailingly kind human. She has the talent to be doing just about anything, yet she chooses to help people like me tell the stories of their heart to the world.

The good folks at Tor, who work very hard to make dreams come true. They deserve more credit than they get.

All of my beta readers and dear friends who have helped me along the way. Kyle Van Wagenen and all of the Van Wagenen crew. The Remote Writers Guild homies. Christine, Molly, and all of the book pros who have given me their time and honest feedback. All of the fellow authors and industry folk willing to answer an email, join a writing support group, or even just talk to me at a convention. There are far too many to name, and all make my work and my life better.

Finally, to everyone reading this: It is a privilege to share this story with you. I hope you found what you needed.

ABOUT THE AUTHOR

SCOTT DRAKEFORD is a longtime lover of fantasy fiction. He had his first taste of "the good stuff" in his younger years from his father. Later in life, Scott was tricked into becoming a "responsible adult," getting a degree in engineering, and living the corporate life in the technology industry. He currently lives in the Boston area with his tech wizard of a wife, their tenacious daughter, and two dogs. *Rise of the Mages* is his first novel.